Chee-Soo Kim

About the Author

ISAAC ADAMSON was born in Fort Collins, Colorado, during the Year of the Pig. He plays soccer well, guitar poorly, and is currently living in Chicago. He doesn't know his blood type. Find out more at www.billychaka.com.

Also by Isaac Adamson

Tokyo Suckerpunch

FIRST VERSE

I've got no place to go
Nowhere I should be
If I knock on your door
Will you come along with me?

—Saint Arrow ("Love Happy Weekend")

1

Nine times out of ten, I'm a nice guy. I believe in nonviolence, intellectual discourse, artistic freedom and all that other jazz. Though I wouldn't go so far as to say I'm open-minded. Like I tell my comrade Sarah, open-mindedness can be a crutch. And objective distance? That's a sucker's game. I'm the kind of journalist who likes to mix it up, go toe to toe, engage the subject in a little *kumite*. Trashing a Saigon hotel room with lisping rock bad boys the High Deathibles, playing strip go fish with caretakers of the Forbidden City palace grounds, arm wrestling Triad triggermen for the last Dexedrine pill—there's not much I won't do in the line of duty.

Including slapping a movie director in the face.

When it happened I told Ed, my editor, that I couldn't go around worrying about hurt feelings and get the kind of stories my worldwide audience of faithful teens expects with every copy of *Youth in Asia* magazine.

Ed said he agreed in principle, but that you couldn't run a magazine on principles. Then he sent me on vacation. Mandatory R&R in some nowhere town in the mountains of Hokkaido. Sending me to Japan for vacation was like sending Dean Martin to Vegas for rehab, but when Ed gets an idea he clings to it like a winning lottery ticket.

I was thinking about Ed's ideas when something brushed against the back of my neck.

Whirling to confront my attacker, I made a quick catalog of potential weapons in the room. A cheap ceramic lamp in the shape of a cat, one unwieldy wooden chair, a black lacquer vase stuffed with fake tiger lillies. Nothing to rival my own hands and feet. Nothing except maybe the whalebone nunchaka. They were a gift from the Water Dragon Alliance, a union of tuna fishermen and would-be poet-warriors in Tsukiji. I'd judged their annual *tanka* contest in '91 and was invited back every year, but a guy can only read so many poems about tuna fish.

The nunchaka wouldn't help me now, though. They were buried in my briefcase along with my writing supplies. I hadn't been forced to use the weapon since the Ping-Pong riots in D'Nang, but I carried them like a talisman. Funny the things we get attached to.

Once I saw my attacker, I figured the chucks wouldn't be necessary. My mute assailant just looked at me from atop the carpet-covered post. You'd think this cat had seen it all before. Maybe it had. This was a hotel cat, after all, sharing my room at the Hotel Kitty.

The cat licked his paw, the one he'd just brushed against me, as if trying to clean itself of my presence. Weird cat. Of course, if you lived your entire life in the same room with strangers coming in and out of your home day after day, it's bound to affect your personality. Even if you're a cat.

I reached out to pet the animal, but it leapt off the post and trotted off under the bed. At the Hotel Kitty, you get to choose from all thirty-three breeds of cats officially recognized by the Japanese Cat Fanciers Association. Abyssinians, Egyptian Maus, Chartreux, Selkirk Rexes, Norwegian Forest cats. Pixie Bobs, Ragamuffins, American Wirehairs.

You can room with a male or a female. It really didn't matter to me. Like I'd told the Day Manager, I'm no cat fanatic or anything.

"No shame in being a cat fanatic," the Day Manager had told me in his northern accent. "Most of our visitors fit quite comfortably in that category. Not being one yourself, well that makes you a rare breed around here. A rare breed, indeed." Then he'd smiled and given me a key and told me all about the cat I'd be sharing a room with.

She was a six-pound female Japanese bobtail of distinguished-merit parentage. Her short fluffy tail was what aficionados called a clown's pom-pom. She liked water and liked to talk. The Day Manager said that as a writer, I'd probably be interested to know that cats were originally brought to Japan from Korea in order to protect important manuscripts from nibbling mice.

"Cats have always been writers' allies," he said.

Then he talked about allowable outcross breeds, and how to tell a Balinese from a Javanese and the difference between lilac point and seal point noses. But thinking about it now, I'm pretty sure he never told me the cat's name.

I spent time wandering around the hotel and marveling at how far they'd taken the cat motif. Each floor of the Hotel Kitty was devoted to a different type of cat. The third floor was called the Domestic Suite and its hallway was lined with framed photographs of somnolent house cats, all white fluff and soft focus. The Rural Cat Ranch on the second floor featured Norman Rockwell–style paintings depicting lean farm cats hunting field mice and chasing each other through tall blades of grass.

My floor was called the Feline Metropolis, and was decorated with a cartoon mural depicting a cat cityscape. There were hepcats hanging out at jazz joints, biker cats on motor-cycles, business cats taking subways, alley cats having a switchblade fight, even cats lined up outside a theater to see a production of *Cats*.

All the cat fare was a little over the top, but nothing beyond the stereotypical Japanese love of kitsch. It wasn't that much different from the Yokohama Carp Hotel or the four-star Sleepy Monkey Inn in Oita, really.

Or so I thought until I saw the swimming pool. It was lorded over by a Macy's-sized balloon of a Chinese beckoning cat. The kind you always see in shop windows, waving you in with their paw. The pool was filled with water that had been colored white somehow, so that from a distance it looked like a giant bowl of milk.

The Day Manager insisted the water was perfectly safe. Just conventional food coloring, he said. It would wash right off with a quick rinse, no problem. He swore the pool adhered to the highest codes of health and safety, and encouraged me to take a dip.

I didn't swim anymore, not since I'd saved actress Anna Wong's pet bonobo chimp from pulling a Brian Jones during the post-premiere party for *Wing-Chun Sex Ghost IV*. Of course, I didn't tell the Day Manager that. I just thanked him and told him that if a drunken chimp ever fell in the water, it was best to leave him to his own devices. The Day Manager just nodded, like he'd suspected the same thing all along.

The one hotel feature that really got my hairs up had nothing to do with cats or swimming pools. It was the stairs. They were temporarily off limits because they were being "fixed." I don't know how you fix stairs, but that's what the sign said. *Stairs off use. Broken. We are fix. Staff of Hotel Kitty thanks you!*

So there I was on the fifth-floor Feline Metropolis, looking at the paw-print carpet, waiting for the elevator. I've always avoided elevators. My long-standing aversion to them is not as irrational as it may seem, but that's another story. Let's just say in my line of work you make resourceful enemies.

The elevator doors opened to reveal a gaunt old man dressed in a burgundy porter uniform. The suit was immaculate, right up to the pillbox hat tilted perfectly on his head. Even with his stooped posture, the man was tall for a Japanese his age, which looked to be the other side of sixty judging by the thinning strands of whitish hair sticking out from under his hat. He leaned out of the elevator, his upper body curled like a wave about to crash as his lips struggled into a smile that fell apart twenty years ago.

"I am the Night Porter," he said.

I nodded and got in the elevator. I probably should have bowed, but the idea of taking an elevator made me forget my manners. They were forgettable as it was—which was okay since I was *gaijin*. Anything short of poking my hosts in the eyes with chopsticks was considered polite for an American. The door closed behind me.

The Night Porter and I shared the elevator with a scrawny shorthaired cat barely older than a kitten. He was a sketchy little runt, puny and jumpy as hell. The type of cat Steve Buscemi would play in the movie. He was probably always getting suitcases dropped on his tail, or maybe traveling up and down all day messed up his equilibrium. I didn't envy the little guy. He looked disoriented, like a teenager in a room without television.

As we descended I felt the Night Porter studying me. His mouth parted every so often as if he were about to speak, but he'd only inhale noisily and smack his lips. The first couple times he did it, I half turned around. He'd stare at me, I'd smile weakly and drop my eyes back to the floor. Then he'd start making the smacking sound again.

We stopped on the fourth floor. The elevator doors opened, but there was no one waiting. Just twin marble cat statues and an empty hall. The elevator doors closed again, and we continued down. Then the Night Porter spoke.

"I thought you already checked out."

He didn't look at me when he talked, but stared at the numbers over the elevator door, the ones people always stare at. Amazingly, no advertisers had bought up the space yet.

"I'm sorry?" I said.

"I thought you checked out."

"No." I chuckled. "Just checked in yesterday. I won't be checking out for a while."

He smacked his lips again. A wet sound like meat being pulled from the bone. I just smiled as he leaned toward me for a closer look, scrutinizing me like some strange object he'd found washed up on the beach.

Just when it was turning into the longest five-story elevator trip in the history of the world, the doors parted to reveal the lobby. With yet more cat statues and cat paintings and just plain cats hanging around, it wasn't exactly your everyday hotel lobby. But compared to the elevator, it was a veritable oasis of normalcy.

"*Dewa mata,*" I said to the old man as I stepped out of the elevator. I remembered to bow this time. The Night Porter didn't move except to lower his head a few degrees. With his stoop, that was all it took to bow.

The two Siamese cats that always hung out at the front desk eyed me as I walked by, that haughty, superior expression all over their pointy faces. Their names were Lieber and Stoller, but Leopold and Loeb would have been more fitting. The Day Manager saw me and gave me a big grin. I did what I could to return it and kept walking toward the front door.

"Is everything satisfactory, Mr. Chaka?" he called out.

"Excellent." I had my hand half raised to wave good-bye, but he wasn't letting it go with that.

"You've met the Night Porter, I presume? He'll be on duty tonight to take care of anything you might need."

"Great," I said, inching toward the door.

"And all is well with your roommate?"

"The cat? Cat is great. Great cat."

"She is really something, isn't she?" He beamed. "Coat white as the year's first snow. We aren't allowed to play favorites here, but I can't help loving that cat. I love all the cats, in their own way, but she is especially divine. She has the manner of a princess, don't you agree?"

I forced a smile.

"You know," the Day Manager continued, "one thousand years ago Emporer Ichijo witnessed five white kittens being born and decreed that they be raised in his palace in Kyoto, treated as if they were real princesses. With her coat and carriage, it wouldn't surprise me if your cat were a direct descendant of Ichijo's royal cats."

The cherubic Day Manager smiled broadly, amused by the thought.

"Pick of the litter," I said.

He fought to keep his smile in place.

"A good evening to you, then, sir."

I nodded, and walked out the door.

I walked around the little town without passing anyone on the street. I didn't find a single place of business. Not even a noodle shop. Before I knew it I found myself back in my room at the Hotel Kitty.

Out of nowhere, I started wondering if I was getting old. Just like that.

My editor had been hinting that maybe it was time for me to go work for *Generasia X*, our new sister Web publication that catered to the 20–31⅓ demographic. He said it was the next logical step for me. I told him *Generasia X* was a stupid name for a magazine.

It's not a magazine, he pointed out. It's an *e-zine*.

It's *generasiax.com*.

Even Sarah—Sarah who'd come to *Youth in Asia* as a plucky nineteen-year-old, pierced punk rocker whose one driving ambition was to die with more holes in her body than John Dillinger—even she was about to go over to *Generasia X*. And though she vehemently denied it, in an unguarded moment I'd even caught her using the word *career*.

Ed said that *Generasia X* could give me a fresh perspective, a chance to explore more challenging subject matter. By clicking through the screens once or twice, I'd ascertained challenging subject matter was stuff like how to get raises _click here_ *for McMahon's bestselling "Who's Your Daddy? How to Make Your Boss Say Yes!"* how to wear suits _click here_ *for 20% off at Big and Large,* how to get your abs in shape _click here_ *for a 40% discount at Jim's Gym,* how to pick up girls in bars _enter your zip_ *for bars in your area,* have more sex and better sex _click here_ *for tips from porn queens* and buy the perfect car stereo _click here_ *to eavesdrop on lesbians!*

I told Ed that the day I start writing about crap like that was the day I snap my pencils in half and join the holdout Khampa guerillas in the mountains of Tibet.

You can't keep the world from changing, Ed said. Just think about it.

So here I was in some goofy hotel on mandatory R&R in nowhere Hokkaido, thinking about it.

Had I known it would come to this, I may not have "assaulted" the visiting Japanese film director at the Chicago Film Festival a few weeks before. But I probably would have.

His name was Ishao Tonda. His movie *Wildman for Geisha!* was loosely based on my life, specifically on a strange episode that happened a few years ago in Tokyo. I'd never given anyone permission to make a movie about me, though, so they had to change a few details.

In the movie, I worked for a magazine called *Wild Teenager.* Instead of being the highly respected teen publication *Youth in Asia* is in reality, *Wild Teenager* was a soft-core rag popular with middle-aged middle managers with *rorikon*—Lolita complexes.

I wasn't called Billy Chaka. The character based on me was named Randy Chance. He didn't wear black slacks and white shirts either, the kind that made Sarah call me the human yin-yang symbol. Randy Chance dressed in technicolor suits. And instead of my ordinary wingtips, he wore custom-made silver Doc Martens.

The final scene saw Randy Chance taking an elevator to the top of the Sunbeam City Building to enjoy a game of rooftop minigolf with the gorgeous geisha he's just saved from the yakuza.

Golf.

You bet I assaulted the director.

I can take a little kidding. And yes, people are free to interpret things their own way and follow their artistic vision. I probably would've forgiven even the golf scene if it wasn't for the way the film treated the two loves of my life.

Sarah was written off as a mousy, mixed-up womanchild who idolized Randy Chance. A passionless bimbo hopelessly disconnected from reality. Randy Chance's little blonde cheerleader. In other words, nothing like the Sarah I knew— she of the ferocious personal critiques, she of the scathing feminist deconstructions. She who was so jealous—of a city no less—that every time I went to Tokyo she visited a certain disreputable dentist in Cuspidoria, Ohio, and got one of her teeth pulled. She did it for the medication, she said. She did it to forget about me.

And Tokyo—my beloved Tokyo, the city I loved enough to mess up my life for weeks and months and going on years on end—Tokyo didn't fare much better.

Back when I'd first heard about the project, I used my connections to insure Tonda didn't get a permit to shoot in greater Tokyo. I figured that would stop the film. It didn't. Instead, all the exteriors were shot in Osaka. Osaka looks like Tokyo like Philly looks like New York, but with all the digital trickery available these days, a talented filmmaker could pull it off.

Tonda was not a talented filmmaker.

And as it happened I only ended up slapping the untalented little bastard inside the Drake Hotel. One weak little open-handed love tap on the side of the face. It was a mild rebuke, at worst. As it turned out, he couldn't even handle that.

It turned into a big deal. An *incident*. Lots of phone calls back and forth and so on. But I never apologized.

Sarah thought I was out of line. She said it was just a movie, and slapping the guy was something Randy Chance would have done, not Billy Chaka. I said I was just trying to defend her character. She said she could defend her own character, thank you very much.

Then *she* slapped *me*.

My editor had put up with a lot over the years, but all this slappery proved too much. I have a troubling suspicion the real problem was that Ed actually *liked* the movie. But I'll give him the benefit of the doubt. After a long argument, Ed suggested in no uncertain terms that I take a vacation.

I didn't want a vacation.

Take one or you're fired, he said.

He couldn't have meant it, but the next day there was a plane ticket on my desk with an itinerary enclosed. Two weeks in a mountain town at someplace called the Hotel Kitty. There was a note, too, attached to my hotel reservation slip. The handwriting wasn't Ed's.

> *A caterpillar*
> *This deep in fall*
> *Still not a butterfly.*
> *—One of your beloved Japanese poets.*
> *Think about it, caterpillar boy.*

I was the one who forced haiku on Sarah, so I guess it was my own fault. Still, you gotta hate it when people use poetry against you. I knew I was supposed to sit around and contemplate a reply, but I didn't feel contemplative.

So here I was trying not to think about *Generasia X*. Trying not to think about the silly director I slapped, and most of all trying not to think about Sarah. That didn't work, so I tried not to think at all. As any Zen student will tell you, it's like washing blood with blood.

When the not-thinking fell through, I did the next best thing and turned on the TV. Sure enough, I didn't have a thought for some ten or fifteen minutes until an ad for *Wildman for Geisha!* came along and ruined it.

I shut off the TV, yawned and rubbed my eyes. Then I slapped my face a few times in order to tighten up the loose skin around my mug. I have no idea if it actually works, but as with most rituals it doesn't really matter. The point is just to do something. Next, I did some three-fingered yoga push-ups. I'm no fitness geek, but the body needs routine main-tainance so I did what I could.

The cat watched me from atop his little perch, listless as ever. I'd probably been the most boring guest he'd ever had. Not only was I not a cat fanatic, but I clearly had no business in this hotel. No secret amorous rendezvous, no family vaca-tion, no tantric ritual that called for a private room and a cat. Hell, I hadn't even watched the porno channels on the TV. So why, the cat seemed to say, are you at the Hotel Kitty? To do push-ups?

Outside, the last of the daylight struggled against the encroaching darkness of the winter sky. The mountains were losing their shapes, blurring into shadows. Even though it was right outside my window, the whole scene struck me as hopelessly remote, impenetrable. Some austere virtual reality projected onto a screen.

I tried to envision a future spent looking out the windows of strange hotels, with only a nameless cat for company. A future like an Edward Hopper painting. *Has-Been with Feline.*

This vacation thing was killing me.

2

The cat pricked up its ears at the sound of the elevator bell. I sat up in bed and listened to the soft parade of approaching footsteps down the hall. They stopped outside my room.

A sharp knock at the door sent the cat leaping from atop the television. She landed noiselessly, bounded to the door and began warbling a language restricted to *a*s, *w*s, and *r*s. I got out of bed and dragged myself across the room.

I turned the knob and gave it a pull.

It was the Night Porter.

He was swaying in a circular motion, engaged in a slow struggle with gravity. His eyes stared off into space and he had fresh towels in his hands, the ones I'd requested about four hours ago. I'd forgotten all about them.

"Domo arigato gozaimasu," I thanked him, trying to sound wide awake as I reached out to take the towels. My words had the effect of reversing his sway. He rotated in the opposite direction while my hands hung there in the air, empty. The cat began rubbing his back against the man's legs.

"I want to talk to you," the Night Porter said.

"Would you like to come in?"

"I want to talk to you about immortality."

I was awake now and besides, there was no chance of getting to sleep with the jet lag. No harm in humoring the old guy. The day might come when I would be an old man wandering hotel halls and wanting to talk to strangers about immortality, or the apocalypse, or how expensive tangerines were these days.

"Immortality, huh?" I said. "I'd better clear off a chair."

I turned on the lights. He stepped into the room as I turned around and moved my briefcase from the chair. "Would you like anything to drink?" I asked over my shoulder.

The answer was a single dull thump.

I turned around to find the Night Porter sprawled out on the floor. He somehow looked taller that way.

I rushed over to him as the cat scurried under the bed. I asked him if he was OK. He didn't reply. I reached beneath his arms and lifted him up to sitting position, propping him against the wall. He weighed almost nothing.

"Are you hurt?"

His eyes were closed. He was still breathing, but only just. Not even realizing what I was doing, I grabbed his wrist and felt for his pulse. The bones in his arm felt like they would crumble in my hand.

He began fumbling for his breast pocket with his other hand, trying to dig something out.

Pills. I dropped his wrist and reached into his pocket, already feeling a little relieved.

But there were no pills. Instead, I pulled out a laminated card, some kind of ID badge with a picture of the Night Porter. The reverse side featured a stylized black logo of a bird. Next to it, a phone number.

"Call," the old man wheezed.

I nodded and dashed to the phone. I punched the number and waited, watching the old man, putting the events in order in my head, readying to speak to the emergency people. I didn't know what to say except that he'd fallen down.

There was no answer. I tried the number again. The old

man's head was rolling slowly side to side, his chest still rising and falling with the same rhythm. I let the phone ring ten, twelve times, watching him and trying to figure out what to do next.

He opened his eyes suddenly and looked up at me.

"They're not coming," he said.

It fell somewhere between a statement and a question. His eyes seemed less clouded, his voice was steady. I took his lucidity as a good sign.

"I'll call the front desk," I said. "Hang in there." I stuck the card with his picture and the phone number in my shirt pocket and called the front desk.

I can't say for certain, but I'm pretty sure it was between the second and third ring when the Night Porter died.

Good hotels have a death mechanism in place, an entire set of preexisting protocols used to deal with guests who check out prematurely. Japanese are nuts about drills, and if the Hotel Kitty was like other hotels they probably conducted death preparedness exercises at least twice a month.

But the Hotel Kitty wasn't like other hotels.

I rang downstairs several times without getting an answer. I toyed with calling the authorities but decided against it. It wouldn't look good for the cops and ambulance people to come busting in while the hotel staff was completely unaware of the dead man in 523, and I had no desire to embarrass the hotel. Besides, it wasn't an emergency anymore. No one could help the Night Porter now.

I decided to go downstairs and see if I could find one of the staff wandering around. Certainly they wouldn't have left the old man to tend to the hotel all by himself, even if there were almost no guests.

When I stepped outside the room I was seized with a new dilemma. I couldn't decide if I should leave the door open or closed. If I closed it, I felt as if I were deliberately concealing the man's body. Closed doors implied a vague duplicity. On the other hand, if I left the door opened, there was a chance that another guest would see the body, get freaked out and notify the hotel staff. But since that's what I was trying to do anyway, having two people looking for a staff member might mean finding one sooner. Still, there was the chance that a person might see the corpse and get right on the the phone to the authorities, ruining my plan of preserving the integrity of the Hotel Kitty. Worse yet, a staff member could be making the rounds and spot the body. What kind of idiot would leave the room with a dead body just sitting there for everyone to see, he might wonder.

I was thoroughly annoying myself. Finally, the cat helped me decide. I figured if I left the door open, the cat might escape. The Day Manager told me they have a very strict policy about keeping the cats separated. If his little princess escaped, he'd go into conniptions, and I might well have another corpse on my hands.

I stepped out of room 523 and closed the door, leaving the cat and the Night Porter shut inside.

The halls were deserted. The only sound I could hear was the insectile buzz of the lights interrupted by the occasional whimpering of some lonely animal locked behind one of the doors.

I hit the button and waited for the elevator.

When it came, the scrawny kitten was still inside. He wasn't so jumpy this time, though. He clawed at the carpet leisurely, hardly aware of my presence. The carpet was patterned with an intricate geometry of tiny cat heads, like something M. C. Escher might have dreamt up while smoking cat-nip. I hit the lobby button and readied words for the staff. I'd tell them how the Night Porter had come into my room, said a few words, fallen over, said a few more and that was it. Dead. All in less time than it takes to watch a television commercial.

The elevator doors opened onto a view across the lobby. The huge windows at the hotel entrance afforded a great mountain vista, according to the Day Manager. But tonight I couldn't see the mountains, only a few streetlamps casting a pale orange glow, diffusing into the night.

Inside was almost as silent. There was no one at the hotel desk, not even a sleeping cat. The big room was entirely empty save for the furniture looming in the shadows.

Off to my left, toward the bar, I heard voices. Through the window embedded in the half-closed door I saw a flickering blue light. Television. With that I felt a palpable sense of relief at having ushered the secret of the man's death safely through the hotel, at having fulfilled my sad duty.

A young woman was sitting with her back to me in the darkened room. Next to her stood the bartender, also facing the other direction. They were both staring at a TV mounted above a long mirror at the bar. I walked into the room and cleared my throat.

The woman swiveled on her stool. I caught only a glimpse of her face before she turned her attention back to the television. She looked like she'd been crying. She was hunched over, clutching something to her chest.

The bartender was dressed in a white shirt with a black bow tie. He gave me a sympathetic little nod, then turned back to the TV. I walked up and stood next to the woman.

"Have you heard?" she said. "He's dead."

I glanced at the bartender. He nodded concernedly, as if to say *yes, it's true.*

The TV flickered in the dark. Light danced over their still faces. At length, I was able to drag the obvious question from the morass of my thoughts.

"How did you know?"

"It's all over the television," the woman said sadly, shaking her head. Before I could look at the TV, she handed me the picture she'd been clutching to her chest. She did it delicately, as if afraid it would break.

It was a framed photograph of her standing next to some longhaired guy a leather motorcycle jacket. The picture was taken in a bar. She was beaming while the guy stuck out his lips in a showy pout. His face was flushed with drink.

I didn't get it.

On TV a woman holding a microphone stood in front of a big building. The building was definitely not the Hotel Kitty, and clearly wasn't in this town. I was trying to figure out what part of Tokyo it was when the image suddenly switched.

The screen was filled with a photo of an androgynous-looking guy with big red hair that matched his lipstick and eye shadow. He wore a thin black shirt with fishnet sleeves and a long silver chain around his neck, his head tilted at an angle just between god-I'm-sexy and god-I'm-bored. Two dates were printed below, a difference of twenty-seven years.

I knew who he was. Anyone who'd been in this country during the last five years would have. I'd seen his face more times than John Hinckley had seen *Taxi Driver*, and the only reason I didn't recognize him in the young woman's photograph was because he almost never appeared without his stage makeup.

His name was Yoshimura Fukuzatsu. Everyone knew him simply as Yoshi, the leader of Japan's most popular rock band, Saint Arrow.

Of course he was all kinds of other things, depending on

who you asked: a pop mastermind, a no-talent glamster, petulant genius of the pituitary set, the worst thing to happen to Japanese rock music since MTV, just another drug addict, a totally gorgeous *iro-otoko* like completely to die for, a terrible-influence-on-slash-fitting-symbol-of the listless Japanese youth raised in the "forgotten decade" of the nineties.

And now Yoshi the dead rock star, unplugged at age twenty-seven.

For some reason I wanted to laugh.

The young woman swiveled around and regarded me with painful sincerity. Maybe it was the shock or the juxtaposition of the two deaths that gave me a laugh impulse, because there wasn't anything very funny about two dead people. I handed the picture back to her.

"I'm sorry," I said.

"Were you also a Saint Arrow fan?" she asked, choking on tears.

"They were OK."

She recoiled slightly, her sympathetic look going sour.

"Look," I said, "I don't know how to tell you this, so I'll just say it. The Night Porter . . ."

"He forgot your towels," the bartender said, shaking his head. He had already snapped to attention and started launching apologies. "You must forgive his—"

"No," I interrupted him. "It's not that. He's just died. In my room."

I confronted their bewildered stares for a second then looked away again to the TV. The coverage of Yoshi's death was being interrupted by a shampoo commercial.

Things moved pretty quickly after that. Guys in hospital gear arrived and hauled him out of the room without so much as asking a single question. It was all done very quietly, as if everyone was afraid of waking the hotel guests. Assuming there were any.

The Day Manager was called in and arrived looking tired and shaggy by his standards, which meant he looked about like I did on my best days. He offered profuse apologies and begged me to take another room. I told him I didn't feel like moving all my stuff, that it wasn't a big deal.

"Very well," he said finally, "you're a braver man than I."

The cat stayed under the bed during all the excitement, causing the Day Manager to worry that the event had traumatized her. I lied and told him the cat slept through the whole thing, never even saw the Night Porter come in. I don't think the Day Manager believed me. He gave me his home phone number and told me to call if the cat princess needed anything.

The young woman and the bartender hovered in the hall outside my room, watching it all. Their attention seemed to be torn between the death in the hotel and the tragedy unfolding miles away in Tokyo. They looked confused, their grief interrupted, compounded and split by the Night Porter's uncanny timing.

As for Yoshi, the TV wasn't giving many details, but I'd worked enough Dead Rock Star stories to know when one dies at twenty-seven drugs and suicide are the silent contenders. Armies of reporters would be chasing the words like ghosts through the floating world of Tokyo nightlife. Kids everywhere were probably ringing each other up, sharing the bad news. Rumors would be exploding in Internet chatrooms worldwide. By morning, there would be more information generated about Yoshi's death than there was about Japan's wartime atrocities, and the circumstances surrounding it would get foggier with each rumor. Like samurai scribe Yamamoto Tsunetomo once wrote, the occurrence of mysteries is always by word of mouth.

As for the Night Porter, no one seemed surprised. No one wondered at the cause. *Kowaiso,* they all sighed, a phrase that simultaneously meant too bad, poor thing, that's his fate. It was as if the hotel staff were half expecting it, had been for some time. It was nearly 3 A.M. by the time everyone cleared out of my room. I shut the door quietly. The cat came out from under the bed and started pacing, pausing in odd corners and rubbing up against the wall where the man died, as if trying to understand the events through tactile sensation.

I was getting undressed when I felt the card in my pocket. I'd neglected to mention it to the hospital guys who'd come for the body, and had even left out this detail when talking to the Day Manager. I didn't recall ever deciding not to tell them, but for some reason I just didn't.

I looked at the number and wondered who the hell he'd been trying to call, who he thought could help him as he felt his chest constrict, his breath shorten. I thought of the look on his face when he realized it didn't matter who he called.

They're not coming.

I considered dialing the number again to see if I would get an answer, but it was 3 A.M., and if anyone answered I wouldn't know what to say. I thought about ringing up the Day Manager at home and telling him about the card, about the immortality thing. Just thought you should know, I'd say.

But I didn't. Let them think he died without even realizing what was happening to him, I thought. Let them think he went humbly fulfulling his duty with a smile on his face, fresh towels in his hand.

I slipped the card into my wallet and shoved the wallet into the nightstand drawer, next to *Gideon's Bible, The Teachings of Buddha* and volumes one and two of Soseki's *I Am a Cat.* I turned off the light. Sometime later, I fell asleep.

$\ni$et to Tokyo."

It was Ed's smoky rasp, straight outta Cleveland. I grunted and hung up the phone. My vacation was finally over.

I was anxious to get back to work and there is no place to work like Tokyo. Besides, I figured I'd experienced all the Hotel Kitty had to offer.

But I didn't like Ed's attitude.

Sure, he was my boss, but there must be some teen periodical union rule against forcing people to go on vacation and then calling them at six in the morning and telling them to get back on the job.

So I lay there for a moment, waiting for Ed to call again with a different tone. It was maybe fifteen minutes later when he did. I allowed him to talk this time, answering him in monosyllables, letting him dangle. I wanted to see how far he would go, test his groveling capacity. A good editor knows when to beg.

Whatever else he was, Ed was a good editor. He apologized and apologized and explained himself silly. I waited for him to take a breath, then unleashed a rapid-fire list of demands.

I told him I'd do the Yoshi story, but only if I could go full Billy. That meant if I wanted to approach Yoshi's life and death solely by writing about his vintage tennis shoe collection, that's how it would go down. If I wanted to limit my story to the night of his death or the day of his birth, I would. And whether my research called for slapping someone in the face or delivering a Jeet Koon Do finger strike to the throat, I wasn't gonna hold back.

I also demanded *Youth in Asia* accountant Chuck grant me a 20 percent increase in my per diem. Just for fun. And finally, I wanted Ed's word that he would print my review of *Wildman for Geisha!*

No way, he'd said. Forget it, that's what started this whole thing. Just get over it. I told him the only way I was going to get over it was to write about it. Out of the question, he said.

Well, I said, I guess you'd better just send Sarah then. He told me I knew damn well that Sarah won't do Japan, thanks to me. I'd ruined an entire country for her because of my inability to control myself within its borders.

I told him I could do the movie review in four hundred words.

The number of words aren't the point, he countered.

Guess you're screwed then, I said, and hung up. I went to the bathroom, brushed my teeth and started packing my bags. Ed held out for almost half an hour.

Three hundred words, max, he sighed.

I considered haggling for three hundred fifty, but I'd put him through enough for one morning. He liked to point out that before I worked for the magazine, he didn't even smoke. Now he was up to almost two packs a day.

Ed told me that Saint Arrow's bassist was having an invitation-only press conference at some Muay Thai kickboxing gym just west of Tokyo's Ikebukuro neighborhood. Ed had already made arrangements for me to attend.

Just before I walked out the door, the cat leapt up onto the coffee table and eyed me quizzically. It had probably seen guests pack their bags enough to know what happened next. Maybe I'm a sap, but I think the cat was a little sad to see me go.

I paused in the doorway, trying to conjure some friendly parting advice, some clever farewell. But I couldn't think of anything liable to help the animal live a more productive and satisfying life, couldn't even think of some little gesture to brighten its day.

"See ya, cat," I said and walked out of the room.

The Day Manager refused to believe my checking out of the hotel was unrelated to the Night Porter's death. He went through a litany of apologies and propositions, stopping just short of offering to bring the Night Porter back to life if I would stay a few extra days.

Just as the Day Manager was bidding me farewell, the lounge cat leapt up on the counter. It looked a lot like the cat in my room. They could have been sisters.

"Too bad people don't have nine lives, huh?" I said to the Day Manager as I lifted my bags.

"Well," he sighed. "I rather think people do. We just have no way of knowing how many lives have already passed, and how many we have left. We're in such a hurry that the beginnings and endings run together."

"Maybe," I said.

He bowed to me and then waved as I hurried out of the lobby, off to Sapporo to catch my flight. I wasn't sure if it was a beginning or an ending or both.

SECOND VERSE

Yoshi takes the stage
Thousands of people screaming
At one silent man.

—Rino Hana (submitted for the Saint
Arrow unofficial fan club's
biannual haiku contest)

Killing time on planes is murder. I couldn't write, because I spread stuff around when I compose—source material, drafts, the whalebone chucks. Couldn't read either, because you open a book on a plane and everybody knows what kind of guy you are. You can almost see thought bubbles over their heads. *"Oh my God, he's reading* Tales of Genji, *that stupid book I had to read in high school. This plane goes down, I'm not saving that geek."*

Sarah says this is world-class-caliber pathetic self-consciousness, but I know how people on planes think. If a guy next to me is thumbing through *Chicken Soup for the Executive Soul* or *The Seven Habits of Extremely Wealthy People*, I'm already planning to steal his floatation device before we even hit turbulence.

Since I couldn't read and I couldn't write, I made lists. I'd list every martial arts technique named for an animal, all the Tora-san movies, punch lines to sumo wrestling jokes, the twenty stupidest books read by people on the plane.

This time I took out a piece of paper and wrote "Dead Rock Stars." I came up with twenty-seven names without pausing to think. I started going down the list and noting the causes of death. Air disasters were represented to an uncomfortable degree. Ritchie Valens, Buddy Holly, the Big Bopper.

Otis Redding, the Bar-Kays. Ronnie Van Zant, Stevie Ray Vaughn, Randy Rhoads. Patsy Cline—though technically she was country.

I put away the list and thought about Yoshi and how the hell I was going to write anything new about Another Dead Rock Star.

"Live fast die young" was a concept about as novel as political corruption and just as ubiquitous. The average American probably thought young Japanese were still dressing up like Elvis and doing the twist—which, admittedly, some were. The slightly more informed Westerner knew something about the *aidoru* phenomenon and the prefab bubblegum pop that dominated the world's second biggest music market.

What most didn't know was that genuine domestic rock was alive and well in Japan. Even as the economy sputtered, kids were spending an average of a hundred dollars a month on CDs, two-thirds of which went to Japanese acts. Every international musical substrata ever invented was well represented, from Delta blues to So. Cal. surf punk to British rudeboy ska to Jamaican dub reggae to Congolese guitar pop—not to mention the homegrown varieties like *minyo* folksongs, *kayokyoku* MOR, Okinawan pop, Shibuya-kei and the earsplitting Osaka industrial noise rock. To Yoshi's well-publicized chagrin, Saint Arrow was usually lumped in with a movement called "visual-kei," a genre that combined elements of glam, goth, pop-metal and a weird strain of neoromanticism into a theatric package that was uniquely Japanese, right down to the unfathomable faux-European names. Cloix de Mickey, Ne'vell Vagû, LeDravenzi, Vox D'merlow—the names were nonsensical enough to make even a hard-core Dadaist cringe.

Not surprisingly, Japan had also cultivated its own canon of musical corpses, lest anyone doubt they rocked as hard as the West. And in true rock fashion, Japanese stars weren't content to simply jump in front of the Chuo train or wander off into the suicide forest of Aokigahara. They went for spectacular, show-stopping deaths.

One morning in 1995, Naked Ape guitarist Hideto Fujiwara drove out to Chiba, rigged up a ligature and hung himself from the flagpole of his childhood elementary school. Around that same time, Nagoya ska drummer Kenji "2-kick" Tanaka calmly padlocked himself into a batting cage, bought a bucket of fifty balls, and kneeled at the plate. By the time horrified onlookers finally got the manager to shut off the power the bucket was already empty. Tanaka was in a coma six days before he died.

Just last year, teen idol Jusan Ozuko flattened a few fifths of canned heat and decided to sleep it off in a Dumpster. It was a cold night, and he covered himself with garbage to stay warm. The garbage man didn't see him the next day, and Ozuko got trash-compacted. Though autopsy results revealed Ozuko was already dead of hypothermia, hard-core fans blamed the Tokyo Municipal Waste Removal Union. Packs of angry teenage girls attacked garbage collectors. Poorly constructed bombs were found in Dumpsters across the city and armed police had to accompany garbagemen on their duties until the hostility died down. Even today you'll still see the odd garbage can spray-painted *Remember Ozuko*.

And now Yoshi.

It wasn't exactly a surprise. He lived with such an unwavering devotion to rock and roll mythology that it was probably the only ending he knew. On paper, his life looked pieced together from bits of every predictable rock tragedy since Robert Johnson sold his soul to VH1's *Behind the Music*.

Yoshi experiences unhappy childhood. Develops obsession with his early musical idols. Maintains poor scholastic record. Purchases used guitar in epiphanic moment at fifteen.

Jump ahead four years.

Saint Arrow becomes the biggest underground live act in Tokyo. They release their first album. Cool people in cool clubs in Shibuya listen to Yoshi's band. Their cool younger siblings scribble his name on notebooks. Big labels fight over him. One wins. Second record gets nonstop hype on TV, radio, magazines, and Web sites as it goes silver goes gold goes platinum. Endless tours, constant video shoots, magazine spreads, television appearances and advertising tie-ins.

These years are a blur.

Alienation first from family then friends then fans then self. A personal life that's neither personal nor life. Idealism becomes realism becomes nihilism. A backstage parade of Interchangeable Nameless Groupies. A tabloid circus of Interchangeable High-Profile Girlfriends. Cameras broken, paparazzi punched. Expensive cars wrapped around telephone poles. Lawsuits filed against management. Impending band implosion. Drug busts, paternity suits, high-rent rehab.

These years are lost.

Then a tanned, rested, ready-to-rock reemergence. Sobriety lip service, virtues of exercise and spiritual maturity extolled. Talk of eagerly anticipated don't-call-it-a-comeback album.

And after the commercial, tragedy strikes.

I arrived in Tokyo at 3:34 P.M. and already felt like I was coming back to life.

Tokyo, my beloved Tokyo.

My love for Tokyo is one of those boozy, bare-knuckled

kind of loves that makes normal people uneasy. A gritty love like a kung fu noir written by Tennessee Williams. The city and I had done a lot of damage to each other over the years, but I always came back, and she always accepted me. Dysfunctional, yeah—but with a place like Tokyo and a guy like me, how could it be anything else?

Tokyo wasn't so much a city as a fractal explosion, a sprawling megalopolis of inhuman scale. It was a wilderness of hideous beauty, a jungle forged from iron and pulsing with neon, at once a sensory playground of endless lights and relentless noise and a dead gray wasteland of oppressive ferroconcrete tenements and faceless skyscrapers. Tokyo made an oxymoron of the phrase "urban planning," turned buzzwords like "managed growth" into bureaucratic gallows humor. Buildings begat streets begat highways begat subways begat buildings. It was impossible to imagine Tokyo was constructed by people. Harder still to believe it was made *for* people. Tokyo seemed the result of some constantly mutating virus, or a parasitic growth run amok—some being wholly indifferent to the health and welfare of human beings, yet dependent upon them for its survival.

Yet for all that, the city wasn't some dystopian nightmare. There were beautiful parks, clean streets. There were ancient temples and shrines, forgotten neighborhoods that still possessed an antique charm of days gone by. Crime was low, trains ran on time, and twenty million people mostly tolerated twenty million other people.

And whenever possible, I joined them.

Which is not to say I harbored gaijin fantasies of turning Japanese. Hell, even the Japanese had a tough time being Japanese. But over the years I'd covered so many stories there that I was probably more a Tokyoite than a Clevelander. Still, Sarah may have been right when she said I love Tokyo the same way people love Disneyland or prison movies. They love it, she said, because they don't have to live there.

Then again, maybe Sarah was just jealous.

My editor had arranged a limousine to pick me up at the Tokyo Haneda Airport and take me to the Isamu Suda press gambit. Isamu Suda was Saint Arrow's bassist—and more importantly, Yoshi's longtime second banana and partner in crime. It would have been quicker and cheaper to take the trains, but since the star treatment was bound to last about as long as a junior high romance, I tried to enjoy the ride.

It was a crummy day in Tokyo, unseasonably heavy clouds and light rain creating an army of umbrellas on the sidewalks as the limo moved north through the city. Anywhere else and you'd think it was the last shopping day of the year, but for Tokyo it looked like a ghost town. The riot of video screens and neon ads was still blinking dutifully, but no one paid much attention. All that advertising, wasted on a lousy day.

During the ride, I listened to the radio. I heard the name Yoshi six times before settling on a station. The program I stopped on featured grieving teens calling in asking the DJ whether life was worth living now that Yoshi was gone.

Well, there are probably a lot of you out there right now asking yourself the same kinds of questions. And that's important—to realize that you're not alone, that in wishing Yoshi was still here you are expressing love. A great big love for not just Yoshi, but everything he meant and for all the other people who love Yoshi the same way you do. Yumiko, as long as you still feel love, Yoshi will never really die. You bet your life life is still worth living. Now let's go to Midori in Kobe, who wants to know if it's OK to cry when she listens to the song "Fallopian Utopia."

Miraculously, there were no suicides blamed yet on

Yoshi's death, but I knew they were coming. Thousands of lonely souls would be aching to end their unformed lives. If entrance exams, schoolyard bullies and abusive teachers didn't do the trick, kids could always kill themselves over pop stars. The more feverishly the adults implored kids to stay calm, to call hotlines and talk to their teachers and their guidance counselors, the greater the danger of a suicide epidemic. The media would create a circus the kids would want to join, if only to finally belong to something.

Legend had it that the day he met Suda, Yoshi himself was about to jump off a bridge into the Ooka-gawa River. While he stared down at his watery death, Suda strolled by wearing a trench coat with a Happy Brigade button pinned to the lapel. Yoshi and Suda got into a conversation about the album *Anhedonia,* and soon Yoshi forgot about killing himself. Instead, he and Suda went to Kentucky Fried Chicken together and talked about forming a band.

If the story was true then it acted as a blueprint for their future relationship. Suda wasn't a musical collaborator so much as he was Yoshi's caretaker, baby-sitter, cheerleader and emergency medical technician. I remembered a picture taken during an infamous Fuji Festival gig where Yoshi collapsed in the middle of a seventeen-minute guitar solo. With weary exasperation Suda is reaching down with one hand to grab Yoshi's limp body as it falls. Suda wears a sweat-drenched T-shirt that says "MOMMY," in English, while the bass guitar dangles from his body like a vestigial appendage.

On the radio the DJ told one Yoshi fan after another things were going to be OK, that perhaps some good could even come out of it. He hoped that Yoshi's death could *teach kids out there that life is precious, not something to be wasted.* The DJ concluded his sermon and put on the Beach Boys'

"Wouldn't It Be Nice?," a song Saint Arrow used for chase-out music at the end of their shows.

Golden California harmonies filled the limo. I thought about the Beach Boys back when they were a bunch of baby-faced surfer kids in matching striped shirts. Smiling and riding the wave, oblivious of the undertow about to take hold.

The clouds above finally made good on their threat, opening up onto all the umbrellas as we passed the shoppers outside the big department stores of Ikebukuro. It wasn't Beach Boys weather, but they kept right on singing, anyway.

Suda was holding his press conference in a little gray concrete box called the Yokohama Kickboxers Pavillion II. It wasn't actually in Yokohama, like the original, but in a northwestern Tokyo neighborhood known as a decent place to go for a knife wound.

The curbsides surrounding the building were clogged with tiny beat-up cars bought before the bubble burst, vehicles perfect for racing after ugly stories in the bad parts of town. Amidst the Tokyo dailies crowd, the limousine stood out like a tiger shark in a goldfish pond. Right away I was spotted by a small band of reporters smoking cigarettes near the entrance. They eyed the limousine for all of two seconds before they got an instinctual group impulse, moving so fast you'd think they'd been choreographing it for months.

And suddenly it wasn't just the guys by the side entrance coming at me. Reporters started popping out of cars, mini-vans and even racing out the front door of the YPKII. In mere seconds, the limo was completely surrounded.

My driver suddenly turned around and began studying me. "You famous?" he asked.

"It depends," I said. "You ever heard of Billy Chaka?"

He thought about it for a moment, then shook his head.

"How about Randy Chance?"

He laughed. "You're not Randy Chance."

A flurry of cameras and microphones clattered against the car. Yelling, shoving, people banging on the hood. Faces like bloated fish pressed against the window then were torn away, replaced by others.

"Maybe they think you're Yoshi," he said. "Come back from the dead."

Suddenly the shouting and the shoving took on an organized form. The jostling chaos abruptly ended with two columns of reporters split down the middle by a swath of clear pavement. I half expected someone to roll a red carpet down the center of the aisle.

Everyone settled into a hushed silence.

I checked my reflection in the rearview mirror. No star quality whatsoever. I decided I'd better go out and face the music before the scene turned into a reportorial Altamont.

I opened the door and stepped out of the car.

The sidewalk exploded.

Cameras whirred and flashbulbs popped staccato. The reporters' faces were a severe uniform of overearnestness, their speech stripped to an ugly core as they shrieked questions. At least, I think they were questions. The sound waves piled on top of each other, merging in an indecipherable, muddled roar. Volleys of crackling white light erupted from all angles, as if the air itself was being torn apart.

Then it was all over.

The crowd went absolutely still. I stood there, grinning from ear to ear, confronting a hundred blank stares. I'd never disappointed so many people all at the same time.

Some of the reporters tilted their heads quizzically. Others lowered their cameras to make sure their viewfinders weren't lying. All eyes scanned me, searching desperately for any hint of fame and not finding it.

My fifteen minutes was over in seconds.

The crowd dispersed with mumbles and disappointed curses. A few of the reporters shot me accusing glances, as if I had planned the whole thing to make them look like jackasses. Then everyone wandered off, grousing and slouching their way inside the YPKII like schoolkids after rain cut recess short. I followed them into the building before I got all wet.

The YKPII oozed hard-nosed martial arts asceticism from the barren gray cinder-block walls that enclosed the grimy little space. Punching bags dangled from the low ceiling of corrugated steel like malformed, bulbous stalactites, while wooden wing-chun dummies huddled in the corner like beaten prisoners. In the center of the room stood a small boxing ring, its canvas floor a monochromatic pointillist painting done in rust brown. Closer inspection revealed the brown specks to be dried blood.

Sullen faces peered out from identical hooded gray sweatshirts. Several kickboxers prowled the area, observing the reporters with a mixture of curiosity and reserved contempt, like captive wolves glaring at fat tourists through the zoo bars. Groups of reporters stood in clusters, not knowing what to do with themselves. Some inspected the training equipment as if they were museum pieces, while others gave their own shoes the same treatment.

An older guy with scrub-brush silvery hair cut to military specs and a neck like a tree trunk emerged from a door at the rear of the facility and made his way toward the ring. He was flanked on either side by bigger, younger versions of himself.

The guy on the left was a six-feet-three slab of muscle and had a nose like a crushed beer can. The guy on the right was practically a walking caricature of his buddy—thirty pounds more meat and two more kinks to his beak.

The two heavyweights lifted the ropes and the older guy climbed inside. The reporters silently made their way toward the ring, crowding around its edges.

"I have an announcement from honorable Isamu Suda," the old man said. I half expected a mic to drop from the ceiling into the center of the ring like before a big fight, but his booming voice didn't need amplification. He put on a pair of glasses that looked like something made for a myopic Barbie doll and clumsily unfurled a scroll. His hands were all bumps and calluses, claws of meat permanently curled into arthritic half fists. The bags may not have been able to hit back, but over time they got their licks in.

"Esteemed Members of the Exulted, Glorious Press Corps," he began, barking out the words. "Thank you for attending. I realize that many of you have questions about Yoshi's unexpected passing. Though at this early juncture I have very little knowledge of the circumstances surrounding this tragedy, I would like to take this opportunity to address your concerns as best I am able. However, please understand there are certain topics I am not at liberty to discuss. Listen closely."

The old man cleared his throat. From the sound of it, his throat was a pretty crowded place. He spit at his feet as the two big guys on either side of him glared over the crowd, daring anyone to notice. The old guy continued reading.

"I will not entertain any questions regarding cocaine, amphetamines, heroin, hallucinogens, marijuana, alcohol, nicotine or other drugs including but not limited to those sold over the counter or by prescription, or any substances illegal in either this country or any country where Saint

Arrow recordings are available. I will not address questions about rumored girlfriends, groupies, underage women or anything that may or may not have occurred in Thailand. No questions about any former or current member of Saint Arrow, or any other artists or producers that may have collaborated with Yoshi—excluding myself. No questions about any assaults, altercations, lawsuits or other disputes in which Yoshi was allegedly involved. No questions pertaining to hair dye, hairspray, makeup, piercings, tattoos, scarification or other aspects of Yoshi's personal appearance. No questions about Santeria, esoteric Buddhism, Pluto Shine, foot-reading cults, Goodbuddy Beer, UFOs, or any political, religious or social views or commercial products allegedly espoused or endorsed by Yoshi. No questions about back-masked lyrics, subliminal messages, voodoo hexes, hoaxes or practical jokes. Finally, no questions that call for me to speculate on Yoshi's cause of death."

After rattling off the items like a series of quick jabs, the old guy took another well-earned pause. The reporters listened patiently, some even jotting down the guidelines just to be safe.

The old guy continued on to the next round.

"In my fragile emotional state, I regret that I am incapable of facing a large gathering such as yourselves. Therefore, the press conference shall follow this unique format: individual reporters shall be escorted by members of the gym to a location on the facility where they will be granted a private audience and given the opportunity to ask me a single question. If the question does not violate the guidelines stated above, I shall attempt to answer it. Should it violate the guidelines in any way, shape, or form, the offending reporter will be escorted from the premises."

The old guy stopped and glared out over the crowd. His

kickboxing days were probably behind him, but he was still deadly with his eyes. Everyone was motionless, quietly poised on his every word.

"Silence!" he bellowed.

I guess the speechwriter must have anticipated some kind of commotion, but there wasn't any. The old man smoldered some more and then told everyone to form a single line against the back wall.

Gray-sweated kickboxers descended from all sides. A hand like a brick nudged me between the shoulder blades and I went where it indicated. I enjoyed breathing and didn't feel like quitting over nothing.

In a matter of seconds I found myself in a neat, orderly line against the rear wall. The old man strode out of the ring flanked by his big friends and they walked to the other side of the facility and disappeared behind a door. A few moments later, I saw the first reporter being escorted by two smaller kickboxers into the same room.

I stood in line, thinking how stupid it was. All the other reporters looked like they were thinking the same thing, but everyone just put up with it. Japan's public schools had taught them that quiet resentment is the cornerstone of civilized society. America's hadn't taught me much of anything, so I don't know what my excuse was.

It was my turn before I'd even had a chance to think of a question.

All around the world, locker rooms smell pretty much the same. They triggered foggy memories of junior high gym class and all the stuff that went with it. Snapping towels, dirty jokes, wondering when the hell I was gonna sprout some pubic hair. Now that I had my pubic hair, I always felt a vague sense of accomplishment walking into a locker room. Whatever else happened, at least I got my pubic hair.

Suda was sitting on a bench at the end of the center aisle, boxed in by two rows of pale green metal lockers and the two giants who'd been in the ring. Up close, they still looked like flawed clones. The old thick-necked sensei was nowhere in sight.

Suda wore the same gray sweats as everyone else. The kickboxer look was ruined by his long blond hair, high-lighted with red streaks and gathered into a tight ponytail that exploded at the end like a cat-o'-nine-tails. I couldn't remember the last time I had seen him, but it was probably on stage with Yoshi—in which case it was no surprise I didn't recall how the bassist looked. Emperor Akihito could have shown up in a schoolgirl uniform and all eyes would still be on Yoshi and his fabulous flying fingers.

"You must be the guy from *Rolling Stone,*" Suda said in a mellow, friendly voice. Before I could correct him, he told me to have a seat. "Would you like some PowerPop?" he asked.

I declined and sat down across from him on the wooden bench. Suda put down the PowerPop and began rolling a bamboo stick over his shins, an old kickboxing treatment used to create tough calluses and make the bones better weapons. Hair aside, he looked about as rock 'n' roll as a suburban aerobics instructor. He wore one of those hangdog, loser's grins, like the kid who always gets picked last but can't help smiling that he was picked at all, and his move-ments betrayed an adolescent unease with his body.

"You come all the way from America for this?"

"Sort of," I said.

"Yoshi always wanted to tour the U.S. An American label, Toreador Records, was going to distribute *Detonation Under-*

pants. We would've done shows from San Francisco to New York. A regular fourteen-city tour. But the deal fell through."

"It's just as well," I said. "With his habits, Yoshi would've never made it out of California."

Just then one of the big kickboxers stepped forward, a serious look on his face. "Janis Joplin died in California," he said.

"So what?" said the other one. "So did Sam Cooke and Notorious B.I.G."

"And Dennis Wilson and Hillel Slovak," the first hissed. "And Randy California."

"Bullshit," the smaller one spat. "California drowned in Hawaii."

"Who's Randy California?" I asked.

"Guitarist for Spirit," the bigger one replied.

"He played with Hendrix before Hendrix was Jimi," the other added. "Back in sixty-six."

"His real name was Randy Wolfe . . ."

". . . and he died in Hawaii. Not California," the smaller guy said, scowling at the bigger one. The fierce one-upmanship gave it away—they had to be twins.

"Meet Aki and Maki Fuzotao," Suda said, gesturing toward the pair. "I met them at the original Yokohama Kickboxers Pavillion. Their dad—the guy who read the statement—he's my sensei. Aki and Maki have been working security for Saint Arrow for years now. They're geniuses at crowd control."

I didn't doubt it. They didn't have the lithe, sinewy bodies typical of Muay Thai kickboxers. These guys looked like bulldogs, and were big enough to be bouncers at a sumo wrestlers' bar.

"Their mother couldn't stand to see them in the ring against each other," Suda continued. "So Aki became a heavy-super-heavyweight while Maki stayed a heavy-middle-heavyweight. Plus, Aki's broken his nose more. Three times, I think?"

"Four," Aki said proudly.

"Keith Richards broke his nose once," Maki interjected. "He smashed it on a speaker cabinet. Passed out in the studio after being awake for nine days."

"So what?" his brother said. "Pete Townshend busted his nose all the time."

"Bullshit," Maki huffed. "It just looks that way."

"They know everything about rock except how to play it," Suda chuckled, nodding at the twins and twisting the cap off another muscle drink. He smiled sheepishly, his eyes drooping so low they looked ready to slide off his face.

"You may as well ask your question," Suda said. "You know the rules."

I didn't have a question and I didn't like the rules, so I improvised.

"Yoshi wrote all the music, right?"

"Mostly. I split credit on a few."

"He penned the lyrics, too?"

"Yeah. Those were all Yoshi."

"Yoshi recorded all the instruments himself on the albums, correct?"

"Just on the demos. I usually played the bass parts on the albums, once I learned them. But yeah, Yoshi could play everything except for drums. Machines usually did that on the albums," he said. "That's more than one question though, dude."

"OK. Just one last quickie. If Yoshi did all of this stuff himself, why did he need you?"

Suda stopped flattening his shins. He picked up his bottle of jock juice and took a sip. The two big guys started getting excited. I could hear their muscles flexing.

"You mind repeating that?" Suda said. "I can't hear so well sometimes. OHL."

"Occupational Hearing Loss," Maki said.

"Rocker's ear," Aki clarified.

So I gave it to him again. Not word for word, but close enough. The situation was probably supposed to be tense, but I was too tired to notice. The worst thing that could happen was a bumpy ride out of the YKPII. The whole Q&A session was a joke anyway.

Suddenly, the twins both came at me. I let them. They grabbed my arms. I let them do that, too. They hoisted me off the bench with my implied consent.

"Wait," Suda said.

They held me there in the air. They could have tossed me around like a beach ball or folded me into an origami crane if they wanted. Suda went on rolling his shins for a moment, then stopped. He scratched his head, as if deciding something.

"Put him down," he said.

The twins let go and I landed on the bench, hard. Suda looked me in the eye and spoke, the words coming out as gently as a kidney Stonehenge.

"You. You're the first guy to come in here tonight," he said, pausing before trying again. "You're the first guy that I can respect, you know? You understand conflict. I think that all great art—and every great kickboxing match—I think they're based on conflict."

His voice rose like he wasn't sure. I just nodded, regretting my strategical error. Suda had mistaken my disgust with the proceedings for a kind of hardboiled honesty, a no-nonsense approach. I was trying to be a jerk and he thought I was being gonzo. The difference is subtle to a layman.

"All these other reporters in here, they're just a bunch of sheep, you know? Nice guys, but they don't get rock. They wear the same suits, ask the same stupid questions. But you're an outsider. You're a maverick."

"Look, don't get the wrong—"

"It's cool, man. That whole speech out there wasn't my idea. I don't care what people ask. Attitude, man. That's what rock is all about, what Yoshi was all about. He would have liked you. He would have tried to kick your ass, but he would have liked you just the same. I like you, too."

I didn't know what to say to make him like me less. I just sat there feeling liked and not liking it much. Time to get out of there before I started liking Suda back. I had to retain some critical distance, at least until I figured out what angle I wanted to take on the Yoshi piece.

"You've got a lot of reporters to talk to," I said.

"Clowns with tape recorders," Suda slurred. "Do you know what it feels like to be asked the same two or three questions all day long?"

I was about to tell him I'd had enough run-ins with Tokyo cops to know all about the feeling when a startled look flashed over Suda's features. I heard footsteps behind me and turned around.

The guy in front had a potato-sack face and a sloped forehead decorated with two crescent scars resting above his right eyebrow like tired slugs.

Teeth-mark scars.

An Osaka prison kiss.

Behind him, four fresh-faced dudes in conservative navy-blue suits bowed over and over, never quite able to sync up their movements. I knew the type—good company boys, dependable as a hangover, crazy about unpaid overtime. They probably shopped at Group-Feeling Menswear, had MBAs from Waseda U., lots of connections and the collective imagination of your average two-by-four.

Not that I judged people by their looks.

"Grief, baby," Prisonkiss said to Suda.

Prisonkiss wore sunglasses darker than Sylvia Plath on a rainy day and had on a razor-thin tie under a cobalt-blue suit cut to intimidate. The getup worked well with his fussy Caesar haircut, and he knew it. Guys who say "baby" a lot tend to know all about what kind of haircut goes with sunglasses and flashy suits. He shook his head sadly and spoke again.

"You must be feeling a lot of grief."

Suda glanced at the kickboxing twins before turning to Prisonkiss with a blank look. "What are you doing here?"

Prisonkiss flashed a lopsided grin. His teeth were even sharper than his suit and you could tell he'd put a lot of work into unsheathing them.

"Mr. Sugawara wishes to express his deepest sympathy."

"All of us," one of the Navyblues behind him chimed. "A tragedy."

"Mr. Sugawara wants to express his sorrow."

It took me a while to figure out that they were talking about *the* Sugawara. A legend in the record industry, he lived one of those rags-to-riches stories as oft-repeated as it was rare. Sugawara started Seppuku Records in the early eighties, and within a few years he'd turned the company into the most successful independent record label in the country. While most indie labels were niche driven—specializing in Cantonese rap or Viet reggae or Okinawan psychedelia—Seppuku was created to beat the majors at their own pop game. With a supernatural ability to hear a hit, Sugawara signed acts no one else would touch, jumped on bandwagons that weren't even built yet and always got off just as the road was getting bumpy.

He was famous for finding talent, and infamous for keeping it. With bigger labels always trying to lure acts away, it was perhaps inevitable that dark rumors would spread regarding how Seppuku maintained artist loyalty. It was the kind of stuff that never made it into any newspaper but was well known among the Tokyo rockerati.

Whatever his secrets, Sugawara was bent on keeping them. He hadn't even done any press for nearly six years. Of course, now that he was overseer not only of Seppuku Records but Seppuku Films, Seppuku Television, Seppuku Video, Seppuku Books and Seppuku Special Promotions, Seppuku Unlimited, Ltd., and seppuku.co.jp, he probably didn't have much time to talk with lowly reporters.

"Mr. Sugawara extends his regards," Prisonkiss announced. "Heartfelt regards. On behalf of everyone at Seppuku."

"Yoshi was like family," a Navyblue mumbled.

The others sang a chorus of similar platitudes until Prisonkiss held up a hand to silence them. They shut up. He took off his sunglasses and stared at me as if he'd just noticed I was in the room.

"You a reporter?"

"Journalist," I said.

Prisonkiss narrowed his eyes, throwing his forehead into a series of ridges that crumpled his scars.

"Please understand," one of the Navyblues said. "This is not the time for journalists."

"We must ask you to leave."

"So much sorrow."

"So many condolences to exchange."

"Please understand."

While they stood there waiting to be understood I glanced over at Suda. He was still sitting on the bench, looking like he didn't understand any of it.

"No disrespect," I said. "But this was billed as a press conference."

"So it's settled," a Navyblue chimed.

"We value your forgiveness," another said.

Prisonkiss motioned them to be quiet and took another step forward. "Maybe you got a name, journalist?"

He spoke in a rough Osaka dialect. Osaka was Tokyo's tougher kid sister, the kind of place where typical polite Japanese wasn't typical. *Making any money?* was Osakanese for hello. *Maybe you gotta name* was the way he said pleased to meet you.

"Billy Chaka," I said. "*Youth in Asia* magazine."

He rolled it around in his head. A funny look came onto his face, but not the kind that makes you want to laugh.

"I know you. You did an article about some weirdo geisha chick, right?"

I nodded, surprised he'd read it. Forty-something record execs were hardly *Youth in Asia*'s target demographic. Then again they probably used the magazine to keep tabs on what was hot with the kids. It was easier than actually interacting with them.

"You got a card or what?"

I thought he'd never ask. In Japan, you can hardly get the time without exchanging *meishi*, a tradition that must have been dreamt up by the printing industry. After running through about fifteen hundred cards in the last two years, I decided printers would have to depend on someone else to fund their golf vacations.

"Sorry," I said. "Gave them all away."

"The bona fide Billy Chaka," he said, grinning knowingly.

He must have been a loyal reader. My op-ed about *meishi* insanity dated way back to April of last year. It wasn't one I was real proud of. After all, why would teenagers want to read about business cards?

"My card," Prisonkiss said. He didn't make a move.

Instead, one of his blue-suited cronies pulled out a stack at least three inches thick, peeled off the top one and handed it to me.

Yatsu Kizuguchi
VP, Artists & Repertoire
Seppuku Unlimited, Ltd.
13-4-2 Ginza, Chuo-ku
03-3581-4111

"Come visit Seppuku Records," said Kizuguchi. "Tomorrow. I think Mr. Sugawara would enjoy meeting you. And we just might have some business to discuss."

I turned to look at Suda to see if he knew what the hell was going on. He just shrugged, a look on his face like he didn't want to be looked at. There were too many people, the room was too small and everything was moving too fast. Maybe I'd been away from Tokyo longer than I thought.

"Where you staying?" Kizuguchi asked.

I told him I just got into town.

"Been to the Akasaka Prince?"

"Sure," I said. "They've got a cute acupuncturist. Chinese gal. Does it Qi Gong style. But I'm banned from the Prince. Long story."

"Take Billy to the Royal," Kizuguchi barked at the twins. "His stay is on Seppuku Records."

Aki and Maki kowtowed, their heads bobbing alternately like twin pistons. They seemed to like taking orders. Either that, or they were anxious to get out of the room. Before I could protest, the Navyblues started in again.

"You'll like the Royal," one blurted.

"It a fine establishment," another echoed.

"Never heard of it," I said.

"The Royal," Suda sighed, "is just like the Prince, but the

furniture is cheaper. In case you feel like breaking any-thing."

Maybe it was the kind of thing rock stars actually look for in a hotel. Whatever the case, it was clear I was history, kicked out of a sham press conference with a free hotel room and an appointment to meet with the founder of Seppuku. It sounded a whole lot better than it felt.

"You never answered my question," I said to Suda.

"Now is not the time of journalists," a Navyblue started.

Another echoed something, but I didn't hear it. I turned and followed Aki and Maki out of the locker room before the conversation went into heavy rotation.

After a short trip through a narrow hall we walked into a garage housing a sleek black BMW with smoked windows. We all climbed in. Aki took the wheel while his brother rode shotgun.

"What part of America are you from?" Maki said as Aki revved the engine.

"Cleveland, mostly."

Maki nodded.

"Walkin' Talkin' Bill Hawkins," Aki offered.

"Alan Freed," Maki said.

"Edwin Collins . . ."

". . . Agent Double-O Soul."

"WAR! Hunh!"

"Good God!"

"Been to Rock and Roll Hall of Fame?" said Aki.

I told him I didn't go in much for museums. He looked at me like it was an odd thing to say. The garage door rose and we backed slowly out into a narrow alley full of puddles. Maki scanned the territory. He motioned to Aki and Aki gunned it.

My head lurched back and we rocketed down the alley. As we neared the corner, the mass of reporters spotted us. There were hundreds of them now. Some bereft young fans had also gathered, mostly girls. There were a few more inches on their platform shoes and a few less on their skirts, but it looked like the fashions hadn't changed much since I'd last been in Tokyo. More likely, they'd changed five or six times and were now revisiting the old stuff.

With the fans came the police. Uniformed cops spread out in an arc, doing their best to restrain the kids while the cameras snapped away. The kids were giving the media lots of anguish and the media responded with the attention kids craved. From a distance it looked like a mutually beneficial relationship. From the same distance, you might think people raised cattle out of the goodness of their hearts.

Suddenly a reporter pointed toward our car.

A girl screamed.

The police line broke and the mass came charging toward us.

Aki peeled around the corner, nearly clipping a fast-running photographer. The guy leaped to safety, holding his camera aloft, snapping pictures of the sky.

I turned around and stared out the back window. As we tore away, people stumbled over each other in a hopeless effort to catch the speeding vehicle. Most of them gave up after a few steps.

Then one teenage girl burst out of the crowd. She was wearing a sailor-style school uniform with baggy white socks bunched around her ankles. Even from far away you could tell she was kind of plain looking. She huffed down the road, moving as fast as her chunky legs would carry her and flashbulbs exploded as all the photographers smelled poignancy. I couldn't hear what she was screaming, but as her face receded in the distance, her tears looked real enough.

Aki flipped on the stereo and the concussive drum intro of the Saint Arrow B-side "Sputnik Diary" thundered through the car, obliterating everything outside.

5

My room at the Royal Hotel was four stories up, on the F floor. The F floor was actually the fourth floor, but some hotels in Japan didn't call it the fourth floor because the word for four was *shi*, which also meant death. Four was considered such an unlucky number that some Japanese rock quartets added a superfluous fifth member to play the tambourine or just dance around onstage.

The room itself was pretty much what I'd expected. The furniture was cheap, just like Suda had said, but it was roomy by Tokyo standards. I walked over to check out the view and I found myself face-to-face with a flat wall of concrete. Cram twenty some million people together and not everybody gets a view. On the wall there was a big painted advertisement for Mamoru brand condoms. A cheery-looking purple cartoon condom man puffed out his ribbed chest while the speech bubble above his head said, "I will protect and defend you as long as I live!" It was a famous phrase in Japan, since those were the exact words Crown Prince Naruhito used when proposing to Princess Masako. The Yamato Dynasty must have wondered what other indignities the new century had in store for them.

Unpacking took me all of three minutes. When I finished, I started in on my contacts list to see if anyone had any good

Yoshi information. I got a lot of wrong numbers and a lot of she-got-marrieds and a few he-doesn't-work-here-anymores. Seemed like everyone was onto something new. When I'd exhausted the list, I decided to call Takeshi at *Marquee*.

I was that desperate.

Marquee used to be the kind of bare-knuckled entertainment rag that kept its lawyers as busy as its copy boys. After it was gobbled up by the massive Tubushimi conglomerate, an internal memo was issued listing affiliated companies and people too important to libel. The memo was thirteen pages long—two columns, single-spaced. At the end of the memo was a curt note informing reporters of their ten percent pay cut and welcoming them to the Tubushimi family.

Most of *Marquee*'s best writers left or were forced out after that. My pal Takeshi was still pushing his pen for *Marquee,* though. He was never much of a writer, but he was one hell of a guy. And if it happened in Tokyo, Takeshi knew about it.

I dialed his number. The phone rang six times before he picked it up.

"Goddamnit," he said in a low voice. "Enough already. You can't keep calling me at work. Do you understand? I'm doing everything I can. Just give me some peace."

"It's Chaka," I said.

"Oh?"

"What the hell was that all about?"

"Nothing," he chuckled. "I thought you were somebody else. It's kind of a joke, very difficult to explain. So how are you doing, Billy? Heard you suckerpunched Mr. Tonda. Broke his jaw, huh?"

I didn't answer. I was too busy trying to remember who's law it was that lies always travel faster than the truth.

"I don't blame you," Takeshi said. "Did you hear what he did to Anna Wong's pet monkey? I haven't been able to even *look* at a banana since I heard about it. Not pretty. Not pretty at all."

"I'll take your word for it," I said. "You still a box man?"

For the last year or so, Takeshi had been living in a cardboard box in Shinjuku Central Park. He'd constructed a regular two-room apartment, complete with a living room of sorts, kitchen and separate sleeping quarters. It was insulated against the weather by a blue tarpaulin and had reinforced cardboard walls at least as thick as the average Tokyo dwelling. By homeless standards, he'd done well for himself.

Takeshi's living situation was something a polite Japanese wouldn't bring up. From Billy the gaijin, it was more or less expected. I actually think he liked me broaching the subject, only because no one else would.

"Well," Takeshi sighed, "you understand how it is."

I'd met Takeshi's wife, so I sort of did. He referred to her as ōkura-shō, "the Ministry of Finance," and her spending habits had more or less bankrupted him. She insisted on living in an expensive high-rise apartment in Ebisu, but claimed the place was too small for the two of them. I didn't understand why Takeshi didn't divorce her. He tried to explain it to me once, using all the classical words for sacrifice and duty and responsibility. When I still didn't get it, he just sighed and told me I wasn't Japanese.

"How's that little lady you used to run with?" Takeshi said, satisfaction practically dripping out of his voice. "Sarah, wasn't it?"

"Never better. She's gonna quit *Youth in Asia* and accused me of being a caterpillar."

The other end was silent for a moment.

"A caterpillar, huh," he said at length. "That's rough. I guess you can't blame her, though."

"What's that supposed to mean?"

"Enough about you," he said. His voice rose a notch, coming back to life. "Heard any good gossip about people who really matter?"

"Yeah. Heard Yoshi left the building."

"*So desu ka*? I'll be damned."

"Know anything about it?"

"Maybe. But this is the age of information. Just giving it away is bad economic policy. Screws up the balance of trade."

"Fine," I said. "You heard of Hideto 'Punchperm' Matsuka?"

Matsuka was head of the Yamagama-gumi crime syndicate. The type of guy who golfed with cabinet members, lunched with CEOs and started gang wars whenever he felt a midlife crisis coming on.

Takeshi grunted.

"Did you know he's a hermaphrodite?"

Takeshi grunted again. A curious grunt this time.

"Medical records," I teased. "I might even be able to get pictures."

I could feel Takeshi weighing it like a rock in his hand, wondering how big a splash it would make. He let loose with a whole series of grunts before speaking.

"How'd a guy like you stumble onto this?" he said.

"You wouldn't believe how many whiskey nipples the average nurse in Nagasaki can drink."

After a few grunts more he graduated to grumbling. "*Marquee* would never print it. The Yamagama thugs would trash our offices, threaten our advertisers. I'd probably end up with a samurai sword in my ass. Besides, we're an entertainment magazine."

"What's more entertaining than a crime boss with both sex organs?"

"A long, healthy life with all my original limbs."

"You're getting soft, Takeshi."

"You know what they say. *The reed that bends with the wind does not break.*"

"Only bent reeds say that."

His end went silent. Maybe I was riding him too hard. He wrote for *Marquee* and lived in a cardboard box, after all. Besides, the story about the yakuza hermaphrodite would probably get him killed, then he'd become some kind of hero and I'd be responsible for turning a lousy writer into a journalistic martyr. It'd happened before.

Before I could apologize, Takeshi started talking.

"There's nothing much to tell about Yoshi," he said. "He's been keeping a low profile since he got out of rehab in Hokkaido. The official word from the Seppuku camp was that he'd been busy recording demos for the new album. Whatever he'd been doing, he was being very quiet about it. We'd been trying to dig up a scandal on him for months—he's usually good for at least three a year. Had photographers staking out his house, watching some of his favorite bars. Nothing."

"Guess you got your story now."

"Yeah," he said. "We're just hoping the authorities can wait a few more days to announce the cause of death. That way we're free to speculate and cast aspersions. Conjecture always outsells the facts."

I couldn't debate him on that one.

"One other question," I said. "You know anything about a guy named Yatsu something-or-other? Two scars on his head, works for Seppuku?"

"Yatsu Kizuguchi," Takeshi said. "He's a tough cookie. Used to run with some yakuza outfit in Osaka years ago. Got busted, did some time. Moved to Tokyo when he got out and used his connections to get a loan for a construction company front. That was before the *jusen* crisis. Then he spent the money on stock in a handful of big companies and started his own *sakaiya* gig. Industrious guy."

Jusen was shorthand for the massive bad-loan scandal that had all but crippled Japan's banking system. Compared to the national *jusen* scandal, America's S&L crisis was lost lunch money. Somehow I wasn't surprised Kizuguchi managed to get involved. Neither was I surprised to hear he'd engaged in a uniquely Japanese form of racketeering, *sokaiya*, which involved buying minuscule amounts of stock and threatening to disrupt company shareholder meetings unless big cash payments were doled out. Companies were so paranoid about losing face that bowing to blackmailers was seen as routine spin control.

What surprised me was that a guy like Kizuguchi managed to get into the record biz. I said the same to Takeshi and he almost burst out laughing.

"Everybody knows there isn't serious money to be made in *sokaiya* anymore, not with the government crackdowns and the bad economy. But no matter how the Nikkei is doing, kids still buy records. My guess is he got sick of freelancing, learned a few Seppuku secrets, and blackmailed his way into a respectable day job."

I suppose it made sense. Kizuguchi had been involved in so many rackets it was inevitable that he got around to the record biz eventually. Something about it still bothered me, but lots of things about the record industry did.

"Anything else I can get?"

"For free?"

My turn to grunt.

"OK," Takeshi sighed. "I've got one Yoshi sighting, unconfirmed. The night he died, Yoshi was supposedly seen at the Purloined Kitten—some grind house in Kabuki-cho. Guy can get any girl in the country, and he hangs out in Kabuki-cho. I don't get it."

"You know the saying. *Fish will not live where the water is too clear.*"

"I know the saying. But I still don't get it."

This coming from a guy who'd rather live in a cardboard box than confront his wife about her lavish lifestyle. I managed to keep the thought to myself this time, though. I didn't want him bringing up Sarah again.

"Speaking of things I don't get," he said. "How come Sarah never comes to Japan with you anymore?"

"Later," I said and hung up the phone.

I pictured Takeshi in his office, staring at his phone, mildly insulted. For some reason, it didn't give as much of a kick as it might have. Rather than ponder why, I headed down the stairs, out of the lobby and off after the ghost of Yoshimura Fukuzatsu.

Rickety bookshelves supported the bowed ceiling and the floor was littered with battered cardboard boxes stuffed with magazines. Stacks of yesterday's manga were jammed next to musty textbooks with yellowing pages while trashy *bunko* novels battled with obsolete business books and incomplete encyclopedia sets and still more comic books. I imagined future rescue workers digging through the avalanche of books after the Big One hit, trying to find survivors under all the words.

I'd ducked into a used bookstore in Jinbocho to wait out the rush hour. Claustrophobic as it was, the shop was still a paradise of open space compared to rush hour on the Yamanote line. Besides, the Kabuki-cho wouldn't be hopping for a while and I'd already spent about a quarter of my adult life doing nothing in hotel rooms.

I squeezed between the tight rows of shelves and made my way to the rear of the store. In back, a youngish guy in wire-rimmed Lennon glasses sat next to an antique paper lamp that did little but illuminate a few dust particles. He was reading a tattered, untranslated edition of *My Antonia*. Why a young Tokyoite would want to read a sonorous account of Nebraska family life was beyond me, but at least it wasn't Ayn Rand.

I walked up to the counter and gave it a rap with my knuckles. He grumbled and carefully marked his place in the book, then took off his glasses and rubbed the lenses with a linen cloth.

"How's the book?" I asked.

"Sweet," he said in a monotone. "Willa Cather is the bomb."

I couldn't tell if he was serious. It reinforced my belief that I was not the guy to write for generasiax.com's 20−31⅓-year-old demographic. For all I knew, they were all nuts over Willa Cather.

"Did you get to that part where they milk the cows?" I said. "I love that part. Cather wields prose like a fucking machine gun."

"Is there something I can help you with?"

"You have a magazine section?" I asked.

He pointed to a cardboard box lying in a heap at the far corner of the room. "The newer ones are over there."

I didn't really have a craving for used magazines, but there was a lot of rush hour left. I thanked the desk guy and waded back through the store, stepping over boxes in various states of decay until I reached the box labeled "magazine-new."

New was a relative term. The most recent offering I spotted was an issue of *Youth in Asia* from February two years ago. I didn't have any features in that one, since at the time I was deep into a story about a seventeen-year-old kid in Hong Kong who was revolutionizing ventriloquism. Unfortunately, he pissed off the Triads during one of his routines and they got to him before I did. They even mutilated the dummy.

I flipped through and found my monthly column had been torn out of the magazine. Maybe a high school instructor clipped it to use as an example of persuasive writing, or a young romantic enclosed it in a gift to his sweetheart on White Day. Just as likely, it had been rolled into spitwads to shoot at the fat kid.

I browsed through a couple other magazines but nothing really caught my eye. Besides, by the time a magazine got hold of a teen trend, it was already on life support. In fact, the very act of writing about a new scene helps kill it. I'd personally euthanized a burgeoning Chinese campus nudist movement, a Pakistani competitive yo-yo craze and even the bloody underground turtle fights that swept Bangkok in the late nineties.

A six-month-old copy of *Nippon Cool* I thumbed through proved the point. I opened up to the magazine's "Too Hot Five." Said five had since disappeared. Ancient history. I might as well have been reading a weekly from the Meiji era. Or Willa Cather, for that matter.

I was about to go razz the clerk some more when I spotted a box of *Power Chord Japan* magazines on the floor. *PCJ* was a rock rag slanted heavily toward guitar jocks, filled with fret-head esoterica and endless debates about the merits of certain string gauges and who stole what riff from who first. It was mostly tablature and equipment reviews—strictly for the guitar *otaku*.

Yoshi was on the cover of this issue, looking up at me

seductively from inside the box. His big black hair mush-roomed out like a weeping willow and he had on more eye makeup than a teenage girl with low self-esteem. He wore leather pants with a pair of handcuffs for a belt buckle, and a shimmering sleeveless purple shirt revealing his arsenal of stock tattoos. Big metal bracelets battled for space on his emaciated wrists and a burning cigarette hung limply out of one side of his mouth, the finishing touch on his portrait of the young rocker as old cliché. Compared to the elaborate space alien costume he'd worn for last year's annual Red and White Song Contest, it was a real Monday-morning look. Yoshi keepin' it real.

Then I noticed the bird.

It was on his left shoulder, prime real estate when it came to tattoos. I narrowed my eyes for a closer look. The tattoo was pretty plain. No shading, just a filled outline, solid black, like something the Nazis would've put on a medal. I'd definitely seen it before, but not, I suddenly realized, on some biker's leather jacket.

It was the logo from the Night Porter's ID card.

I tucked the *Power Chord Japan* magazine under my arm and made my way toward the counter. The clerk wrinkled his brow, looked up at me curiously, then down at the maga-zine I'd placed on the counter.

"I play guitar," I lied. "Prewar acoustic slide Delta swamp jump blues mostly. Texas swing style. Rudebelly, Blind Skunk Johnson, Gatortooth Willy. Real old-school stuff. But sometimes I just like to plug it in and shred."

He ignored me and picked up the magazine. His lower lip curled under as he thumbed through the guitar mag with exaggerated diligence, as if assessing some antique tome for market value.

"Twenty thousand yen," he pronounced finally, putting

the magazine down and looking me squarely in the eye. It was the equivalent of two hundred dollars American.

"C'mon, pal," I said. "This isn't a first edition of *Death Comes for the Archbishop*."

"Look at the date."

I did. It was dated one month in the future.

"That magazine is a rare item," he said. "A friend of mine works at the press where *Power Chord Japan* is printed. When Yoshi turned up dead, *PCJ* stopped the run. This edition is never gonna make the newsstands. In fact, my guy assures me that there are only fifty or so of these in existence."

"So why do you have it sitting in an old cardboard box?"

"Must have been misplaced," he said with a shrug.

"Listen," I said. "Ten years from now, five or more Yoshis will have already come and gone in his place. If history is kind to him, then maybe—just maybe—Yoshi will be immortalized as a game-show question. Besides, *Power Chord Japan* isn't exactly gonna fetch a big price at the Antiquarian Asian Periodicals Convention. Still, I like you, so I'll give you seven thousand yen for it."

"I don't like you enough to give it to you for less than fifteen thousand."

"Do you like me enough to give it to me for ten thousand?"

"Not really," he said. "But I'll do it if you promise to leave."

The kid was the rudest shopkeeper in Tokyo, so I couldn't help but like him a little. I thought it over, picturing Chuck the accountant's facial tic back in Cleveland as I patiently explained why I'd needed a one-hundred-dollar guitar magazine.

"You've got yourself a deal, kid."

He worked a calculator and I plopped my money into the rubber tray on the counter. Then he carefully wrapped up the magazine in about four layers of delicate washi paper, stuck the magazine in a thin box, stuck the box in a brown paper bag and stuck that in a larger bag with the bookstore logo printed on the side. I figured he'd probably just killed about eighty trees.

I stopped short of introducing him to the concept of environmentally friendly packaging and made my way out of the store, squeezing back through the shelves of forgotten books.

"By the way," I called back to him. "Her kid dies at the end. Consumption."

"We're all dying of consumption," the kid said. "And it's obvious you've never read this book. Nor a great many others, I imagine."

I had to admit he wasn't bad. Sure, I could've zinged something back, but sometimes you have to let the kids win. Tucking the hundred-dollar guitar magazine under my arm, I walked out of the store and pointed my wingtips in the direction of the nearest train to Shinjuku station.

In the last twenty-four hours, I'd hung out with kickboxing rock stars and bought rare music ephemera. Now I was headed to a strip bar in the sleazy part of town. At the right angle, my life looked almost glamorous. A cheap glamor, sure, but it wasn't my fault the country was in a recession.

6

The Kabuki-cho was a network of skin joints, love hotels and pachinko arcades close enough to the big government buildings for a guy to have a quickie after work, far enough from the big Shinjuku department stores to keep him from bumping into his wife or daughter. The area was awash in pink neon advertising soaplands, cabarets, take-out hostesses and even something called "fashion massages." It was one of the few places in Tokyo that tourists were warned to steer clear of after dark, in part because it was a favored battleground for yakuza and the Chinese and Korean gangs that were muscling in on their turf.

The Purloined Kitten was on the second floor of a building that looked straight out of a sci-fi comic book. As I walked upstairs, some guy in last year's trendy suit tried to lure me into Sexy Words Tere Kure below. It was a telephone club—a place where you get a private booth, a phone, a list of girls' numbers, and rarely, lucky. I just shrugged at the guy and mispronounced *wakarimasen*, I don't understand. It wasn't far from the truth.

I kept walking up the narrow hallway and nearly bumped smack into the Purloined Kitten doorman. He came from nowhere, stepping out of the shadows and into the dull throb of the neon sign overhead. The sign featured a purring pussy-cat with big cartoon kitty titties. I wondered what the Day Manager would make of it.

"You know the password?" the doorman said.

I took a shot. "Meow?"

"Welcome to the Purloined Kitten."

He grinned. I paid my cover and went inside.

Most of the clientele were *madogiwa-zoku*. They were called the "window tribe" because they'd been shuffled off to corner offices to look out the window all day and await retirement. The window tribe was a shrinking one, a cultural vestige from the days of employment for life. Busted-bubble economics had the managers trimming fat, and even senior salarymen were getting the axe. The possibility of losing their pensions gave them plenty to drink about, as if they'd ever needed a reason.

The club itself was a miniature version of a Western-style strip bar, the kind that popped up everywhere in Tokyo during the eighties. A faux-marble-tiled proscenium stage complete with vertical pole jutted out into the audience. There was a disco ball, a strobe light and bad music played at high volume. Not the kind of place you'd expect to find one of Japan's biggest rock stars, or anyone else under forty.

That the guys were all old enough to be Yoshi's father might have been significant. His dad was an American who'd swept Yoshi's mother off her feet before being shipped out on a one-way journey to Vietnam when Yoshi was only two years old. That's the story Yoshi told interviewers, anyway. None of them noticed that the Vietnam War would already have been over by the time Yoshi's dad supposedly went off to fight. The way Yoshi told it, he knew his father only through his record collection. Yoshi's pop belonged to several record clubs and long after he'd gone the records kept coming, a new one every week. Little Yoshi would listen to them over and over, as if they were secret messages from his father sent from some faraway land. Yoshi was almost eleven when he figured out his father wasn't sending the records home. The realization did nothing to change the way he felt about the music.

But I scratched the father-figure scenario off the list. What brought Yoshi to the Purloined Kitten was less poignant, perhaps, but it was the same thing that brought everyone to the Purloined Kitten.

Strippers.

Given his strict adherence to the rock-and-roll code, Yoshi would pretty much have to date an actress, a model, or a stripper. *Dancer,* that is. Now that every code geek called themselves a guru, every CEO was a visionary, every Web designer an artist and every ad copy boy a writer, a stripper calling herself a dancer didn't sound as absurd as it used to.

I sipped my scotch as the woman onstage went through the compulsory poses and a strobe light kept bad time to an updated version of Gloria Gaynor's "I Will Survive." There wasn't much new in the song. Basically, they just took out the keyboards, upped the tempo and stuck in some techno bells and drum-'n'-bass whistles. Gloria's vocal was the only track that survived untouched. Which proved her point, I guess.

I watched the dancer cavort around for a while and then watched the men watching her. They stared at her intently, working their jaw muscles and sucking down cigarettes like they were going for some kind of record. There was none of the hooting and hollering you get in American strip clubs. If these guys were having fun, they were careful not to show it.

Disjointed images of the girl's life outside of work came to me. A cute little ashtray overfilled with lipstick-stained cigarette butts. A miniature ironing board. A fashion magazine folded to a half-read travel article about Brazil. Piles of gray laundry. Daytime television turned up too loud.

Not the kind of imagery she was paid to arouse in customers.

I tried to picture her dressed as an elevator lady, or maybe like those college students in Hongo. In a dental hygienist's uniform. Nothing really worked. Funny, you see an attractive stranger on the street and all you can do is try to picture them naked. Then you see an attractive stranger naked and the mind starts putting clothes on them. There was Zen in there somewhere, but I let it drift on by.

The music came to a bombastic close and the woman bowed deeply at the waist, mindful to give both sides of the audience the reverse angle. Then she scampered offstage with tiny steps that made her buttocks jiggle comically. There was a smattering of applause followed by an infinitesimal silence.

I was beginning to wonder what I was doing there when a thin waitress made a beeline to my table in the corner. I put my hand over my drink and shook my head no thanks. She kept coming.

When she got to my table, she spoke.

"Calico wants to see you."

The name didn't register.

"In back. She told me to get you." The waitress acted annoyed, putting one hand on her hip while she balanced a tray of drinks on the other.

"Calico?" I said, hoping the sound of it would kick-start my memory.

She glanced around like a nervous bird, then leaned over and said with hushed insistence, "Ca-li-co."

When that didn't work, she sighed and said, "Olga."

"Solskjaer?"

She nodded and repeated the name, mispronouncing the hell out of it.

I tossed back the remaining half of my drink and ordered another before the last sour drops made their way down. You don't meet with Olga Solskjaer without a little backup.

"Billy! Motherfuck, how did you know I am here? It is good you come see me! Here, asshole!" she squealed. She threw her arms around me and I got a noseful of the pink feather boa draped across her shoulders. Her Japanese was as broken and Swedish-sounding as ever, but she'd picked up some new curse words since I'd seen her last.

The big reunion show seemed to be for the sake of the woman sitting on the stool just behind her, the one I'd just seen onstage. She was smoking a cigarette, still naked except for a pair of oddly modest blue underwear, something out of Victoria's Secret for Grannies.

The dressing room was just a mirror, a makeup counter, and a paint-speckled stool. A tiny costume closet stood in the corner, a jumbled mess of glitter, leather and animal prints that took up about a quarter of the space.

Olga took my hand and drew me into the middle of the room, a distance of two small steps, then pulled the door closed behind us. The air was heavy with her peculiar perfume, a dense mixture of alcohol and rotting orange blossoms. It brought back memories.

"Billy," she said, "this is Tabi. Tabi, Billy." I nodded to the woman and she nodded back and exhaled a puff of smoke. "Tabi is not a *real* name, but a cat name," she added. "Tell Tabi what you thought of her dance."

"It was nice," I said. That sounded too stupid so I added, "Do you pick your own music?"

"You can," Tabi said. "I don't. I just do it to whatever."

"This is why your act is not clarity," Olga admonished. Tabi rolled her eyes and puffed on her cigarette. Olga turned to me. "When you saw the routine, Billy—what kind of shit did you thinking?"

Making people uncomfortable was a hobby with Olga. I certainly wasn't going to say that watching Tabi made me think of ironing boards and daytime TV.

"It was a dense piece," I said. "I'm still digesting it."

"Ha!" Olga boomed, turning her attention to Tabi. "The fucking audience is indigestion, because dancing of you has no thematic unity."

Tabi wrinkled her nose in disgust and tapped some ashes into a cute little ashtray, not unlike the one I'd pictured.

"I thought her unity was just fine," I said.

"Fuck off, Billy," Olga snorted. "You're old to Tabi, anyway."

I didn't take offense. That was the kind of Japanese you picked up in places like this. Funny thing was, I don't even think Olga knew she was cursing half the time. I'd seen her very politely call Ginza shop girls "bitch" as if it was a synonym for "honey" or "darling."

Tabi had heard enough. She left her cigarette smoldering in the ashtray and rose from the stool. I tried to give her some room, but her bare body brushed against mine as she squeezed by.

"Nice meeting you," she said and then strolled out of the room, still naked except for her sky-blue underpants. The door closed behind her. Guess my intimate fantasy of seeing her in street clothes would remain unfulfilled.

I took a seat on the stool Tabi had just vacated and

indulged in a long pull at my drink before setting it down on the counter amid the mess of cosmetics.

Olga was looking at me now, a mischievous smile on her face. I noticed the crow's-feet just beginning to get a grip around the corners of her eyes. For years, she'd been waging an expensive war against aging. The geography of the multi-front struggle was constantly in flux. If bags showed up under her eyes, she'd counter with a butt lift. If her breasts started sagging, she'd react with a teeth bleaching. She had to realize she'd lose eventually, but it didn't deter her. She was practically the Fidel Castro of youth preservation. I admired her stubbornness.

"You remember when we met?" she asked suddenly.

I did. Star Festival Night in Ikebukuro. An overcast sky, two lonely foreigners and a whole lot of alcohol. The story I was working on had stalled out, and I was going deaf from hanging out in pachinko parlors all day. So I ducked into the Sunshine City Building and hit the Wild Strawberry to drink and watch the rain bounce off the windows.

"I thought it would never stop. Rain coming and coming down." Olga started to get that faraway look in her eyes, and she shook her head slowly, thinking of the rain.

I remembered, too. It was still raining when we left the Wild Strawberry and it kept on raining the whole three days we spent together. We never left her flat except to pick up take-out Chinese and more cheap bottles.

"You know what I remember for you?" she said sadly.

I shrugged.

"You leave with two Italian men."

The fact is, I was working on a story about a video-game pirating ring. I'd left the flat to meet my tipster for ten minutes, and the next thing I knew I was shipped off with a crate-load of Mario Bros. cartridges bound for Hong Kong. By the time I got back five days later, it was too late to explain. I tried, but her English was worse than her Japanese and my Swedish was nonexistent.

"Yeah," I sighed. "You'd understand if you met Mario."

"You were bastard, huh?"

A long time ago, Sarah told me that until I knew what I was after, I would always end up being a bastard. She even drew up this weird diagram that showed what would happen when a directionless, unpredictable person like myself collided with the normal trajectory of people's lives. I always told her people wouldn't collide with me if their own trajectories were so normal. She said I didn't understand the diagram.

"You were a bastard, but I forgive," Olga sighed. "I meet so many bastards there is no counting. As bastards are, you're not the worst."

I smiled, good bastard that I was.

"So," she said, moving on, "your life is the same, you're at a shithole like this."

I nearly pointed out that she was the one working here. But as I was on assignment, I was working here, too, if only for the night. I guess neither of our lives had taken much of a turn. Perhaps we had trajectories after all.

"You still plan on getting back to Sweden someday?" I said.

Olga had come to Tokyo some ten years ago. Like all the other foreigners in the *mizu shobai*, she'd planned on amassing a quick fortune and then returning home, the conquering hero. Like almost everyone else, she'd had some bad luck and some bad habits and the rest pretty much took care of itself.

"I go back, very soon," she said. "Ugly, this business now. Not like before, when I was hostessing in Ginza. There was money then, ne? Class. Now is all ignorant girls from Thailand, Vietnam. Scuzz bag steal their visas, loan sharks make them slaves. Poor girls desperate, they do anything. A good girl as me can't compete. So what are you doing? Plan on keep writing for the teenager?"

"The question seems to be on everyone's mind lately," I said, shifting on the stool. "I always thought I was lucky to find a calling early in life."

"You're so lucky, why are you doing here?"

I flopped my copy of *Power Chord Japan* down on the makeup counter and pointed to Yoshi sneering from the cover.

Her smile left in a hurry.

"I'm doing a story on this guy. You know him?"

"Yoshi is a bastard," she said in a low voice.

"A bastard like me, or a different kind?"

Just then, the door swung open and Tabi barged in. The baby T she had on still didn't quite count as clothing. She looked distressed.

"Jingle Bells," Tabi said.

"Fuck," Olga whispered. She grabbed me by the arm and pulled me from the stool with considerable strength. "Billy, quickly. You go. Now."

"Jingle Bells?" I said, halting our flow toward the door.

"Get out before he sees. Holy fuck!" Her hands were jittery on my arms as she pushed me out the door and into the dark hallway.

"Tabi, slow Santa!"

"How?"

"Be sexy!" Olga hissed. Tabi grumbled something, but turned around to do as told. Olga grabbed my arms and pulled me back into the room. She spun me around and pointed at the closet.

"In there. Go!"

"You couldn't hide a baby leprechaun in there."

"Get in! Billy, hurry ass!" She followed up with a barrage of Swedish that sounded about as delicate as her Japanese. I moved quickly toward the closet and pulled out an armload of clothing to try to make room.

"Put this," Olga said. I turned around and she snapped a black stocking over my head. Camouflage, I guess. Then she shoved me into the closet.

I sat on the floor and pulled my knees up to my chest while she buried me beneath a flurry of bras, transparent camisoles, G-strings, T bars, tassled pasties and rubber schoolgirl uniforms. She muttered curses, moving frantically and looking over her shoulder.

"Olga?"

It was a gruff-sounding voice, deep and male, coming from the hallway. Then a knock, and the voice said her name again. "Olga Olga Olga, let me in, Olga. Trust me, we need to talk."

She took one last look at my hideout, adjusted a pair of leather underwear on top of my head, then turned and skipped toward the door.

"I'm coming. Chill you fuck," she said in an edgy voice.

From my position in the closet, if I squinted one eye I could just barely see through a pair of crotchless panties covering my face. I watched her walk over and open the door.

The guy burst through as the knob was turned. He trundled to the center of the room, then turned a half circle like he'd forgotten something. He was decked out in a shiny red warm-up suit supplemented with lots of senseless jewelry. Big gold chains dangled from his neck and gold-encrusted barnacles studded his beefy fingers. His hair was slicked with enough gel to lube an elephant. The outfit would have looked dopey on a suburban American kid. On a chubby, fortyish Japanese man it signaled a severe identity crisis.

He made such a bombastic entrance I almost didn't notice the little guy in blue denim sneak in behind him. He was about five feet four and had a body like a bamboo shoot. How his frame could support the massive reel-to-reel tape recorder strapped over his shoulder was a mystery.

"We need to talk," the red guy said in a messy voice. "Boy oh boy oh boy do we ever need to talk." The dude stopped yapping and rolled his tongue around inside his mouth so vigorously you'd think it was part of some weight-loss program. His jaw shivered and he smacked his lips. Then he turned to face the little guy in blue. "Hey, Towa, turn that damn thing off for a second."

Towa didn't react.

"Hi, Towa," Olga said, smiling at him.

Towa still didn't react. He was lost somewhere inside his headphones.

The red sweat suit reached over and pulled off the headphones.

"Turn it off," he said. "No recording right now, OK?"

Towa flipped a switch, put his headphones back on and stood there like a mannequin, still extending the microphone.

"Do you have any gum any chewing gum I could use a piece of gum right now if you have one," the man in red said. Before Olga could answer he reached into his sweat-suit pocket and pulled out a packet of green Gumi100 muscat-flavored gummies. "Never mind forget about it," he said, shoving the candy into his mouth. "Have the police been here?"

"No," said Olga. "Why do they?"

The answer calmed him, but not much. He ran a hand through his hair and wiped it on his red sweatpants. Olga moved in between the guy and the closet, blocking his view. It partially blocked mine, too.

"They're gonna find out Yoshi was here that night he was here and they're gonna want to talk to you, trust me."

"So what." Olga yawned. "Cops, I like. Good money."

The guy smacked his lips twice, blinked about thirty times then smacked Olga across the face.

Olga recoiled.

I felt my muscles tense, and readied to spring.

Before I could Olga walloped the guy with a left. He wasn't expecting anything like it. His jowly flesh was still bouncing around his face as he stumbled against the makeup counter, knocking over bottles of fingernail polish and hairspray. *Power Chord Japan* fluttered to the floor.

He regained his balance and put a hand to his cheek. His eyes burned and he clenched his hands into little balls. Towa was still in full waxwork mode. Olga just stood there, hands on her hips, waiting. I got ready to do some domestic conflict management, Shaolin Panther style.

The guy straightened himself, sucked in a couple of deep breaths, and tested out his jaw muscles. As he unclenched his fists I could hear the skin sticking from the hair gel.

"Boy oh boy oh boy," he wheezed. "I deserved that."

"The fuck is problem!"

The guy held out his hands, shook his head. He didn't know what the fuck was his problem. In all likelihood, it wasn't the first time he'd been asked.

"You quit the speed shit, Santa," Olga smoldered. "*Shabu* is headfuck on you."

"Don't call me Santa."

"Yoshi call you Santa."

"Yoshi's dead," he said. "And we gotta get our stories straight because something isn't right about this whole thing and sooner or later the police are gonna come asking questions, trust me, because they're gonna want to know what I want to know and what I want to know is just what the fuck happened that night and something tells me you know."

I felt myself getting dizzy.

"Me?" Olga huffed. "I'm not the person sell to him drugs."

"Look look look," he stuttered. "This is not about blame and this is not about who sold what to who and you're angry and your anger is perfectly natural because you didn't want him to die and, trust me, nobody wanted him to die and hell I loved the guy loved him like family like he was my natural-born little brother like he was—"

"You would give to your little brother heroin?"

"Let's deal with some bona fide reality here okay your boyfriend liked his drugs *loved* his drugs and knew the risks and if it wasn't me it would have been someone else selling him shit and there's some bad shit out there Olga, trust me, and he was lucky to have me because I always looked out for the guy like he was my brother."

"You leave him in hotel. Alone."

"Olga. Olga Olga Olga listen to me. Yoshi said he promised he guaranteed he wasn't gonna shoot up until I got back there and dropped you off which brings me to my fucking point if you'll just shut up and let me think of what my fucking point was here for a second."

Olga glared at him. Santa shoved another piece of muscat candy into his mouth and ran his hand compulsively over his oily hair, slicking it back again and again. His eyes were the same red as his suit, bulging out of his pale, fleshy face like they were trying to escape. Towa, the one in blue, noticed the magazine on the floor. He picked it up and started thumbing through it.

"What I need to know is this," Santa said. "I need to know if after he left here that night did Yoshi call you?"

"Why it matters?"

"I repeat I repeat I repeat—did Yoshi call you?"

"No."

"No. You're saying no, no he definitely did *not* contact you after leaving this club?"

Olga rolled her eyes.

"Boy oh boy oh boy I don't fucking get it," Santa muttered.

"What's to get?"

"Listen to this. Listen to this and see if you can make some sense of it because it doesn't make any sense. Okay— the hotel where they found Yoshi's body? The one in Sanya?"

"Love Hotel Chelsea."

"Right right right. But *that wasn't where I dropped him off.* I left him at the Hotel L'Charm and not the Love Hotel Chelsea and they're not even in the same part of town not even close and so I'm thinking if he suddenly decided to go to another hotel in Sanya fucking *Sanya* of all fucking places he would have called and told you and so I'm asking again did Yoshi call you or not?"

"I already answer."

Santa snorted, then bowed his head and closed his eyes. "Impossible," he said quietly. "Impossible impossible impossible."

"Why it's impossible he switch hotel?"

He dismissed her question with a wave of his hand. His own questions weren't so easily dealt with. He walked a tight circle, pacing like an inmate awaiting a call from the governor and munching his Gumi100 with enough energy to light up Tokyo Tower. Meanwhile, Towa disinterestedly flipped through the magazine. As for me, I didn't know how much longer I could last in the closet. My legs were starting to cramp and the erotic camouflage of undies and bras and rubber fetish costumes oozed a heady mixture of sweat and cheap perfume, making me lightheaded. Still, it wasn't as bad as the time I'd been forced to spend the night in a waterfront storeroom crammed with dried tiger penises during a story about the aphrodisiac black market in Taiwan. I reeked for weeks, and the zaniness that followed convinced me the power of the tiger's organ was more than just another Asian superstition.

"That night," Santa started. "The night it happened did he mention anything to you about Seppuku Records? I mean about anything strange going on or maybe I don't know how the new album was shaping up or anything like that related to Seppuku Records?"

"The new album."

"Yeah," Santa said. "You know because I know he just finished recording demos for the new album and I'm just curious if he mentioned anything about the writing-recording process or maybe if he liked the final outcome if there were some hit songs maybe—"

"Hit songs," Olga repeated, her voice sharper now.

"Right," the guy said. "I guess I'm thinking I can't understand what the hell happened that night and I'm just wondering if—"

The look on Olga's face stopped him cold.

"I'm sorry," Santa hiccuped. "You're right wrong time and wrong place but sometimes I just think without speaking I mean *speak* without *thinking* and I'm just well we're all just pretty shocked here in a bona fide state of shock so let's just forget this discussion and pretend it never happened."

"Fine," she said. "Leave. *Now.*"

"Right," Santa said. "I'm leaving now but you're coming

with me because there's someone here who boy oh boy oh boy I almost forgot all about him someone who wants to talk to you waiting in the car outside and I totally almost forgot all about him I can't believe it."

Olga shook her head.

"Olga this is not your decision and it's not mine either, believe me, this guy wants to talk you'd better talk so get dressed and let's get out of here because I don't want to drag you kicking and screaming but I will if I have to, believe me."

Given the way Olga had walloped him, I figured he'd be the one kicking and screaming. Still, I considered making a move before the situation escalated. Then Olga shot me a glance telling me to stay put. Trouble registered on Santa's oversized face as he followed her sight line.

"What are you looking at?" he said, jerking his head toward the closet. "You were looking at something is there something in there?"

"The hell is look like," Olga said, a note of tension in her voice. "Clothes in there. Is fucking closet."

Santa slicked back his hair again. Then he took two quick steps across the room. I measured an uppercut to his groin and was just about to release it when he grabbed a fur coat from one of the hangers and tossed it to Olga. The empty wire hanger clanged and rattled overhead.

"Put it on and let's go let's go," he said. "The guy outside doesn't enjoy waiting to the point that you could say it's a bona fide character flaw in his character."

"Who is outside, this man?"

"You'll find out soon, believe me, so let's you and I get out of here so I can get this over with and maybe just hear myself think for one goddamn second is all if that isn't asking too much."

Olga draped the coat over her shoulders. Santa glanced toward the closet again, then turned and motioned to the catatonic guy in blue. Towa tossed the guitar magazine onto the counter. As he did, Olga lowered her hand to her side and made a circle of her thumb and forefinger, a hint of a smile playing over her face as she flashed me the okay sign.

All three of them headed out the door. I listened to their footsteps recede down the hall, then I hopped from the closet and shook loose the errant undergarments. I was about to dash into the hallway when I caught my reflection in the mirror. The black nylon was still over my head, pinching my features into a pummeled, meaty grimace the color of a bruise. I yanked off the nylon, grabbed my hundred-dollar copy of *Power Chord Japan* and made for the door.

By the time I hit the street they were already gone. I could've stuck around, I suppose, but I had no idea when or if they'd be coming back. While I stood in front of the Purloined Kitten building watching groups of drunk guys wander by and wondering what to do, a tout in a sandwich board approached and told me through a bullhorn about Club Shojo Densha, a pink club made up to look like the inside of a train. Patrons would pay to "ride" the train, where they would be free to fondle women dressed as schoolgirls without fear of prosecution. I didn't know whether to laugh or use the guy for a trampoline, so I decided to go back to the Royal Hotel and do neither.

The first thing I did when I got back into my room was go to the closet and look through my jacket, my pants, my shirts. I finally found the ID card in a shirt pocket. As I dug it out, I thought of the Night Porter, slumped against the wall in a room not unlike this one.

I walked over to the nightstand and plopped the card down next to *Power Chord Japan*. There was no doubt about it. The dead rocker's tattoo matched the logo on the dead Night Porter's card. I picked up the phone and dialed the number printed on the card, the same number I'd called from Hokkaido nearly twenty-four hours ago.

I got a busy signal.

I spent the next half hour giving the redial button a work-out. When I figured I had the busy signal about memorized, I called up the operator and asked her to give me all the listings for Solksjaer in Tokyo. She gave me exactly zero. No listings for anyone called "Santa" either. I hung up the phone, flipped off the light and tried to get some shut-eye.

But my brain wouldn't stop squirming. I kept wondering just how well Yoshi and Olga had known each other. Well enough for Santa to call him her boyfriend. Well enough for her to call Yoshi a bastard. I wondered about Santa, and how such an obvious speed freak could be so fat. I wondered about his silent sidekick in blue. I wondered who had been waiting for them in the car outside. I didn't have those answers, but I had learned something. Yoshi had died of a drug overdose. And from the way Santa was acting, the overdose was anything but the end of the story. It was probably only the beginning.

Which meant I had a real story.

Which meant I couldn't sleep.

I flipped the light back on. I picked up my rare guitar magazine, opened it to the interview with Yoshi. The interviewer opened up with nice easy one about analog vs. digital effects, not knowing it would launch Yoshi into an exhausting, incomprehensible tirade about technology and the future of music.

For the first three pages he used stoner math to demonstrate that the perpetual recombination of existing notes and chords would soon reach its finite rhythmic limit. When this happened, music would come to a temporary standstill, and the art would suffer a dark age of overt cannibalism and veiled regurgitation—an era Yoshi believed we were entering this very moment. For the next three pages, Yoshi talked about how songs, instruments and even notes as we know them would have to be abandoned as musicians strove to break through the concept of sound divided by time in order to seek "aural tones of atemporal, post-finite contextual purity."

It was a lot to swallow from a guy who's biggest hit was "Love Happy Weekend." The words that most immediately sprang to mind were those of another musical visionary— *shut up and play yer guitar.*

I flipped to a random page and spent about fifteen minutes trying to decode an instructional section riddled with fret-head slang. The stereotypical Japanese love of gadgetry coupled with guitar technofetishism rendered the equipment reviews doubly baffling. I figured out the difference between a rotovibe and an E-Bow, but was still foggy on what a phase shifter run through a parametric EQ with a sweepable mid-frequency and two-channel selectable 10dB filter would sound like.

I sighed and tossed the magazine to the floor. I stared up at the ceiling for a while and thought some more about Olga. Then I started thinking about Sarah, back in Cleveland. My gaze shifted to a mirror on the far wall. From my angle on the bed, I couldn't see myself in the glass. The mirror cast a still reflection of the silent, empty room.

7

I woke early the next morning, took a long shower then sat around my room planning how to make the most of the day ahead. I figured I'd start by going to Ginza to visit the offices of Seppuku Unlimited. That was as far as my plan went. Like Zen Master Dōgen said, *Dig the pond without waiting for the moon. When the pond is finished, the moon will come by itself.* At around eight o'clock I headed out of the hotel and started toward the train station, giving myself a big head start on the moon.

It was a blustery morning. The wind came in small aimless bursts, rattling the trees then vanishing. Just when you started to get a little chilly, it would suddenly die out, only to come again from some unexpected direction.

I hadn't walked a block from the hotel when a lime-green-and-tangerine-colored taxi pulled up beside the curb. The rear passenger door swung open.

"Mr. Chaka?"

She was dressed in a long gray overcoat and sat in the back of the cab, her doll-sized hands folded primly in her lap. Her dark eyes shone in her round face for just a moment before she dropped them to the floor. I watched her lips part to speak.

"I'm sorry, if it isn't too much trouble, I would appreciate a small moment of your time." The wind nearly stole her voice before it got to me. She kept her eyes turned down.

"Have we met?" I asked.

"We're strangers. I think it will be easier for us to . . . please come inside the car. I'm very sorry to disturb you, but we must speak."

A gust of wind blew her hair around, covering her face. I tried to get a read on her body language, but she wasn't offering much. She just sat there, still without being rigid, quiet but not making any obvious effort to be silent.

I thought of a story from the ancient *Gekkan Sodai* about a famous kenjutsu master hanging out in a garden with a bunch of his students. One of the students starts daydreaming about launching a surprise attack on his master. Suddenly, the master bolts upright. He looks at each of his pupils. He walks over and looks behind the bushes. Perturbed, he retires to his room. The pupil later asks what was bothering him, and the master says he was sure someone was planning to attack him in the garden. Amazed, the student confesses it was himself. The master has a good laugh, finally able to relax.

I sensed something there on the sidewalk, but it wasn't anything I could put a name to. Besides, the story was probably apocryphal and I'm no kenjutsu master, anyway. I knew all about the dangers of getting into cars with strangers and it was nothing compared to the threat of getting caught in the flood of morning subway commuters. I decided Seppuku could wait and got into the car.

Miles crawled by without a word. She didn't even say anything to the driver, but I guess he knew where we were going. I spent most of the ride stealing glances at her as she stared out the window, a distracted look on her face like she was trying to count how many businessmen on the sidewalks carried their briefcases with the left hand, how many with their right.

She wasn't a gorgeous woman, but she wasn't unattractive. There was a certain softness to her features, a looseness. She looked like the type of gal who might go for twenty- minute jogs two or three times a week then reward herself with ice cream and Pocky sticks. She was probably a big believer in genetics, could talk a blue streak about her metabolism. Likely, she had a decent education, a decent job, and a decent personality. A decent gal all around. In other words, not the type to spend her morning cruising for foreign journalists.

"Didn't you want to speak with me?" I asked finally.

She glanced up at me briefly, flashing me again with those big dark eyes. They moved from me to the cab driver and back again. She raised a gloved index finger, pressing it lightly against her lips.

I looked for clues as to what she might do for a living, where she might have come from, who she might be. She was too old to be one of my fans, too young to be a parent coming to me for advice on a teenage daughter who'd shaved her head and changed her name to Rock Candy. Her ordinary attire and conventional hairstyle made me guess she was one of Tokyo's ubiquitous OLs, the beleaguered office ladies working thankless secretarial jobs in Japan's big corporations and government bureaus. But she didn't have that terminally worn-out expression you see on many OLs. She was in her late twenties or early thirties perhaps. Overall, she looked startlingly normal, which, had I been thinking about it, wasn't normal at all.

Eventually the car pulled over and stopped. She slid out as soon as the automatic doors popped open, not even bothering to thank the driver. I took out my wallet.

"The lady took care of it," the cabbie said, waving his hand. I shrugged and put my wallet away.

For a moment, the two of us just stood there near the entrance of some park, looking around. It felt like I'd been here before, but I wasn't sure. Tokyo transformed itself with such blinding speed you could never count on things looking the same from one year to the next. She turned and began walking down a gravel path. I followed.

It was a weekday in winter so the park was virtually deserted. We strolled nearly shoulder to shoulder along the path, hemmed in by barren trees sadly earthbound against rows of jumbled apartment buildings dominating the skyline. The park itself felt like an oversight, a space they simply forgot in the rush to pave every square foot of the Kantō plain.

We went over a small hill. At the bottom was a Western-style duck pond with a bench by the shore. Millions and millions of people and nobody in sight. Even the water in the pond looked somehow abandoned.

She turned her head quickly as if to say something, then thought better of it and continued down toward the pond. She walked with such determination I had a vision of her going straight into the water, moving with measured steps until the water reached up to her neck, up to her head, until she couldn't be seen at all.

Instead, she sat down on the edge of the bench. I sat down next to her. She took a couple of deep breaths, removed her gloves and stuck them in the pocket of her coat. I watched her throat rise and fall a couple of times with false starts. She folded her hands on her lap and studied the pond.

I considered the possibility she may never actually speak, that she'd brought me all the way here only to lose her nerve. Since I didn't even know where to begin with the usual brain-racking, I just sat there watching the wind ripple the surface of the water. Beneath the wind, you could hear the hum of faraway traffic, a dull throb punctuated by the occasional siren. But for the city, it was downright pastoral.

"This was my grandfather's second-favorite place in the whole world," she suddenly said.

I didn't turn to look at her or say a word, fearing the slightest of movements might throw her off course, halt the flow of her words. I waited for her to continue.

"Grandfather took me here, I think twice when I was a little girl. When I was older, we would often come here. Of course, my grandmother had long since died by then. Grandfather would feed the ducks. No ducks here today, but they still come around sometimes. In the summer, I think."

I nodded thoughtfully, picturing the ducks.

"He told me this was his second-favorite place in the world when I was a little girl. I remember I thought he was being funny. But about two years ago, he told me the same thing. *This is my second-favorite place on earth.*"

She lingered on the thought. I looked around again, trying to gain a fresh perspective, but the place still felt like a stifled yawn. I wondered absently what Grandpa's favorite place had been.

"I lived with my grandfather for three years, after my mother got ill. He may have already told you this."

"Forgive my asking," I said. "But do I know your grandfather?"

Now it was her turn to look dumbstruck. She turned toward me, searching for something.

"You know him from the mountains," she said. "The mountains in Hokkaido."

She looked away and then looked back.

"He died in your hotel room."

.   .   .

Ed, my editor, was born an orphan. He'd worked out a whole scenario whereby his mother gave him up because she couldn't contact his father. It wasn't that the father left or that the mother simply didn't want to keep little Eddie, but something completely random—a lost phone number or a late train. Some tragic missed connection, a twist of fate. The story lacked specifics and I doubted it was true, but you can't go around calling an orphan a liar. Especially if said orphan signs your paychecks.

Perhaps because of his own missing lineage, Ed was hypervigilant about families and responsibility. Which was fine and admirable, except for one thing: he assumed that every anonymous woman who called the magazine was pregnant with my love child, and saw it as his moral obligation to give them my phone number and detailed directions to anywhere I might be staying. In reality I was neither as promiscuous or reckless as he imagined—not since I'd given up geisha—but he'd long ago decided that I was just like the father who abandoned him, and he wasn't going to let it happen to someone else.

Once when we were drunk he called me Dad. No irony, no humorous intent. My editor, my senior by fifteen years. It was one of those moments we never talked about.

This was how the woman had tracked me down. She would have talked to the Day Manager at the hotel, wanting to know some details of her grandfather's death. The Day Manager would have been his chatty self, and probably dropped something about a reporter from *Youth in Asia* without even meaning to. Even if he didn't give her my name, she would have had enough. She could have called Ed back in Cleveland, said something about *a journalist for your publication staying at the Hotel Kitty*, and that would've been all it took.

Her name was Setsuko Nishimura, she finally told me. She hadn't seen her grandfather for almost two years prior to his death and didn't even know that he lived in Hokkaido until she got the call. They used to be very close at one time, but recently had some kind of falling out. A rift, she called it. She told me this in the park, on the bench by the sad little duck pond.

I'd told her about how he came into my room with the towels and collapsed on the floor. I didn't tell her about how he'd wanted to speak to me about immortality. I didn't tell her about the ID card or mention his final words.

She just nodded in her quiet way, and apologized several times for intruding on my morning. I did my best to reassure her that it was no problem, told her I wished I knew more about her grandfather, but like I'd said, we only exchanged a handful of words. He seemed like a nice guy, though, I said.

Then she asked if I'd seen his spirit leave his body.

When I told her I hadn't, the uneasy conversation sputtered to a complete stop. We both just sat there on the bench. After a while, she turned her back to me and started quietly crying.

I almost brought up the ID and the phone number, but something stopped me. It seemed her grandfather's death had given her plenty to think about for the time being without bringing the ID into it. True, she might have been able to tell me something about what the bird logo meant, and how it could possibly have appeared on Yoshi's shoulder. But you just don't think to ask many questions to a woman crying on a park bench.

After a long silence, Ms. Nishimura suddenly stood. She said she was sorry and started thanking me and found herself saying sorry again.

"Can I call you sometime?" I asked. "In case I remember anything else?"

She bit her lip and looked around at the duckless duck pond and all the leafless trees. Then she took a pen out of her handbag and wrote on a Hello Kitty sticky note. She handed me her number and turned to leave.

I hopped from the bench to walk her out of the park.

"Please," she said quietly. "I think maybe, yes, I need to be alone for a moment. I'm sorry . . ."

I nodded and sat back down. I stared at my wingtips. They were smeared with blades of yellowing grass. I tried to picture the Night Porter sitting on this very bench and getting a real kick out of it. Of course, I couldn't picture him in anything but his porter's uniform, so I had to make do with that. A gaunt old man in a pillbox hat, sitting on a bench tossing bread crumbs to the ducks.

Another picture bumped that one out of the way. It was the Night Porter again, this time slumped against the wall in my room at the Hotel Kitty. *They're not coming*, he says. His eyelids close, his hands uncurl.

I got up and made my way out of the park.

8

Seppuku Records was at the outer edge of the Ginza 13-chome, at the intersection of Jikoku-dori #1 and Jikoku-dori #2. Jikoku #1 was home to a row of upscale art galleries selling paintings no one understood and fashion designers making clothes no one wore. Jikoku-dori #2 housed corporate headquarters for lots of familiar international conglomerates, as well as large investment consultants, accounting firms and a few advertising agencies.

It would have made for some nice symbolism to say that Seppuku Records existed exactly at this crossroads of art and commerce, but it wasn't exactly true. Seppuku was in a medium-sized building standing about half a block down Jikoku-dori #2, the corporate side of things. Maybe it made for nice symbolism after all.

One of the label's newest rap acts was doing his thing on the giant video screen outside the Seppuku building, jumping around in a puffy white coat that made him look like the Michelin Man doing Tae Bo. By the time I crossed the street and ducked into the Seppuku Entertainment Corporate Headquarters, I'd already seen the six-second clip looped three times.

I breezed by the greeting committee and took the stairs up

to the eleventh floor. As stairwells go, this one was pretty well kept. They even piped in elevator music. Actually, it may have been stairwell music. Right now a lounge version of Zeppelin's "Stairway to Heaven" was keeping time with my ascent. Next maybe they'd put on Frank Loesser's "Down the Stairs, Out the Door" or that gospel number "Goin' Upstairs." I tried to think of others but my brain hit a dead end. I'm sure Aki and Maki Fuzotao could have rattled off fifty or so stair songs, but they weren't around.

The office I was headed to was halfway down the hall, across from a giant, unfinished art deco–style mural depicting the history of the company. From the way the artist painted it, you'd have thought Sugawara made Seppuku the number-one independent label in Japan solely by his ability to hand out gold records as musicians beamed up at him gratefully.

The mural made me think about Fasthand Furizake.

Hayaite "Fasthand" Furizake won all kinds of awards, but he was nowhere on the painting. An *ereki*-style surf guitarist of blinding skill, he'd been a session man before Sugawara signed him and launched his solo career. Three years ago, Furizake won best new artist at the Oricon awards and landed a blistering metal-surf track as the theme song for the hit TV series *Park Mom Wrestling*. He was set for an opening tour slot with Austrian opera-rock behemoths Wagnervosa when his career took a sudden turn.

One night he was abducted by three hooded men. They broke both his hands. Then they cut off two of his fingers and dumped him under a Shuto Expressway overpass. No one was able to prove who did it, but an interesting fact surfaced. Furizake's agent had been negotiating a new deal with Sony Entertainment. Fasthand wanted to leave Seppuku.

You could still catch Fasthand playing the clubs once in a

while. Only he played slide guitar now, and had developed a facial tic that hurt his stage presence a little. He'd never be a big star again, but he was one hell of a musician, and pretty nice guy. He was a natural storyteller, too, had lots of yarns about the zany rock-and-roll life.

But he hardly ever talked about Seppuku.

And like everyone else in town, he never talked about Sugawara.

I buzzed the security intercom outside the door and gave my name. The door whizzed open and I walked into a shimmering expanse of white. White floors, a white desk and big white letters spelling *Seppuku Enterprises* against a white wall. I'd been in igloos more colorful. Just to the left of the unoccupied desk, a uniformed security guard stood at attention, staring across the room like a toy soldier.

Then a woman walked into the room. Underneath her mousy glasses, modest black skirt and no-name blue blouse she looked plenty capable of ruining a guy's life. If it was a music video there would be a montage of her taking off her glasses and her conservative clothes, putting on makeup, a miniskirt and high heels and all but writing *I've uncovered my latent sexuality* in lipstick across the mirror as she transformed into a modern party girl ready for a night on the town.

Instead she just motioned me to an unmarked white door. She buzzed the intercom next to it and it barked back some white noise.

"Chaka-san!" she squealed. Her voice was so high even the stoic security guard flinched. The door popped open and I walked into Sugawara's office.

. . .

The legendary Sugawara stood with his back turned, peering out the window across the intersection below at all the people hurrying around with shopping bags. Maybe he was wondering how the country could be in the middle of a recession with so many people buying so much junk. Of course, that would've meant he was thinking the same thing I was, which meant I wasn't an original thinker. So he must have been thinking something else.

Kizuguchi rose and bowed. "You're late," he said. I caught myself staring at the scars on his head and looked away.

The three guys in navy-blue suits paid their respects in exact change, bowing minimally. The fact that they sat down at the large, round conference table before offering me a chair told me even more about how they felt. The tabletop was occupied by a white, old-fashioned rotary phone.

I looked up again at Sugawara. He was wearing a creme-yellow sweater that would have looked good on Mr. Rogers. Not the kind of sweater you'd expect to see on a guy who had the hottest ears in showbiz. He hadn't budged from his place at the window.

"Sit," Kizuguchi said, pulling out a chair. It was right next to the Navyblues. In fact, all the chairs but one were bunched in the same area of the circle. "Get comfortable."

The arty chairs didn't allow you to do that, but I sat down anyway and did a quick survey of the room. In the far corner a row of fax machines drooled reams of paper. There were lots of gold and platinum records hanging on the walls and a large shelf housing the entire Seppuku CD catalog. The CDs were unopened, still shrink-wrapped in cellophane. Looking around the room, I didn't see anything to play them on.

My eyes eventually circled back to Kizuguchi. He gave me a pretty decent prison stare. Apparently he'd picked up the basics in the Osaka lockup and kept it in shape over the years. Then I looked over at the blue suits. They all seemed to be sharing a single thought, but I had no idea what it was.

"Sugawara is nuts to meet you," Kizuguchi said.

I glanced at Sugawara's back.

"I told him all about you," he continued. "He thinks the same thing I do."

"What's that?"

"That you're the man for the job."

I could've asked him what job, but I figured sooner or later Mr. Sugawara would have to tell me himself. Maybe I figured wrong. Sugawara was only a few feet away, but he might as well not have been on the same planet, much less in the same room.

"This is a very important time for Seppuku," one of the blue suits said.

"Pivotal," another added. "There's so much on the line."

"What say you guys shut up," Kizuguchi said. His tone was even, flat. The Navyblues nodded and took turns glancing toward the window. What felt like several minutes passed. Everyone sat around the table, doing nothing. Kizuguchi gave me a blank stare.

Suddenly, Sugawara turned around.

Except the way Sugawara looked it couldn't have happened suddenly. His face was kabuki white, blanketed with thick layers of powder and cream, but it wasn't enough to hide the muted liver spots dotting his skin beneath. His jet-black moptop wig wasn't fooling anyone either, not with the two white eyebrows trailing over his forehead like wisps of smoke. He looked more like a painting than the hallway painting of him did.

"Hello, hello!" he said, clapping his hands together. "My name is Mr. Sugawara. I am very pleased to meet you. Everyone, let me introduce to you the one and only Billy Chaka!"

Apparently, he didn't realize that I'd been in the room for nearly ten minutes. The blue-suit flunkies bowed dutifully enough, but couldn't match Sugawara's level of enthusiasm. He held a smile in place like he was waiting for a picture to be taken, his thin lips only the slightest shade darker than his face. With a stately gait he made his way to the head of the table and settled into the single empty chair. I tried to figure out just how old he was, but it was tough. His face was out of time with itself, full of anachronisms. He clasped his hands together and put them on the table. Ageless hands. Then he looked to each person in turn before settling his smile on me.

"I'll tell you something," he started in English, before switching back to Japanese. "I am indebted to Western people. You gave me the word. Gave me some of that rock and roll music. Everything I am today, I owe to rock and roll."

Looking at him, it was hard to believe he knew rock 'n' roll as anything but a distant concept. But if what he said was true, Sugawara may have been the persuasive argument against rock parents had been searching for during the last fifty years. No kid would wanna wind up looking as uncool as him.

"Are you aware how seriously we take your visit?"

I wasn't even sure why I was there.

"Let me tell you how it will be," he said.

He grabbed the phone in front of him and lifted the receiver off the hook. He placed it gently on the surface of the table and gave me a meaningful look. I could hear the dial tone droning quietly.

He made a slight motion to the others. They reached into their jackets and tossed their cell phones onto the table. Then their pagers. Then their handheld computers. Then their other cell phones. One of the Navyblues strolled over and flipped a switch on the wall. The fax machines went dead.

"I am utterly disconnected now," Sugawara said. "We're all utterly disconnected."

No kidding, I thought.

"I shall remain disconnected, Mr. Chaka, until you and I have reached an understanding."

I started to ask something and was interrupted.

"I must apologize," he said, bowing his absurdly black head. "I have never read this publication for which you write. But my colleagues tell me you are toppermost of the poppermost."

"The deadline poet of the bubblegum set," a blue suit said.

"Hard-boiled laureate of literate teen," another added.

I shifted in my chair uncomfortably and looked around at all the gold records hanging on the wall. I'd come hoping to get a glimpse of the kind of guys running Yoshi's career, but from all the compliments it was clear they had an agenda, too.

"I know you'll get to the heart of things." Sugawara smiled. As he spoke, his words alternated from English to Japanese and back again several times. "You've got that something. I think you'll understand. True, recent events leave us all a bit shaken. And though the news was rather sad, we may find slight solace where it comes. Ignorance and haste may mourn the dead. I've always believed in making the best of things. Only time will tell if I am right or I am wrong."

I was trying to figure which way to take it when a blue suit handed me the traditional Japanese death notice—a white card bordered in black. The name in the middle was

Yoshi's. Actually, it wasn't Yoshi's name so much as it was Yoshi's logo, the same stylized characters rendered like I'd seen on countless Saint Arrow T-shirts and stickers. It was as if the icon were dead rather than the person. Somehow, though, I got a feeling the commodity Yoshi never felt better.

"In two nights," Kizuguchi said. "Private memorial concert. A tribute gig. The farewell party he never had a chance to throw. We're keeping it secret until two hours before the show. Then we're gonna announce it on a couple fan sites on-line."

"It's the way he would've wanted it," said a blue suit.

"It's an invitation," Sugawara trumpeted. "And a good place for you to begin the project. I've contacted Isamu Suda personally and he told me to say he's in complete agreement with the book. You know you should be glad."

"There's just one problem," I said, tucking the death-notice-slash-concert-flier into my pocket. "I haven't got a clue what the hell you guys are talking about."

Sugawara leaned forward in his chair, a strained look of expectation on his face. Maybe he didn't hear me. I was about to say it again when Kizuguchi spoke up.

"Saint Arrow bio," he said. "Behind the scenes. In-depth look at Yoshi and his band. The history, the hits. The gossip, maybe some of the truth."

"The project was born a long, long time ago. Long before what happened," Sugawara intoned, brimming with sadness. "We've tried many ghost writers, but you know it ain't easy. You know how hard it can be."

"Bunch of hacks," said Kizuguchi.

"With every mistake we must surely be learning," Sugawara continued. "And now we know what we want. A book of a thousand pages, give or take a few. A work of scholarship, not one of those sleazy books that piles scandal upon scandal like endless rain into a paper cup."

So now I knew why they'd brought me here, and why Kizuguchi had insisted on paying for my room at the Royal Hotel. I wasn't sure why they thought I was the guy to pen the Yoshi biography, but I decided I'd better tell them why they were wrong.

"Sorry," I said. "I'm already spoken for. I write feature articles and a monthly column for teens. I do it well and I have no desire to change careers."

Sugawara looked confused. Kizuguchi made a vague gesture and Sugawara returned it. They were taking the legendary Japanese science of nonverbal communication to a whole new level.

"Working for peanuts is all very fine," said Sugawara.

"This could be a big step up," Kizuguchi said.

"And teens *are* our primary market," a blue suit cut in.

My protests fell on deaf ears. I couldn't think of much else to change their minds except a flat-out uh-uh, no way, forget it. But that kind of Japanese was too rude even for me. I tried another course.

"You should at least wait until the autopsy comes out," I said. "I've got a sneaking suspicion that Yoshi overdosed on heroin. And the circumstances under which it happened might turn out to be pretty ugly. I'm not gonna make it any prettier."

Kizuguchi lifted an eyebrow in Sugawara's direction. Sugawara lowered one. My heroin news didn't seem to rattle them one bit. Guess the idea of Yoshi overdosing wasn't exactly earth-shattering.

"It's Yoshi's life that interests us," Sugawara said. "How did he feel at the end of the day? What did he see when he turned out the lights? Did he think happiness was measured out in miles? In years? Did he need anybody? Could it be anybody? These are the kinds of questions we find quite fascinating."

They were also the kinds of questions I was in no position to answer. Sugawara and Kizuguchi exchanged another round of inscrutable glances. At its conclusion, Sugawara lifted the receiver off the table and held it about seven inches over the cradle.

"Life is very short. There's no time for fussing and fighting, my friend." He was all smiles, staring hard at my mouth. "Can we work it out?"

I spent another thought or two wondering why they'd picked me. I'd envisioned my *Youth in Asia* story as the standard rags-to-riches-to-death pop star retrospective, but I was starting to get the idea that maybe Yoshi's life, and especially his death, were a bit more complicated. Going along with Seppuku's plans, at least outwardly, would give me better access to the key players. Until they put a paper contract in front of me, I figured I was safe.

I nodded to Sugawara.

He smiled and made a joyful ceremony of hanging up the phone. The moment the receiver hit the cradle, all the blue suits snatched their cell phones and started checking their messages. Someone flipped a switch to start the fax machines chattering again.

"There is one more thing I'd like to show you," Sugawara said, rising from his chair. Kizuguchi's face went stiff, and he shook his head slightly. All the blue-suit guys stared hard at the table.

Sugawara laughed. "My associates tried to persuade me against it," he said, amused by their discomfort. "I say yes, they say no. They say stop, I say go! I can see them laugh at me—but, after all, I am the boss. They must indulge me from time to time. Besides, half of what I say is meaningless."

His eyebrows did a little dance. Kizuguchi shifted in his seat. I wondered which half.

"When I was younger—so much younger than today—the Beatles were quite popular," he said. "You've heard of them?"

"Once or twice," I muttered.

Sugawara leaned forward, as if he didn't hear my answer. I noticed the whites of his eyes seemed to have a slight blue tint. I'd never seen eyes quite like them.

"Well, no matter," Sugawara said. "I once had a dream, or should I say, a dream once had me. The dream was to start a band. My band would be called the Tigers, and we would play songs by the Beatles. Not just the standards, but all of their wonderful music. But alas, it was not to be. For someone else started a band called the Tigers, and what's more—well, suffice it to say it was simply not meant to be."

He laughed, shaking his head. "You see, Mr. Chaka—I know what it is to be sad. Life doesn't always happen as we imagine it will, but dreams are curious things. It's getting hard to be someone, but it all works out. That is I think it's not too bad."

He grinned at me and nodded to Kizuguchi. Kizuguchi gave me an apologetic, embarrassed look. One of the blue suits stood up and walked over to the CD shelf. He pushed a button on the wall and the shelf slid back. A scratchy recording started.

In the hidden alcove behind the shelf stood four full-sized Bengal tigers. Three of them were posed on their hind legs, the fourth stuck behind a drum kit. They were all stuffed.

Oh yeah, I'll, the music went, *tell you somethin'* . . .

Kizuguchi lowered his eyes, refusing to meet my gaze.

I think you'll understand . . .

The tiger with the Hofner slung around his neck—Paul, I guess—swiveled with the music. Tiger John jerked robotically side to side, his glass eyes black and hard. Ringo moved his paws up and down, out of time with the song. Tiger George didn't do much of anything.

When I say that somethin' . . .

I'd seen enough tigers to know that these weren't fakes. They were fully grown Bengals, killed, stuffed and expertly mounted. Beautiful animals, endangered species no less, gutted, filled with robotics and fitted with musical instruments. Each had the same ridiculous Beatles wig propped on its head. Probably the same one Sugawara himself wore.

I WANNA HOLD YOUR HAND!!!

A bountiful smile erupted on Sugawara's face, almost putting color in his cheeks. The blue suits tried to sink into their chairs, but the chairs wouldn't give. The tigers kept jerking around, the Beatles kept singing. My mind was a total blank.

When the music stopped, the blue suit hit the button again and the shelf slid back into place. Everyone went about pretending nothing had happened while Sugawara stood there in his yellow sweater, feeling happy inside.

9

I made my way out of the Seppuku building and walked about three blocks, a heavy plastic bag dangling at my side. As a parting gift Sugawara had given me a copy of every Saint Arrow recording available. Four albums, two EPs, fourteen maxisingles. He'd even given me the karaoke version of each disc, in case I felt like singing along.

As I strolled down the street, hardly a thought went through my shell-shocked head. A chorus of anticlimax blaring from the newsstand finally brought me to my senses. You could almost feel the relief in the headlines, the numb comfort of confirmed suspicions. The language was final and decisive, leaving no room for messy interpretations. At any rate, it was suddenly apparent why the Seppuku crowd hadn't flinched when I'd mentioned heroin.

Yoshi OD'd

Overdose Official

Yoshi Dead of Heroin

And from the *Tokyo Daily Gambler—*

Cash Your Bets: Heroin Wins!

I grabbed the *Yomiuri Shimbun,* plopped down my yen and went to a nearby coffee shop called the Blind Dog. It was one of my favorite Tokyo caffeine pits, which meant it would probably disappear by this afternoon. I ordered a cup, took a seat and tried to get Sugawara out of my mind. It was like trying to unring a bell. The best I could do was shove him way to the back. I didn't much like the thought of he and his tigers roaming the shadowy corridors of my consciousness, but getting him out completely could take years.

"I Want to Hold Your Hand" was pretty much wedged in there, too. Every time I got a song stuck in my head I thought of Yunbo Umezawa, the lead singer of Autumn Wind. During a free show in Yoyogi Park back in the eighties he was leaping around stage and cracked his head on the mic stand. He tried to soldier on, but they had to stop the show because the only song he could remember was "Postcards from Fuji." The condition didn't improve. He ended up visiting neurologists, Zen masters, Shinto priests, African witch doctors, Mongolian shamans, Malibu astrologers and when all else failed even a licensed psychiatrist. But it never got better. He could talk just fine, and even managed to write new song lyrics, but every time he opened his mouth to sing, out came "Postcards from Fuji." His loyal bandmates tried to make the best of it. They went into the studio and recorded the fifteen different versions of "Postcards from Fuji"—including a spoken-word version dubbed "Phone Call from Fuji" and a techno remix called "E-mail from Fuji." Of course, Umezawa still sang the word "postcard" rather than "phone call" or "e-mail" in all the choruses. The album *Messages from Fuji* managed to chart, thanks to an ingenious marketing tie-in campaign featuring a booklet of actual postcards of Mt. Fuji designed by famous artists, but it was a trick you could only pull once. The band split. Yunbo, last I heard, was working at Mt. Fuji as a tour guide.

I drank my coffee slowly and read the official story of Yoshi's death. According to the paper, the long-awaited coroner results were released during a hospital press conference at 8:30 P.M. yesterday. Yoshi had been admitted to Akasaka Hospital at approximately 2:20 A.M. on Sunday, after his body was discovered in a love hotel in Sanya. He was pronounced dead on arrival from respiratory failure caused by overdose of a controlled substance. The coroner found 1.52 milligrams of morphine in Yoshi's bloodstream, administered by injection. Having conducted a thorough examination, the police ruled out foul play, and the death was labeled an accident by misadventure. A public memorial service would be held at the Tsukiji Hoganji Temple. The article was accompanied by a map showing which streets would be closed off, advising drivers of alternative routes.

Other than Yoshi, it was the usual uplifting news. The Nikkei was down, schoolyard bullying was on the rise. Five more scandalized bank managers had killed themselves in the last four months. Children's test scores continued their downward trend while teenage boys spent an ungodly amount on cosmetics this year in what was being called the "groom-boom." There were four books on the bestseller list with the word "failure" in the title, and *Wildman for Geisha!* was killing at the box office.

I was reading a story titled "Elephant Missing in Tokyo Suburb" when I noticed an ad for *Marquee Weekly*, the magazine my pal Takeshi worked for. "Yoshi—The Last Photos" said the teaser. The cover for this week's issue featured the same shot that graced the cover of *Power Chord Japan*. But I noticed one major difference.

The bird tattoo was gone.

I finished up my coffee and went to find a pay phone.

Takeshi didn't want to talk. Not over the phone. Instead he told me to meet him in two hours at a place called the Last Hurrah. It was a stand-up bar across town, in the Golden Gai. Then he hung up before I could get a single word in. I killed some time walking the streets of Ginza and admiring all the pretty women admiring all the pretty window displays along Chūō Dōri Street. Nothing like wandering Ginza to make you feel underdressed and underpaid. When I figured I'd given my wingtips a good enough workout for one day I hopped on the Marunouchi subway line and headed northwest toward Shinjuku station.

The Golden Gai, a.k.a. Piss Alley, was a Lilliputian maze of two-story ramshackle drinking hovels near the Hanazono Shrine. The place belonged in Shinjuku like an outhouse belonged on the space shuttle, but that was part of its charm. Developers constantly threatened to buy up the land, convinced Tokyo needed more department stores pushing staggering quantities of every product known to man. The real estate crash had taken the piss out of development plans for now, but Piss Alley didn't stand a chance against the bulldozers in the long run.

But for now it was still standing. I arrived around six-thirty and wandered through the narrow rows, squeezing past jumbles of parked bicycles and passing cinder-block stalls named Situationist, Happy Ghetto, Phrygian Mode, La Joli Mai. Even one called Cleve Land. Nobody seemed to notice me, caught up as they were in exchanging toasts and jokes or just sipping whiskey and watching the sky slowly darken.

I must have walked right by the Last Hurrah three times

before finally noticing the place. It didn't look much different from any of the other stalls. Green potted plants out front, gray pipes running every which way, walls spider-webbed with cracks. Behind the bar stood a wiry man with graying hair and a moon-shaped face. The kind of tranquil face an earthquake couldn't shake up.

I walked up to the bar and leaned on it.

"Are you a regular?" he asked, though he knew damn well I wasn't.

"Irregular," I said. "Came to meet a guy called Takeshi."

The bartender nodded about three centimeters. Newcomers weren't often welcome at places like this, but apparently Takeshi's name was enough for him. "Would you like something to drink?" he asked.

"Gimme a beer."

"Sorry, no beer."

"What do you have?"

"The Seven Faces of Happiness."

"Give me one of those."

The bartender propped a glass in front of me. The surface of the wooden bar had seen lots of unskilled hands carving names into it over the years, a scarred monument to boredom and knives. While I wondered how many of the guys were still around, the bartender waved seven different bottles of liquor over my glass. Some of the stuff made it inside, some didn't.

I took out my wallet to pay and the bartender stopped me. "Your friend has an account," he said.

A large crow was perched on the roof of the place directly across. Two stalls down, a cat sat on a wooden railing eyeing the crow. I raised my glass in a silent toast to all the cats eyeing all the crows. I was nearly finished with my drink when I heard someone behind me call out to the bartender.

"You start letting barbarians like him hang out here, you're gonna start losing customers."

I turned to see Takeshi beaming at me. He was clean-shaven and was wearing a pressed black suit. You had to really look closely to notice the frayed cuffs and small tear near the collar. Overall, the suit was remarkably clean and wrinkle-free for a guy who lived in a cardboard box.

"You're looking pretty good," I told him. "Even lost a little weight, I see."

"Cooking your own food will do that for a guy," he said.

"You build a kitchen in your box?"

"Nah," he said, taking a seat. "Bought a little oil stove. Not much, but it works. Best thing is, if I happen to burn my house down, I can build another one for less than the cost of that Seven Happiness you're drinking."

"Sounds like a good deal. Any chance I could get a place there?"

"You'd have to take it up with the officials of the Shinjuku-koen Neighborhood Association," he joked. "I don't know if they'd allow a foreigner to live there. It's a pretty exclusive shantytown."

Good to see Takeshi still had a sense of humor. Given the shape his life was in, I suppose he'd have to. The bartender poured him a Seven Happiness and Takeshi and I drank to each other's health. That didn't seem funny enough, so we drank to our vast wealth and unlimited futures. Then he proposed a drink to Sarah back in Cleveland. I countered with a toast to his wife, the Ministry of Finance. He was midway through a salute to the director of *Wildman for Geisha!* when I told him maybe we should get down to business.

"Fine," he sighed. "What's this tattoo nonsense you were trying to tell me about?"

I nodded suspiciously toward the bartender.

"Don't worry about him," Takeshi chuckled. "He's cool."

I placed *Power Chord Japan* upon the bar, then set the ad for *Marquee Weekly* beside it. I pointed to the missing tattoo and explained to Takeshi how the guitar magazine's run had supposedly been canceled. Takeshi nodded along as I spoke, inspecting the twin photos.

"I thought that's what you said," Takeshi remarked. "In fact, I looked into it for you after I got off the phone. Talked to a guy in graphics production. He told me they got the photos from *Power Chord Japan* all right. They're owned by the same company we are. But my guy claims he didn't airbrush the picture or do any digital work on it. He said they ran it exactly as they received it from the guitar guys. So if there was any doctoring, they're the ones who must've done it."

"Don't you find that strange?"

Takeshi nodded. His expression shifted slightly as he took another sip of Seven Happiness. "That's not the only thing I find strange. Something isn't right about this whole thing. Yoshi's death, I mean. I think there's more going on than what the authorities have said."

"Like what?"

"Well," Takeshi said. "We listen to police scanners. You know, so we can be first on the scene and all that jazz when things go down. So get this—the night Yoshi was found dead, there were actually two different emergency calls about him overdosing."

"What's so weird about that?"

"They were made almost ninety minutes apart," he said. "And they directed the cops to two different hotels. In two very different parts of town."

I thought about Santa's conversation with Olga. He'd been wondering much the same thing, but he hadn't mentioned any calls to the authorities. I wondered who else could've known Yoshi's whereabouts that night.

"So someone was expecting Yoshi to overdose," I mused. "They made an emergency call without actually seeing him do it, not knowing he'd gone to a different hotel to shoot up."

"Maybe," Takeshi offered. "Or maybe Yoshi overdosed at the Hotel L'Charm. Someone witnessed it, fled the scene and called the cops. But before the cops could get there, someone else came along and dragged his unconscious body across town to the Love Hotel Chelsea."

"Why would anyone do that?"

"I dunno," Takeshi said sheepishly. "I never got that far."

"Why don't you write the story. Tell about how there were two different emergency calls. You know—beat the grass to startle the snakes."

"Yeah, right," he said. "As if *Marquee* would ever run anything disputing the official police version."

I understood the problem. In Japan, official press clubs had exclusive rights to most news conferences. Run a story counter to the official version and you risk getting kicked out of the press clubs. Getting banned from press clubs meant you'd no longer have access to any information. It was a big reason the ostensibly free press in Japan wasn't so free. I didn't have to worry about getting booted from the press clubs, though. Foreigners weren't allowed in them in the first place.

"So what are you gonna do?"

"I'm gonna look into it, anyway," Takeshi said. "Visit the Hotel L'Charm in Shibuya. You know how those love hotels are, though."

I did. Most love hotels were designed to protect the anonymity of the guests. There were no clerks, no bellhops, no one to witness patrons' comings and goings. They were favored by young couples and people having affairs. Lately the yakuza had been running a scam that involved causing car accidents with patrons exiting love hotel parking garages. The exiting guests weren't likely to go to court and have it known that they were visiting a love hotel, thus the yakuza were able to demand compensatory payments on the spot—even though the accidents were their fault to begin with.

In other words, love hotel patrons typically weren't fountains of information.

"But maybe I can dig up something," Takeshi continued. "Something so big *Marquee* would have to run it. Even if they don't, I just wanna find out what happened. For my own curiosity."

"I never had you pegged for a Saint Arrow fan."

"Nah," he said. "Me, I'm a jazz guy. Coltrane, Miles Davis, Charlie Mingus. But Yoshi seemed like an OK guy. He understood being misunderstood."

I nodded and took another sip of the Seven Happiness. The sun was dropping now, the air getting cooler. The crow had taken off. The cat was still on the ledge, his eyes opening and closing like he couldn't decide whether staying awake was worth the effort.

"How about we make a deal?" I said.

Takeshi raised an eyebrow.

"You see what you can find at the Hotel L'Charm. I'll call up *Power Chord Japan* and see what's going on with this tattoo. Either of us finds anything, we share information. What do you say?"

"I thought you were *ippiki-ōkami*. The lone-wolf type."

"Then we'll be like Lone Wolf and Cub."

Takeshi rolled his eyes at my reference to the classic comic book then took another drink while he considered my offer. He finished and placed his empty glass on the bar.

"OK," he said. "One condition."

"Name it."

"You gotta promise me that you'll try to patch things up with the girl back home. Sarah. You're made for each other. Maybe I only saw the two of you together once, but I could tell. I'm sure you're secretly still crazy about her. And I bet she feels the same way. Someday all this cat-and-mouse stuff has to end, you know?"

"I'm not even sure who's the cat and who's the mouse."

"You're equals, then. So much the better."

I laughed, but maybe Takeshi was right, maybe Sarah and I were made for each other. I wasn't sure if that was a comforting thought or a terrifying one. While I pondered it Takeshi ordered another round of Seven Happiness. This time we skipped the toasts, and there was no more talk about women troubles. No talk about dead rock stars. We sat under the moon, laughing and trading stories, talking about the good times, about the way the world looked when we were young.

10

I woke up and saw the smiley Mamoru condom man peeking through the curtains, pledging to protect and defend me. I got out of bed and walked across the room to grab myself a glass of water. You can never go wrong with water, I thought. Have a little cartoon guy saying it and you've got a regular high-priced ad campaign.

If yesterday was a day of questions, the cyclical nature of the universe dictated today would be full of answers. With that in mind, I decided to call Setsuko Nishimura and tell her about her grandfather's ID card with the bird printed on it. Even if she had no idea what I was talking about, I figured I had nothing to lose. I dug up the Hello Kitty sticky note she'd given me and dialed her number. Four rings later a tired voice answered.

"*Moshi moshi . . .*"

"Is this Ms. Nishimura?"

"What's left of her," she said. "Who's speaking?"

"This is Billy Chaka."

"Oh?" A short silence followed. The signal was thin, staticky. It sounded like she was speaking from the other end of a long tunnel. "That's really weird. I was just thinking about you."

"No kidding?"

"I was thinking I'd probably never hear from you again."

"I guess you were wrong."

"Yeah, but isn't it strange? The exact moment you popped into my head the phone started ringing. Or maybe it isn't strange at all. Maybe it's like an omen."

"I can call back later, when I'm out of your head."

"Go ahead and joke, but I think it means something."

I didn't have the courage to ask what it meant, and I doubted she'd be able to tell me anyway, so I asked instead, "Are you at work right now?"

"No," she said. "I took a few days off. I need more time for things to sink in, you know? That's why I'm at the park again."

"The one with the duck pond?"

"Uh-huh."

"Any ducks yet?"

"I'm not here for the ducks," she said quietly.

"I didn't mean anything by it."

She let out a long sigh. I imagined her sitting in the forlorn park, staring at an empty pond and thinking about her grandfather as the rest of the world rushed about its business. Funny thing was, I couldn't imagine anyone sitting on a park bench thinking about Yoshi. Everyone I'd met was too busy planning biographies, throwing secret memorial gigs, wondering how he got from one hotel to another, hoping the police wouldn't come asking questions. It was nice to imagine that when I died, someone, somewhere would sit on a bench and think about me. But if my chaotic life to now was any indication, my death wouldn't inspire much quiet contemplation.

"Why did you call, anyway?" Setsuko asked.

"I thought maybe we could get some dinner. Are you free tonight?"

Her end went silent. I tried listening for the pond lapping the shore in the background, but of course I couldn't hear it. When she spoke again her voice was hesitant.

"I don't know. I'd feel kinda weird about it."

"It's not what you think. I want to talk about your grandfather. There are some things you should know. About when he died. Things I didn't tell you the other day."

That brought her to life.

"I knew it! I knew you were holding something back! Don't ask me how, but I did. I can sense things like that. I'm very in tune with people that way, you know? Practically clairvoyant."

"Sure." I was starting to get the feeling she might be very out of tune with people in other ways. "Can you meet me tonight?"

"OK. Where?"

"You name it."

She thought for a moment, then gave me the name of an Italian restaurant in Roppongi. She told me she'd call and make reservations for two. "See you at seven," she said.

Then she hung up.

Seeing as things were going so smoothly on the phone that morning, I decided to dial up the number to *Power Chord Japan.* I listened to a voice-bot read me fifty-six extensions then hit the numbers 5 and 6 followed by the star key. The voice-bot thanked me and reminded me to look for the new issue of *Power Chord Japan* on stands this Tuesday.

"Picnic in the Abyss" played while I was on hold. It was an older Saint Arrow tune, the kind of blistering dirge perfect for moshing on someone's grave. A DJ interrupted the song every twenty seconds to tell me it was on the *Ninjaborg II* soundtrack, available in stores everywhere. Finally, a real live person answered. He did his best to sound like a recording.

"I respectfully wish to inquire about a photo that appeared on your most recent cover," I said, putting on my polite Japanese.

"The one featuring Koi Koi Klub? We've been getting a tremendous response to that cover. In fact—"

"No," I interrupted. My politeness threshold was pretty low today. Blame it on last night's Seven Happiness. "I'm talking about the one featuring Yoshi."

"Oh? That one isn't available yet. It should be out—"

"I have an advance copy."

The other end crackled with static. Maybe it was just the sound of the guy thinking.

"That *is* highly unusual." He made a few troubled noises and then asked me to describe the cover of the magazine.

So I did, in loving detail.

"Please hold, sir." From the cheer in his voice I could tell he'd found a way to shuffle me off to someone else. I buckled up for a long ride on the *tarai mawashi,* the revolving barrell, a.k.a. the royal runaround. Every country has one, but Japan's is frustrating in such a unique way I was surprised the government hadn't declared it an Intangible Cultural Treasure.

Another click and I was listening to "Picnic in the Abyss" again, hearing Yoshi joyfully tear his way through a solo with the wanton glee of a juvenile delinquent tossing his first brick through a window. He held a high note, torturing it ever so slowly higher before plunging in a whirlwind down the neck that landed with a teeth-chattering rumble. He let some feedback build before racing back up in a bubbling cascade that explo— *That's Saint Arrow with "Picnic in the Abyss," from the sizzlin' new soundtrack to* Ninjaborg II.

"*Power Chord Japan,*" a new voice chimed. "How may I help you to rock?"

This guy had me go through my conversation with the last guy, voicing affirmative grunts as I relayed the details. When I'd finished he said, "Sir, may I ask where you purchased this edition of the magazine?"

"Didn't buy it," I said. "Uncle died and left it to me."

"I see," said the guy on the other end. "Kind of an odd thing to bequeath someone, isn't it?"

"He's an odd guy. *Was* an odd guy. We even called him Uncle Odd. Odd old uncle Uncle Odd, bequeather of odd things."

"I see," the guy said again. A short silence followed, and I thought I could hear him grinding his teeth.

"The specific edition of the magazine you are referring to is a regrettable mistake. It never should have been distributed. In order to rectify the situation, I'd like to reacquire that magazine."

"Reacquire?"

"We're willing to offer thirty-five thousand yen for it."

I'd expected to talk to at least three or four other people before anyone even admitted the magazine actually existed, much less used the word "mistake." The $350 part barely registered.

"We will replace your magazine with a legitimate version, in addition to the money. If you wish, we can supply you with the next month's issue and a free T-shirt of our featured artist. Are you a big fan of the KKK?"

"The who?"

"Koi Koi Klub."

"Who isn't?" I said. "But I'm more interested in Yoshi. On the cover of your magazine, he's got a tattoo on his left shoulder. Some kind of bird. I was wondering if you could tell me about it."

"I certainly can't claim to be an expert on the various tattoos musicians wear," the man said nervously. "So I'm afraid answering your question would be very difficult."

Very difficult. Standard conflict-avoidance Japanese for *take a flying leap.*

"Be that as it may, you must know something about this tattoo. Because I couldn't help noticing it was airbrushed out of the pictures run by *Marquee.* They're a sister publication of yours, I understand."

"I assure you I have no information on the tattoo," he said emphatically. "None whatsoever."

"Then why did I get transferred to you?"

"Please understand," he said, shifting his tone. "The edition you own should never have fallen into anyone's hands. Whoever sold this to . . . *your uncle* . . . was breaking the law, and more importantly, distributing a flawed product. We are very embarrassed. We'd like to rectify the situation."

"Good. You tell me who ordered the bird tattoo to disappear, I'll give you your magazine back."

From his end I heard only an empty whooshing sound, like he was standing near a jet runway. Maybe they were product-testing some new guitar gizmo in the background. When the guy finally spoke, his voice was quieter than before, his confidence gone with his volume.

"You put us in a very difficult position."

"Uncle Odd used to say that difficult problems often have simple solutions," I said. "They were his dying words, actually. Difficult problem, gasp gasp, simple solution."

Another long pause.

I knew I had him when the guy started talking about the weather. I agreed that it was nice for December. I even implied that the fine weather was somehow a result of the excellent customer service at *Power Chord Japan.* If I wasn't careful, I'd wind up going out to flirt with bar hostesses and destroy Sinatra tunes with him.

"I appreciate your understanding in this unfortunate matter," the guy finally said. "Perhaps we can meet somewhere to bring this business to a conclusion."

"How about Smash Guitar?"

There was another long pause. He asked if I'd mind holding. I held. Ninjaborg II also featured hot new tracks from Paincake, the Furopi Gentlemen, Clown D'Arc and Satori Headbutt. It was available wherever cutting-edge music was sold.

"Smash Guitar is suitable," the guy said. "You bring the magazine, we'll supply you with the information you require. I'll send our intern, Juzo-san. He's got bright silver hair and will be wearing a black Bloody Dolphins T-shirt. Juzo-san will be playing "Toccata and Fugue" on the guitar in the amp room."

"Is that on the *Ninjaborg II* soundtrack?"

"You'll recognize it. Thank you for your interest in *Power Chord Japan*," the guy said, automatically defaulting back into his sugary customer service tone. "We wish you the best in your efforts to rock."

Stepping out of the Akihabara train station was like stumbling into a semiotician's fever dream. An explosion of kanji, katakana, hiragana and romanji of various sizes, colors and voltages battled for attention from the ground to the sky. Every surface was covered with messages—from hand-painted signs on the lower levels to the latest animated characters dancing and singing on the giant video screens hovering above like motherships. On the far end of the intersection the Marlboro Man stared out from a billboard, an expression on his face like he was lost.

Akihabara had all the chaos of your average Asian fish mar-

ket, minus the smells. A longtime mecca for Tokyo's DIY elec-
tronics geeks, it started as a black market for the ham radio
crowd during the MacArthur years. These days it was overrun
by computer *otaku* bent on building the cheapest PC on the
block and amateur roboticians trying to construct the ultimate
fighting machine for the annual Robocon tournament.

As I fought my way through the discount madness on the
sidewalk, seven different guys touted the cheapest RAM in
Tokyo, while a bunch of cheerleaders in flourescent green
windbreakers bounced up and down on a makeshift stage,
enthusiastically singing about some new handheld computer
called the Mini-Sexy-Cool. A shill with a Santa Claus hat
begged me through a megaphone to take a look at a shipment
of beat-up American flat monitors *just off the jet* and got all
sore when I asked him if the jet crashed. Cell phones were
everywhere, growing out of peoples hands, displayed in neat
columns or laying in jumbled piles on folding tables like
multicolored ears of corn at the farmer's market. It was hard
to imagine people really had that much to talk about, but it
hardly mattered now that phones were used as stock tickers,
global positioning systems, Internet browsers, address books
and game systems. Actually talking on the phone was as
unimaginative as sex for procreation.

I stopped by Kinko's and made a few color copies of the
Yoshi cover. There were some other folks I wanted to ask
about the tattoo, so I wasn't about to surrender all evidence
of its existence. After Kinko's, I turned the corner and spotted Smash Guitar across the street. Even with the ten million
competing signs it was tough to miss the giant cherry-red
neon six-string lit up over the entrance. The instrument's
fretboard was divided into TV screens, each showing a different guitar hero silently wailing away.

The electric doors whizzed open as I stepped through. No

one hollered the mandatory *irrashaimase* to me, but I didn't take it personally. Around thirty kids with guitars and basses plugged into the amps were generating the kind of high-volume discord that made you envy deaf people. Trying to greet a customer was like whistling in a tsunami.

Strains of some kid giving the Hendrix treatment to Japan's national anthem wrestled with thick buzzsaw metal riffs à la Super Junky Monkey. A kid with the pictogram for "vacant" shaved into the back of his head worked a drum machine, punching buttons until it sounded like the amplified beating of hummingbird wings. A skinny burnout next to him banged mercilessly on a bass string, snapping it over and over without the slightest variation. On the other side of the room, a pretty girl in a sky-blue jumpsuit rocked autistically on a wah wah pedal while some kid who looked like Buddy Holly gone glam rested his head against the amp, a sweet smile waltzing over his face with each noisy burst from the girl in blue.

None of the kids looked at each other. They acted as if they were all alone in their bedrooms, lost in fantasies of sold-out Budokans.

I was getting disoriented, almost physically losing my balance as sounds assaulted me afresh, first from one side and then another, like I was the ball in a brutal game of sonic Ping-Pong. An employee strolled back and forth on the sales floor with his arms crossed. He looked pleasantly bored, like he was trying to decide what to do when his shift ended. Poor bastard must have already gone deaf or mad or both.

Then I heard it.

That famous opening immortalized in a thousand horror movies, the song done so many times that they might as well flash the words "spooky music" on the screen.

I followed the tune through crowds of kids ogling the latest digital effects racks and 8-track recorders, past the jumbled stacks of African percussion instruments and Australian didgeridoos, through racks of instructional videos with serious-looking ponytailed dudes in cheesy vests on the covers.

The kid sat atop a Marshall half-stack, perched like some silver-haired elfin king on his throne. His small frame curled around a massive translucent hollow-body guitar that looked like a petrified jellyfish. I walked up to him and stood there, but he was too into his Bach to notice. When I reached up and touched him on the shoulder, he jumped, nearly dropping the jellyfish.

"Nice lick, kid," I shouted over the ruckus. "You play funerals?"

He gave me a throwaway look to match the comment.

"I'm here about the magazine," I said. He nodded blankly, bobbing his silver mane as he launched into "Toccata en Fugue" again, upping the tempo.

"I called on the phone," I yelled. "Talked to your boss."

He eyed me like I'd just asked if he had any homework. The kid didn't miss a note, just went right on playing, increasing the speed with every measure.

At his pace the song couldn't last much longer, so I just sat back and waited, watching his nimble hand scuttle up and down the neck of the guitar like a mechanical dancing crab.

He finished the song and I gave an appreciative nod. It only enhanced his disdain for me. He put down the guitar and stood. With hairspray he was about five feet five but a little rain would bring him down to four feet eleven.

"I've got the magazine," I said. "What have you got?"

He reached into his German army jacket and produced a thin envelope with the *Power Chord Japan* logo printed on the front. I took out the magazine still in its brown paper bag, bowing and offering it to him with both hands just to irk him with formality.

He snatched it out of my hands, then tossed me the envelope. From the look on his puckish face the effort nearly killed him.

"Thanks," I said. "Keep polishing your chops."

Some of the contempt went out of his glare, like maybe I might be all right for an adult.

"Remember to play with feeling," I added. "Don't bother trying to play as fast as Yngwie Malmsteen, don't waste time trying to learn 'Eruption' note for note and don't use effects pedals as crutches. The important thing is to discover your own style. And just in case the world decides it doesn't need another guitarist, stay in school. School is cool. You dig, daddy-o?"

His mouth fell open and his face turned the color of a tomato. Here he was, he seemed to be thinking, face to face with the unhippest man in the world. I stood there staring at him, a big grin on my mug. He gingerly put down the guitar and made his way to the door, fighting the urge to break his loping pimp roll and make a mad dash to the exit. I'd probably ruined his street cred for at least a month, just by being an adult and talking to him in public. It felt good.

11

I called up the Royal Hotel to check my messages. After punching in my room number and security code, I heard Takeshi's voice speak the seven words I wanted to hear. "We're onto something," he said. "Call me back immediately."

So I dialed up Takeshi at *Marquee*. He wasn't in. The message I left on his answering machine consisted of only three words.

The Phoenix Society.

That's the name I'd found when I opened the envelope the kid had given me at Smash Guitar. Thirty-five thousand yen and a copy of a fax with most of the information marked out in black ink. *Power Chord Japan* had held up their end of the bargain I guess, but only just.

The Phoenix Society.

The gist of the fax was that the company was requesting Yoshi's bird tattoo be removed from the cover. The Phoenix Society claimed it represented a trademark infringement. The language was polite and nonthreatening, but the implications were clear. If *Power Chord Japan* didn't remove the tattoo from the photo, they could expect legal action to be taken. An American magazine might have laughed and said "see you in court," but things were different in Japan. Courts were used only as a last resort, since even the simplest of lawsuits could drag on for years and years, bankrupting both parties in the process. Besides, Japanese companies naturally tended to avoid conflict whenever possible, and from the *Power Chord Japan* standpoint, they didn't have anything to lose by airbrushing out a tattoo.

The Phoenix Society.

I slapped it around in my head for a while, but couldn't make it talk. But at least I had the name. A name will make itself into all kinds of things, given time. I gave it the rest of the day, then decided it was time to head to Roppongi for my meeting with Setsuko Nishimura.

Roppongi was a seedy nightlife district within walking distance of many of the Tokyo international embassies. As such, it was the one place in the whole of Japan where I could count on seeing fellow whiteys. Back in the eighties and early nineties, it was *the* trendy hotspot, the place to come for Western-style sex, drugs and rock and roll. In the years since it had turned into somewhat of a dump, a Tokyo version of Tijuana.

Sarah once said I didn't like Roppongi because seeing all the other foreigners shattered the myth that I was somehow unique. Maybe there's something to that, but I'd say I don't like Roppongi because most ex-pats who regularly hung out there were the types who'd travel halfway around the world to spend all their free time sitting in a sports bar and complaining about backwards Japanese social customs while they hoisted pint after pint of Guinness and screamed for Manchester United or the San Francisco 49ers.

When I arrived that evening Roppongi was pretty quiet, but once the imported beer started flowing it wasn't likely to stay that way. I followed the directions Setsuko had given me to a restaurant called Chez Bologna, a well-known place with a decidedly strange history.

Back in the sixties, Chez Bologna—or Guisseppe's, as it was then called—had been a pizza joint with rumored mafia connections. But in the early eighties it was bought by a wealthy real estate speculator as a gift to his wife—a well-traveled, highly educated woman named Yumi Tsukiyama. Tsukiyama loved Italian food but for some reason didn't like the language. She decided to change the restaurant's image to reflect her tastes, renaming the joint Chez Bologna and giving all the Italian dishes classy-sounding faux-French names.

Chez Bologna made an easy target for the foreign contingent, who often complained that to the Japanese, all of Europe was one big homogenous country—which, come to think of it, was pretty much how most Americans viewed Asia, Latin America, Africa and anywhere else without enough white people—but for all their grousing, the ex-pats knew that Chez Bologna offered the best Italian food in south-central Tokyo.

As far as the restaurant decor went—well, that was a whole different story. Suffice it to say that Yumi Tsukiyama wasn't a big fan of French or Italian interior design. She preferred what she called the Lisbon school, which, as far as I could tell, had something to do with fish.

Ms. Nishimura was already half an hour late according to the clock above the aquarium. The tank mounted in the wall was about the size of an elevator car turned on its side and was crammed with eels, octopi and a bunch of fish I couldn't name. There were so many fish they couldn't even swim, just wriggle in place like commuters on the Tobu subway line.

The hostess seated me with so much courtesy I figured she must've mistaken me for someone else. I sat at the table waiting for Setsuko, listening to smooth jazz drift through the room and wondering why someone who'd gone through all the trouble of learning an instrument would play smooth jazz. A few must've had guns pointed to their heads, I figured, but what about the rest of them?

"I'm sorry," Setsuko said, making me jump a little. I hadn't seen her come in, lost as I was in contemplation. "I know I'm late."

She was dressed in a gray wool skirt and a thin white sweater over a white turtleneck. Her makeup looked freshly applied, as if she'd touched it up on the way over. The outfit was remarkably unremarkable, urban camouflage you could assemble in five minutes at countless *depato* stores across the city. But it looked good on her in a way an expensive evening gown or trendy clothing never would.

I stood up and pulled out a chair for her. She sat with her legs drawn together, her black handbag resting neatly in her lap. I took my seat across from her.

"I hope I haven't kept you waiting."

"Quit apologizing," I said. "It makes me feel important."

A waitress came by. Setsuko ordered some cold barley tea, I asked for a Coke with no ice. I usually take it with ice just like everybody else, but I decided today I was going to be interesting.

"You look nice," I said, amending it instantly with, "I mean, you look like you're doing well."

"You're too kind," she said with a slight blush. "The truth is, I haven't been getting much sleep lately. I guess that's normal, right?"

I nodded. Insomnia, sleeping all day, loss of appetite, eating like a pig—any reaction was normal when it came to grieving. The only things that could shake up your life as much were falling in love and quitting smoking.

The waitress delivered our menus. Setsuko hid behind hers, studying it as if it contained secret instructions on how to make nice conversation with a foreign stranger who saw your granddad die. Her shyness reminded me of Mae Ling Chow, grand champion of the Pan-Pacific Women's Bloody Knuckles Finals back in '92. Chow was a meek girl, but charming once you got her talking. Unfortunately, most people couldn't take their eyes off those two fearsome chunks of meat she called her hands. She was made painfully aware of them at all times, and it crippled her socially. Chow started wearing gloves and soon resorted to keeping her hands clasped behind her back where no one could see them. Eventually she couldn't take the attention and gave up bloody knuckles altogether, retiring to her father's pig farm outside Ankang. I trekked through the mud for three days to get her version of the story. When I reached her she just looked at me like I was an idiot and said *pigs don't care what my hands look like.*

"Is something wrong?" Setsuko said.

"You ever play bloody knuckles?"

She looked sideways at me.

"I'm sorry, but are you one of those weird kind of guys?" she declared timidly. "It's okay if you are. I don't have anything against weird. My grandfather was weird. Maybe you knew that already."

"Weird is probably a prerequisite for working at the Hotel Kitty."

"I've never been there. How long did you stay?"

"Two days."

"Why were you there, anyway?"

"Vacation."

She frowned. "You went all the way to a little town in Hokkaido for a two-day vacation?"

"It was a sudden vacation. I was forced."

She pursed her lips and wrinkled her brow. *Definitely a weird kind of guy*, she seemed to be thinking. "So what are you doing in Tokyo? Another forced vacation?"

"No. I'm working on the Yoshi story."

"Who?"

"Yoshimura Fukuzatsu, vocals and guitar for Saint Arrow. A rock star who died recently. The same night as your grandfather, as a matter of fact. You've never heard of Yoshi?"

Before she could answer, the waitress strolled by to take our order. Setsuko opted for something called La Belle Dame Sans Fromage, whatever that was, while I ordered a plate of plain old spaghetti sold under the moniker Les Nouilles Discrètes du Bourgeoisie. The waitress smiled and backed away from our table with tiny steps, as if she was wearing a kimono instead of tan slacks.

For a time Setsuko and I tried making small talk. The weather, the big news in Japan, the big news in the United States. Clumsy as our conversation was, I was still happy to be enjoying such an everyday scene. No kickboxing rock stars, no Swedish strippers, no scar-headed record executives or drug dealers named Santa. Just a normal guy and a normal girl at a normal restaurant. Bad jazz lilted harmlessly through the air, so quiet you almost didn't notice it. As pleasant as the scene was, though, I knew it couldn't last. I could feel the normalcy beginning to slip away as Setsuko turned the subject back to the Hotel Kitty.

"My grandfather told me there were many cats at the hotel," she said. "Cats are very spiritual creatures. And very wise. They understand much more than they let on. I heard that all writers love cats. Cats, they say, are a writer's best friend."

"So they say."

"Maybe cats are wise because they get to lead so many lives, whereas humans only get to lead one," she said. She thought for a moment before resuming. "I don't really believe that, though. That we only live one life. I think we lead many lives. No beginnings, no endings. Our lives just run together, on and on until the end of time."

"It's a nice idea," I said. Something in her words sounded familiar. Then I figured it out. The Day Manager back at the Hotel Kitty. He'd said more or less the same thing when I was checking out. Maybe it was a popular belief.

"What do you think happens to people when they die?"

I shrugged.

"You're not curious?"

Before I could think of something nice and neutral, she leaned over the table and whispered, "Well, I just told you what I think. But there's another part of it. See, I think sometimes things *go wrong*. When that happens, the dead get stuck. Their spirits are left to wander among the living. They see what we do, how we live. They are forever there, silently witnessing the choices we make. Always watching."

Kinda like marketing researchers. I managed to keep it to myself. "Setsuko," I began. "About your grandfather—"

"That's why you called," she said. "Like I told you, I have an intuition for this sort of thing. A gift. I know why you felt compelled to speak to me today."

"Why's that?"

"My grandfather's spirit contacted you."

She stared intently across the table, awaiting my reaction.

"Not exactly" I said. "At least, not that I know of."

"That isn't why you called?"

I shook my head. Setsuko looked disappointed, whether because she'd guessed wrong or because her grandfather's spirit hadn't contacted me, I couldn't say. I didn't know where to begin, so I took out the Night Porter's laminated photo ID and pushed it across the table. She picked it up with both hands, turning it over and looking at it hesitantly.

"What is this?" she said.

"I think it's some kind of emergency medical ID. Setsuko, the night your grandfather died, he was reaching for this card. I thought he wanted me to call the number printed below his picture. So I called—several times—but no one answered. There's something else I want to show you."

I took out the photocopied *Power Chord Japan* cover and handed it to her. As she studied the paper, I watched the color drain from her face. Her eyes went from the card to the photocopy and back again.

"I don't understand," she mumbled.

"Look at the tattoo. The bird. That guy wearing it is Yoshi, the rock star who died the same night as your grandfather. But that particular picture of him never made the news. I think somebody ordered that tattoo erased from the photo. And I found out the bird logo belongs to some group called the Phoenix Society. Does this mean anything to you?"

She closed her eyes and shook her head slowly side to side. "None of this means anything," she said. A busboy appeared. Neither Setsuko nor I spoke until he'd refilled our water glasses and scurried away.

"Some strange things happened the night Yoshi died," I said. "I think this group, the Phoenix Society, just might be involved. I can't say how or why yet, but—"

"Please," she whispered. "I don't care about this Yoshi person. Please stop telling me these things."

"But don't you see? It's not only about Yoshi. Just before your grandfather died, he said something that struck me as odd. I didn't think much of it at the time. But as I was dialing that number, he said *they're not coming*. Do you have any idea—"

"Stop! Why are you telling me these things? None of this helps! Don't you see? None of this helps me now!"

She was trembling. Tears welled up in her eyes.

Everyone in the restaurant was watching us now. Even the eels seemed to be gazing at us from inside the aquarium. The jazz kept piping, a sax solo started.

I thought of the famed monk Senshu, who once said silence is always the appropriate response. I agreed with Senshu in principle. But like Ed said, you can't run a magazine on principles.

"Setsuko," I began, speaking in a low whisper. "I'm not trying to upset you. I know this is a difficult time for you. I know this is probably confusing, hearing about what happened this way. I know—"

"You know nothing," she hissed. She was gritting her teeth, struggling to control her tone. "You know nothing about my grandfather. You know nothing about me. Maybe you're just trying to help. But you're not helping. You're not helping one little bit."

Before I could say a thing, she popped right out of her seat, the skin under her chin bouncing with the movement. She looked at me as if she was about to say something more, but instead turned on her heel and stormed out of the room, nearly colliding with a waitress on her way out. I watched her charge through the exit, thankful there was no way to slam a revolving door.

Then I sat there staring at the table in disbelief. The sax solo kept playing, a sound like a big gray elephant swaying his trunk side to side in a heavy lament. The waitress came by and asked if I'd like the meals to go. I said something or other and asked for the bill.

That's when I noticed the Night Porter's ID was gone. Intentionally or not, Setsuko had swiped it from right under my nose. I wasn't sure what to think of it any more than I knew what to think of Setsuko. I knew one thing, though. I was really starting to hate the Phoenix Society, whoever they were.

12

The doorman studied my passport, moving a toothpick from one side of his mouth to the other. He glanced up at me and shined a flashlight in my face. I squinted and tried hard to keep a positive attitude. I wasn't keen on returning to the Purloined Kitten, but there was no way around it. I had to talk to Olga. Find out who this Santa character was and just what happened the night Yoshi died. I was also curious to know who had been waiting in the car, and just where this mysterious person fit in.

The doorman put down the flashlight, took out a big walkie-talkie and spoke into it. It crackled back some static. He put the walkie-talkie away again and smiled at me.

"*Chotto matte*, OK?"

I gave him a moment. Last time I'd breezed right in, but the way things moved in the Kabuki-cho they were probably already under new management and had redone the whole place as a gay karaoke roller-disco. Thanks to a secret verbal gate-crashing technique I'd learned from a family of exiled *rakugo* comedians on the island of Sado, I wasn't worried about getting in. But it's a dangerous technique, something you don't just use on a whim.

A second guy emerged from inside the club like he was

stumbling out of bed. He looked me over, yawning and rubbing his eyes.

"Can I see some identification?" he asked.

"Your friend with the toothpick has it."

His head bobbed like it was falling off and he took the passport from Toothpick. He looked at it for a long time, holding the walkie-talkie to his face like a pillow. Limited range, crummy sound quality, bulky and only good for talking. Either Sleepy was even more old-fashioned than me or retrotech was becoming chic.

"OK," he said, drowsily handing my passport back to me. "Welcome and all that."

The same crowd of older company guys from two nights before sat around drinking and looking worried. I scanned the room for my pal Santa. Even if he wasn't wearing the red sweat suit, I knew he'd still be wearing the jewelry. Guys like him would no more leave home without their big gold chains than without their genitals. They had the two confused in sometimes complex ways.

No, Virginia, I thought, making one last sweep of the room. *There isn't a Santa Claus*. Not in this room. Not tonight.

My seat in the corner was already taken, so I was forced to sit up front, so close the proscenium lights spilled onto my table. Dancers went on one after another, fretting and strutting their three minutes onstage. Two Thai girls who looked drugged to the gills came out for some languid simulated lesbianism to a disco-fied version of an old enka ballad.

The girl I'd met named Tabi was next. She dutifully put in her time to a jungle version of a song called "One-eyed Daruma." Daruma were traditional good-luck dolls. You paint one of the doll's eyes when you make a wish, the other when it comes true. The guy in the song lamented his life was filled with one-eyed darumas.

Still no sign of Olga. It struck me that I'd only seen her onstage once or twice over the years. I'd never really gotten used to the idea. Memories of her on that big futon in that tiny apartment still lingered, even if they didn't come around much anymore. Even good memories disappear sometimes. They're like those friends you just drift apart from, for no reason whatsoever.

Lately, I'd been thinking of Olga in a whole new light. Trying to imagine her as Yoshi's girl. My imagination wasn't up to it, though. I'd hoped seeing her again would help, but it looked like Olga wasn't around. There was nothing to do but finish my Kirin lager and leave.

I'd taken the last sip when Tabi emerged in a loose-fitting white yukata with a sleek black cat embroidered on the back, claws tearing through the Purloined Kitten logo. Wearing nothing more than the glorified bathrobe, she made her way straight to my table.

"Would you like a private performance?" she asked.

"Thanks, but I came here to see Olg— Calico. Is she around?"

Tabi's eyes darted toward the entrance. Her small body tensed beneath the yukata.

"Would you like a private performance."

This time it wasn't a question.

I followed her past the stage, out of the room, down the tiny hallway. We went past the dressing room door and proceeded farther into the darkness. She looked back at me just before we reached the end of the rear exit, then pushed open a beat-up-looking door to our left. I stepped into the room and she followed, closing the door silently behind us.

The place was pitch black. She took my hand, moving in

the dark, pulling me toward the center of the room. Then she stopped. With a click the room was bathed in an eerie crimson. There was nothing to mask the naked walls, and only a broken-down weight bench upholstered in torn vinyl and an upended plastic paint can in the corner for furniture. The room needed emergency feng shui.

She turned me around gently and moved me onto the weight bench. Then she took a step back, looking down at me.

"Olga is gone," she said.

"Gone where?"

"I don't know. She said she had to get away. She knew you'd come, though. She wanted me to give you something. A good-bye gift."

Her brow wrinkled almost imperceptibly. She loosened the belt of her yukata. It fell open, exposing her breasts and the smooth skin of her stomach. Whatever kind of gift she had in mind, I decided to play along. After all, I was a guest and in Japan it's very impolite to reject gifts.

She reached inside the robe. A smile swept over her face. It looked a little ghoulish in the light, like something from a carnival funhouse.

"Here you go!" she chirped, and dropped a piece of small, cold metal into my palm. She took a step back and did up her robe again.

It was a key.

"What's this?"

"It's a key." She frowned.

"To what?"

"Olga said you'd know."

"I don't."

"She said you wouldn't at first, but that you'd figure it out. She said to think of the night you met."

"She say anything else?"

Tabi shook her head.

I squinted at the key. There was a number on it, 910, but nothing else. I was a long way from figuring anything out. I decided to ask what I'd come to find out about.

"What happened the night Yoshi died?"

"I don't know," she said. "He's dead. She's gone. I've given you your gift, and that's that for me."

"What can you tell me about this Santa guy?"

"I've gotta get back to the floor," she said, turning and making her way toward the door.

I leapt up from the bench and blocked her path.

"Yoshi was here the night he died," I said. "Santa took him to a hotel and Olga was supposed to meet him there later. But something went wrong. I'm starting to think Yoshi may have been murdered."

Hearing myself say it, I suddenly realized it was possible.

"You didn't even know Yoshi," she said. "Why do you care?"

"Personally, I don't," I said. "It makes no difference to me whether Yoshi overdosed, was murdered, or got killed by a cartoon anvil falling from the sky. But I have a responsibility to the readers of *Youth in Asia*. They deserve the truth."

She rolled her eyes. "I don't know what happened to him. All I know is that before Yoshi left he was talking with Olga. In the dressing room. I overheard him say something about a man named Kizuguchi. Yoshi said Kizuguchi had a big surprise coming to him. Something about the new album. I couldn't hear much of it. But at some point, Olga became very upset. She was crying. She told him not to go with Santa. He told her everything would be all right, not to worry. Then he left. Santa was supposed to come back to pick up Olga, but he never did. And that's all I know. I really gotta get back to the floor, or people are gonna start wondering about me."

"Is Olga still in Tokyo?"

"Just let it go," she said in an almost motherly tone. Then she grabbed the doorknob and pulled. I put a hand against the door to keep it in place. She grimaced and stepped away from the door. Then she reached into her robe and produced a key chain. Who knew a yukata had so many pockets. Tabi pointed to a small red button on the key chain.

"I don't want trouble," she said. Quiet but firm.

Apparently it was some kind of panic button to get the bouncers bouncing if a customer tried to get more than he paid for. I looked at the silent tired plea on her face and it was easy enough to imagine what kind of assholes she had to deal with every night.

"Sorry," I said. "I don't want trouble either, but trouble is nuts about me. Thanks for the key."

I let go of the door and forced myself to smile.

"Untuck your shirt and mess your hair up a little before you go out to pay," she huffed. "It wouldn't hurt if you were a little out of breath, too."

She brushed against me as she opened the door and strode quickly out of the room. I guess she didn't notice that my shirt was already untucked and my hair wasn't exactly in pristine condition either. Still, I undid a couple of buttons on my shirt and pushed my hair around a little. The hard breathing part was easy.

By the time I stepped into the dark hallway, she was already gone. Instead, two bulky shadows lingered halfway down the hall, between me and the main area of the club.

The sleepy-looking guy stepped forward.

"Thirty-five thousand yen," he said.

The huge figure threw me for a loop. I was worried that if I didn't haggle, they'd suspect something. I was worried that if I did, they'd get nasty.

"Didn't anyone tell you the bubble burst?" I asked. Maybe no one had. They didn't look like the kind of guys who'd pore over the *Nikkei Weekly*.

"You're funny," the sleepy one said. "Kenji, do we have a funny guy discount?"

"We used to," Toothpick said, pulling his mouth to one side. "But like the man said, the bubble burst."

The sleepy guy shrugged in apology and held out his hand, waiting for the money. Toothpick nodded.

I dug into my wallet and grabbed a wad of bills. I was doing the dollar conversion rates in my head when the first blow landed in my stomach.

It stopped my math cold. Sleepy wound up to kick me, but I managed to step back at the last second, sending his foot into the wall with a thud.

Toothpick came at me again, grabbing a fistful of collar. I snatched his wrist and gave it a nice twist in the wrong direction. I could have done just about anything I wanted with him, but nothing came to mind. Fighter's block.

Sleepy lunged at me with his fist—you'd have to be charitable to call it a punch—and I used my free hand to redirect the blow into Toothpick's face.

Toothpick made a bleating noise as Sleepy's fist slapped his cheek, and I gave his wrist some torque to make sure he didn't get too comfortable. He could've made it interesting if he'd remembered his free hand, but pain was clouding his thoughts.

Prolonging the situation was cruel and unnecessary, the combat equivalent of putting a ten-minute drum solo in the middle of a song. I decided to bring the transaction to its conclusion.

I released Toothpick's wrist. Dumb relief swept across his face for a microsecond before I clocked him with a forearm shiver. He hit the floor in a way that made my conscience tingle.

Sleepy looked down at Toothpick in utter confusion, as if he'd just awoken from a terrible dream only to find reality was even worse. I considered the quickest way to send him back to sandman land.

Once in Taipei I'd seen a cuckholded kung fu master KO the number-one oboe player in China with a mere finger flick to the nose. But that guy was like an umpteenth dan blacker-than-black belt. Come to think of it, if he would have spent less time in the dojo and more time with his wife, he wouldn't have had to worry about oboe players.

My version was less exotic but no less effective. I faked with a high left hook then popped him with a good ol' USA uppercut right where the jawbone meets the skull.

I caught him by his jacket as he rag-dolled and eased him to the floor next to Toothpick. It always amazes me the way thugs look when sleep takes away all their anger and bitterness. This guy was innocent as a baby in his crib, not a care in the world. I felt like taking a picture and sending it to his mom.

Suddenly, the walkie-talkie came to life, squealing from its place on Sleepy's hip.

"Nebosuke? Nebosuke!" it said. "Goddamnit. Nebosuke!"

I picked it up. Some Mariah Carey song boomed from the main room, echoing through the hall.

"Yeah?" I said.

"Keep him there make sure he stays," a voice crackled. "I'll be there in ten minutes I'm on my way there."

Then it went dead. I put the walkie-talkie back in Sleepy's hip holster. After a moment's consideration, I decided against keeping myself there. I had a pretty good idea who was coming to town, and didn't think he'd be bringing me any presents.

13

By the time I finally got back to the Royal I was ready to face-plant into sleep. During the cab ride my brain had already started going into dream mode, imagining all the lit-up kanji signs on the buildings as electric insects jittering to life, ready to swarm the night sky the moment I took my eyes off them. A motorbike gang sped by on Day-Glo rice rockets, looking for all the world like anime characters come to life. Every now and then the moon winked at me from behind passing clouds, always seeming on the verge of whispering its secrets, always remaining silent in the end.

I was having such a hard time keeping reality safely within its boundaries that when I saw three sinister types hanging out in front of the hotel, I figured they were just nightmare figures who'd made a premature entrance. It wasn't until they stepped in front of me and blocked my path to the door that I realized they were flesh-and-blood thugs.

"You Billy Chaka?"

The guy speaking had a large black mole stuck on his left eyelid. A thick hair grew from the center of it, like a fuse on a cherry bomb. The rangy guy on his left smiled, his two front gold teeth glinting in the moonlight. The third man looked one hundred percent normal, no distinguishing facial features whatsoever. Just goes to show that not every thug is colorful.

"Lemme guess," I said. "You guys want autographs. Maybe a couple of pictures to bring back to your wives and daughters. Well, sorry, fellas. Seems I don't have a pen on me. And it looks like you forgot your cameras."

The three yakuza deliberated and reached a unanimous decision not to laugh. The one with the golden choppers stepped forward, withdrawing a card from his pocket. He handed it to me without saying a word.

YATSU KIZUGUCHI
VP, Artists & Repertoire
Seppuku Unlimited, Ltd.
13-4-2 Ginza, Chuo-ku
03-3581-4111

"I've already seen this one," I said. "Besides, you guys don't look like Seppuku Records A and R men."

"We're not," said Goldtooth. "Just Kizuguchi's friends."

Moleman snatched the card out of my hand. Mr. Normal pointed to a Mercedes waiting across the street. "If you don't mind, we should probably get going. Mr. Kizuguchi has been waiting all night. Not to bad-mouth the guy, but he's not the most patient person I've ever met. I'm not criticizing him, I mean nobody is perfect, right? I know I'm sure not. Anyway, we've been standing out here for a couple of hours, and I think I speak for the other guys when I say we're all getting a little cold. So if it's okay with you, can we go now?"

"Sure. See you later."

"I'm sorry," Mr. Normal sputtered. He spoke in sincere, unironic tones. "But when I said *we*, I was including *you*. We want you to come with us. I mean, that's why we've been waiting here the whole time. Sorry if I wasn't clear on that. I can understand how you might misinterpret my request, being that it was a little ambigu—"

"Get in the goddamn car," Moleman interrupted.

"That's more like it," I said.

"See?" Moleman said to Mr. Normal. "Don't ask. Don't explain and never apologize. Just tell the man what to do."

"Okay," Mr. Normal sighed. "I guess it's just, I dunno, I feel kinda funny, like *ordering* people around. I mean, what gives me the authority to—"

"Reach into your left coat pocket," Moleman said. "Tell me what's in there."

"A gun?"

"Wrong. That's your authority. Now try it again."

Mr. Normal steeled himself and turned to me. "All right, mister. Why don't you go inside that car over there?"

"Better," Goldtooth grumbled. "But you're still phrasing it as a question. And you're using too many words."

"And don't say *mister*," added Moleman. "Say asshole, or dickface or something like that."

"Better yet, be specific," said Goldtooth. "Tailor your insults. Like this guy here is a foreigner. So you might want to call him butter-stinker, or pale-face. Pointy nose. Hairy-assed ape, round-eye, burgerchomper."

Moleman nodded in agreement. "Good point. And if you can make it personal, so much the better."

"Sarcasm is good, too," chimed in Moleman. "If the guy is short, call him stretch. If he's bald, call him curly. Ugly bastard? Call him pretty boy."

Moleman and Goldtooth kept up their tutorial as I walked across the street. The doors of the Mercedes were unlocked, the key in the ignition. It would be fun to steal the car, but I couldn't think of anywhere I wanted to go at this time of night, and besides, I'd have to come back to the hotel eventually. So I just got in the back of the car, sat down and looked out the window, watching Mr. Normal nod along eagerly as they spoke. It took the three of them nearly two minutes to notice I'd left. When they did, they started panicking, turning small circles and scanning the streets.

"Over here," I yelled, rolling down the window.

The sound startled Mr. Normal. As he spun around, the gun fell out of his pocket and hit the pavement. Luckily, it didn't go off. It still didn't go off when Moleman accidentally kicked it as he turned, sending the gun skittering across the sidewalk and into a rain gutter. For the next several minutes, all three of them took turns trying to reach through the grate and retrieve the gun. I just sat in the back of the car wondering whatever happened to old-school yakuza like Kodama Yoshio and Susumu Ishii and Jirocho Shimizu. They may have been sociopaths, but at least they knew how to kidnap a guy without turning it into comedy.

Half an hour later we stopped next to a garish building that looked like a miniature version of the Taj Mahal. It was situated under a highway overpass in some working-class neighborhood where everything had closed down hours or maybe years ago. The free-standing building was painted a sandy copper color, draped with fire-engine-red curtains and had a sign out front reading "Sento Ganges." My hosts opened the Mercedes door. Moleman stepped out to guide me inside. Cars roared by, one after another, on the expressway overhead.

I was led into the lobby of the public bathhouse and told to take off my shoes. After I did, Moleman handed me off to a thin man in a high-collared white tuxedo. The man in the tuxedo motioned me through a curtain decorated with the pictogram for "Men." After a short trip through the hall, we passed though an arched doorway that opened onto a scene like something out of a Fellini film. Romanesque columns supported a high ceiling painted in gold. A large, marble-tiled pool took up the center of the room, and through the steam I could vaguely make out the figures of several men half submerged in the black water. The color of the water lead me to believe the pool must have been on an *onsen*, a natural hot spring, bubbling up right in the middle of some run-down Tokyo suburb.

Murmurs of conversation rose with the steam. Without warning a man emerged in front of me, clad only in a towel. As he passed I saw a massive dragon tattoo covering his entire chest. Peering through the haze, I noticed all the men were covered in ink, and started suspecting the public bath wasn't so public after all.

The man in the tuxedo marched me through another short hallway, finally stopping in front of an ornate door with an elephant tusk for a handle. As he pulled the door open a thick, vaporous plume unfurled with a blast of heat. Someone back in the *onsen* laughed, the sound echoing through the hallway. The tuxedoed man motioned me inside.

A broad-shouldered figure was sitting alone in the dark sauna, swaddled in a towel and cloaked in steam. The moment the tuxedoed man closed the door I started to sweat. The thickset man motioned me to sit opposite him, on a low bench in the middle of the room. Walking across the sauna was like wading through a bowl of miso soup. Only when I'd sat some six feet away from the man could I see well enough to confirm that he was, in fact, Kizuguchi. And even then I could see little more than his lumpy form hunched above me on the second level of the three-tiered wooden benches.

"You must've had a long night," Kizuguchi said. "So I'll try to make this fast. We're both busy men and I'm not a big fan of chitchat. Have you ever been in prison?"

"Not for long," I said. "Couldn't stand the food."

"I liked prison," Kizuguchi said. "Lot of men aren't cut out for it, but it didn't bother me. Only thing drove me nuts was the constant chitchat. Convicts always try to fill time with their bullshit. No respect for silence."

I nodded, and showed my respect for silence.

"But being incarcerated taught me a lot. About myself and the world. Prison strips away all the meaningless crap. What you're left with is truth. The fundamental nature of reality. Being an inmate ain't so different from being a monk, really."

He scooped a ladle full of water from a bamboo bucket resting by his feet and dumped it over the hot rocks. The rocks let off a hiss of steam. I was starting to get the idea that prison had been a life-defining experience for Kizuguchi. The way serving in Vietnam or seeing *Star Wars* was for some other people. I wiped the sweat from my brow.

"One thing prison taught me was the nature of secrets," he said. "The secret of secrets, you might say. It's real simple—they don't last. *Ever*. Two guys kill some punk in the showers. Then it's a race to see who can rat out who first. Or some queer brags to his bitch about knocking over a pachinko parlor in Kawagaseki back in the day. I don't care what great lovers they are, the moment the bitch hears it, he's already scheming to use it to his advantage. That's human nature, something you learn a lot about in prison."

As a drop of sweat rolled down my nose, I wondered why thugs always thought human nature revealed itself only in prison, and not in, say, karaoke bars or bowling alleys or day-care centers or at bus stops. I suppose it depended on which parts of human nature you were drawn to.

"Before I got into the record business I was into *sokaiya*," Kizuguchi continued. "Corporate blackmail. I'm not afraid to tell you that. You probably knew already, and I don't care. I'm an open book. Besides, what's blackmail when you think about it? Just taking advantage of someone's failure to realize the nature of secrets—*that they don't last*. If our country's companies weren't run by a bunch of frightened children, they'd realize their secrets are going to get out eventually. In the meantime, I took their money. Why not?"

"You consider your boss, Mr. Sugawara, one of these frightened children?"

He laughed, the air from his lungs momentarily clearing a hole in the steam. I got a peek at the tooth-mark scars on his forehead until the vapor enclosed him again.

"Mr. Sugawara believes in managing with the intellect," he said, sidestepping my question. "Me, I believe in *hara gei*. The art of the belly. Music is a gut business. A business of emotion. Passion. Loyalty. And loyalty I know. I am loyal to my artists. When I find out my artists aren't showing me the same respect . . ."

He trailed off and went for the water ladle again. My shirt was sticking like a second skin. For a guy who didn't like chitchatting, Kizuguchi was doing a lot of talking. It must have been almost two in the morning, but I couldn't be sure. The face of my watch was all fogged up.

"Yoshi's pal, that bass player," Kizuguchi resumed. "Isamu Suda. I think he has a secret. A big secret he's trying to keep from me. And from Seppuku Records. He won't be able to do it, of course. Not for long. Because of the nature of secrets. But it offends me that he's even trying. A personal affront. A slap in the face to me and everyone at Seppuku

Records. The very family who have nurtured his career. The people standing by him even now that Yoshi is dead."

I thought about what I'd learned at the Purloined Kitten, about Yoshi telling Olga that Kizuguchi had a big surprise coming to him. I wondered if the big surprise was related to Suda's alleged secret.

"What kind of secret are we talking about?"

"That's not important," he said. "But that he would have the belly for that kind of disrespect? That's why you're here. I wanted to talk to you before the Yoshi memorial concert tomorrow. So that you could talk to Suda."

"Wouldn't it be easier to cut out the middleman?"

Kizuguchi emitted a one-syllable laugh. "Look—I'm gonna level with you. We need a middleman right now. You really think Seppuku wants you to write a Yoshi biography? There *is* no Yoshi biography. Besides, we could get anyone to write the kinda mindless crap kids read. No disrespect."

I'd thought the bio project was a little cockeyed from the start. But Kizuguchi's revelation begged the obvious question of what Seppuku Records really wanted from me. I hated to see a revelation go begging, so I asked the question.

"You're to observe," he answered. "To observe, and try to help Suda do the right thing. Suda may be smart, but he likes you."

"And I thought the two were mutually exclusive."

"Suda's a lot like Yoshi," continued Kizuguchi. "He has a weakness for foreign things. To him they mean freedom. Why else become a rocker? Why study Thai kickboxing, instead of the superior Japanese martial arts? Why surround himself with those yammering Western jukeboxes he calls body-guards? Suda likes you. To him, you're exotic. Like a figure out of a movie. Like friggin' Randy Chance."

His laughter boomed through the sauna. The room had

grown so sweltering I was one bead of sweat away from becoming a puddle on the floor. I tried to think of some polite way to tell Kizuguchi what I thought of his plan, but I didn't have enough energy left for politeness.

"You want me to hang around and observe Suda, fine," I said. "I'd be doing that anyway. But I'm not going to be answering to you or Mr. Sugawara or anyone else but my editor back in Cleveland. And as far as bringing Suda in line with the Seppuku vision, that's not my job. You think he has a secret, you'll have to find it yourself or hope it shows up in the pages of *Youth in Asia* magazine."

"Perfect," he said. "Keep talking like that, Suda can't help but trust you. Speaking of *Youth in Asia*, what's your story about? You find an angle?"

"My story is going to be about the night Yoshi died."

I wish I could've seen the expression on his face right then, but of course I couldn't. Kizuguchi remained litte more than a disembodied voice, a ghostly figure only half visible in the haze. He reminded me of Taka-okami, a Japanese rain god depicted as a mountain dweller enshrouded in mist and clouds.

"Not the most original approach," he said at length. "But good luck. Let me know if I can help."

"I do have one question for you," I said. "What did you get locked up for back in Osaka?"

I watched as Kizuguchi's form shifted. "A misunderstanding. I was working for a loan-shark outfit back then. Some clown refused to make good. We beat him up. Stripped him naked and dumped him in a dry canal. We didn't know it, but the guy had a bad heart. Medication was in his pants pocket. But he didn't have his pants. He was too ashamed to call for help, so he died. Anyway, the judge was a friend of a friend. He saw it was basically an accident. A misunderstanding. I got off with five years. Anything else you want to know?"

"One thing," I said. "How did you convince Mr. Sugawara to hire you as the head of Artists and Repertoire for Seppuku Records? You don't exactly fit the company profile."

I could almost feel him grinning through the steam.

"That," he said, "is a secret."

Before I could remind him secrets didn't last, he clapped his hands together three times. Suddenly the sauna door swung open, and there was the man in the white tuxedo. Apparently, he'd been standing outside the door the whole time.

"I'll be seeing you tomorrow," Kizuguchi said. "At the memorial concert. The twins will be by early to pick you up. Hang out with Suda. See what you can see. Good night, Mr. Chaka."

I reflexively told him the same and rose from the bench. As the steam escaped through the opened door, the veil was lifted and I got my first clear glimpse at Kizuguchi.

It wasn't a comforting sight.

The teeth-mark scars prominently displayed on his forehead were duplicated all over his body. There were bite marks on his back, his shoulders, down his chest, on his legs. The thicker scars were purple and rubbery, others looked like sketches done in pink crayon. There must have been nearly fifty of them, but I looked away before I could count. Either Osaka prison had gotten a lot more vicious since I'd visited, yakuza had graduated from tattoos to ornamental scarification, or Yatsu Kizuguchi was into some weird shit.

I tried to block out the image as I dripped my way out of the sauna, past the Roman *onsen,* out the Sento Ganges and into the cool December morning. I tried to forget about the whole evening as the trio of bumbling thugs drove me back to the Royal Hotel. But I wasn't too successful. Back in my room, just as I was nodding off to sleep, the image of Kizuguchi popped into my head. The scars were alive, writhing and tunneling into his skin like worms.

CHORUS

In carefully scrutinizing the affairs of the past, we find there are many different opinions about them, and that there are some things that are quite unclear. It is better to regard such things as unknowable.

—Yamamoto Tsunetomo
(*Hagakure: The Book of the Samurai*)

14

Elephants conjoined at the belly.

That's what the fish-eye lens of the peephole made them look like. One big blob in a gray sweat suit. Aki and Maki were standing in the hall outside my hotel room, waiting to take me to the secret Yoshi memorial gig. The show didn't start for hours, but Kizuguchi had arranged for me to hang out backstage all day and "observe" Suda and his entourage. I relaxed the Ten Claws of the Mongoose stance I'd learned from the Shanghai Peace Faction, a sort of kung fu version of Up With People, and opened the door.

"One of you guys oughta wear a different color," I said. "Make it easier to tell you apart."

"Suda-san is waiting," the one with the triple-twisted nose said. Aki, I think. No, make that Maki. Either way, they were in no mood for twin jokes. I'm pretty much always in the mood for jokes, but the needs of the community outweigh the needs of the individual. Particularly the needs of the Fuzotao Brothers, who outweighed me by a good five hundred pounds.

We headed down the stairs and found Isamu Suda waiting in front of the hotel. He was in full rock-star mode, reclining in a camouflage Hummvie limo as long as Godzilla's tail and wearing a outfit that took eclectic to a jarring new level. Foppish black Edwardian overcoat on top of a

T-shirt featuring Marvin the Martian speaking in wingdings. Scarlet-and-gold matador pants tucked into knee-high silver spaceman boots. Purple lipstick, a painted teardrop halfway down his cheek. The pièce de résistance had to be his hair, a blond-and-red affair that fanned over his face in stiff spikes like the dorsal fin of a sea dragon. Of all the things you might mistake him for, a kickboxer wasn't on the list.

I got in the car, a Fuzotao on either side of me.

"Tell him your joke!" Suda said to Aki.

"What did Mark David Chapman say to John Lennon just before shooting him?"

"What?"

"Fuck you, Ringo," Maki cut in.

Suda busted up laughing.

I think I got it, but not as much as he did. Dead rock stars seemed an odd choice of comic material the day of Yoshi's memorial gig. But if you buy the notion that people joke about things that bother them, I guess it made sense.

A slender woman with a destroyed beehive hairdo and torn fishnet stockings was sprawled out asleep on Suda's lap. On her back there was a grisly tattoo of St. Sebastian. He was tied to a tree, bleeding from all the arrows stuck in him. It was a picture lifted from Saint Arrow's first EP, titled *Beauty Full of Shafts.* I'm sure the double entendre was unintentional.

Another young woman in smeared makeup and a nylon ligature choker drowsily traced invisible patterns on her friend's back. Her long crimson nails were straight out of a vampire movie and she wore a thin white bra decorated with bloody handprints.

The women weren't groupies. They were the dual leads of Body Dump, the group everyone was anointing The Next Big Thing.

Their press kit described them as a Japanese version of the Shirelles meet the Boston Strangler. Body Dump sang sweet Motown-style harmonies dropped into a minor key, half-speed requiems with dark lyrics romanticizing serial-killer victimhood. Tate-LaBianca Matsumoto, the one asleep on Suda's lap, would perform bound in a plastic bag with leaves and twigs sticking in her hair and every Body Dump show ended with guys dressed as homicide detectives walking onstage with flashlights. The audience would scream for an encore before the fake ambulance guys came out with a stretcher and carted her off. Needless to say, Body Dump weren't exactly Pink Lady. All the negative press was pushing their album toward the top of the charts.

"How's the kickboxing life?" I asked Suda.

"Rest day, man," Suda replied with a lazy grin. "You know Tate-LaBanca and Dahlia Kuroi?"

"Heard of them," I said, smiling at Dahlia. She didn't smile back.

"They're finishing up a one-month tour of Asia and just flew in from Hong Kong," Suda said. "They've given four magazine interviews, done two TV spots and three impromptu photo shoots. That's just this morning, since they landed. Now they've gotta get to Sour Note for a soundcheck, record a series of promo spots for XFM, approve the new artwork for the *Sad Clown Painter* cover, look at storyboards for the *One Shoe Highway* video, do a signing at Tower Shibuya, play a forty-five-minute set at the gig tonight, go to the post-party schmoozefest with the Seppuku weasels, then fly back to Hong Kong for a show the next day. So if they seem moody, don't take it personally."

"Soon they won't need the makeup to look dead."

"A two-month tour takes five years off your life," said Aki.

"Seven," Maki countered. "Ozzy Osbourne told me so."

"You never met Ozzy!"

"You don't know everyone I've met."

Aki dismissed him with a wave of his hand. "It's five years. Not seven. Five."

I was doing the math, trying to figure out how long ago the Rolling Stones croaked when Suda spoke. His voice was low and halting.

"Yatsu Kizuguchi tells me you're working for Seppuku now. Some Yoshi biography project. Is that true?"

Aki and Maki shifted restlessly in their seats. Suda gazed out the window as the limo merged into traffic. He didn't seem too happy at the idea of me working with Seppuku. I wasn't too happy with him having the idea. Buddha teaches that absolute happiness is impossible in this life, and I didn't think I'd prove him wrong with what I said next.

"There is no biography," I told Suda. "Kizuguchi just wants me to hang out and observe you."

"Observe me?"

"Kizuguchi thinks you're keeping some kind of secret," I said. "But I told him I wasn't working for Seppuku. If the two of you have a problem, you're gonna have to work it out yourselves. I'm a journalist, not some kind of intermediary."

"You told him that?"

I nodded. I wondered if I was making a mistake being so upfront with Suda, but I couldn't have him clamming up because he thought I'd become a Seppuku flunkie. Besides, the guy had one of those faces you couldn't help but trust. Sarah said I had one of those faces too, and that's why I was so untrustworthy.

Suda thought about it for a moment. The situation hung in the balance. When that loser grin started spreading over Suda's face I knew I was in the clear.

"Cool," Suda said. "You told Kizuguchi off. Very cool. Be

careful though, man. He's a scary dude. If even half of what they say is true, he's capable of just about anything. From what I hear, he'd kill his own mother for a parking space."

"Speaking of killing," I said. "Have you thought about the possibility that Yoshi may have been murdered?"

Aki and Maki exchanged nervous glances. The Body Dump girls paid no attention. Suda pretended to look shocked, but he wasn't much of an actor. He'd obviously thought about it plenty.

"Why would someone want to kill Yoshi?"

I shrugged. "Why would someone kill John Lennon?"

"Or Sam Cooke," Maki blurted.

"Or Bobby Fuller," said Aki. "Or Peter Tosh or—"

"I get it," Suda said. He picked at something in Matsumoto's hair and looked out the window some more. Tate-LaBianca Matsumoto snored to wake the dead while Dahlia Kuroi kept up the fingernail tracings.

"Yoshi wasn't murdered," Suda said. "At least not in the traditional sense."

"Which makes him what—nontraditionally murdered?"

"I'm not sure how to say it," Suda said. "But even if nobody actually killed him, there were people who looked the other way. Accomplices in his suicide, you could say."

"Suicide. You think Yoshi meant to kill himself?"

"Some people think that's what Yoshi was about from day one," Suda said glumly. "And he toyed with that image, encouraged those stories. Even his love songs had pretty miserable lyrics when you really listen. Yoshi liked to play the sensitive, suffering, brooding type. He thought he was Lord Buylawn."

That one had me puzzled, until I figured out what his accent was doing to Lord Byron. "But it was just a pose?" I prompted.

"Difficult to say," Suda sighed. "Yoshi was different people at different times, you know what I mean? Sometimes I felt like I was the only one in the world who knew the real Yoshi. Sometimes I felt like I didn't know the real Yoshi at all. Sometimes I felt there was no real Yoshi."

"But you think the overdose was intentional?"

"The autopsy said they found 1.52 milligrams of morphine in his system. That's a lot of heroin. And despite what you might've read in the weeklies, Yoshi was not a hard-core drug addict. I mean, being a heroin junkie is like a full-time job, you know? Maybe you can buy it on every street corner in America, but that stuff is pretty hard to come by here."

What he said was true enough. Except for alcohol and tobacco, Japan was famously drug-free. Speed was the illicit chemical of choice, though many used it for work rather than for recreation. But Japanese rock stars were like rock stars everywhere. Sure, the laws were tough and the prices high, but where there's a will there's a way. Tokyo wasn't Singapore yet.

"Yoshi never had the discipline needed to be a serious addict," Suda continued. "He was what they call a chipper, a joypopper. He didn't know what the fuck he was doing half the time—that's what made him dangerous. He OD'ed more than once. I had to give him a naloxone shot myself once in Hakodate, right out in the goddamn alley behind a club. I remember it was freezing cold that night, snowing. My hands were shaking so bad it's a miracle I didn't kill him."

Suda glanced down at his hands as if they might start shaking again. Then he turned his head to look out the smoked-glass window. Even the sunglasses couldn't hide the fact that he was trying hard to conceal his emotions.

After a time, he cleared his throat and asked in a weak voice if we could talk about something else.

"You know a woman named Olga Solskjaer?" I asked.

He shook his spiky head.

"A Swede at the Purloined Kitten. Also goes by Calico."

"Some woman of Yoshi's, right?" The idea brought back his customary hangdog grin. "There's a saying that you can't make a good album without losing a girlfriend. Well, Yoshi made a lot of good albums. In fact, he couldn't even record a single without cutting loose some girl. Six or seven steady girls a year. Yoshi was always introducing me to his latest flame, telling me she was *the one*. At one point, I had a bunch of T-shirts made. I gave his new girl a T-shirt with the number 22 printed on it. Then she was gone and there was another in her place. When Yoshi declared that *she* was the perfect girl for him, I gave a her the #23 shirt. After about #34, he started giving away the shirts himself. It became a big joke. There's even a song on the *Pissing in the Bitstream* compilation called "Number One Girl #42." But she wasn't even the last."

And Suda couldn't understand why anyone would want to kill Yoshi. I just nodded, wondering what number Olga would have worn.

"Funny thing is, he wasn't really a womanizer," Suda said.

Dahlia Kuroi rolled her eyes. Matsumoto let out a muffled giggle into Suda's lap. Suda kept his face straight, but the effort was taking a lot out of him.

"He wasn't," Suda protested. "I mean he didn't act like that for kicks, or to prove anything. He was just hungry for experience, you know? He'd just throw himself head-first into things, then burn out. Lose interest. He was like that with everything, not just women. Always trying to live as many lives as possible, to be as many things as he could."

"What's wrong with just being a rock star?"

"Nothing," Suda said. "As long as it's a dream. Something you're pursuing. But once you actually become big, everything changes. You've got money and fame and women and all this shit, which is cool for a while, but then you're like, *now what*? Think about it this way—you accomplish everything you've ever wanted by the time you're twenty-four. All your dreams have come true. In a very short time, you've experienced things most people never will in their entire lives. But you still don't feel, I don't know, *complete* somehow. There's still like this emptiness, and rock music—this pursuit you've devoted your whole life to, this thing that was supposed to be *the* answer, the only thing you know—just won't fill it anymore. That's a scary fucking proposition. So what do you do? Well, Yoshi joined a Buddhist monastery. Lasted three days. Then he tried to become an actor. Couldn't memorize more than two lines and refused to cut his hair. Then he got on a science kick, which was completely insane given the dude couldn't pass junior high chemistry. He started subscribing to all these off-the-wall journals and at one point even hired a famous biologist to clone his cat. After that, it was fringe sports. Deconstructionist bodybuilding, dolphin polo, sky-chi—"

"Dolphin polo?"

"Just like water polo, but on dolphins. Anyway, after the skydiving tai-chi thing he moved on to more traditional martial arts. That's when he started kickboxing. He quit that, too, but not before he got me into it. For me, kickboxing was the answer. It filled the holes."

I pictured Yoshi and Suda adorned in all their theatric rock foppery, prancing little circles around each other and trying to look tough. Would've made a funny video, but Saint Arrow wasn't the kind of band that made funny videos. Not on purpose.

"It was the same with his music, you know? He approached it with a mad desperation. Yoshi'd get all into slow-core prog samba fusion for a while and then it was lo-fi trance-a-billy ambient jazz. He'd tire of that after a few weeks, and go into grindcore enka ballad mode, try to mix it with shoegazer-flavored Tibetan chant-hop with a kind of cocktail Moog *kayokyoku* skiffle thing going on underneath. Once he wanted to release an album where he just sang numbers, but those kraut-rockers Algo and the Rhythms beat him to it."

"Funny," I said. "It all sounded like rock 'n' roll to me."

"That's because of Seppuku," Suda said. "They'd water everything down in production. And they refused to release a lot of his music. What did they call it? Satirizing the market. . . ."

"Saturating?"

"Yeah. Saturating the market. And so Yoshi always got talked into falling back on the same old rock formula. That's why he was thinking about leaving the label after the next record."

Dahlia Kuroi stopped her fingers. Tate-LaBianca Matsumoto lifted her head from Suda's lap. It took Suda about four more seconds to figure out why everyone was staring at him.

When he did, his face went as stiff as his hair. He leaned back in his seat and scratched his chin, trying to look nonchalant. Guitar advice from *Power Chord Japan* came to mind: *In the right place, a sustained note creates tension.* I let it hang in the air, and thought about what Tabi had told me last night. *Kizuguchi had a big surprise coming to him.*

"Who else knew about this?" I asked.

"I don't know," Suda stuttered.

But it was clear he was wondering about the same guy I was. Kizuguchi didn't seem like the type who enjoyed surprises. But killing Yoshi wouldn't exactly solve the problem of him leaving the label. And it didn't explain all the hotel nonsense, or the Phoenix Society or the guy in red and his mute friend in blue. Which reminded me . . .

"You know a guy named Santa?"

Suda looked at me like something that just bit him.

"Hijime Sampo?"

"Wears a lot of jewelry, flaps his lips a lot."

"How did you find out about *him*?"

"You play bass, I find stuff out."

"I don't play bass anymore. I kickbox."

"I still find stuff out," I said. "And then I ask more questions and find more stuff out. When I've found out enough, I sit down and write. I like to sit in a cheap metal chair at an expensive wooden desk with a nice view of Lake Erie, but I don't always get the luxury. Tell me about Santa."

"First of all," Suda mumbled, "don't ever call him Santa to his face. It's not a nickname he likes much."

"A fat man in red can hardly expect to be called anything else. Especially in December."

"That's not how he got the name," Suda said. "See, he likes to have little kids sit on his lap. Teenaged boys. At least, that was the rumor. He's a talent scout. Or *was* a talent scout. Put together boy bands. Song-and-dance shit. Parents of one of his would-be idols a few years back threatened to sue him for sexual misconduct. He managed to keep them quiet, but it was nasty business. Pretty much killed his career."

"What's he do now?"

"Goes through the motions. You can find him trolling for *tarento* in Yoyogi Park, hanging out near Omotesando or at the Hachiko statue in Shibuya. Where there's girls, there's boys. Where there's boys, there's Santa. Him and DJ Towa."

"The headphones guy?"

"Yeah," Suda said. "Towa, he had the hottest beats in Tokyo, man. Motherfucker worked turntables like Bruce Lee. Knows his way around the mixing console, too. Back in the day Towa twiddled studio knobs for just about everybody. Then he went to Europe. Got heavy, I mean *heavy*, into the rave scene. Spent a lot of time in Amsterdam, if you get my meaning. Then Goa, in India. He eventually returned to Tokyo, but not all of him made it back. He hasn't spoken a word in five or six years."

"What would these two be doing hanging around Yoshi?"

"One guess."

"Santa moonlights as a drug dealer."

"*Pinpon,*" went Suda, imitating the sound of a doorbell. "You got it. Small-time, very discreet, a few loyal customers. Just enough to keep his so-called talent-scouting business alive. I suppose he's the one who sold Yoshi the heroin?"

"It looks like it," I said. "But there's more to the story than that. Which brings me to my next question. Ever heard of the Phoenix Society?"

More trouble piled on his face. He took off his shades and looked out the window. Then, in a hollow voice addressed to no one in particular, he wondered:

"How come we're not moving?"

I followed his gaze to a car on the right. Then I peeked through the front windshield. A car was stopped in front of us. Another one directly behind us. We were hemmed in by a concrete highway divider wall on the left.

A traffic jam in Tokyo wasn't exactly headline material. But there was no traffic jam—the other lanes were zipping along just fine. The part that really made it special was that the three cars pinning us in were identical late-model Hondas.

Suda shook Tate-LaBianca Matsumoto.

"Hey . . ." she groaned.

"Wake up. *Now.*"

She mumbled something and Suda lifted her head from his lap and shook it. Dahlia Kuroi laughed and put her lipstick away.

Aki and Maki popped their muscles, ready for action. They looked at the girls, then at Suda, then at each other. A moment of twin telepathy. Maki opened the door and exited the limo without a word.

He was met outside by a guy in a charcoal-gray suit a size too small. Any size would be a size too small on him. Even next to Maki, he looked big. Big and unhappy. He and Maki chatted for a moment. A second guy got out of the lead vehicle. Two more emerged from the car on our left.

These guys didn't bother with suits. They had standard-issue cop uniforms, right down to the pretty white gloves.

Aki got out of the car in a hurry and went to help his brother chat. Our driver turned around and made an odd gesture with his finger. Suda nodded and turned to the girls.

"Give me your candy."

"What candy?" the sleepy one said. The girls looked at each other and cackled.

Suda grabbed Matsumoto and started shaking her. "Give me that shit right now!"

"Ow! Fucker . . ."

Laughter dripped from Dahlia Kuroi. She reached languidly into Tate-LaBianca's beehive and pulled out a prescription bottle. Suda snatched it from her hand.

"C'mon! All of it. Now."

"I thought kick-boy didn't do drugs anymore," she cooed. That set the girls giggling again.

Suda shot her a hard look and held out his hand.

It was a real drag. She sighed, went back into Matsumoto's hair and dug around until she found an aspirin bottle. From the way Suda grabbed it I doubted it was filled with aspirin. He chucked the drugs to the driver. The driver was busy removing a false panel inside the door and didn't see it coming.

The inside of the car became a series of freeze frames taken the moment before a collision. Eyes gone wide, faces paralyzed with expectation as the bottle spun in midair, people looking so nakedly human their terror was almost funny.

Bottle hits driver.

Loose lid opens with a pop.

Out spill yellow pills.

An ungodly number of them, enough to keep the whole roster of Seppuku artists high for weeks. The lengthy prison sentence rolled around the leather seat, bouncing like miniature pachinko balls as the driver tried desperately to scoop them up.

There was a knock on the back window, next to Suda. He whimpered almost inaudibly. Maybe he was thinking about his bullfighting pants and how cute all the convicts would find them. I had a lot to think about myself. I might have been in a car with two women who made a living singing about murder and a guy wearing spaceman boots, but when it came to drugs I was the obvious scapegoat. I was gaijin, after all.

The window came down about three centimeters.

It was just Aki.

His eyes darted around the interior of the limo. Everyone

stared back at him, faces like question marks. Eventually Aki's bewildered eyes settled on me.

"They want him," he said.

Now it was Suda's turn to look perplexed. The Body Dump girls followed suit, parting their lips in perfect little *o*s. My turn would have been next, but I skipped it and got out of the car.

15

Just a formality.

That's what the big guy who introduced himself as Inspector Imanishi told me over and over. Coordinating four cop cars to corner a gaijin in a limo seemed a little heavy-handed for a routine check of my work visa, so I started in with the questions. But trying to rattle Inspector Imanishi proved tough work. Tough and unrewarding, the type of work I'm a sucker for. Eventually, Imanishi got sick of my questions and cited a prefectural ordinance against annoying behavior to shut me up.

Finally, we got to the station. Not some neighborhood *koban*, but *the* station, cop central. Inspector Imanishi left me with one of his underlings, a fresh-faced kid right out of the National Police Academy. The kid was on the fast track to be an inspector himself. He inspected my passport, inspected my signature and inspected my fingerprints. He took my picture with a digital camera so he could inspect that, too. Then he turned his monitor around proudly to show me what I looked like on-screen. It wasn't the best picture, but maybe I just wasn't a digital kind of guy.

I started in on the questions with the kid, but the academy trained him in that, too. He just kept saying "routine" in English, and assuring me that I wasn't under arrest in Japanese. When I asked him if that meant I could leave, he got a real serious look on his face and asked if I wanted a translator.

After that, I was taken to a waiting room filled with a bunch of other foreigners sitting around on undersized folding chairs. There were so many white people in the room I thought I must have died and gone back to Cleveland. I noticed most of the guys were around the same height as me and had the same dark hair. For variation, there was a colossal Aryan übermensch right out of a gay Nazi fantasy, and a burly rugby type with roosterish red hair and a face like a speckled marshmallow. I counted eleven of us altogether. No one in the room looked like a hardened criminal, but I wasn't sure what hardened criminals were wearing this season.

Two uniformed officers strolled into the room and told us to make a single-file line. Human beings had a long history of making each other line up, so it was one of the easier cross-cultural exchanges. Everybody got in place. One cop took the front, the other fell behind us and we marched down the hall.

They took us into a narrow, well-lit room with nothing but a wall on one side and a huge mirror on the other. A one-way window. The cop told us to turn our backs to the wall. We did. There was nothing to do now but stand there while someone behind the window looked us over. So we stood there.

I looked at the reflection of all eleven of us lined up next to each other like a soccer team full of pregame nerves during the national anthem and knew this wasn't routine. These weren't random foreigners pulled out of some pub in Roppongi or tourists picked up outside the Sensō-ji Temple— there wasn't enough variety for that. Other than the redhead and the blond, we had the same height, the same build and hair color. Someone put some effort into the lineup.

I didn't think I was the guy they were looking for, but with all the laws on the books it was tough to be sure.

Back in the waiting room, we all resumed waiting. Periodically, a cop would come in, point at someone and take them away. The ones they took didn't come back. I didn't know if that was good or bad.

They called me fourth.

I was led into a small cubicle with a flimsy desk. A detective named Arajiro sat behind the desk in a swivel chair that needed replacing ten years ago and looked at me like it was my fault. I sat in the wooden chair opposite him. We peered at each other over a teetering mountain of paper.

I knew Arajiro. He was a good cop, one of the best who'd ever annoyed me. A little sadistic for my tastes, but very thorough. He'd throw me in jail every so often trying to teach me how to talk. My last lesson was a couple of years ago when I accidentally messed up his Balinese cockfighting sting operation.

"What the hell is that?" I pointed at a big blue button on his shirt of a cartoon mouse smiling like he'd won a lifetime supply of cheese.

"Pee off," Arajiro mumbled.

Pee off? Payoff? I didn't get it. Either Arajiro wanted me to bribe him or his cussing skills had really gone downhill. He noticed my disappointment and sighed.

"P-E-O-F-F," he said. "A combination of the words *People* and *Officers*. He was created by the Tokyo Municipal Police Department Public Relations and Recruitment Division."

Japanese cops in general and Tokyo cops in particular needed all the good PR they could get. Recent front-page debacles involved everything from amphetamine use to ritualized hazing of new officers to public drunkenness to bribery to shoplifting to taking pictures up schoolgirls' skirts. Add those to the perennial complaints of cronyism, neglect of duty, interrogation-room torture and internal cover-ups and it was shaping up to be one hell of a new century for the boys in blue.

"Peoff here helps show the public we're good guys," Arajiro continued. "Normal, everyday citizens."

"I wouldn't be so sure," I said. "She really is adorable, though."

"Peoff is a he."

"Then I commend your progressive spirit. You must be the first police force in the world to adopt a gay mascot."

Arajiro squeezed a smile onto his face. It fit like tutu on a sumo wrestler. His composure came back soon enough though, and he settled back into the bored-bureaucrat demeanor he'd perfected. He tapped his pen a couple of times. Even the pen sounded bored.

"Enough nonsense. Let's get down to questions."

"All right," I said. "First question—who was the blond guy? I think he's trying to impersonate Dolph Lundgren. That a felony or misdemeanor?"

"I'll be the one asking the questions," Arajiro said. "Please state your name."

"That hurts, Arajiro-san."

"This is official business, Chaka. Name?"

So I gave it to him. Then he asked to see my passport, asked my occupation, asked my employer. When I answered *Youth in Asia* he looked up from his notepad.

"Still writing kids' stuff?" he said. He seemed either amused or irritated. I picked irritated, only because I wasn't sure he had the capacity for amusement. I didn't bother responding.

"You have a business card?"

"I'm seriously considering taking them up again, soon."

He didn't like that. Not at all. It earned me a hard look and an awkward silence. When he felt I'd done my time, he asked where I was staying. I told him.

He grabbed the phone, punched some numbers and did some muttering to establish I was indeed staying at the Royal Hotel. Satisfied, he hung up.

"Where were you last night?"

I had to think about it. Last night may as well have been the Heian period. Then I figured it out. Sleepy and Toothpick, the two guys I'd battled at the Purloined Kitten, must have decided to press charges. What was the world coming to when you couldn't get in a little scuffle at a skin joint without the cops becoming involved?

"I was a few places," I said. "Ended up at a place called the Purloined Kitten. Strip club in Kabuki-cho."

He nodded and wrote it down on his clipboard.

"Hang out at strip clubs a lot?"

"I was working on a story," I said. "You hassle kids on skateboards, I write features and columns for a magazine. You might say we're part of a system of checks and balances necessary for achieving a healthy society and sustaining the global economy."

He smirked and scratched the words "media-asshole" on his notepad. It got my pulse up a little, but I managed to keep quiet.

"What story you working on, Mr. Chaka?"

"Story about Yoshimura Fukuzatsu. I'm trying to find out what happened the night he died."

"Hate to be the one to tell you, but you've been scooped. The story is all over the papers. Yoshi died of a drug overdose. I guess you can go back to America now, huh?"

"I'd miss you too much."

Arajiro grumbled and put down his clipboard. He rubbed his eyes with the heels of his palm. Then he leaned back in his chair and eyed me coolly before speaking.

"Every New Year's Day I go to the shrines," Arajiro said. "The temples, too. Some years I even go to a Catholic church in Yotsuya. I listen to the 108 rings of the temple bell and all that. I buy the trouble-sweeping brooms, the votive candles, the evil-destroying *hamaya* arrows. I purify my hands, offer the gods *mochi* cakes, eat those Jesus cookies. The whole deal. I'm a regular New Year's fanatic. And then, when I've done everything I can think of to appease the gods, I pray. You know what I pray for?"

"That Peoff will come to life to help you fight crime?"

"I pray that this will be the year you finally get into real trouble," he said. "The year you slip up and I can have Billy Chaka barred from Japan or locked up. Same prayer, every year. I have dreams about these prayers coming true. Usually, I dream in black and white—but these dreams are in color. It's true. Deep, radiant colors, more vivid and real than life itself. Dreams are so captivating my wife has trouble waking me."

"Have you told the police psychologist about it?"

It took all the professional training and personal experience he had to ignore my comment. "Unfortunately," Arajiro said, "it looks like it won't happen this year. But another year is just around the corner. Which puts me in an optimistic frame of mind. So let's be civil to each other. Just for today."

I looked sideways at him. "I'm not in trouble?"

"Strange, isn't it?" he said. "As long as you answer my questions, you can be out of here in under an hour. You're not the man we're after this time. We're after a man named Takeshi Ishikawa."

"Takeshi?" I blurted. "The reporter Takeshi?"

Arajiro answered by opening a folder, withdrawing a photo and passing it across the desk. I picked it up and had a look. It was my pal, all right. He was posing next to Donald Duck in front of the Cinderella castle at Tokyo Disney. He had a big smile on his face, almost as big as Donald's, and was wearing the same black suit I'd seen him in two days ago. The suit looked better in the picture, practically brand-new. I don't know why someone would wear a new suit to Disneyland, but that question was pretty far down on the priority list.

I handed the photograph back to Arajiro.

"When did you see him last?" the inspector said.

"Place called the Last Hurrah, in the Golden Gai. I'm guessing whoever you had looking at the lineup told you the same thing."

"What did you talk about?"

"Mostly the Yoshi story. He'd discovered that Yoshi was reported overdosed in a different hotel than the one his body was later found in. Two emergency calls, two different hotels, separated by ninety minutes. Didn't make much sense."

Arajiro shook his head, disgusted. "Meaningless."

"Something was going on, you ask me."

"I didn't ask you," Arajiro said. "You reporters, always trying to find an angle, stir up controversy. It's pathetic. I was on the Yoshi case, as a matter of fact. You think we didn't already look into the two phone calls?"

"How do you explain it?"

"Simple. The first call was a prank."

"A prank?" I said.

He showed off his prizewinning deadpan. I tried to get him talking again. Over the years I'd found the best way to do it was to insult him.

"I gotta hand it to you, Arajiro. Most people couldn't deliver that line without a laugh track running underneath it."

"I don't need to justify our conclusions to you," he said. I guess Arajiro had learned a few things over the years, too. "Let's get back to your friend Takeshi Ishikawa. Did he ask to borrow money?"

I shook my head. I kept shaking my head as Arajiro laid out one question after another. Had Takeshi mentioned going on a trip, had he given me any alternative address or phone number where I could reach him, had he mentioned relatives in the countryside, had he grown a mustache, dyed his hair or undergone plastic surgery? My head wagged back and forth like I was table-side at the Beijing Invitational Ping-Pong tournament. By the time Arajiro stopped asking questions I was in danger of dislocating my neck.

"Very well," Arajiro announced. "Thank you for your cooperation. You're free to go."

"Hold on a second," I said. "I wanna know what's going on."

"I bet you do," he said smugly.

"What does that mean?"

"Nothing," he said. "You can go. See you around."

"Is this some kind of new torture you learned in a workshop or something?"

"Look, Billy," he said. "The trouble with you Americans is that you're concerned only about yourselves. About protecting your all-important individuality. All these years, you act like I bring you down here because I enjoy it. Because I like to hassle you. That I'm a real guy trying to do a real job to help a community—that's right, *community*—of real people is a fact that never fit into your juvenile worldview. So you stonewalled me, year after year, time after time. I can't remember how many times you withheld information from the police."

"I had my reasons."

"Maybe so. But now the wind has shifted. I'm the one with the information, and you're the one with the questions. But unless you apologize to me, I'm not gonna tell you anything."

"Apologize?"

"That's right," he said. "Apologize. Maybe there's no word for it in English. But finding words won't be a problem. See, I've already prepared your apology for you."

Arajiro smiled maybe the first genuine smile in his whole life. He reached into his desk drawer, then handed me a legal-sized sheet of paper. The writing was tiny, running off the margins, filling up both sides of the page.

"Fine," I said. "Where do I sign it?"

"You don't sign it. You read it. Aloud."

The smile grew even wider, just in case I thought he was kidding. This was the low-down dirtiest thing that Arajiro had ever pulled on me. Worse than the Chinese urine torture, worse even than the time he piped Hibara Misora's greatest hits into my isolation cell for three days straight.

But I had to find out about Takeshi. So I swallowed my pride, chased it down with a gulp of air, and read.

The document was a regular trip down memory lane. I listened to myself apologize for the cockfighting sting fiasco. For the time I'd disabled a loudspeaker at Hamayama beach that incessantly reminded swimmers to avoid drowning. For endangering citizens' lives by racing motorcycles against a teenage *bosozuki* gang in Harajuku. For spreading superglue on the mouthpieces of bullhorns used by right-wing nuts outside the Yasukuni Shrine. For depantsing the Minister of Education during a charity soccer match, for unlawful use of a photo booth, stairwell trespassing, repeated violations of Meguro-ku's Morning Courtesy Act, assaulting a stand-up comic in Roppongi. The speech went on and on, listing my alleged crimes in detail, begging forgiveness using the most florid, self-abasing verbiage in a language known for florid self-abasement.

When I finally finished I looked up to see Arajiro leaning back in his chair. His eyes were closed, his features softened into a blissful mask. I dropped the written apology back on his desk. He savored the moment a second longer, then let out a long sigh and opened his eyes.

"Wonderful," he said. "Absolutely wonderful. Care for a cigarette?"

"I don't smoke."

"No? Well, just sit tight while I bring the rest of the force in. And when you read it again for them, really try to put some *feeling* into it. . . ."

Once the Tokyo cops get what they want, you won't find a nicer bunch of guys. A cop named Shibomo gave me a ride to the Sour Note and even offered to buy me some hot chocolate along the way. I declined as politely as I could, but he seemed a little disappointed. He kept talking about how good hot chocolate is on a cold day like today. In fact, he said, he loved cold days because they made him think about hot chocolate. I told him he should move to Cleveland. They have plenty of cold days.

When he found out I was from Cleveland, he had to know all about some washed-up pitcher from the Indians who was currently collecting a paycheck from the Nippon Ham Fighters. I wasn't able to answer many of the questions, but the cop didn't seem to mind. It gave him a chance to tell me all about how he played against Ichiro Suzuki in junior high. Just for fun, I asked him who Ichiro Suzuki was. The rest of the trip was pretty quiet.

I spent the ride thinking about Takeshi's disappearance.

Inspector Arajiro eventually told me Takeshi had been reported missing. The bartender at the Last Hurrah called the police when Takeshi hadn't shown up for his usual after-work drinks. He hadn't shown up for work yesterday, either. His wife hadn't spoken to him, none of his neighbors in the Shinjuku Park shantytown had seen him. Sometime after we'd met for drinks, he'd simply vanished.

According to Inspector Arajiro, Takeshi had accumulated some truly staggering debts. Turns out he'd been living in the park mostly to avoid yakuza loan sharks. His wife's place in Ebisu was actually paid for by her wealthy father. She'd been living there under a fake name ever since Takeshi started having money problems three years ago.

These facts coupled with the timing of the disappearence led Arajiro to believe Takeshi had pulled a *yonige*—a midnight run. Every year increasing numbers of Japanese were trying to escape their debts by changing their identities and going on the lam. Because loans are traditionally repaid before the New Year, December was the prime season to disappear.

My heart sank as Arajiro relayed the news in his professional, detached tone. I found myself wishing Takeshi would've told me about the real nature of his problems, but then he wouldn't have been Takeshi. And he certainly wouldn't have taken my offer to help. That's just how he was.

But the more I thought about Takeshi, the more I started doubting he'd run for the hills. Debts or no debts, he didn't strike me as the type to just suddenly pack up and leave. Especially if he was about to break a big story. As I recalled his excited voice on my answering machine, another possibility reared its ugly head. Maybe Takeshi's vanishing act hadn't been his idea.

First Olga, then Takeshi. I doubted there was anything linking their disappearances. Unless the thing was me, and that was a thought I didn't feel like thinking.

Instead I thought about the key Olga had left. I took it out of my pocket, held it in the palm of my hand and stared at it. It shone blue in the daylight, a color I couldn't have noticed in the red haze of the Purloined Kitten back room. I wondered where Olga had gone, and why. Mostly though, I wondered what the key was for. Olga told Tabi I'd figure it out, but I had no idea where to start.

When I got sick of looking at the key I picked up a newspaper someone had left in the backseat and read about a guy in Ginza who was making a living getting beat up by strangers. He wore a helmet and a thick protective rubber suit and charged people a thousand yen to go at him for thirty seconds. Women got a fifty percent discount. Business, he said, was good.

Tucked in the middle of the paper was the one headline I'd hoped not to see. It had to happen sooner or later, and all things considered I was surprised it took this long. The papers had probably already written most of the story and were just waiting for reality to catch up so they could fill in the names.

Hers was Rino Hana. She was fourteen years old, lived in the Chuo ward, got good grades and was involved in the drama club. All her friends knew her as a quiet though generally cheerful person and as a huge fan of Saint Arrow—especially Yoshi.

Her mother found her hanging in the closet by a noose made from an extension cord. No ambulance would have made it in time. There was no note. Her parents said she was a happy kid overall, but her best friend said that Rino had been distraught over the recent death of the musician Yoshimura Fukuzatsu.

The article was accompanied by a sidebar where some esteemed psychology professor was quoted at length about the phenomenon of copycat suicide. He liked to call them sympathy suicides, and noted that it was not an uncommon occurrence among younger people, especially when someone they thought of as powerful or charismatic ended their life unexpectedly. The prof had learned this through a lifetime of study.

Another sidebar took a preventative approach, giving parents a list of warning signs that their kids might be contemplating a sympathetic suicide. They were advised to watch for changes in appetite, listlessness, sullenness, a loss of interest in the world around them. It described roughly half the kids on the planet.

I put down the paper and stared out the window. Outside the world went about business as usual. Without Rino Hana, without Yoshi, without the Night Porter. Just as it would without me.

16

Several *gomigyaru* in their late teens and early twenties were loitering outside the Sour Note, yapping on their cell phones and fidgeting against the cold, cigarettes bobbing between their blue lips. Some of the "garbage girls" sat hunched in loosely formed circles on the sidewalk, blocking pedestrian traffic as they picked at their platform shoes and brushed the bangs out of their eyes. Many of them had *chapatsu,* hair dyed muted tones of reddish brown, a shade just ambiguous enough to frustrate school dress codes. The rest of their outfits weren't as subtle. Like their idols in Body Dump, the *gomigyaru* dressed to look like victims of violent death, some sporting latex neck lacerations and painted black eyes while others had plastic bugs glued to their torn clothing and bits of broken candy glass stuck in their hair. Aside from being an homage to Body Dump, the look was a reaction against the kindergarten cuteness of the popular *kogyaru* look and the wannabe blackness of the *gangyaru* look—a trend some kids took so far as to paint their faces in brown magic marker and pay for four-hundred-dollar Angela Davis perms.

One look at the kids and it was easy to see why the older generation had started to refer to them as "space aliens." All over Japan, pundits and regular people alike were declaring the death of common decency with accusing fingers pointed squarely at today's youth. Minor offenses included everything from letting their bra straps show to kissing in public to using cell phones in crowded commuter trains. But a string of shocking, violent crimes had recently elevated the concern over juvenile delinquency beyond the usual generational whining. Motiveless homicides, grisly matricides, escalating schoolyard brutality—all over the news, the message was clear. *The kids are not all right.*

But in the hysteria, a simple fact was getting lost. The vast majority of kids *weren't* nihilistic criminals. The vast majority of kids were just fine, thank you very much. And between society labeling them amoral monsters and an economy that didn't give them much to look forward to, it wasn't a great time to be a teenager in Japan. Though maybe it's never a great time to be a teenager anywhere, until you aren't one anymore.

I strolled past the leather-clad scalpers openly hawking tickets a short distance from the entrance. Club security had to put up with the *dafu-ya* because busting their scalping operation could have serious repercussions. Most scalpers claimed connections with the yakuza, and a few actually had them. A couple scalped tickets weren't worth a wrong guess.

Two bouncers stood just inside the entrance, both wearing tight-fitting black Sour Note T-shirts that showed off their gym muscles and baggy black jeans bunched at the ankles. I told one bouncer I was on the list, and gave him my name.

Moments later Aki and Maki showed up at the door. They weren't in their kickboxing sweats this time, but were wearing matching black motorcycle jackets and Joey Ramone sunglasses. Somehow the leather made them look even bigger.

Aki and Maki motioned me to follow them. We trudged up a dimly lit, narrow flight of checkerboard-tiled stairs populated by cigarette butts, discarded concert flyers and a few metal bottlecaps. The bass was thumping, bouncing off the walls and making the whole passage vibrate. About halfway up, a girl huddled with her back to the wall and her knees drawn to her chest. Her face stayed blank as we stepped over her and continued our ascent.

We got to the top of the stairs and Aki and Maki pushed through the double doors. A concussive sonic blast pressed my face against my skull. My view of the band was obstructed by a thick cloud of dry ice, cigarette smoke and boozy, evaporated sweat. Under the multicolored flashing lights I could just make out the army of bodies pogo-ing around the pit, careening into each other like excited molecules.

Aki and Maki cut a swath through the perimeter crowd as they ushered me toward the left side of the stage. The size of the Brothers Fuzotao inspired cooperation, but the kids were curious what was going on. Muscle-bound twins escorting a foreigner backstage wasn't something you saw at every Body Dump gig.

We passed another headphoned bouncer and made our way to a door guarded by a big bald guy with a Fu Manchu mustache and a physique like the Great Wall of China. The kids' collective interest grew as we got closer to the door.

"Is that Ricky Martin?" I heard one ask another as I passed. The side area was dark, and the kid was probably on drugs, but it still stung plenty. At least he didn't call me Randy Chance.

The dude with the Fu Manchu pulled the door open and pushed us through. Carefully folded notes, bouquets of flowers, cassette tapes and a necklace made from what looked to be chicken bones rained down on us as the fans near the backstage entrance hurled tokens of their desperate affection through the opening. The door slammed shut behind us and we went down the narrow hall, avoiding the thick crisscrossing cables taped to the floor.

Halfway down the hall, a guy in a long trench coat and wide-brimmed fedora smoked a cigarette and leaned against the wall. I pegged him as one of the fake homicide cops who bagged Tate-LaBianca Matsumoto and carted her offstage when the show was over.

He was standing by a half-opened door with a sheet tacked to it that said "Body Dump." I peeked inside and saw Dahlia Kuroi sitting in front of a mirror, watching herself get worked over by a fussy team of makeup technicians armed with brushes, combs, hairspray and fake blood.

At the end of the tunnel was a metal door with a gold star and the word "Relax" painted in English. Aki and Maki pushed it open and motioned me inside.

There were upwards of twenty people in the room. Some sat on sofas quietly sipping fruity drinks while others milled around the catering table, picking it apart like a team of ants. A few people spared us a cursory glance but it was hard to tell how many because most of them wore sunglasses. For people relaxing, they didn't look very relaxed.

Even with the glasses, I was still able to recognize a few of the celebs. Avant-garde filmmaker Ronji Tsujui was chatting up rising starlet Mei Tsudako, trying to persuade her that starring in a four-hour 8mm nonnarrative film about light, shadows and the nude human form getting destroyed by power drills would win her the artistic respect she craved. Shirtless Yokohama rap sensation Kuzo Real was sprawled all over a designer bean bag, yawning unconvincingly to underscore how chill he was. Across from him, famed Eurotrash shoe designer Italo Rosseti sat riveted by the big-screen TV projecting a lightning montage of pornimation, seventies soccer highlights, and black-and-white Nazi propaganda clips. He kept rewinding to a shot of soldiers goose-stepping outside the Berlin stadium during the '36 Olympics. It gave me a pretty good idea of what the runways would look like when he unveiled his new boots next spring in Milan.

"How the hell did those guys get in here?"

It was Suda, appearing in front of us out of nowhere. I followed his nod to the far end of the room where two sharp-dressed guys with faces like used cutting boards posed with their hands in their pockets, silently surveying the party. They stood out like Kimodo dragons in a petting zoo. No wonder everyone was having trouble relaxing.

"They're with Seppuku," Aki said.

"Do they look like Seppuku guys?" Suda huffed. They didn't. And these yaks were in a whole different class than the bumblers Kizuguchi had sent the other night. If the way they carried themselves was any indication, they were plenty competent.

"They had passes," Aki said. "Said they were with Mr. Kizuguchi. You want me to give them a hot-foot powder?"

"I'll upset their backbones," said Maki.

"Put their kidneys to sleep, break away their livers—"

"Dare their hearts to beat—"

"Never mind," Suda groaned, his voice wavering slightly. "Just keep an eye on them." Suda reached into his Edwardian coat pocket, worming his hand like he was searching for something. A weapon maybe?

I couldn't tell. I studied the thugs and thought about the short, happy career of Fasthand Furizake.

"How are you doing, Billy?" Suda said, seeming to notice me for the first time. "Cops weren't too rough with you?"

"Kittens."

"What was that all about, anyway?"

"Missing person."

"You better take this," he said, pulling the object out of his pocket. "In case you get in a jam with the cops. Or anybody else."

It was a cell phone with the Saint Arrow logo decorating the faceplate. Ed had given me a cell phone once, but I'd lost it going overboard in my coverage of the Fiji Islands Sixteen-and-Under Pearl Diving championship. It was probably ringing at the bottom of the ocean right now, irritating all the fish.

"It's preprogrammed," Suda said. "In case of emergency, just hit one."

There weren't any other numbers on it. Just a big green button with the number 1. I remembered a story about Yoshi missing a show in Hiroshima when he'd tried to rescue a young prostitute from some soapland. During subsequent tours, he'd worn a special bracelet fitted with a microchip so tour security could locate him before curtain time. They also banned *Taxi Driver*, *Pretty Woman*, *True Romance* and about fifty other films from the tour bus.

I wondered if my new phone had a similar tracking device, but I couldn't imagine why Suda would want to keep tabs on me. Besides, you start worrying about things like tracking devices, and next thing you know you're checking your underwear for microphones and worrying about hidden cameras in showerheads. I shrugged and said thanks and slipped the phone into my pocket.

When I looked up, Kizuguchi was standing right in front of us. The two yakuza toughs stood behind him, hands in their pockets, cigarettes pinned to the corners of their mouths. Somehow they'd made their way across the room, but they couldn't have simply walked. They looked much too cool to even consider such a mundane activity.

"How you doing, Suda?" Kizuguchi asked.

"Doing all right."

"That's good," he monotoned. "Real good. Enjoying the show so far?"

"The show hasn't started yet."

"Right," Kizuguchi laughed. He glanced over his shoulder at the two goons. All three of them smiled like they were sharing a private joke. "You're right. The show hasn't even started yet."

I wondered what the comment was supposed to mean. I looked at Suda to see how he was interpreting it. His face had gone pale.

"Hope you don't mind that I invited some old friends," Kizuguchi said. "They just took the bullet train in from Osaka. I thought I'd take them out, show them a good time. They're convinced everyone from Tokyo are a bunch of pussies. Especially rock and rollers. Not true, I told them. Why, I know a guy who even kickboxes. So whaddaya say, Suda? Wanna show them some of your moves?"

Suda shook his head, his hangdog grin nowhere in sight. In its place was something disquieting, jarring in away I couldn't pinpoint. Like his personality had gone out of tune.

"No?" Kizuguchi said. "But I told them all about you. What a tough guy you were under all the makeup. You're not trying to make me look bad in front of my friends, are you?"

The room fell so dead you could hear ice tinkling in glasses and the nervous crackles of burning tobacco. Everyone was pretending they didn't notice the scene unfolding in front of the door, but suddenly no one was talking. No one was even moving. Save for the cigarette smoke curling lazily toward the ceiling everything had gone as still as a photograph.

"I save my moves for the ring," Suda managed.

Kizuguchi clapped his hands together and smiled at his Osaka pals. They didn't smile back. "Good for you," he said. "Anyway, don't mind me. I'm just having a little fun. I think Yoshi would've wanted everyone to have fun tonight, don't you?"

Suda nodded. Kizuguchi turned his attention to me.

"You keep talking to this guy," Kizuguchi said, tilting his head toward Suda. "You'll learn everything about Saint Arrow you need to know. See, Suda's a loyal guy. That's why we like him. That's why we're gonna make sure he always has a place in the Seppuku family. Because we know that he'd never do anything untoward. He wouldn't want to harm Yoshi's reputation. Suda shares the Seppuku vision. Isn't that right, Suda?"

"That's right," Suda mumbled.

"You're right it's right," Kizuguchi said. "Anyway, just wanted to drop by. Pay my respects. Make sure everything was running smoothly. These unannounced gigs can get gummed up sometimes. I hope we don't have to have any more memorial shows for a while."

With that he pushed between Aki and Maki and made for the door. The two Osaka yakuza followed him. Aki and Maki looked ready to pounce on them, but they kept their instincts in check. As soon as Kizuguchi and his goons had left, the room started coming back to life. Before I could ask Suda what that had all been about, he leaned over and grabbed a beer resting on a nearby table. He cracked it open and drained about half of it in one swallow.

Pandemonium exploded as soon as we exited the backstage door. The girls in the cheap seats screamed and rattled their jewelry and the excitement rippled through the crowd, trav-

eling around the house to the other side of the stage. Even
the boys were hopping up and down trying to get a view.
Kids jostled and craned their heads Suda's way, paying about
as much attention to the band onstage as they would to a
panel of guidance counselors.

Security ushered us up a winding metal staircase to a
roped-off corner of the balcony. In case the velvet ropes didn't
work, about fifteen guys with matching black T-shirts and
headsets stood with their arms crossed, facing outwards
toward the crowd. There were three tables, two of which
were occupied by kickboxers from the gym and their girlfriends. The YKPers were trying their damnedest to look rock
'n' roll, but in pressed jeans, polo shirts and do-rags they
looked more like narcs frozen in 1985. Their girlfriends
mostly ignored them, eyes fixed on Suda through a haze of
Thin Duke cigarette smoke. As I passed, all the pretty young
things glanced up at me curiously, saw I was nobody, not
even Ricky Martin, and went back to their Suda gazing.

A nebbish-looking guy in a blueberry pullover sweater
rose as we reached the third table, near the balcony railing.
He was all jitters and shakes.

"Hey, Suda dude. What happened, bro'? I thought I was
on the list," he said, peppering it with nervous tics.

"Who is this guy?" Suda asked Maki.

Aki whispered to him from the other side.

"Sorry, man," Suda groaned. "Have a seat."

The guy's head shook side to side a few degrees, as if his
shit-eating grin was throwing his equilibrium out of whack,
but he managed to sit down.

As if to acknowledge Suda's presence, the band below
launched into a Saint Arrow tune. It was one of those
feather-and-anvil numbers where the guitars meander around
with lots of subtle, echoey sounds during the verses then

suddenly hit you with a crunching blast of distortion. An old formula, but then so is haiku.

I took an empty seat to Suda's left. The pullover guy on the right seemed a little miffed at sharing what little of Suda's attention he had, so I figured I should introduce myself. I did, and instantly knew we'd never be pals.

"I am a writer, too," he said. "Überscribe for a guitar magazine."

"*Power Chord Japan*?"

"Fuck those guys," he spat. "My pen rocks for *Nippon Axe Bender*." The way his eyes danced around, you could tell he thought *my pen rocks* was damn clever. The guy stopped admiring his own nimble mind long enough to take out a pack of smokes and offer me one. When I declined he looked suspicious, like maybe I wasn't a real writer.

The song ended and the guitarist took a break to guzzle bottled water. He took a couple of sips then tossed the plastic bottle out into the crowd. He was a spitting image of Yoshi, right down to the pretty cheekbones and big poetic eyes. At a second glance I noticed his outfit was a replica of the one Yoshi had worn in a controversial photo shoot where he posed in front of the Diet Building with a group of retarded kids dressed like samurai.

"Look, dude," Suda said. "There's me!"

He pointed to the bass player, who sported a fan of red-and-blond hair just like Suda's and was wearing the famous MOMMY shirt beneath a frilly cloak Merchant-Ivory could have turned into a whole movie.

"Who are these guys?" I asked.

"Dark Essence," the guitar hack said.

Even I recognized the name. It was taken from a Saint Arrow advertising tie-in song for Nocturne perfume. Radio wasn't a real big player in the Japanese hit-making scene. To get a hit, you needed to get a song in a commercial or write a theme for one of the big TV shows. The Nocturne perfume/Dark Essence tie-in was instrumental in launching the band, even though the perfume stunk.

"Dark Essence is one of the two or three best Saint Arrow tribute bands around," Suda said. "We once sent them out for an encore at Fuji Fest and nobody noticed. They were one of two groups we kept on standby for when Yoshi was too wasted to show up for rehearsal. Them and Hope Springs Infernal."

"You school 'em?" the überscribe asked.

"Shit, they play most of our songs better than we did. I told the bassist if he wants to make the show authentic, he's gotta screw up more. Get off time coming out of the bridge and shit like that."

Suda laughed again. At his lead, everyone laughed again.

"How is the Yoshi taking Yoshi's death?" I asked.

"He's not," Suda said. "I ran into him backstage today. He says singing Yoshi's tunes has given him a window into Yoshi's mind. According to him, Yoshi isn't really dead. He's just hiding out somewhere and waiting for the music scene to catch up, so he can come back and lead us all to some rock utopia or something."

Suda stopped talking. Onstage, the drummer clicked off the countdown with his sticks before assaulting the kit with brutal precision, his simian arms flying into the air while his knees popped up and down. It looked more like the drums were playing him.

The fake Yoshi stepped forward and pounded out a bludgeoning, monotonous metal riff. After wanking it for fifteen or twenty seconds, he began adding a note here and another there until the simple pattern had taken on a dazzling complexity. The guy had obviously mastered his Yoshi licks.

"Makes you wonder why he doesn't start a real band," I said to no one in particular.

"They've been working on some original tunes," Suda said.

"Originals? That guy is a rote player," the *Nippon Axe Bender* scribe said. "No subtlety. No style. Anyone can play like that if they spend seven solid years aping riffs in their bedrooms."

I just nodded. Maybe it was true, but it's a well-known fact all music journalists are failed musicians. Of course, I was a teen journalist, so what did that make me?

"I'm hitting the chilled bevvies," the writer said. "Check ya in a few." He threw us a peace sign and rose from his chair, ducking under the red velvet rope and getting the security wall to let him through.

Suda studied the Yoshi clone hard. I wondered what was going through his head. He hadn't shown much remorse about losing his best friend, not around me anyway, but I tried not to read too much into it. Many Japanese keep their private feelings—their *honne*—tightly under wraps. Hell, people from all countries did it to some extent. Maybe when alone Suda wept uncontrollably. Maybe he was too broken up to even shed a tear, or maybe he just figured Yoshi was dead and with or without tears the beat goes on.

"That writer wants to interview me about why guitarists smash their instruments," Suda said, just to be talking. "I've been avoiding him for almost two years. Don't ask me, I told him. I play bass. Used to anyway. Let's talk about kickboxing, I said."

"You're really never gonna play again?"

Suda shrugged and got a pinched look on his face. "I was never any musician, man. I learned my parts and played them, but I was never, I dunno, *an artist*. I was in the band because I believed in what Yoshi was doing. Fuck, I had nothing else to do and it was fun. But you outgrow fun if you're normal."

For the sake of kids everywhere, I promised myself never to repeat what Suda had just said.

"All this shit," Suda said, gesturing at the stage, "it's so superficial, you know? It's *unreal*, a total mindfuck. That's what I like about kickboxing. It's just you and the other guy in the ring. No one to take your beatings for you. Your money and your girls and everything else doesn't mean shit. It's only what's in your fists, in your feet. In your gut. There's a beauty in that. A simplicity. If it wasn't for kickboxing, I might have ended up just like Yoshi."

He half smiled, like he wasn't sure I was buying it. I leaned over the railing, watching the vertiginous swirl of bodies moshing below. The writer from *Axe Bender* returned with an armload of beer bottles and unloaded them on the table in front of us. Suda popped one open and took a healthy chug.

"Carbo loading," he said with a dull wink to his kickboxing chums. They all shone back at him, though there was no way they could have heard what he'd said.

"Hey," the writer blurted, "you still never told me if Yoshi ever broke a guitar in the studio."

Suda burped. The writer kept going.

"Through my research I've discovered that rockers break guitars for at least fifty-seven distinct reasons, you dig? Each of those can be grouped within five general categories."

"Oh no," Suda whimpered. The writer didn't hear him.

"*Category number one, Maintenance of Street Credibility*: to prove they're still raw, that they haven't sold out, cashed in, gone soft. To show they ain't wimpy folk singers, noodling jazz geeks or fossilized crooners. They're rockers, man—musical powderkegs. *Category number two, Show-manship, Spectacle and the Art of Misdirection*: smashing a guitar at the end of a show is fireworks. A grand finale. I mean, you'll never see some cat smash his axe during the opening tune, right? And smashing a guitar can also be a cover-up for technical problems. Kinda like when movies get stuck, they just blow something up. Kinda like mystery writers use red herrings and surprise endings. The live musician has a guitar for smashing if the audience needs distraction. *Category number three, Transformative Rituals and Traditional Displays of Hierarchical Status:* Hendrix did it, Page did it, Townshend did it, Cobain and Hideto Matsumoto, too. If you don't do it, there's something wrong with you. Smashing guitars is an initiation, vandalism as ritual of graduation. Taking it to another level. It's a hierarchical trip. A display of status. Field researchers have found some serious similarities among the primates. Mating behavior that correlates. Wild chimpanzees smashing sticks against jungle trees. You know what I'm saying?

"*Category number four, Impotent Rage and Acknowledgment of the Finite Powers of Rock*—the Rock Star Tantrum trip. Anger with the fans, bandmates, bouncers, managers, the amp tone or—check it—anger at their own inability to articulate the depth of their feelings through music alone. Deep shit, taking it down to the bone. Raw emotion overpowers the musical vocabulary and is transformed into brute physicality. Into an epiphanic episode of total fucking destruction."

Suda shot the guy a look of pained boredom, but he wasn't stopping for anybody. He was literally talking to beat the band. His eyes were bulging and he kept chopping one hand into his palm as if demonstrating in miniature the act of breaking a guitar.

"*Category number five, Existential Idol Smashing and Brechtian Aspects of the Performer/Audience Dynamic:* The complexities of rock in a post-everything world engender in the performer a certain disdain for the industry machinery, you know what I'm saying? The rocker comes to view the kids not as fans but as *consumers*, and thus part of the very mechanism that both defines and confines him. Subsequently, the star develops a complicated love-hate-love for those screaming voices in the dark, the ones that make him everything he is and everything he ain't. The rise and fall goes like this—early on, alienation makes him a rebel. Rebellion makes him famous. Fame makes him even more alienated, but then what? How do you rebel against the establishment when you're a millionaire? So check it—the performer plays the only card left, and attempts symbolically to shatter the Svengaliesquitude, to break the cycle of soul-sucking symbiotism, to descend from the throne from which there is no descent. By smashing his guitar, the performer is announcing *I'm not your god, you dig? I'm just another motherfucker, this guitar just another object, unworthy of your worship.* Fuck fetishism. He's breaking the spell, yanking back the curtain to expose the little man pulling levers, you know what I'm saying?"

"Enough," Suda said. But it was too late.

"That's what rock music is really all about, see? Breaking down the damn walls. But, paradoxically, even acts of rock rebellion have become codified over the years, rendering true defiance ever more difficult to define and achieve. Check out some of these historical rules and codes of conduct I've compiled in relation to axe smashing."

Suda raised a single finger into the air. Across the room, standing by the iron stairwell, Aki and Maki both nodded silently. Aki began making his way over.

"Rule number one—no one smashes vintage guitars. Even busting a hollow-body is pretty rare. And acoustics? Uh-uh, no way. Not unless an actual fight breaks out onstage. And check this—my research proves that Fender Stratocasters are the most smashed guitars, followed closely by Les Pauls. They're the most popular guitars, too, so whaddaya expect? Dig this, though—guitarists who smash their instruments outside of the performance arena, whether in studios or when practicing, tend to have some heavy psychological shit going on. Statistics prove that these guitarists tend to have shorter lifespans than their performance-only guitar-busting brethren. Which is why I wanted to know whether Yoshi ever—"

Aki appeared behind him.

The writer caught me looking at Aki. It must have been the first thing he noticed for the last ten minutes.

"What's up?" he asked.

"You are," Suda answered.

Aki hoisted him cleanly out of his chair without even bumping the table. Then the guy was over the balcony, plunging silently to the moshing crowd below before he even had a chance to scream—or vocally express his displeasure, as he probably would've put it.

The band kept right on playing. Suda took a sip from his drink while the flock of would-be groupies looked on in awe, more in love than ever. Aki walked back toward the stairwell to join his brother in standing around looking tough and bored.

"I guess he forgot a reason," I said.

"Huh?" Suda scowled.

"Category number six. Because they can."

Suda put down his drink.

"That guy was full of shit."

"So what? This whole business is full of shit. That's why you like kickboxing, right? Just you, your fists, your feet and your guts. No one to fight your battles. No one to toss annoying reporters over balconies."

He crossed his arms over his chest and stared down at the band. The Yoshi wannabe had one foot propped up on his monitor and was leaning out over the crowd as he sent the guitar squealing like a dying pig. Arms reached up toward him, trying to grab him, to touch him in all his cover-band glory.

"I always hated this fucking song," Suda sulked, and took another sip from his beer. It was clear that it would be the last thing he said for a while.

I hung around, finishing my beer and watching a couple more songs. Maybe I was being too hard on Suda. It was plain to see that backstage episode with Kizuguchi and the silent Osaka criminals had spooked him. And I wouldn't have even cared about the big limo, the flock of ornamental admirers, the writer getting tossed or any of the rock-star antics if it weren't for Suda's self-reliant kickboxer spiel.

Then again, hypocrisy is one of those unalienable human rights.

I got up and made my way toward the restroom. Suda didn't seem to mind. He might have been contemplating having me thrown over a balcony next.

Getting through the crowd took a lot longer without the help of Aki and Maki, but it was somehow refreshing to be lost in a crowd of kids gyrating to the big rock sound. Made me wonder if there really was something to those vials of Legong dancer's sweat they sold as a youth restorative on the Balinese black market.

I looked around but didn't spot the writer guy anywhere.

I hoped that he didn't just get trampled underfoot. It seemed unlikely, but it was a pretty good concert.

I circled the club about three times before I found the bathroom. There was no sign on the door except a hand-painted note that read *Don't even think about doing drugs in here, you junkie scumbag.* I pushed the door open.

I was unzipping myself when someone tapped me on the shoulder.

I turned my head and was face-to-face with a young kid in a Hanshin Tigers replica baseball jersey. Behind him stood four more, each with a fresh face and a pretty hairdo. They all had matching jerseys, like they were getting ready for a scrimmage. I smiled and turned back around to zip my fly back up before it started.

It started with a stinging jab to my kidney.

I managed to twist around in time to miss a rabbit punch aimed at the back of my head and let loose a quick backfist. It tagged one of the ballplayers right on the fleshy part of his nose, snapping his head back.

A good backfist really can never be overrated, I mused as I sidestepped a clumsy haymaker from a kid wearing the number 7 jersey. The movement sent a fresh wave of pain through my kidney.

"Strike one," I grunted, sending my knee into his thigh, hard. He clutched his leg like he was trying to squeeze off the pain before it reached his brain. It didn't work. He let out a long yelp and stumbled around, grabbing the sink for support.

Number 5 threw a decent roundhouse kick at my face, so close I could see the bubblegum stuck to the bottom of his shoe. I caught his foot as it passed, giving his ankle a nice little twist. His support leg went skyward. His head bonked against a urinal, dropped a couple more feet and bonked against the floor.

"Strike two," I whistled. One of the smaller guys came at me in a flurry. His punches didn't land, but they were effective enough to brush me back, right into one of his teammates. The guy behind me wrapped me in his arms and gave me the old squeeze play.

I caught a left hook to the side of my face. Two or three years ago, I probably would have dodged it, but that's life. I stomped on the catcher's foot and sent an elbow into the middle of his strike zone. All the air rushed out of his lungs, across the back of my neck. He pitched forward, clawing at my legs. He didn't catch anything but a mulekick to the jaw. I wasn't sure what to call it.

"Foul ball?"

Two more came at me, charging in from either side. I waited until their momentum was unstoppable, then dogded the pickle by stepping backwards. They cracked heads like something right out of a bloopers reel and dropped. The sound echoed off the bathroom walls like a slow-banging drum.

Double play.

They'd gone through their whole rotation. The first guy I'd hit was back up now, wobbling around like he'd just been beaned.

"You wanna go another eight innings," I said, "or you want to tell me what this is all about?"

I hoped he talked. I was running out of baseball metaphors.

The guys looked at each other from their various positions of defeat and reached a silent consensus.

"We're supposed to take you with us," the first guy said.

"Says who?"

"Mr. Sampo."

"Who?"

"Hijime Sampo. Our manager."

I started to ask something, then I figured who they were talking about. "All right," I said. "Just give me a second."

I turned back around towards the urinal, unzipped myself and let loose.

17

They drove a second-hand white midget van the size of your average phone booth. Not surprisingly, it had a big Tigers logo painted on the side. When I got a closer look, I saw it wasn't the Hanshin Tigers logo after all, but one exactly like it that said *Handsome* Tigers. Same thing with their jerseys.

We all piled in. The bigger guy did the driving, while I squeezed in back with the rest. As soon as we got in the van, the guys crowded into the rearview mirror, jostling for position as they mapped their faces for signs of damage. It was like the girls' bathroom on prom night.

"Does my nose look swollen, Teshio?"

"Your nose always looks swollen."

"At least I don't have a caterpillar crawling across my forehead," he replied haughtily.

The first guy pushed him out of the mirror, reached into his pocket and yanked something out. It glinted in the darkness. I got ready to snatch the knife away, but realized it wasn't a knife. He flicked a switch and shoved the electric razor against his own face, shaving the hair between his eyebrows while he gave the slow burn to his comrade.

"There," he said, clicking the razor off. "Now my eyebrows look just fine, and your nose *still* looks like a *tengu* mask."

Razorboy opened his mouth to laugh and got it filled with a blast of hairspray. He choked and sputtered as Nosey sat there holding the aerosol can.

"That shit stinks!" another one yelled.

"You stink!"

"Knock it off, dumbasses!" the driver said.

Razorboy spit on the floor and glared at Nosey. Nosey glared right back.

"Not bad," I said. "You guys are gonna be the biggest comedy troupe since the Tokyo Shock Boys."

"We're not comedians," Razorboy said. "We're musicians."

"I'm impressed. What do you play?"

"I sing," he said.

"We all sing," Nosey chimed in, "and we all dance. And we all act. The Handsome Tigers are gonna be bigger than SPAM."

SPAM stood for Super People Awesome Music. More a commodity than an actual group, the rotating cast of megapopular performers took the prefab concept to dizzying new heights. They had their own brand of bubblegum, their own nightly variety show, their own line of video games and still managed to release a new album every two months.

"Santa's gonna make you big stars, huh?"

"Don't call him that," the driver said. "It's not funny."

I sighed. The kids had probably all dropped out of high school to pursue their big dream only to end up attempting bungled abductions for their washed-up, so-called talent scout. I wondered how long the Handsome Tigers would stick it out before they were dragged back into reality with their tails between their legs.

Of course, who knew? Maybe in six months the stores would be full of Handsome Tigers action figures, complete with big noses and caterpillar eyebrows.

The driver popped a CD in the stereo and cranked it up high. Break-beat hip-hop filled the tiny car, and some evil-sounding dude started rapping in Japanese about how he'd been dissed all his life by his parents, his teachers, the cops, the establishment, and now even his girlfriend, his true love, his darling, his baby. He didn't care, he said, because it made him hard, and you had to be hard to survive.

I looked around the van. Nobody bobbed their heads or tapped their feet. There wasn't room for it. They just stared out the window at the colored lights racing by as we rocketed down the expressway toward the glow of Shibuya blurring in the soft winter light.

The Handsome Tigers van pulled into a parking garage up the hill, just past the 109 Building. They tried to get into the elevator, but I wasn't having it. I told them the high-speed vertical transportation would give their complexions the bends. They didn't buy it, but we ended up taking the stairs just the same.

We exited the stairwell on the seventh floor and journeyed down a long, soft-lit hallway. At the end of it was a glass door with a sign that read "Launchpad Talent and Productions" in a futuristic font that already looked dated. Behind the door was only darkness.

A Handsome Tiger rang the buzzer and the door swung open with a sharp beep. I stepped inside and heard the door close behind me. Turning around, I saw the Tigers on the other side, looking through the door blankly at me. More likely, they were studying their cheekbones in the glass. It would have made a good group photo for the press kit.

"Boy oh boy oh boy if it isn't Billy Chaka."

I turned and followed the voice into the darkness.

. . .

Moonlight spilled into the room through slats in the vertical blinds over a large window. Actually, it wasn't moonlight, but the neon from what seemed like hundreds of electric bill-boards lighting up the sky surrounding Shibuya station. The moon didn't stand a chance.

Santa was sitting in a plush leather executive chair in the middle of a room decorated with posters of androgynous young men, their shirts unbuttoned to reveal the smooth skin of their chests. He wore the same unflattering red Adidas track suit, this time complementing it with a Gilligan hat. He probably thought the clothes and the jewelry gave him street cred with the kids, which meant he thought the kids were pretty dumb. If I hung out with the Handsome Tigers, I'd probably think the same thing.

The furniture was scattershot—a desk here, a chair there, a monitor but no computer. I couldn't tell whether the room was being taken apart or put together.

"I'm glad you arrived intact," he said. "I hope the boys weren't too rough with you because they can be pretty rough when they want to be rough."

"They didn't serenade me if that's what you mean."

Santa grinned using every tooth in his mouth and sprung from his chair. "Some people think talent is inborn. That it emerges fully formed like some gift from the skies but, believe me, that's a load of fish entrails because talent is something produced something crafted something nurtured by an army of people by physical trainers and fashion designers and cosmetic surgeons and songwriters and photographers and voice coaches and dance instructors and hairstylists and lip-synch consultants and I could go on forever and ever."

I didn't doubt it.

"These people are the truly talented ones which is not to say that the boys don't matter, believe me, they do because without raw material you've got nothing to produce craft and nurture and the Handsome Tigers are quality raw material but they definitely need a little more polish before they're market-ready so I'm in complete agreement there with your assessment of the situation as far as their singing goes."

"How about me? I got the raw material to be a star?"

"Too late too late," he said, the maniacal grin riveted on his face. "You should've come to me ten years ago and I might've been able to make something of you back then but then again maybe not because young girls prefer the non-threatening look *bishonen* tragic and tender boys whose hearts are easily broken and, believe me, you don't look fragile and wounded enough not by a long shot."

"So why am I here?"

"Trust me I'll tell you why," he said.

But he didn't.

Instead, he walked over to the window and looked out. Then he took off his floppy hat and twirled it around on his finger, a cryptic grin on his face like the act was supposed to mean something to me. He casually let the hat fly and watched it sail across the room.

It landed on Towa's mic. Towa was standing motionless in a darkened corner, doing his best impression of a hat rack. It was a pretty good one, because I hadn't even noticed him. He had on the same denim prison blues and was still carrying his tape recorder and microphone.

"Don't mind DJ Towa," Santa said. "He's a mummer a mute virtually catatonic hasn't said a word in years not a word but he can mix a mixing board like you wouldn't believe, believe me, Towa Towa Towa is my ears and if something is gonna be a hit he knows it right away he can tell."

I could picture them in the studio. The Handsome Tigers slap-fighting in the sound booth. Santa sweating and babbling and looking on anxiously as Towa stomped twice for gold, three times for platinum.

"Nice to meet your ears," I said, waving to Towa.

Santa twittered and ran his hands over his slick hair. I started wondering if he actually put gel in it, or if it was a substance that oozed out all on its own. Before I could decide Santa started speaking again.

"There are people Mr. Chaka," he said, "who are working very hard round the clock to see me fail people you could call bona fide scumbags who go around spreading lies and rumors and innuendo to fuck with my livelihood. Trust me, this business is all about connections and connections are based on trust and when trust is undermined by scumbags spreading lies my livelihood suffers due to a lack of trust."

"Dope dealing is a tough racket."

His face puckered and a vein popped out on his forehead. He ran his hand over his scalp. It seemed to calm his vein.

"That lie is exactly the kind of lie I'm talking about."

"The child-molesting stuff, too, huh?"

His features darkened. "Understand there are powerful powerful people who want to wipe me off the face of the earth so they started this rumor this lie this innuendo this completely fabricated made-up falsification that had no basis in the truth. At the time I was in no position to force the issue so I had to keep quiet and act like DJ Towa over there to play the mummer the mute behaving in a catatonical manner and this silence damaged me, believe me, and now they're trying to set me up again for a fall but this time I'm fighting back."

He turned to look out the window again, eyes scanning the city for signs of trouble, peering at the neon glow with a worried expression like a sea captain looking at storm clouds gathering in the distance. Apparently deciding he was safe for now, he turned again to face me.

"I hear you've been hanging out at my place my joint my—"

"What joint is that?"

"I shouldn't call it *my* joint *my* club not anymore so much has been taken away from me so much but I used to own part of the Purloined Kitten and somehow it still feels like mine just like when you lose your leg and it still itches and what's that called again?"

"Shitty karma."

"No there's a specific term a phrase a word—"

"Phantom limb."

"That's it. Phantom limb." He pondered for a moment, then said, "Boy oh boy oh boy phantom limb that'd be a great name for a band *phantom limb* what do you think?"

"I think you didn't bring me here to talk about band names."

"True true true. I can see you're anxious to conduct business not the most sociable guy in the world which is fine by me so I'll just come right out and say it get to the point cut to the chase *burie ko de hanashimasho* so here's the deal the nitty gritty brass tacks actual factual of why you're here and it's real simple so let me spell it out to you in words you can understand in no uncertain terms—"

"Enough!" The shout knocked him momentarily speechless. "Just tell me, in ten words or less, what you want."

"I need the key."

"What key?"

"The key key key and I forgot to say please I need the key Olga left last night please."

"She didn't leave me anything," I said. "No key, no kiss good-bye, nothing. Just up and broke this lonely heart of mine."

Santa frowned.

"Don't play with me because I know what's going on here and I've looked long and hard at this situation from every possible angle of possibility, believe me, and this is my big opportunity the break I need a great chance and I'm not gonna blow it and you're gonna hand over that key, trust me, besides the key is useless to you it means nothing."

"Not if you want it," I said. "I'd say that makes it worth quite a bit."

"You want money," he said. "I'll give you money fair is fair tit for tat I'll pay in the name of fairness what's your price how much you asking?"

"I want to know what happened to Yoshi."

"Yoshi?" His nostrils flared to the size of a ten-yen coin and even vigorous hair-slicking was unable to calm his vein. "Yoshi Yoshi Yoshi. He was like a little brother to me and I wish there was something I could've done some way I could've helped him save him, *believe me*, but he had a drug problem with drugs and I told him straight I said *Yoshi* I said *I don't wanna see you anymore until you straighten yourself out buddy* I said *and until you do I don't want—*"

"You were with him the night he died. You sold him the heroin."

"No no no," he said. "I don't know who told you that but—"

"You did."

So much confusion filled his face there wasn't room for all of it. It spread to other parts of his body, corrupting his posture and forcing him to pace the darkened room.

"That's a bona fide impossibility seeing as how we've never met it's impossible." He scurried over to the window again. "I admit it I'm baffled pickled stumped perplexified but I haven't got time to worry about that right now because there's no time because I'm totally one hundred percent completely focused on one thing and one thing only and that's getting the key so come over here and look at this because I think it's something you're gonna want to see to help you change your mind your attitude your tune."

He raced across the room, stopping in the corner, next to a closet with sliding doors. A smile snuck onto his face. "Come on over," he said. "Have a peek it's free this one's on me."

I shot a look to Towa. His face wasn't giving anything away. Mentally, he was probably still grooving at some Euro rave, standing in a muddy field, watching the sun come up. I half wished I could join him there. Instead, I walked over to the closet. Santa slid the doors open and backed away.

She was naked, bound with black electrical tape and gagged with a wad of cloth taped over her mouth. Her wrists were clasped together, hanging from a hook on the ceiling of the closet while her feet rested on the ground, wrapped tightly at the ankles. For some reason, I fixated on her toenails. They were a sparkling blue, shimmering in the neon light. My hands balled into fists.

"So about that key key key," Santa started.

I ignored him and searched Olga's body. No blood. No visible bruises. More than terrified or shocked Olga simply looked annoyed. She made a face like a kid forced to dress in ridiculous clothes for the school picture. Her blonde head tilted slightly back and to the side, and her eyes were hard and alert. She didn't look tortured, not physically, and she didn't look doped.

I tried to communicate a silent message of reassurance, but it was hard to tell if Olga registered it. She kept glaring, and I didn't blame her.

"You know, Santa," I said, stepping toward him, "you go

around doing sick shit like this, people are liable to start another rumor."

He saw my fists and cowered, scrambling backwards and only regaining a measure of composure when he got to a desk and put his hand on an electronic panel.

"Not so fast slow down cowboy," he said. He was trying to sound tough, but the speedy quiver in his voice ruined it. "If I push this button the door opens and to the left of the door is an umbrella stand and in the umbrella stand are five baseball bats and my boys the Handsome Tigers have been instructed to do whatever is necessary to insure I get the key they'll do whatever is necessary."

"Send them in for batting practice if you want. But you're gonna be disappointed. I didn't bring the key."

He shook his head.

"I think you would have mentioned that before."

"Maybe I was just trying to find out how much you wanted it."

"You're about to, trust me, you will."

Just as his finger went down, I lunged.

We both plummeted to the floor, tumbling across the carpet. He rolled away, shrieking and kicking wildly and talking through all of it. I didn't know if he'd hit the button or not, but so far I didn't hear his elves rushing down the hall.

I hopped to my feet and readied a nice instep kick when I was stopped by the frenzied gargle of Olga's moans. I turned around.

"Hvuhuh huaaal!" She repeated it over and over, her blonde hair bouncing all around as her body writhed in fury. I spun and yanked the intercom panel off the table. Santa rolled into a corner, appealing to Towa for help as he struggled to his feet.

Suddenly Olga lifted herself off the ground. She swung

back and forth, bounced up and down. The hook popped out, bringing part of the ceiling with it in a rain of white dust.

Santa's eyes lit up and he stopped babbling.

Olga reached her bound hands to her mouth and pulled out the cloth gag. She shook her hair out and spit a mouthful of dust.

"*Jävla skit, skithål*!" she said. She must really have been angry, because I'd never heard her use Swedish before. "Just give to him the fucking shit key!"

I looked at Santa. He was just as surprised as me, but in a happier kind of way.

18

Once you're in Tokyo it's hard to get out. The city goes on and on, concrete spreading as if it were a living thing, an amoeba or a cancer bent on devouring everything in sight. High-rises seem to spring up by the side of the road as you watch, giving one the impression that the city is monitoring your movements, expanding in whatever direction you're trying to flee. The sign by the road said we'd left Tokyo behind fifteen miles ago, but I didn't believe it.

Olga Solskjaer lit a cigarette. I decided when she finished it I'd start talking. There were too many things I had to know and not many miles left. What was the key for, why did Santa want it, what had Olga and Yoshi fought about the night he OD'ed, had Yoshi told Kizuguchi he was planning to leave Seppuku Records, how did Yoshi get from one hotel to the other, who called in the first overdose call, who called in the second, why were there two in the first place, and why did Olga have a Norwegian last name when she was from Sweden . . . ?

The questions clambered over one another, squeezed and squirmed, threw elbows and shoved and pushed and made a general racket as they jostled for position in my mind. And when I finally got them all settled down, the Phoenix Society questions muscled their way in and set off the whole fracas all over again. I hadn't said a word in nearly an hour, afraid if I opened my mouth all the questions would come flooding out in a gush that made Santa's speeches look concise and well reasoned if not downright taciturn.

During my silence Olga had put on her clothes and we'd hightailed it out of Santa's office, leaving him grinning and holding the key under the diffused neon light, scrutinizing it like he was inspecting a diamond for flaws. The Handsome Tigers posed smugly as we passed them in the hallway. Then they saw the look in Olga's eyes and thought about their careers and kept their beautiful mouths closed.

We took a cab to her apartment, where her bags were already packed and waiting. Olga loaded them into her VW Beetle, all the while muttering curses to stop herself crying. The tears would come suddenly, sporadically bursting through fissures in her wall of protective anger. I'd never seen her like this. The last few days had led me to believe there were all kinds of ways I'd never seen her. Where we were going meant it would probably end that way.

"Fucking asshole fuck Santa," she hissed, flicking her cigarette butt out the window as the car raced down the Keiyō Expressway. "Fuck him. Fuck *me*. I can't believe I am this stupid. I should always known."

I waited for the rest to come. She took a deep breath, let most of it out and delivered the news in a tired, quiet voice as she stared at the road stretching into the distance.

"Santa is kill Yoshi. Murder him."

She started crying again, and probably would've kept crying, but there are only so many tears a person can shed in one night. If people could just cry and cry until they no longer felt the need, Tokyo and every other city in the world would've long gone the way of Atlantis.

"Santa was give to him pure heroin," she resumed. "Uncut, one hundred percent. Santa has make a deal with Scar Head Man to sell Yoshi overdose. To kill Yoshi. But something is go bad. Santa give to Yoshi the drugs, but then Scar Head Man change his mind. He calls to Santa and tell him don't give to Yoshi the drugs. But now is too late. Santa, he call police, call hospital, call 119. Tell them to go to Hotel L'Charm. But when they go, Yoshi is gone. Nobody know why. If he was stay, he is still alive."

But for how long, I wondered silently. We passed a sign reading "Narita Airport 30 KM." I realized I didn't have time to think through what she told me. I needed to get answers, fast. There would be time later to figure out what they meant.

"The guy you call Scar Head Man," I said. "Was he the one waiting in the car the night I was hiding in the closet?"

Olga narrowed her eyes. Her hands tensed around the steering wheel, fingernails digging into the flesh of her palms, knuckles gone white.

"Yes," she snarled. "I don't know then about Scar Head Man and Santa make plan to kill Yoshi. I thought Yoshi just stupid overdose, ne? But that night you are in the closet, I go to car. Scar Head bastard tell Santa and Towa to wait outside, so we can private talk. Then he drive away. Scar Head tell me he sorry about Yoshi and is terrible tragedy and all some shit like this. He tells to me this is private conversation, only for him and me. Forget Santa, he says, Santa is not a smart man, not powerful man. I tell to him everyone know Santa is stupid bastard motherfuck. Then Scar Head Man, he tell to me take his briefcase from backseat. 'Open the briefcase,' he tell to me. So I do. More goddamn money I have seen in my life! He is say to me, we can cooperate. We can be team. I tell to him I don't understand. He tell to me, 'this money you can have, you give to me what I want.' I tell to him I don't know what he wants. He laugh and tell to me, 'Is OK, I don't think you would. To Yoshi you are just *abazure*, just another loudmouth whore.' I get so angry I spit on him!"

"You *spit* on him?"

"I spit on him!" She sniffed and wiped her eyes with the back of her hand. A nervous laugh escaped and rattled around the inside of the car. "He drive the car off the road and grab my hair. I punch his face, pow pow pow, like this, then I push open the door and run away. I keep running and running. I get to home and decide no more. No more Tokyo. The next day I go to club, give the key to Tabi, tell her to give to you. Later Santa knows this. Send his baseball bastards to capture me."

"Why does Santa want the key?"

"Because he is crazy stupid bastard! He thinks Yoshi gives to me some tape recordings, some music. He thinks that I hide them. He thinks this is why the key."

"Is that what you and Yoshi fought about the night he died?"

Olga let out a big sigh and dug another cigarette from her purse. "No more questions," she said, exhaling the words with the smoke. "I finished think of Yoshi now. I finished think of all this. My head, it is over the ocean almost to Sweden. This highway and this lights and this whole fucking place. Even you are already disappearing."

Even at this time of night Narita International Airport was bustling with people, all of them red-eyed and worn-out-looking. None more so than Olga. The ugly flourescent light was revealing sags and lines in her face I'd never seen before. She looked not merely exhausted from the night's events, but fatigued in a deeper sense. I wondered what she must have looked like all those years ago, stepping off the plane into this very airport, a beautiful young woman come to conquer a big foreign city where rich men liked blondes. She couldn't have known how long the next ten years would be, how she'd be kicked by the recession into less and less glamorous gigs, how she'd have a fling with a strange journalist, fall for a rock star and eventually find herself bound and gagged and hanging in a closet. But it was stupid of me to even think in those terms. Aside from a few instances where our trajectories had crossed, Olga had a whole existence I knew nothing about. Maybe she'd look back on her Tokyo years as a wonderful adventure, as the greatest time of her life. If anything, the last few days had taught me I never really knew Olga Solskjaer.

She got an open seat on a flight to Paris. From there she could get a connecting flight to Stockholm. The plane left in forty minutes.

There wasn't much time left, and besides, I didn't like the idea of grilling her after all she'd been through. I waited with her by the departures entrance. She didn't cry anymore. Her eyes glassed over as she silently watched the people arriving and departing. I got the impression that her last moments in Japan may also have been her quietest. But again, there was a lot I didn't know about Olga.

When they finally announced her flight was boarding, she handed me her car keys.

"*Omedetō*," she congratulated me. "You win car. Make sure to wash. It likes washing."

"Don't worry," I said. "I'll keep it nice and shiny until you come back."

She smiled sadly and then turned to go take her place in line. As she walked away, I called out to her.

"So what's in the locker?"

"Ah?"

"The key you gave me. What's in there?"

"But Santa has the key."

"I know. But I'm curious. I mean, how was I supposed to even find the locker?"

She looked at me like I was ruining a perfectly good good-bye. Then she sighed and tilted her head.

"You remember the song play when we met?"

I thought for a moment. "Of course," I said unconvincingly.

She nodded her head slowly. Her eyes never left mine as that sad little smile came and went. "But it doesn't matter now," she said.

She turned and walked off toward the line of people headed to France and destinations unknown. I stuck around and watched her disappear through the security gate. Then I sat there for a while longer, looking out the window and watching the plane taxi to the runway as the first rays of light struggled over the horizon. When the plane was out of sight, I sat there some more. Finally, I got up and headed out to the parking lot, into the car and back toward Tokyo. I had to move fast, before I thought twice and booked a flight to Stockholm myself. Or Nairobi or Buenos Aires or Cleveland or anywhere no one had ever heard of Yoshimura Fukuzatsu.

Encroaching daylight didn't afford much of a view on the way back to Tokyo. Miles of power cables, concrete embankments and ugly factories lined the highway, as if Japan was trying to lure arriving foreign investors with its loose environmental laws.

During the drive I thought about everything I'd learned.

Olga's story cleared some things up, but it wasn't the easy solution I was hoping for. I now knew for certain that Kizuguchi had wanted Yoshi dead, and that he'd used Santa to make it happen. But I didn't know what to make of the fact that Kizuguchi had tried—too late—to call off the murder.

And the new information did nothing to clear up the greater mystery—the one that had troubled Santa, the one that alerted my pal Takeshi, the one that Inspector Arajiro dismissed as the result of a prank. I still couldn't figure out how—or why—Yoshi had left the Hotel L'Charm to go to the Love Hotel Chelsea. Who did he meet there? Because he must've met somebody. And that somebody placed the second emergency call.

And on top of all that, I'd made no progress in figuring out who the hell the Phoenix Society were and why they'd had the tattoo removed from Yoshi's photo and what, if anything, they had to do with the rest of this mess.

But maybe Takeshi knew.

Maybe that's why he disappeared.

For the first time in my life, I hoped the cops had outsmarted me. I hoped Arajiro was right, that Takeshi had simply run out on his debts. Hell, I hoped Takeshi was hanging out on some island down Okinawa way, sunning himself on a beach and sipping Seven Happiness.

But I had a feeling he wasn't.

To keep myself from thinking about it, I concentrated on the night I met Olga. Star Festival Night, the fifty-eighth floor of Sunshine City, rain tapping against the window. I thought of dozens of songs, but not the one I needed. I couldn't even remember what type of music they played at the Wild Strawberry. Mostly, I remembered the rain.

The only thing that cheered me during the miserable

trip back into Tokyo was feeling Olga's blue key hidden in the insole of my left wingtip. That and picturing Santa, sweat pouring out of his fat head as he tried in vain to jam my YMCA gym locker key into a nameless locker hidden somewhere in the city Olga had finally escaped.

19

I ended up driving back to the city and spending the night in a capsule hotel, a practice I'd sworn off years ago. The capsule hotels were basically locker storage for humans, coffin-sized crash pads for salary-men who'd missed the last train home. Every time I slept in one, I worried I'd wake up years in the future to find the earth overrun with aliens or Chinese.

But I couldn't live in a pod forever just because some drug-addled former talent scout would be looking for me. I rolled out of the capsule, paid for my two hours of pseu-dosleep and fought my way through the hordes of commuters doing their best to make rush hour live up to its name.

The sidewalks outside of Ueno station were almost as crowded. People shuffled on by, thinking about their fami-lies, their careers, something they saw on TV or what they felt like eating for lunch later. Everyone kept their heads down, eyes on the pavement. The sky above didn't offer much distraction. The sun was a dry smudge, an eraser mark in a dull gray pencil sketch.

I hopped in Olga's VW and headed back to the Royal. I flipped on the radio, but the consolation DJ was nowhere on the dial. The only station that came in well was FEN. Some American R&B singer was crooning about how he was gonna sex-up his girl. At one point he rhymed "smoove satin sheets" with "bumpin' love treats." I decided to skip breakfast.

I left the car with the valet and ambled into the lobby of the Royal with all the vitality of a damp rag. I got my room key from the front desk and walked up the stairs in a daze. Somehow I managed to exit the stairwell on the right floor and make my way inside my room without a single thought going through my head.

The sight of my room jolted me from no-mind.

Either Zeppelin were on another reunion tour or Santa had decided to come looking for the real key. My briefcase lay gaping on its side, its contents strewn over the floor along with all the black pants and white shirts I'd left hanging in the closet. The bed was torn apart, the cheap wooden chair rested in a crippled heap in the corner. Even the Saint Arrow CDs Seppuku had given me were broken and scattered across the floor. The Mamoru Man grinned from outside the window. So much for him protecting and defending me.

About the only thing they hadn't broken was the answering machine. The little red light flashed impatiently. I waded through the wreckage and hit play.

"The fuck happened to you last night, dude?" It was Suda. He sounded washed out, whether from the morning's kickboxing or last night's inevitable post-gig partying I couldn't say. "Look, I'm sorry about the busting guitars reporter guy. You were right, man. It was uncool. You still got that phone I gave you? Just hit number one. There's something I need to—"

Beep. Cut off.

The next message started with a few moments of empty crackling. I figured it was Sarah. She habitually called and left messages of silence, and depending on the duration and the intensity of the static, I was able to read all sorts of things into her messages.

"I'm sorry," a woman's voice said.

I knew right then it couldn't be Sarah.

"Please call me," the voice resumed quietly. "I'm sorry. I didn't mean to . . . it's been very difficult. Please call me. I've been thinking a lot. About you and about my grandfather's spirit. Please call me."

The machine recorded the clumsy sounds of the receiver rattling as she hesitantly placed it back on the cradle. It was an old-fashioned noise, something you heard back when phones still had cords attached to them. Ten minutes later I found the Hello Kitty note with her phone number lying next to my whalebone chucks. Miraculously, Hurricane Santa had left the chucks undamaged.

I tried calling Setsuko. The phone rang and rang. A perfect soundtrack for the end of the twentieth century. Then I remembered the twentieth century was already over. I hung up and started to pack. After that, I did what I could to tidy up the room, but most of the damage couldn't be undone. It didn't trouble me too much. Americans are seen as a reckless and destructive people in general, and I like to help a stereotype along when I can. Soon I'd be blacklisted from every hotel in Tokyo. Maybe not soon enough.

Before leaving I made one last sweep of the room. I saw the Saint Arrow CDs sitting on the night table where I'd just restacked them. They were neatly aligned like some abstract sculpture, backlit by the bedside lamp. If I was feeling poetic, I might have compared it to a tombstone done in miniature, a paltry memorial to another fallen rock god.

But I didn't feel poetic. They were just plastic discs in plastic jewel cases in plastic wrappers. It was suddenly utterly fantastic that so little plastic had caused so many people so much trouble.

Hanging out with rock stars and industry people is the quickest way to forget what music is about. I was already forgetting about the magic that happens when a tiny light hits the surface of the disc and suddenly illuminates a whole inner world. Forgetting that for a kid just the right age with just the right amount of feeling left, even bland pop music offers a universe of inarticulate truths, a landscape of noise in which he can locate himself, in which he can finally belong. Forgetting that music provides the soundtrack to some of the best and worst moments of their lives, that it is the closest thing to a friend some kids have, that it is more important than their parents, their teachers, their coaches and possibly—just possibly—my advice and features in *Youth in Asia*.

And hard as I tried to remember, Yoshi's life work still looked like a lifeless pile of nothing, a long joke with no punch line. I left the battered CDs sitting on the nightstand, turned off the light and walked out of my room at the Royal Hotel.

I'd already checked out and said my good-byes when I saw Setsuko sitting there. Even though there was plenty of empty furniture around, she was huddled on the floor with her back against a large column, her knees clasped to her chest. She wore a gray sweater that didn't quite match her plaid skirt. Not much would. Her hair wasn't forced into any particular shape today and was reacting with wild abandon, each strand celebrating freedom in its own special way.

I walked over and stood in front of her for a moment, letting her get a good look at my shoes. Finally, she turned her head up to me.

Her eyes were ringed by dark circles and makeup trailed off down her cheeks where the tears had dried. There was no hint of what had done the damage. The emotions had come and gone, leaving only a mess of mascara upon her placid face. I summoned up my best reassuring smile and put as much cheer into my voice as I could find.

"Your aura looks a little blue."

"I'm sorry," Setsuko said quietly.

One of the hotel clerks walked by, closer than she needed to. I caught her eye and her gaze dropped as she hurried off on whatever imaginary errand she'd invented in order to get a better look. I felt like telling her she was too young to turn into a nosy old lady, but I guess even nosy old ladies have to start somewhere.

"Don't sweat it," I said. "You're not the first girl to run out on me at dinner."

"You don't have to treat me like a child," Setsuko said. There was no anger in it, no defiance. She might as well have been saying *there's a forty percent chance of rain today* or *Osaka is the manufacturing center of Japan.*

"Fair enough," I said. "But you look a little childish sitting on the floor like that."

She pushed a strand of hair away from her face. It stayed there for about a second then fell back in front of her eyes.

"You're leaving, aren't you?"

"No. Just checking out for a while."

"Don't coddle me. Please."

For the first time, she glanced away. Her whole head turned, facing out the window, toward the street. She picked at some imaginary thing on her skirt.

"Before you go," she said, "there's something I must do. Something *we* must do."

I got a sinking feeling in my stomach.

"Somewhere we must go. Together. Please understand. It would give me . . . closure."

She said a Japanized version of the English word. Apparently, some clown had brought the word from overseas and infected the whole city, spreading it even to common office ladies. Next thing you knew, they'd all be talking about moral compasses and emotional intelligence and who knows what else.

"Closure, huh?" I said.

She bobbed her head.

Lots of wisecracks made noise in my brain, but for all their fuss they were powerless against some sad, lonely woman with a dead grandfather. I looked at Setsuko and tried to imagine her life with the old man, to understand the bond he'd severed to leave her like this. I couldn't, but thinking back, I realized she'd never even asked about the nitty-gritty circumstances of his death. It was me who brought death into it, with Yoshi and the strange Phoenix Society ID. Maybe that's what had upset her. She wanted to imagine some transcendent moment for her grandfather, one where the light shone down as his spirit languidly waltzed from this world to the next, or from one vessel to another, or whatever it was she believed. Instead, I'd told her about disappearing bird tattoos and a wheezing old man propped up against a wall, too weak to use a telephone.

"All right," I said. "Closure it is."

She stood up and smiled hesitantly before grabbing my hand and pulling me across the floor, out of the lobby. Off toward closure.

I asked the valet to bring Olga's VW around, but Setsuko insisted we take a cab, telling me there was no parking where we were headed. She wouldn't say where exactly that was. She didn't tell our cab driver, either, but gave him directions one at a time—turn left here, turn right at this light, keep going for a while. Other than that, she spent most of the time staring out the window.

"Why are you leaving?" she asked at one point.

"I'm not leaving," I repeated. "Just switching hotels. Too many people know where to find me."

"Like me?"

"Not you. Other people. Long story."

She nodded slowly, still gazing out the window.

"You're a very evasive kinda guy, aren't you?"

I shrugged. Maybe somewhere down the line she'd been convinced everyone was a kinda guy. No matter what you did, you'd be a kinda guy. Rescue a beached whale on the coast of Yaku Island with blowhole-administered CPR, and you'd just be one of those save-the-whales kinda guys.

"Please understand," she said. "I want to thank you. For helping me reach my grandfather."

"What do you mean?"

She smiled at me mischievously and wagged her finger back and forth. All the smiles were unnerving. Parts of her just didn't fit together. First she's shy, then she's throwing fits in restaurants. She started half her sentences with apologies, but was assertive enough to throw herself into the life of a complete stranger, a foreigner. She dressed like the most normal woman in the city, yet believed in things like clairvoyance and wandering spirits. All of it had me wondering just what her concept of closure entailed.

I glanced over at her, sitting plumply in her overgrown sweater and ridiculous skirt. She looked about as manipulative and calculating as a house plant. If it was all some kind of game, it wasn't one I was familiar with. Which meant I was likely to lose.

The cab twisted and turned through a labyrinth of identical-looking streets and back alleys, so that I couldn't tell if we were miles away or had simply been traversing the same territory over and over again. Once in a while, I'd catch a glimpse of the pale sun playing hide-and-seek behind the passing buildings, racing right along beside us.

The cabbie flipped the radio dial, landing on my pal the consolation DJ. He was telling the kids *no matter how bad it seems, it's really not that bad. If Yoshi could have realized this, he'd probably still be with us today, writing great songs and rocking out.*

One kid called and said he'd heard Yoshi never cried, ever. He said if Yoshi was alive to hear all these people whining about him being dead, it would probably kill him, it was so pathetic.

Well, the DJ said diplomatically, *I think he'd probably understand. I'll bet even Yoshi cried sometimes. And maybe he should have cried more. Maybe he wouldn't have felt the need to harm himself if he just could have let his guard down a little. If he'd been able to openly talk about his feelings.*

The kid said if Yoshi was like that, he never would have needed to write songs in the first place. You could hear the DJ tapping his pencil on the desk, trying to think of a response.

20

Stop here," she said.

Whatever neighborhood we'd finally ended
up in was ripe for urban renewal. Broken glass littered the
pavement, glinting in the dull sunlight like jewels. Empty
paper bags and plastic wrappers wandered aimlessly down
the street, tumbling slowly with the wind until they stopped
to rest against a telephone pole or rusted chain-link fence.
The scene reminded me of east Cleveland, which meant it
was the most run-down Tokyo neighborhood I'd ever seen. I
hoped this wasn't her grandfather's number-one place on
earth.

She slid out as soon as the automatic doors popped open,
not even bothering to thank the driver. I took out my wallet.

"The lady took care of it," the cabbie said, waving his
hand. I shrugged and put my wallet away.

I followed Setsuko about five yards before it hit me.

It was the same cab driver. The one who'd driven us to
the park the first day I met Setsuko Nishimura. The air outside felt suddenly cold. The only sound came from a bedrag-
gled figure at the end of the road, a day laborer who looked
like he hadn't found any labor for days. He was loudly belt-
ing out a bad rendition of some military song, but the chorus
proved too much for him. He leaned against a telephone pole

and started coughing, still trying to sing as he gasped for air. You had to admire his commitment to the material.

Before I could ask Setsuko what we were doing here she pointed across the street.

The pink sign above the window read *Love Hotel Chelsea.* A beat-up sign next to that said all payments in advance, cash only, no prostitution, we call police. It had a smiley face on it. I ignored pretty much every voice in my head, crossed the street and followed Setsuko into the tiny lobby of the Love Hotel Chelsea.

The lobby consisted of a vending machine, a dying baobab tree and a lit-up panel of screens displaying the rooms that were available—which turned out to be all of them. Unlike other love hotels I'd been in, this room menu didn't feature pictures of exotic fantasy suites. Just a bunch of room numbers.

"Check us in," she said.

"Setsuko—"

"Room 100. Pay for two hours. Don't worry, it's not what you think. There's something I have to do, something *we* have to do."

"For closure?"

She bit her lower lip and nodded anxiously.

I pressed the button for room 100. A computerized voice told me to insert four thousand yen. A moment later I heard a bell ring and a key slid from a slot at the bottom of the machine. The computerized voice thanked me, and reminded me the key must be returned in one hour, fifty-nine minutes and fifty-two seconds.

Room 100 was in a building across the courtyard, according to the map printed on the automatic key dispenser. Setsuko clutched my arm as we walked across the so-called courtyard, a space no bigger than a sumo ring. Dead weeds surrounded a shallow carp pool. There were no carp in it though. Just a puddle of coffee-colored muck and a few rotting leaves.

I unlocked the door to room 100 and we stepped inside. Setsuko clicked on the light and a single overhead bulb too dim to scare cockroaches cast dull amber shadows over the confines. What little the light did reveal wasn't flattering. There was a small futon on the floor and a large mirror on the ceiling. A bathroom with no door stood off in the corner, taking up roughly one-third of the floor space. That was it. No fantasy elements whatsoever, unless you fantasized about being a squatter. It was hard to imagine anyone had ever been happy in this room.

"This is the spot," she said reverently, looking around at the peeling walls. "An axis of parallel astral planes. A soul portal."

"A what axis?"

"The room where he died. The man you are writing about. I read it in the papers."

I'd recognized the name of the hotel right away, of course, but was still wondering just what to make of it. I'd never been to the Hotel L'Charm, but if Yoshi had suddenly felt the urge to come here instead, he must have had a pretty compelling reason. It was the most run-down love hotel I'd ever seen. I glanced around the place, trying to focus on anything but the miserable futon. There wasn't much else to look at.

"You're not afraid, are you?" she teased.

"I'm not sure what this has to do with your grandfather."

She turned away and spoke into the corner, as if addressing the shadows gathered there. "Do you believe in mystical connections? In people brought together by fate?"

I laid the words out carefully in my mind before speaking.

"Setsuko," I began, finding the words already jumbled. "I like you. I think you're a great gal, and you've got a lot going for you. But one day, you're gonna look back and realize that, well, you're a little mixed up right now. You're going through something very difficult, and complicating your emotions with—"

"You misunderstand."

"Right," I said. "Well, obviously. What I'm trying to say is . . . well, what are we doing here?"

"This is how I see it," she said, turning to confront me. "My grandfather died in your hotel room. While you were *there*. That man Yoshimura Fukuzatsu died in this one, on the very same night. And now you are *here*. Do you understand?"

I shook my head.

"You are the missing link."

"So I've been told."

"I'm not joking! You are the spiritual intermediary. I can only reach my grandfather through you. And you can only reach him from this place. Don't you see? This room is a portal to the other side."

"Setsuko—"

"Don't think I'm attracted to you, OK? Or that I'm trying to seduce you or that I even like you. Truth is, I wish it had been someone else, someone a little more open-minded. Maybe a Japanese would better understand. But fate chose you. And you *will* help me reach him. You will help me and then we must never see each other again. *Ever*. I'm sorry, but this isn't something I can control. This is fate."

I tried to brainstorm an exit strategy, but I couldn't even get a few clouds to gather. So I decided I'd play along. Hell, I'd make ghostly moans and try to speak in the old man's voice if that's what it took. Tell her life in the parallel astral plane was peachy, not to worry. I'd give Setsuko whatever it was she needed, because for better or for worse that's just the kind of guy I was. But I had to admit that I liked Setsuko a whole lot better when she was that sad, silent woman on a bench by the duck pond.

I rolled over onto my back, feeling the cool fabric of the futon through my shirt. I was supposed to be concentrating, clearing my mind. Everyone knows you don't clear your mind by concentrating, but that's what Setsuko told me to do, and it was her show. She kneeled at my side and lit some incense. I was waiting for her to put on a funny robe and start chanting, but so far she was content to sit there looking serious.

So this is where Yoshi died. I pictured him lying on his back, just as I was. Looking in the mirror above him, just as I was, watching his own eyes close as the heroin entered his bloodstream and he nodded off.

"You're supposed to close your eyes," Setsuko chided.

I closed my eyes.

The last thing he saw was himself.

Catchy opener for the Yoshi story, if I ever stopped running around Tokyo and actually got a chance to sit and write the thing. I waited for a follow-up sentence, but nothing came. Setsuko began humming in a strange, low voice.

Here we go, I thought.

No prostitution, no loud music. The sign out front hadn't said anything about incense and séances, or whatever this was. Closure.

"Please keep your eyes closed."

I closed them again.

"Billy, I want you to know something. Can you hear me?"

I was only about a foot away, but maybe she thought I was already slipping through the portal to the spirit world. I nodded, careful to keep my peepers shut, anxious to get this whole silly ritual over with.

"When you see my grandfather, you must tell him I am very, very sorry. It wasn't my decision, it wasn't meant to happen like this. Someday, everything will be made clear."

"Okey-dokey," I said. "That all?"

"There is something else," she said. "Something you should know. I deeply regret any inconvenience this may cause you. And I apologize on behalf of everyone at the Phoenix Society." Before I could process the words I felt a sharp sting in my left arm.

My eyes popped open.

She held a syringe in one hand and a gun in the other. She was trembling all over as she backed toward the door.

"What are you doing with a gun?" I wondered aloud, confused by the sound of my own voice. I tried to stand, and felt something warm spilling through the back of my head, spreading inside my body. She slipped the syringe into her bag and gripped the gun with both hands. I fell back on the futon. It must've been the softest futon in the whole world.

"Hold on a minute." My voice sounded bottomless.

I tried to stand again, but my legs didn't work. They felt great, better than they ever had, but for standing they were about as useful as dolphin flippers. I don't know what I would have done if I could have stood up anyway. Setsuko had a gun. And now she had her closure, too.

The samurai believed that every day you must prepare yourself for death. Of course, they didn't have much else to do but dash off some haiku and practice bujutsu once in a while. Me, I was a busy guy. I was lucky to get a cup of coffee in the morning.

Just before she stepped outside, Setsuko put the gun in her handbag and took out a cell phone. She looked at me one last time, then shut the door. Outside I heard her dialing the phone.

The phone.

I reached into my pocket, numb fingers fumbling in a race against unconsciousness. I found the emergency phone Suda had given me and hit the big green number one. The ringing sounded like a far-off temple bell. I pictured the temple on the side of a mountain, enshrouded in mist. Below, a narrow river wove through a peaceful valley of rolling green hills. A monk rang the bell again and again. A white crane on the bank of the river took flight. I knew I was losing it and struggled one last time to open my eyes.

Look, there I was up in the mirror.

21

I stared up at a wrecked chandelier of wood and wire dangling from the waterstained ceiling and wondered what the guy from *Nippon Axe Bender* would think of it. It was the twisted remnants of what had once been an acoustic guitar, something rockers hardly ever break, according to the expert. *Category number seven—Home Decorating.* I was lying on a fancy antique couch upholstered in gold velvet, a piece that must have fetched a steep price at some swanky Aoyama boutique in its day. But its day was long gone. Now it was spotted with so many cigarette burns it looked like a dying leopard.

"I thought I was through with this shit," Suda said absentmindedly, pacing the room. There wasn't much room to pace. Teetering piles of vinyl LPs fought for space with discarded take-out containers, dirty ashtrays, crushed beer cans, tapes, CDs, guitar cables, books, magazines. A black amplifier big enough to be pro-wrestler Giant Baba's coffin stood in one corner, lording over the five-tatami room.

"I'm shocked, Suda," I said. "I had you pegged as one of those anal-retentive types."

Suda swiveled around, surprised to see me speaking. He wore a white sleeveless T-shirt that showed off where his muscles would be once they came in. His red-blond hair was relaxed, hanging loose over his shoulders, and he had on brand-new fingerless weightlifting gloves—the kind that make me instinctually take a person less seriously. Then again, I'd just been covered in my own puke, which is no credibility enhancer itself. I must have made a mess, because someone had replaced my white button-down with a black Merzbow tour shirt and a leather motorcycle jacket. It made quite a combination with my black slacks and wingtips.

"So you're alive, huh?"

"Like disco," I answered drowsily.

"They say disco is making a comeback."

"Good for me."

"But they've been saying that for years," Suda said. "Dr. Nick is on his way. He said you'd live, but he wanted to check you out. I guess he can look at your nose while he's here, too."

I reached up and felt the nose in question. Pain shot through my brain. My nose was the size of a plum. A big, angry plum that didn't like to be touched.

I wasn't feeling a whole lotta love in the room. Suda was visibly unhappy. Maybe his sense of honor prevented him from asking questions or complaining about being called in the middle of the night to help out an overdoser. Or maybe it was because the routine was old hat, like performing the same hit song so many times you might as well be tying your shoes.

It was 3:35 in the morning according to the VCR clock on the giant entertainment system about four feet away. The stereo clock next to it said it was 1:19 P.M. An Elvis figurine clock gave me a lopsided grin from its prominent place on the wall, but Elvis wasn't saying anything. His arms had been ripped off. I thought I could hear the armless Elvis still ticking, but it may have just been my head throbbing. My nose dripped the occasional stream of blood down the back of my throat and my stomach was twisted like a balloon animal.

"Aki and Maki found you alone, passed out," Suda said. "They had to toss a brick through the window. I guess it hit you in the face."

"How's the brick feeling?"

"Go ahead and joke, but they probably saved your damn life."

It was coming back now. Ms. Setsuko Nishimura and the Love Hotel Chelsea. It's just as well they found me alone. She would have been a tough one to explain. I was still wondering about it myself, especially how I was still alive to wonder. It was probably the closest I'd come to death since last April, when Chinese cult leader Xiaping Lu tried to take me down with his deadly dung beetle powder.

The doorbell rang. It wasn't your normal ding-dong, but a MIDI version of the first three bars of Saint Arrow's buoyant "Love Happy Weekend." Suda took a half step and undid the lock, sliding the door open.

Aki and Maki squeezed in side by side. They were followed by a short wiry bald guy dressed like an Atlantic City showroom. He had on two-tone shoes, a too-large purple jacket and pants made from metallic python skin. Underneath he wore a silk shirt the color of a toy canary, opened low to display the riot of pawn-shop jewelry against his sunken chest. His ears had more rings than a redwood tree and his fingers had plenty to celebrate, too.

"This is Dr. Nicholasowscyz," Suda said. "He's from Armenia. We call him Dr. Nick."

"What's up, Doc?" I said before I could stop myself. If the doctor took offense, he didn't show it. I got the feeling he was the type that could take a sword through the stomach and not show it.

"That's the *peboke*," Suda said, pointing at me on the couch. It was a slang term for heroin addict, the literal meaning something like "person muddled by heroin." I was muddled all right, and heroin had nothing to do with it.

Dr. Nick studied me from the doorway, moving his shiny bald head up and down a few degrees at a time. After he got bored of that, he started toward me. He held his hands in front of him, showing me his empty palms, approaching me like you might a wounded animal.

"I've had all my shots," I assured him. "And then some."

He kept his eyes locked on me as he slithered silently closer, poised on the balls of his feet. As he moved, the chains on his neck jingled a cheap-gold blues. Eight feet and one hundred years later, he eased himself onto the pile of porno mags at the foot of the couch.

"Give me your right wrist," he said. Dr. Nick spoke in a high, musical whisper, serene but earthbound, like the teenage Dalai Lama always sounds in made-for-TV movies.

I did as he said. He held my wrist gently between his thumb and forefinger. He closed his eyes, leaning back and inhaling ponderously. I studied his fingernails. They were nicely rounded, no dirt, no hangnails. Ideal fingernails by any standard.

The doctor opened his eyes and gently let go of my wrist.

"Look into my eyes."

Instead I bounced a look of consternation off Suda.

"Do what he says, man," Suda said.

"Look into my eyes," Dr. Nick whispered.

I groaned and looked into his eyes. He moved his hand slowly up to my mouth, ever so gently cupping my chin, holding it in place. He leaned his face closer to mine and spoke tremulously. "Breathe on me."

"It might kill you."

"Breathe on me. Exhale on my face."

He moved in a little closer, his eyes closed again, his nostrils flared in anticipation like he was awaiting his first kiss. I breathed on him and watched his nose twitch around, pulling at the corners of his mouth. Something in my breath set his eyebrows jumping, but they calmed down soon enough. They stayed like that until I ran out of air.

"Thank you," he said, opening his eyes to their usual languid nonexpression.

"Just don't ask me to turn my head and cough."

"Where did you procure these narcotics?" he asked. He spoke decent Japanese for an Armenian, though it was a bit genteel for my taste. At any rate, I had no desire to share the fact that I'd been injected against my will by a strange woman while supposedly participating in some kind of closure séance. I felt stupid enough already.

"Some *hero kutsu* in Ikebukuro," I said.

"Heroin cave? " He lingered over the sound of his own voice. "Quaint. I wouldn't have thought that particular colloquialism still in use."

"It is with these guys," I replied. "They'll use anything." Ba-dum-bum. He reached up to hold my chin as he searched my face. His fingers were so smooth it felt like he had latex gloves on. I doubted they'd even leave prints.

"Enlighten us further about your associates," he cooed. "Do they enjoy playing a little rough?"

"How do you mean?" I said. I tried to pull my face away, but he caught me in his grip. Not enough to hurt, but enough to keep me still.

"You have a contusion beneath your right eye. Your nose is swollen and discolored."

"It's insured," I said.

He moved his head from side to side, rolled it back a

little, but his eyes never left mine. He was still searching for something. He reached up with the other hand and moved it toward my nose. Then two fingers shot up my left nostril. He yanked out a couple of my nosehairs in one dexterous movement.

It stung like hell and my eyes started watering.

He pinched the hairs between his ideal fingernails, twisting them, holding them up to the light. Satisfied, he dropped them to the floor. I sniffed and wiped my eyes. Suddenly he was on his feet, a purple blur moving toward the door, fast.

"What's the diagnosis, Dr. Nick?" Suda said.

"It's not Chinese molasses, that's certain. In fact, I'd wager it isn't heroin at all. More likely, he's taken pharmaceutical-grade fentanyl. It's an extremely fat-soluble drug sold under the name Sublimaze. This drug was mainline injected rather than inhaled, snorted, or popped subcutaneously. Our friend here doesn't have the physical appearance of a hard-core user, but he apparently possesses a sophisticated knowledge of chemistry and his injection skills are well refined. He knows how to avoid bruising. No surprise, as I'm told they teach safe drug injection techniques in American high schools when they're passing out free needles and sex toys. Oh yes, one other thing—this man is a liar."

"It's the nosehairs," I chuckled, casting a glance to the Fuzotao brothers. "They give me away every time."

Neither of them cracked a smile.

"What should we do?" Suda said.

"I'll proceed to that momentarily. As far as the exterior wounds are concerned, the injury to his proboscis happened very recently. It is fractured, but not broken. There are several minor lacerations covering his head and neck area. Either he's had some sort of contact with shattered glass, or his sleeping area is infested with the Okinawan vampire flea. Given the rarity of the species, I'll wager on the glass."

I rubbed the front of my neck. He was right—it was covered with tiny scabs. Dr. Nick placed one hand on the door.

"The physical trauma is minimal, really. It's his lying that complicates the diagnosis. Candidly speaking, it annoys me. His body is in fine shape, but he's got the well-honed deceit reflex of the chronic addict. He lies, he jokes, he uses subterfuge. Mr. Chaka has married a bloated, juvenile sense of self-confidence to a destructive code of blind self-reliance. It is not a happy marriage."

On and on he went, wagging his chin. I just relaxed and took it, glad he'd exposed himself as a charlatan before I started to take stock in his words. Never trust a doctor who dresses like a pimp.

"His are not the deliberate, exuberant and comparatively exhibitionistic self-destructive impulses possessed by our departed friend Yoshi. No, his are a bit more oblique. He has a tendency to create accidents, to orchestrate the very events he believes beyond his control. One might compare him to a man who tosses a boomerang, and is surprised when it returns and strikes him in the head. A man who then picks up said boomerang and throws it with redoubled force, and is shocked when it strikes back even harder. So he picks up the boomerang again . . . *ad infinitum*."

"You're a quack," I said. "I've never thrown a boomerang in my life."

"Every physical addiction has its psychological components," Dr. Nick continued. "In his case, teaching him to forsake even a single behavior would require a monumental realignment of his core mental processes. It's a very rigid personality before us, gentlemen. One might even say turgid."

Suda nodded as if he'd been thinking exactly the same thing all along. He had that look on his face like, *yep—I knew it. Turgid personality.* I started wondering if Dr. Nick had been comparing notes with Sarah.

"What do you suggest, Dr. Nick?" Suda said.

"Keep him off the streets for a minimum of forty-eight hours. Make him confront the situation, ponder how he got himself here. Whatever you do, don't let him get back into the routine."

"That's a lame prescription," I said. "I feel cheated. Cheated and turgid."

"The simplest solutions are often the most difficult to achieve."

"Where'd you learn that? Fortune Cookie Med School?"

Nobody paid me any attention. I probably wasn't helping my case much, but the whole thing was too ridiculous to take seriously. I wondered if every doctor in Armenia was like this or if they drove him out.

Before I could ask, he was gone. Suda stood there shuffling his feet and avoiding my eyes. Aki and Maki more than made up for it. They stared long and hard at me.

"Who's next?" I said. "A Mongolian proctologist in a Hawaiian shirt?"

I waited for laughs, but they never came.

"You heard Dr. Nick," Suda mumbled. "Better make yourself at home."

"I appreciate it, Suda. I appreciate all of this. I am plainly indebted to you and the Fuzotao twins for saving my life. But I can't afford to waste any more time right now."

Suda looked up at me sharply.

"Do you even know where you are right now, man?"

"It doesn't matter," I said. "I don't plan on a repeat visit." I stood up from the couch to show the spring in my step, the color in my cheeks. The movement brought a wave of nausea.

"This was Yoshi's old pad," Suda said. "Before the apartment in Hiroo, the penthouse in Hong Kong and the beach house in Australia, there was this place. When he wanted to get away from everything, he'd come here. Sit around, think about the good times when he was nobody. Strum his guitar. Go cold turkey."

I glanced at the mangled guitar chandelier overhead. Suda saw me looking at it.

"Cold turkey ain't much fun. You'll see. There are three or four other guitars in the room, if you can find them. Feel free to break whichever ones you want."

"Look, Suda," I said. "A freaky thing happened to me, that's all. I need to get to the bottom of—"

"Something just *happened* to you?" Suda said, his voice getting a little thick. "Heard that tune before. Heard it in this very room. Big hit in its day. Well, you'll get to the bottom. You'll hit a bottom so low and so hard you'll be curled up on the floor wishing you were dead."

"Suda—"

"*I'm not losing another fucking friend!*" he shouted. The words buzzed around the room like angry hornets trapped in a jar. "Maybe you're fine, maybe you've got your shit together. Maybe it was just like you say, an accident. Well, that's nothing but a bunch of maybes. I can't have maybe right now. Or hopefully, or probably or any of that shit. You aren't saying enough, Billy. Dr. Nick says you're lying and I believe him. He says you should stay here, and I believe that, too. You're your own worst enemy right now."

He'd worked himself into a frenzy. The familiarity of the room and the whole intervention scene probably conjured up all kinds of ghosts. I felt like reminding him I wasn't Yoshi.

"Tell me about the missing demo recordings."

He took a step back, regarding me like a cute little puppy who'd just taken a chunk out of his leg.

"That's my business. Nothing to do with you."

"Your business is spilling over into my life. The other night, I got in a little bathroom scuffle with some ballplayers working for Santa. Seems they thought I might be able to help them find some tapes. Then someone came along and trashed my hotel room. I've got a feeling Yoshi left some unfinished business behind, and I think you know about it."

All the air went out of him. The kickboxing twins kept their heads lowered like they were at a funeral. All three of them seemed to wish they were at the gym, delivering shin kicks and forearm blows to a big bag that didn't ask questions.

"All right," Suda said finally. "Yoshi had just finished up recording all the songs for the next album. He'd been locked in the studio for weeks, more or less living there. The night he died, he'd supposedly finished all the masters. But somehow, the tapes never made it to Seppuku. They just . . . *disappeared*."

"Meaning what exactly?"

"I don't know," Suda said. "Usually he has them delivered to Seppuku the second they're finished. But Kizuguchi claims the company never received them. And now even my own goddamn record company thinks I had something to do with it, okay? That's why Kizuguchi sent the creeps around to the tribute show last night. It was a message."

"Why does Kizuguchi think you're hiding the tapes?"

"Simple, man," Suda sighed. "All that fuck cares about is money. He assumes everyone else thinks the same way."

"I still don't get it."

"Guys . . . help me out."

"December eighth, 1980," Aki recited in monotone. "John

Lennon shot by Mark David Chapman. December twenty-first—*Imagine* soars to number one in the charts. *Sgt. Pepper* recharts at number three and *Rubber Soul* finally goes triple plat—"

"Tokyo, April twenty-fifth, 1992," Maki jumped in. "Pop idol Yutaka Ozaki dies drunk and naked in an alley. Less than one month later, *Confession for Exist* is released and soars to number one on the Oricon charts. The following year, *Date of Promise* repeats the feat, selling over—"

"Norway, August tenth, 1993," Aki interrupted. "Count Grishnackh stabs his bandmate Euronymous twenty-five times, killing him. Four days later, their band's *De Mysteriis Dom Sathanas* album tops the Norwegian charts.

"April fifth, next year," Aki continued, stepping in front of his brother. "Kurt Cobain discovered dead of a shotgun wound to the head. *Unplugged in New York* is released that November. It goes platinum in less than a month."

"Cobain was found in the greenhouse," Maki added. "He was wearing Puma tennis shoes."

Aki punched him in the shoulder. "What's that got to do with anything?"

"Well, he was."

Aki snorted. "May second, 1998. Former X Japan guitarist Hideto 'Hide' Matsumoto commits suicide by hanging."

"His single 'Rocket Dive' rockets to number four—"

"And his best-of collection, *Psychocommunication*—"

"I think Chaka gets the idea," Suda huffed. "Posthumous rock marketing 101. Mournful pause followed by all-out blitzkrieg. Raid the archives, reissue, repackage, promote, promote, promote."

I thought it through, but something still wasn't making sense. I directed the question to Suda. "You said Kizuguchi assumes everybody is just as greedy as he is, right?"

"Right."

"Then why would he think you'd try to stall release of the next album? Given what the Fuzotao brothers just said, you stand to make a pretty penny."

"That's just it," he said. "All the songs on the demo are written and performed by Yoshi. Since they're in demo form, nobody touched them but him. He recorded all the parts himself. I've got no publishing rights, no performance points. They get the DATs, hire some cheap session players to beef it up and a producer to mix it down. Then they release it all songs written and performed by Yoshimura Fukuzatsu. I get cut out completely. I don't make yen number one."

"So the Seppuku guys think you're holding on to the tapes until they offer you a percentage?"

"Not exactly." Suda frowned. "They think I'm burying the demos to force them to release a live album, or some of the back-catalogue stuff I played on. They think I'm trying to stall my way into the picture. Because everybody knows whatever is released next will be Saint Arrow's biggest seller ever. They could release a CD of Yoshi singing nothing but 'Sukiyaki' and the thing would still go triple platinum."

"Makes sense," I said. "So where *did* you hide the tapes?"

"Sometimes you take the confrontation thing too far," Suda said darkly.

"Contractually, don't the demos belong to Seppuku anyway? If they really thought you had them, wouldn't they just sick some lawyers on you?"

"Of course," Suda said. "But timing this release is everything. The public is fickle. Lawyers work slow. Gangsters don't."

I thought about it from all the angles, even Santa's. If he got his hands on the tapes, he could force Seppuku to buy them for a big cash payout. One that might be enough to get

Launchpad Productions up and running again. The Seppuku clan wouldn't like it, but they'd do it. Like Suda said, it was all about timing.

"So what are you gonna do?"

For an answer, Suda arched his eyebrows and slowly rubbed his face with the palm of his hand. Suddenly, I started feeling bad for the guy, even as he was about to imprison me in this claustrophobic shithole.

"I don't know what I'm gonna do," Suda said at length. "Satisfied?"

"I might be able to help you find those tapes."

"Right. Down at the local opium den."

"Suda—"

"Yoshi was always his cleverest when he was jonesing. He'd twist you around so many ways, you thought he was looking out for your best interests."

"You can't keep me here against my will—"

"Aki and Maki can."

The twin peaks stared down at me. There wasn't any joy in their gazes, nothing macho or intimidating. Their faces just registered silent affirmation of an obvious fact—they could keep me here. If I had to, I'd put that fact to the test. For now I pursued the middle path. Whining.

"I can't just disappear for two days, Suda. People will get worried."

"Tell me who and I'll give them a call."

I opened my mouth to speak and realized I was bluffing. Calling Sarah or anyone else from *Youth in Asia* was out of the question, unless I wanted a planeload of overreacting Americans invading Tokyo. Maybe they wouldn't form a rescue posse this time at all, but just throw up their hands in resignation.

"Staying here will be good for your little article," Suda

said. "You can experience firsthand just what Yoshi's life was like. You're practically living in the archives. Do some research. Look around. There are pieces of Yoshi everywhere."

He must have felt the weight of his own words, because those big droopy eyes went bigger and droopier. Soft orange light struggled through a tear in the curtains, backlighting Suda beautifully. He looked like an oil painting. *Bass Player in Fingerless Weightlifting Gloves.*

"Who knows," Suda said. "Maybe we'll both get lucky and you'll find the tapes under his bed. But I wouldn't look too hard."

I wondered just what the last comment meant. I was just about to ask when I noticed Suda had already gone. I noticed Aki and Maki had gone with him. I noticed I was fast asleep.

22

The door was locked from the outside, the keyhole filled with superglue to keep me from picking it. I pulled back the curtains to look out the window and found a gridwork of iron bars. Beyond the bars was a beautiful view of a transformer supporting a tangled nest of about nine hundred power cables.

I still didn't know what time it was, and I guess it didn't really matter. But with all the things I didn't know, I had to start somewhere. Finding out the time seemed like it would be an easy one, a good confidence builder.

I waded through all the imported long-format rock videos, self-help books and beat-up cassette tapes littered between the couch and the TV. The giant idiot box was a real state-of-the-art number, so futuristically designed it was impossible to turn the damn thing on manually.

I decided to begin my quest at the coffee table, though I couldn't actually see the table's surface. It could have been just a hovering pile of debris for all I knew. Some book called *The Engines of Creation* was lying open-faced in a pool of coagulated soy sauce. There were Shibuya fashion magazines, Donut Man boxes, bags of wasabi potato chips, half-empty cans of Pocari Sweat soft drinks. Generations of cigarette butts littered the low table. Some had stayed in the ashtray while others had struck out on their own, gone exploring. Some were bent, burned down to a twisted nub, others only half smoked, crushed out carefully at the tip. There were different brands, red lipstick on some and black lipstick on others. The whole spectrum, a diverse rainbow of cigarette butts.

Somehow, though, I knew they were all Yoshi's. Smokers are notoriously brand loyal and no two crush out a cigarette the same way, but Yoshi seemed like the type who'd diversify it just to make a point. Show how complex he was. Give Dr. Nick something to analyze.

Even when it came to cigarettes, Yoshi strove to defy categorization. Not the worst opening line, but it didn't stand a chance against Ed's red pen. Because of his own nicotine demons, he'd banned all mention of tobacco in the magazine. Good-hearted, wrongheaded Ed back in Cleveland. It seemed like another universe.

A tiny refrigerator squatted next to the big amp in the corner. The fridge door was plastered with band stickers—Platonic Sextoy, Ween, United Future Organization, Pinocchio's Alibi, Buddha and the Riflemen. The inside was less happening—a few cans of beer, a half-eaten slice of pizza, a three-pack of Love Donkey condoms and a pair of vintage Adidas tennis shoes still in their original box.

I two-stepped back toward the couch and picked through all the junk on the floor, unearthing a press-kit photo of some wannabe glam metal band Yoshi had been in called Devil's Angel. Their logo was done in cheesy lightning-bolt letters, like something a kid would draw on his algebra notebook, and the whole band wore plastic red devil horns and crepe paper angel wings. Yoshi looked about fifteen years old. The frontman was more than twice his age, an English bloke with a face like a jack-o'-lantern two weeks after Halloween. Anyone willing to wear crepe paper angel wings well into his thirties isn't gonna give up easily. He was probably still rocking out in a nameless dive somewhere, doing covers people only half recognized. Good for him.

Still no remote. I found a big gray duffel bag under the coffee table and unzipped it. It was filled with fan letters mostly, and packages of swag. I opened one of the smaller boxes and found a big foot pedal attached to a letter that said, "We think you'll find the Crack Baby has the most killer, anguished sound of any wah wah pedal on the market."

Just to see how Yoshi's fan letters compared to mine, I opened a letter addressed to Yoshi c/o Seppuku Entertainment. It was from a girl named Kiki in Nakodate.

> *Dear Yoshi-chan,*
>
> *Let me say I am not one of your little fans who are in love with you and scream whenever they see you, sorry, I mean I'm not obsessed. I do think you are very charming and very sweet and your music expresses the way I feel my own self.*
>
> *I would love to meet you someday. It is like my dream. I am 15 years old, type AO positive, and live in Nakodate with my mom. I have short dark hair, and green eyes (with my colored contacts!). I enjoy soccer, rollerblading, painting, swimming, modeling, basketball, writing, guitar, cooking, dancing, photography, ikebana, gymnastics, acting, pottery, and walking my dog. My dog's name is Olivia Newton John.*

Reading about Kiki's busy life was wearing me out. I stuck the letter back in the envelope and checked the postage mark. It was dated over three years ago. Kiki would be eighteen now, probably off at college. Olivia Newton John would be missing her.

I took four steps and landed in the bathroom.

Nothing inside the medicine cabinets but empty prescription bottles and a film canister filled with stale marijuana. Underneath the sink was a garter belt, a packet of Izumi guitar strings, some virgin bottles of cleaning supplies, an unopened carton of Nocturne perfume and a fake rubber snake. Pretty much your standard under-the-sink stuff.

The shower curtain was a canvas of unreadable graffiti and weird multicolored stains. The tub itself was absurdly clean. It'd probably seen less action than ZZ Top's razor.

When I'd exhausted all other options, I lifted up the lid of the laundry hamper and got the full olfactory rock-and-roll experience. Sweat, smoke, alcohol and sex mingled in a nasty funk like wet Phish-heads in a broken-down van. The hamper was chock-full of crusty, glittering headbands, Lycra pants and leathery things I could only guess at. It reminded me of the closet at the Purloined Kitten and I suddenly wondered if Olga had ever been in this apartment. I shut the lid. No TV remote was worth sticking my hand in there.

I turned around and caught my reflection in the mirror. The glass was covered with a dozen lipstick kisses from a dozen different mouths, a congregation of pale reds and faded pinks under a thin layer of dust. If I stood at just the right angle, there were kisses on my big swollen nose, kisses on my cheek, even a big set of lips right on my own. I looked like I was having a real swell time.

Just as I was leaving something on the bathroom floor caught my eye. It was made for catching eyes—four-color print job, embossed logo, die cuts for inserts. Yoshi'd left behind a great leave-behind.

A black bird appeared on the front. Underneath it were the words "Where will you be in 2099?" Underneath that, in small print, "an invitation from the Phoenix Society."

I forgot all about the remote.

PROJECT 2099:
BRINGING TODAY'S VISIONARIES INTO TOMORROW.

Imagine . . .

—achieving what man has always thought impossible.
—being on the cutting edge of modern science.
—living amid the wonders of the future.
—being "born again" in your own body (or better!)
—meeting your grandchildren's grandchildren.

Sound farfetched, like something out of a science-fiction novel? Well, it isn't. It's actually our promise to you, and it's all possible today. The Phoenix Society for Cryopreservation and Life Extension is proud to announce Project 2099: Bringing Today's Visionaries into Tomorrow.

<u>WHAT IS IT?</u>

Have you ever wanted to have dinner with Bach— not a Bach record, but the living, breathing Johann Sebastian Bach? Or maybe you'd like to dance with Ginger Rogers, or have a literary discussion over tea with Tanizaki?

Well, you can't.

But thanks to scientific breakthroughs in the early twenty-first century, you'll be able to rub elbows with great men and women of the future. And they in turn will learn about the past from the movers and shakers of our own time.

How, you may ask, is this possible?

It's called cryonic suspension. Project 2099 aims to recruit the visionaries of our world, top people in all fields—from entertainment to sports to science and politics—and offer them a chance to see the future they've helped create.

HOW DOES IT WORK?

For a donation to the project, those awarded Visionary status are guaranteed a place in the future through cryonic suspension. Cryonic suspension works by cooling the body to -196°C shortly after death, thus minimizing tissue damage. The body is perfused with special cryoprotective agents that preserve vital organs on a cellular level by preventing the formation of ice crystals that can destroy cell structures. Once perfusion is complete, the patient is stored in a specially constructed cryopreservation chamber inside our state-of-the-art Cryotorium, located in a remote region in Hokkaido and carefully monitored until reanimation becomes a technological reality.

IS IT REALLY POSSIBLE?

In the past, people may have asked the same question about landing on the moon. Or about finding a vaccine for polio, or even something as simple as beaming an image of a person thousands of miles through the air—something we all know as television.

The fact is, we can't see the future. But as visionaries, it's not difficult to foresee that the amazing medical advancements made in the last century will continue. Soon, nanotechnology will make it possible to repair minor organ damage to the point of bringing a well-preserved subject back to life. There is plenty of evidence available today that suggests that much tissue damage is reversible, and by minimizing our tissue damage today, we have a wonderful chance to join the people of tomorrow.

AM I A VISIONARY?

You wouldn't be reading this if you weren't. We are making this offer only to a select few individuals we believe will truly be invaluable to the future. Instead of simply targeting wealthy individuals, we have selected those who have made a tangible contribution to the betterment of our own society.

ISN'T THIS A BIT ELITIST?

Before I could get the answer, I heard someone fiddling around outside the front door.

I grabbed a big guitar hanging on the wall outside the bathroom. It was a cherry-red hollow-body Gibson. A real beauty, the kind that usually gets a woman's name. I yanked it off the wall, gripping the smooth maple neck kendo-style, and eased up beside the door.

The door creaked open and I swung.

The blow connected with the side of his face. He dropped

the two plastic bags of take-out he was carrying and stumbled backwards into his brother. All the food and drinks hit the floor. They smelled good.

Maki pushed his brother aside and came in with his hands balled into fists, ready to do battle. His footwork was graceful for a big guy. For some reason, they were both wearing black three-piece suits.

"C'mon!" he barked. "Hit me with your best shot! Fire away!"

"I don't want to hit anybody," I said, still gripping the guitar and backing away. "It was a mistake. Please, just let me out."

Maki looked to Aki. Aki shook the dust out of his head and wiped his jacket. The blow to the face was already forgotten. As far as Aki was concerned, I was a one-hit wonder.

"He's chasing the dragon," Aki said.

"Banging the H gong," said Maki.

"Riding a horse with no name."

"Sister Morphine."

"Mr. Brownstone!"

"Dr. Feelgood!"

"Hold on, guys," I said, moving behind the couch. They were both dancing now, knocking over piles of records as they bounded toward me like a couple of kangaroos. "You don't know what's going on."

"The needle and the damage done," Aki said.

"Every junkie like the setting sun," said Maki.

They circled closer, in full fight stance now. I backed around the couch, gripping the guitar neck tightly. I took a swing to keep them at a distance.

"Relax," Aki said.

"Don't do it," echoed Maki.

"Do you really want to hurt me?"

"Do you really want to make me cry?"

"Cut that shit out," I said, my voice rising, my hands gripping the guitar neck even tighter.

"Just like Yoshi," Aki spat, moving around the couch, forcing me toward the TV. "Yoshi hated eighties music."

"Especially when he was coming down."

"Especially gay bands," Aki added.

If I hadn't whacked Aki in the face, I probably could have been eating right now. I could've enjoyed a few bites of take-out and made a play for the door. Instead, I'd taken a blind swing and now had two pissed-off heavyweight kickboxing twins thinking I was a drug-crazed lunatic. Such is life's rich pageant.

The impasse couldn't last long. It didn't.

Being a little smaller, Aki got to me first. This time I caught him squarely, the whammy bar of the Gibson digging right into his chin. He sailed into the path of his brother. Their feet got tangled up, and they fell headlong to the floor.

As they scrambled to their knees, I brought the Gibson down hard, smacking Maki right between the shoulder blades, dangerously close to his head. Then I windmilled around to catch the smaller Fuzotao, but Aki deflected the blow with a well-timed forearm block. The guitar went careening into the corner of the couch, the sharp edge of the furniture connecting with one of the f-holes.

The body of the Gibson splintered on impact.

A few jagged spikes of wood clung to the neck, fanning out in a pattern that reminded me of Suda's hair. Just as Aki was bringing up his leg for a crescent kick, I jabbed the splintered end right into his thigh, pitchfork-style.

He screamed like a schoolgirl at an idol show.

I let go of the guitar.

Maki started off the ground, but he didn't make it. His jaw fell slack.

The guitar was sticking out of Aki's leg. His own momentum had wedged the splintered edge deep into his outer thigh, the instrument jutting out at a right angle like some bizarre appendage growing from his bloody leg. His nice black slacks were totally ruined.

Maki's shock quickly transformed into fury. He rose from the floor. He tuned up his knuckles one by one and gave me the slow burn as he growled:

"Momma said knock you out."

I leapt onto the couch as he lunged, using it as a springboard to send me sailing through the air.

Maki launched right behind me. His massive body stretched out, going horizontal. It would have been one hell of a flying tackle but I snagged the busted acoustic guitar chandelier, and pulled up as I swung. I looked down to see Maki flying under me, making a harmless play for my legs. A big cosmonaut on an ill-fated spacewalk.

Then he dropped hard, right on top of the low table. Its legs snapped and the table crashed to the floor in a cloud of cigarette ashes and dust.

The guitar mobile didn't fare much better. It pulled out of the ceiling at the height of my swing, just as I was parallel to the ground. As I plummeted downward, I pulled a half twist and cocked my elbow, putting my forearm between me and Maki, seven vertical feet apart and closer all the time.

My elbow caught him right in the kidneys as he tried to roll over. I weighed about 160 pounds. and I'd just fallen almost seven feet, but I didn't need a calculator to figure out the force of the blow. The physics were all over Maki's face.

I picked up the Phoenix Society folder on my way to the door. As I walked out, I grabbed one of the take-out containers that lay scattered on the floor and popped it open. Pork fried rice, burnt and greasy just the way I like it. I tortured my stomach for a while, then shut the lid and put the container back where I'd found it. My stomach returned the favor by torturing me all the way down the stairs.

23

It was warm outside, the sky perfectly clear behind a dizzying mess of crosshatched power lines. A few cats were milling around the narrow alleyway, but they offered no clue as to what part of town I was in.

I rounded the corner, still trying to get my bearings. The street was eerily quiet. All the businesses were closed, and there were no cars parked at the curb. If I listened hard, I thought I could hear singing from somewhere far off, but I wasn't sure.

Someday, everything will be made clear, Setsuko had said. Someday was gonna come sooner than she thought. I was starting to work things out. There were some gaping holes, but like go master and millionaire land developer Kakutani used to say, open space is the mother of strategy.

I turned the next corner and almost tripped over my own feet.

The entire width of the street was filled with marching kids. There were thousands of them, some carrying framed pictures of Yoshi, others with chrysanthemums or flags. About every fifth person carried a placard. *We love Yoshi, Remember Yoshi, Yoshi will never die.* Most were dressed in black, holding lit candles and burning incense. The ones in front were carrying a big banner that said "Yoshi FOREVER

1973–2001." One girl was banging a drum while a guy next to her had a guitar rigged to a tiny amp hanging around his neck. I could barely hear him wailing beneath the chanted chorus. The dreary voices all ran together, blurring the words in a dull roar.

That's why Aki and Maki had suits on. It was Saturday. Yoshi's memorial service.

I looked for an exit, an alley, anywhere I could duck out of the way. Nothing. The kids were closing in. Someone chanted through a megaphone, blaring his grief so loud I could hardly hear myself failing to think.

And then they were upon me. The wave of mourners hit, spilling by on all sides. The first few rows managed to side-step me, but it didn't last. A girl with her eyes closed bumped right into me, knocking me sideways. I went into a big kid wearing a ripped up Broken Inside You shirt. He elbowed me the other way and I struggled to keep my feet as I held the Phoenix Society folder aloft, clinging to it like a low-hanging branch over a swift river. I hopped to my left, tripping over the legs of a skinny girl with Betty Boop eyes. She looked at me in shock and started to go down. I dropped the folder.

I caught her by her sweatshirt and yanked her upright before she got trampled. No sooner did she get to her feet than I got knocked from behind. I tumbled forward and hit the pavement, snatching at papers from the folder, trying to grab at them as they scattered.

Several hands clutched at my leather jacket and reached under my arms. I felt weightless as I was swept up, placed on my feet and moved into the current. It was useless to resist. A young girl next to me took me by the arm. She looked up at me silently, her eyes filled with tears.

. . .

I made halfhearted attempts to escape once or twice, but it was impossible. The human current was too strong, too single-minded. Whether they're hanging around on the street looking bored, playing video games, dancing—whatever—teens have a way of doing things with almost superhuman energy. Grieving was no exception.

I knew where I was now. As we neared the Tsukiji Hon-ganji Temple more and more cops lined the route. They stood with their hands clasped behind their backs, greeting the spectacle with the disinterested gaze they used for noncrimi-nal human activities. TV helicopters buzzed overhead. The street was bordered by remote recording vans sent from NHK, SkyTV, and TBS. Spindly metal beams carried the satellite dishes skyward, jutting up like tent poles at the circus.

A slender young woman I recognized from late-night broadcasts stood atop one of the vans, posing for the live-coverage shot. She was a real looker, no surprise since these days all the big network anchors came from modeling agen-cies. The news might not be getting any prettier but the mes-sengers were cuter every day.

As we passed through the media gauntlet, the chanting faded out. The kids saw all the cameramen poised atop the vans, lined up on the sidewalk and peering through their viewfinders. A stunned silence fell over the procession. The air felt charged, like the moment before lightning strikes.

One brittle voice rose from the center of the group. *Yoshi*, the girl spoke, the sound choked with tears. Soon another voice joined, an octave above. *Yoshi*. A third came in an octave below, *Yoshi*, and the word raced through the crowd. Thousands of voices echoing quiet Yoshis, the sound a bab-bling brook then a gushing river, a flood, a tidal wave.

The reporters took the cue. Floodlamps beamed, flash-bulbs strobed, shutters clicked. The crying turned to sobbing, the sobbing grew to wailing. The girl at my side let loose a high-pitched, earsplitting lament. A kid to my right who'd been looking on with a hardened stoicism suddenly erupted.

"*Long live Yoshi! Yoshi forever!*"

His face puckered as he called the phrase over and over again, the syllables expanding with each cry. His voice rose above the others, pulling the cameras his way.

"*LONG LIVE YOSHI!*"

"*YOSHI FOREVER!*"

And then another voice joined, and another, and another, until the entire mass of kids was chanting in thunderous unison, until the words seemed enough to shake down buildings, to crumble the pavement, to shatter the sun and crack open the very sky above. The TV reporters cupped their free hands to their ears, moved the mics closer to their mouths, then gave up trying to speak into their microphones altogether, forgot they were on camera, and gazed at the kids with a stunned look of fear and wonderment as the booming procession overwhelmed them like an conquering army, a inexorable, unstoppable force.

And as I watched the bewildered reaction from the adults, I suddenly realized just how deeply, how desperately, these kids needed someone like Yoshi. Granted, everything I'd learned about the guy pointed to the indisputable fact that he was a complete basket case, but that was beside the point. I was looking through the eyes of an adult. The deafening mass of kids surrounding me saw something else.

They saw someone who wasn't preaching about responsibility, someone who wasn't trying to keep them off drugs, out of gangs, or away from premarital sex. Someone who would never pester them to clean their rooms, or to study harder, or to start thinking seriously about their futures. Someone who would never call them ignorant or immature, who'd never label them good-for-nothings, failures, slackers, or disappointments. Someone who would never say they weren't living up to their potential, someone who'd never ask why they couldn't be more like that nice Murakami kid down the block. Someone who wasn't dismissing their romances as harmless crushes, their ideas as naive, their dreams as unrealistic.

They needed Yoshi because they needed someone who embodied the idea that life could be more—*is more*—than homework, cramschools, college entrance exams, company jobs, workable marriages, filial piety and sound investments. They needed someone who addressed teenagers as human beings, not as another generation of Pepsi drinkers, or the workforce of the future, or the embodiment of crumbling national values.

And in a way I couldn't quite name, they probably needed Yoshi to die.

The young girl beside me looked up at me with a curious expression on her face, almost as if she had been reading my thoughts. She squeezed my arm and motioned me to lean closer. Perhaps she wanted to share her sorrow, wanted someone to understand her pain, to tell her everything was all right. Cupping her hand over my ear, she whispered.

"What happened to your nose?"

The police had closed the temple gates to prevent the grounds from getting destroyed by mourners, so an impromptu Yoshi shrine was erected all along the length of the fence. Kids placed flowers, hung black-bordered photographs, strung up banners. They hugged each other and they cried. As the crowd fanned out along the perimeter of the temple grounds, I unlinked my arm from the young girl's.

She didn't seem to notice. I fought my way across the crowd and finally broke free of the mourners.

The sun descended as I walked toward the Tsukiji subway station. I tried to hurry, but my legs seemed stuck in funeral pace. When I reached the station everything was strangely quiet. I waited alone on the platform, listening for any kind of sound, staring into the gloomy subway tunnel. It seemed like the train would never come. But of course it did, right on time. I got inside. The doors closed and the train headed into darkness.

24

"Gimme a beer."

"Sorry, no beer."

"What do you have?"

"The Seven Faces of Happiness."

"Give me one of those."

I was back in the ramshackle Golden Gai, at the disintegrating drink stand known as the Last Hurrah. I'd returned hoping to hear some good news about Takeshi, but the look on the bartender's face when I arrived told me there wasn't any. I scanned the scarred surface of the wooden bar, looking for Takeshi's name while the bartender waved seven different bottles of liquor over my glass. Some of the stuff made it inside, some didn't.

I reached into my pocket and withdrew the few crumpled pieces of Phoenix Society literature that had survived the Yoshi memorial march. I smoothed one of the papers out on the bar and began reading.

HOW DOES IT WORK?

For a donation to the project, those awarded Visionary status are guaranteed a place in the future through cryonic suspension. Cryonic suspension

works by cooling the body to -196°C shortly after
death, thus minimizing tissue damage . . .

A few sentences later, I found the passage I'd been looking for.

Once perfusion is complete, the patient is stored
in a specially constructed cryopreservation chamber inside our state-of-the-art Cryotorium, located
in a remote region in Hokkaido and carefully monitored until reanimation becomes a technological
reality.

I recalled Setsuko quoting the Day Manager nearly word-
for-word about humans' lives running together. Right before
she'd walked out of the restaurant, taking the Night Porter's
Phoenix Society ID card with her. I took a sip of the Seven
Happiness and dug out another crumpled piece of paper.
This one was torn, but enough was left to give me some idea
of how Yoshi had traveled from the Hotel L'Charm to the
miserable Love Hotel Chelsea while he was unconscious
from a heroin overdose.

REACHING INTO THE FUTURE

Part II: Emergency Cryonic Suspense Procedures

But death is not always a planned event. When an
unforeseen death occurs, the Phoenix Society is still
capable of carrying out cryonic suspension with a
minimum of ishemic tissue damage occurring.

All members of the Phoenix Society are provided
with medical identification cards, upon which is
printed the number to our emergency response
team. Some may also choose to have the Phoenix

Society logo tattooed on their bodies for purposes of identification in case the card is lost or misplaced. A special "hot-button" pager is available to members of our Visionary Alliance Program, ensuring that even if one is unable to dial a telephone, they may still contact our emergency suspension team.

Currently, the Phoenix Society maintains emergency response vehicles in Tokyo, Osaka, Nagoya, Sapporo, and Fukuoka. Each vehicle is manned by four emergency technicians trained in emergency transport protocol. When a distress call is received, these technicians are deployed to the site of the emergency, where they will load the patient and transport him to a safe location where they can begin cryonic suspension protocol.

Because of the ignorance, prejudice and fear surrounding scientific movements like the Phoenix Society, we choose to keep the whereabouts of our cryonic suspension operations unknown. However, you may rest assured that they're all top-notch, cutting-edge facilities.

It is worth noting that before cryonic suspension protocol can begin, an individual must be pronounced dead by current medical and legal standards. Unfortunately, this means

The rest of the words were torn away. I knew well enough what it meant without having to read more, anyway. I folded up the paper and tucked it into my back pocket, downed the rest of the Seven Happiness and took out my wallet to pay. The bartender stopped me.

"Your friend has an account," he said.

If I'd been in charge of things, my friend Takeshi would have strolled by that very moment. He would have slid up next to me without my even noticing. I would've shown him the scraps of Phoenix Society literature. He would've told me all about what he'd learned at the Hotel L'Charm. We'd both get good and drunk, happinesses multiplying on the bar by factors of seven as we talked about how crazy the whole thing was. And right before we stumbled out of the Golden Gai, I would've turned and asked him what he meant the other night when he said Sarah and I were made for each other.

But I wasn't in charge of things.

Takeshi didn't show up at that moment. He didn't come the next moment or the one after that. I decided to order two more Seven Happinesses, and drank one while the other sat untouched on the bar. The same cat I'd seen the previous night was once again huddled on his perch, looking down over the proceedings.

"How well do you know Takeshi?" I asked the bartender.

"Fairly well." He responded as if he'd been expecting the question for some time.

"He's not the type of guy to just disappear because he owed some people a little money, is he?"

"No. I wouldn't say so. In fact, I would say he is the opposite of just such a person."

I had to agree. The next booth over, someone finished a story with a rapid-fire burst of expletives. Everyone erupted in laughter. Then it fell quiet again.

"You were the one who called the police, right? The one who picked me out in the lineup?"

The bartender nodded. "I'm sorry for getting the police involved. But I am worried for Mr. Takeshi Ishikawa. He is a good man. And he is my only customer. He has been my only customer for years now."

The sinking feeling I'd had all day sank even lower. Even Seven Happiness wasn't helping. Little by little people started filing out of the Golden Gai. I looked up to see what my friend the cat was doing. He was gone. I lingered over my drink. I kept hoping somehow Inspector Arajiro had found Takeshi. I worked out lots of implausible situations, even going so far as to tell myself that the Tokyo cops always get their man. I tried to believe Takeshi was getting grilled by a bunch of inspectors at this very moment. Maybe Peoff was even there. Or that he was in a penthouse in Ebisu, listening to his wife, the Ministry of Finance, haranguing him for running up such huge debts in the first place. But I might as well have been wishing that the Night Porter hadn't died in my hotel room, or that I'd never been assigned to work the Yoshi story, or that I'd never called up Takeshi looking for information, or that I'd never stumbled upon the *Power Chord Japan* magazine. There were so many things to wish once I got started I might never be able to stop.

"Are you and Takeshi pretty good friends?"

"I like him," the bartender said. "He is one of a kind."

"I liked him, too," I said quietly.

The moon-faced bartender's expression shifted ever so slightly. He was the type of guy who would notice I'd changed tenses and wonder why. I reached for my wallet again.

"The account—" he started.

"Please. Let me pay."

He studied me for a long time. I studied him right back as I laid out every bill in my wallet. His face never changed shape, but his eyes looked heavier somehow. He started to protest as the pile of bills on the counter grew next to the untouched drink. I held up a hand to silence him. He knew. We both knew. Takeshi wouldn't be coming back to the Last Hurrah.

I had one more stop to make in Tokyo. On the way out of the alleyway, I said good-bye to the Golden Gai. I always do. I never know when one day it won't be there anymore.

Shibuya was so beautiful at night I was almost able to forget the ugliness that brought me there. Walking out of the station, I emerged into a shimmering world that was clean and bright and unabashedly optimistic. Newly hung Christmas lights were strewn above the Hachiko statue, where crowds of people sat bundled in their winter gear, waiting to meet their dates. People were smiling, people were laughing, people were taking pictures. People looked happy to be there, happy to be alive, happy to be people.

On the giant video screen across from the train station, cute-as-a-button Yuki Yomada was singing a barely recognizable version of "Frosty the Snowman." Yuki wasn't a person, but a virtual idol, a video image made from motion capture computer technology. An ageless beauty who'd never gain weight, never lose her voice before big shows, never try to assert creative control. Not to mention take drugs, threaten to leave her label, or get herself murdered. All this and you didn't even have to pay her royalties. Record execs hoped she represented the future of music, and given all the chaos surrounding Yoshi, I almost couldn't blame them.

I was only minutes away from the Love Hotel Chelsea, the second hotel Yoshi visited that fateful night, the place I now believed he'd died in. But that wasn't where I was headed. Instead, I walked up Bunkamura-dori, past the 109 Building. I ducked into the parking garage. I walked up some stairs, exited on the seventh floor and journeyed down the long, soft-lit hallway leading to Launchpad Talent and Productions.

The glass door whisked open and I stepped into a dark room, deciding if Santa wasn't here, I'd just have to entertain myself. There were a lot of questions I wanted to ask the guy, foremost among them where I could find Olga's secret locker. Because try as I might, I still couldn't remember the song that was playing that night at the Wild Strawberry, and I had to find out what was in the locker before I left Tokyo to play a wild hunch that just might tie everything together.

But I wasn't gonna have to wait for Santa. He was already there in his makeshift office, sitting in a recliner, looking out the window. I walked across the room, and stopped about six feet behind him.

"Nice view, huh?" I said. "I can see why you'd want to stay in this place, even though you can't afford it. I suppose you'd do whatever it took to keep your little operation in business. That's why you agreed to kill Yoshi, isn't it? Because Kizuguchi offered you enough money to quit dealing drugs and get back into the talent business for real. Maybe try to launch the Handsome Tigers. But your plan didn't work out."

He didn't answer, but then I hadn't asked a question. As I took a step forward, he sat rigid in his chair, tense, afraid to move a muscle.

"You took Yoshi to the Hotel L'Charm and left him there with his precious heroin. But on the way back to the Purloined Kitten, you got a call from Kizuguchi. He told you the plan was a no-go, told you to call off the murder. That's when you made the emergency call, alerting the police of Yoshi's overdose. Because now you desperately needed to save the man you'd just tried to kill. But Yoshi wasn't at the Hotel L'Charm anymore. He was all the way across town, at the Love Hotel Chelsea. I'll tell you how that happened in a second, but first let me put together the rest. Feel free to interrupt me if I get anything wrong."

Santa held his tongue. I took a deep breath, lining up all the facts in my head before I unloaded them. I knew I was talking too much, but I didn't care. Maybe it was the drinks, maybe it was the empty stomach, maybe it was everything that had happened since I landed in Tokyo or since I was forced to vacation in Hokkaido or since the beginning of time. I didn't care what Santa knew. I didn't care if he spun around in his chair and pointed a gun at me and I didn't care if he pulled the trigger. Nothing was going to stop me.

"When you screwed up Yoshi's killing, Kizuguchi decided not to pay you. So you had to come up with something else. Somehow you figured out that Yoshi had bamboozled Seppuku. You found out he never delivered the demos. You figured that must've been why Kizuguchi called off the hit, and you figured if you could find the missing demos before Seppuku did, you'd be back in the picture. You and DJ Towa would be . . . where is DJ Towa?"

When he didn't answer, I saw what an idiot I'd been. I was so in love with the sound of my own clever voice unwinding the senseless, sloppy murder that I hadn't realized I was standing at the scene of another one. I crept around the chair, and confirmed what I should've known the moment I walked in the door and didn't find Santa racing around the room and blabbering to himself.

Hijime "Santa" Sampo wouldn't be doing any more blabbering. Someone had made sure of that. His eyes stared into the back of his skull and the front of his red sweat suit was stained a much darker, much uglier red. His open mouth was crusted, caked with dried blood. A small, twisted lump of

279

blackened flesh lay curled on the floor beside him. It took me a moment to realize what it was.

I fought back the vomit rising in my throat as I stumbled out of Santa's office, down the stairs, out of the parking garage and onto the street. It was the wrong place to stumble. The sidewalk tilted as people swirled past in all directions, a nauseating carnival of hair and flesh and teeth and tongues. Tongues licking lips, tongues rolling in cheeks, tongues chewing gum, tongues yammering, tongues chattering, millions of tongues all speaking at once all trying to be heard. Tongues saying so many words they ran together, overlapped, became disconnected, meaningless sounds like tomato plumber sex halter top Thursday boyfriend dishwasher sale history pet cat fuyasu akedo matsuge yasui kokioroshite yakimochi gakuwari pansutoochobo guchimotemoteanatanoshinjinrukekkonshitaiiaigantawago totawagotosannanshimaidechojonoatashidakegamadeurenok orinanoyoimotogawatashinofukuoyokumudandekiteikun odearamataatarashiifukuokattanotoatekosutteyattaanofu fuwaisakaigataenaikarenitaisurukimochiwasukkarisamateshi mataaitsunokanojokaowachinkushadakedoseikakuwatote moiikodekawaiindajibunnodeppagasonnaniiyanara haishadekyoseisureabaiinonikarewajibungasabottebakariitak usenirakudaisasetagakkonisakauramioskitehokoshitafushigi fushigifushigifushigi . . .

I made it to the side of the building, then I lost it.

When it was all over, I stood upright, and felt my surroundings slowly coming back into focus. I sucked in a lungful of air, trying to steady myself. The lights kept flashing, loudspeakers kept blaring, people kept shuffling on by, looking the other direction, pretending they didn't see me standing there, sweaty and pale beside the mess I'd just made. And somehow, Shibuya still managed to look beautiful through the whole thing.

THIRD VERSE (SAME AS THE FIRST)

Catnip is a kitty cat drug
One puff, two puffs
High in a dream

—Shonen Knife ("Catnip Dream")

25

$\mathbf{A}$ backstage pass from the 1986 Hammer of the Visigoths tour dangled from the CB receiver as the truck bounced down the highway north of Sapporo. I'd been riding with Kenji for about fifteen miles. My ears were still adjusting.

"I saw you standing there in that Merzbow shirt, freezing your ass, and I said to myself, well what the fuck, Kenji? Give the man a lift." Kenji laughed and punched me in the arm. He was a bearish guy with broad shoulders and hunkered posture. The thickness of his three-day beard led me to believe he probably had some Ainu blood in him.

I was glad he came along when he did. I'd landed at the Sapporo airport with nothing but a hangover, the leather on my back, ten thousand yen and three crumpled sheets of Phoenix Society literature. I wasn't about to rent a car and leave a paper trail for anyone to follow, but I never would have guessed it would be Yoshi's Merzbow shirt that saved me from freezing on the side of the road. In another few minutes I would've looked like Jack Nicholson at the end of *The Shining*.

As the rig climbed into the hills, Kenji and I compared notes on the greatest metal bands of all time. He did a lot more talking than I did, telling me all about how he used to be a real *gariben*, until he went to see some local band play. That day, he quit being a square. Two years later he dropped out of school and started driving trucks.

"I eat when I want, wear what I want, listen to whatever music I want, it's great!" he said. "And I'll tell you what, man. I've got women from here to Kagoshima and all points in between. All points in between."

He talked on as the sun rose, but I hardly heard what he was saying. A border was slowly etched between the sky and the earth. The mountains defined their edges. Fresh details appeared—a tree here, a rock there, a little more snow now visible on the sides of the hills. By morning light there was a perfectly rendered mountain against a postcard sunrise.

The conversation gradually dwindled, turning to silence the way day turns into night. Miles went by, hours too. The rig climbed into the mountains and I sat there, mind a total blank.

Evening approached from the horizon. The line between sky and earth started disappearing again. I was hypnotized by the snow dancing in the headlights, snaking across the road. I could have watched it forever. It was better than a lava lamp.

It was dark when we came upon the nothing town by the highway in nowhere Hokkaido. I had Kenji pull over.

"You're getting out here?" he said, concern mingling with amusement. "There ain't nothing here but a few hicks and lots of snow."

"And some cats," I said. I offered him some yen, but he refused it. We wished each other luck and all that stuff, then he closed the cab door and started climbing up the winding road, farther into the mountains.

I turned and walked down a road branching off the highway. My cheeks hardened, my nostrils stuck together. With the swelling my nose was twice as big now, so I guess I shouldn't have been surprised it felt twice as cold. I trudged onward, toward the lights of the Hotel Kitty softly glowing at the far edge of the valley.

CLOSED FOR WINTER.
HAPPY CHRISTMAS AND HAPPY NEW
YEAR TO YOU.
SEE YOU IN THE SPRING!!

The sign on the front door had all the cheery flourishes of the Day Manager's handwriting. On the other side of the glass, a cat pawed the window and opened its mouth in silent mews. I pushed my face against the window and peered inside.

A few lights were on, but no one was home.

Before I walked the perimeter of the building looking for other entrances, I decided to give the door a shove just to be sure. It gave grudgingly and I stepped inside the Hotel Kitty.

The lobby smelled like an overdue litter box. I'd hardly moved inside the door when five or six kittens came tumbling at my feet, making a racket like I was their mother. As my eyes adjusted to the dim light I saw cats everywhere. In the farther recesses of the room they sulked like tired shadows, their shapes merging into darkness. Some batted the fake potted plants around while others were clustered on the expensive couches, curled up in sleep. One cat darted under a chair, another darted out. Lieber and Stoller honed their claws on the twin columns near the reception desk, oblivious to the three kittens wrestling on the marble floor behind them.

It was a full-scale feline riot. Getting to the other side of the room without trampling any kittens was like mountain biking through Cambodia without hitting a landmine. They roamed in pesky groups of three or four, each taking turns attacking my shoes. I was starting to appreciate how Godzilla must have felt.

Suddenly, hundreds of eyes shone from the darkness as light swept over the room. The headlights belonged to a white van pulling up just outside the lobby. I watched through the window as a figure waddled out of the car. It was the Day Manager, wrapped up in his winter gear. He took a few steps then stopped, looking at the ground.

My footprints in the snow.

I double-timed toward the stairwell. The door still had the sign on it. *Stairs off use. Broken. We are fix. Staff of Hotel Kitty thanks you!* I thanked the Hotel Kitty right back and pushed the door open.

The stairwell was noticeably cooler. As I headed toward the basement, it felt downright chilly, but I'd trade cold air for cat stink any day. I stopped and listened for any sounds, but there were none. I continued down.

The stairs ended, opening onto a narrow white corridor. The passage was spotlessly clean and longer than a *noh* play. I could just barely see something shimmering way down at the other side. The proverbial light at the end of the tunnel, I guess. Not only weren't there cats in the hall, but the cat motif was gone, too. No paintings, no paw prints on the floor. A completely cat-free zone. Maybe that's what they meant about the stairwell being broken.

I started walking. The sound of my wingtips traveled down the hall, bouncing off the far end and passing me going the other way about five seconds later, followed by an eerie whistling sound. I didn't even realize I'd been whistling until I heard it coming back at me, repeated note for note. After that, I stopped whistling. Every so often I quit walking and listened, just to make sure the only footsteps were mine.

I kept walking and walking, but the end never seemed to get any closer. I figured I'd probably already walked all the way under the Tsugaru Strait, back to the main island of Honshu.

And suddenly, without even realizing it, I'd reached the end.

PUSH THIS BUTTON!

It was a handwritten sign taped under a button in the exact center of a large stainless-steel door. The button was big and red, like a clown's nose. Or mine, for that matter.

I'd read enough comics to know that whenever there's a sign that says *push this button,* it means you're about to have a bucket of water fall on your head or get punched by a spring-loaded boxing glove. But I didn't think the Day Manager had it in him. Sending someone all the way down the hall to get bopped in the nose—that kind of joke borders on genius.

Still, I ducked as I hit the button.

The cavernous room was almost as big as the hotel lobby but not nearly as charming. Instead of cats and plants and inviting furniture, the place was filled with empty stretchers, electronic monitors mounted on wheeled carts, a sink under a dripping faucet, two stainless-steel bathtubs and a complex network of gleaming metal pipes and electric cables worming across the ceiling. Their destination looked to be the four large steel tanks at the far end of the room, giant thermoses huddled together as if to stave off the cold.

I recognized them from the Phoenix Society brochure.

Aluminum dewars, long-term cryostorage units filled with liquid nitrogen chilled to a cool -196°C.

I went down a short metal staircase for a closer look. Underneath the sound of the dripping faucet was an electric hum of high-powered fans. It sounded like the inside of a giant refrigerator. I guess it shouldn't have been surprising, since that's basically what the Cryotorium was.

As I neared the dewars, I spotted a clipboard on the side of the wall. I took it down and looked at a chart.

Cryo canister #1

112805 . . . . Sano Hiroshi
112806 . . . . Watanabe Akira
112807 . . . . Sakamaki Noburu

Cryo canister #2

212808 . . . . Diseni Waruta
212809 . . . . Matsuda Ryu
212810 . . . . Takahara Akio
212811 . . . . Shigoto Mei

Nobody I knew. I flipped to the next page.

Cryo canister #3

312805 . . . . Araki Toji
312806 . . . . Iwatsuki Keko
312807 . . . . Okomoto Yasuji

Cryo canister #4

412808 . . . . Hirohito Nekomo
412809 . . . . Choneko Yoyo
412810 . . . . Ishikawa Takeshi
412811 . . . . ~~Chaka Billy~~ Chaka Billy

My name had been written in, crossed out, then added again. Someone was as indecisive about my future as I was. I'd been right about Ishikawa, Takeshi. But there was no satisfaction in it. Then again, I wasn't in the can yet either. Maybe the fourth dewar was for prospectives. The B-list for Project 2099 in case the top visionaries rejected immortality.

Suddenly, the door whisked open.

I leapt behind one of the giant steel dewars. Footsteps thumped down the metal staircase and headed across the floor. They went the other way, then turned around and came back. They stopped.

From the sound, whoever it was stood just on the other side of the dewar. I heard someone sigh along with a quiet dial tone.

"I'm here," a woman's voice said, echoing off the walls. Was it Setsuko? It didn't sound like her. I remembered the girl at the Hotel Kitty bar, clutching the Yoshi picture to her chest the night he died. I couldn't recall what her voice sounded like.

"Nothing," the voice said. She was talking on a phone. "You sure they weren't yours? All right. I'll go to the bar. You check the pool. Ten more minutes."

The footsteps headed across the floor, then went up the stairs again. I peeked my head out, but only got a look at the back side of a white smock and some short dark hair as the door shut again.

I waited around for about five more minutes before heading out of the Cryotorium. Unless you're into blipping monitors and medical equipment, there wasn't much worth sticking around for. It would be a dull place to spend the next hundred years.

The trip back toward the stairwell seemed much faster. Maybe I was just moving more quickly this time, aware that I had about three minutes to disable the white van. Then I'd get on the phone to Inspector Arajiro back in Tokyo, and hope he had some friends up north. That was about as far as my plan went.

I opened the door to the lobby an inch at a time, making sure there was no one waiting to intercept me. The cats blew my cover, though. Another litter of kittens spotted me and made a bunch of noise on the way over. They had wrinkled peach-fuzz skin, puggish, withered faces and tails like malnourished snakes. Their bodies were scrawny, almost ferretish, while thick tufts of hair sprouted between their toes. They were the ugliest kittens I'd ever seen, but they didn't know it. They went right along doing all the cute kitten stuff, mewing and crashing into my legs.

I heard more mewing across the room and looked up to see the Day Manager come waddling from shadows by the pool entrance. He was carrying two big suitcases. "Let's go quickly. I have a feeling it's that journalist. We must move . . . "

Then he recognized me. He dropped the suitcases.

WWWAWWAEERRR!

A cat's tail was pinned to the floor. His claws scuttled uselessly on the marble as he howled and tried to escape.

"Oh my!" the Day Manager gasped. He lifted the suitcase and before he could apologize the animal raced away to lick his wounds.

"Letting the elephants run the circus, huh?" I said.

"Mr. Chaka, I'm so very sorry," he said, switching into his pleasant hotel manager voice. "As you can see, we're closed for the winter. There's been . . . well, there's been a catastrophe." He shook his left leg and several kittens somersaulted across the floor. They scrambled back to their feet and renewed their attack on his pant leg. One of them climbed all the way to his knee before being flung off. "Somehow, one of the males escaped from his room. I still don't understand how it happened, but Lothario was able to impregnate almost all of the females."

He pointed across the room to a furry heap of utter exhaustion. A lean Oriental cat lifted his leonine head from the ground, squinting at us and rotating his hairless, batlike ears. Then his head rolled back and he stretched out. I took it he was Lothario.

"With a face like that, you should've had him neutered," I said. "Especially with a name like Lothario."

"Oh my!" the Day Manager said. "I've never heard of such cruelty! Lothario was a rare Oriental. Chinchilla silver coat and lynx point eyes. As a stud, he was worth thousands. But he strayed from his allowable outcross breeds. Now he's ruined everything!"

That explained all the kittens with oversized heads, corkscrew tails, floppy doggish ears and rodentine faces. Others had sinewy trunks, abbreviated muzzles and matted coats of wavy ringlet hair. The color combinations were borderline psychedelic. Lothario the Oriental had not only squandered his bloodline, but he'd produced a veritable feline freak show.

It was kind of romantic, really. Lothario frees the Hotel Kitty from the tyranny of arranged inbreeding.

Across the lobby, two cats hissed at each other and arched their backs. "Stop that this instant!" the Day Manager called to them. They stopped hissing and flew together in a whirlwind of teeth, claws and fur. Three seconds later they scrabbled to their feet and trotted off in opposite directions as if nothing had happened.

"I hope you weren't expecting to stay," he said. "I can

make reservations for you a few miles down the highway. There's a wonderful ryokan that—"

"Where's Setsuko Nishimura?" I asked.

"Who?"

"The Night Porter's granddaughter."

"But there is no one here except me. Even the staff has left. I must tend the cats, and watch over . . ."

"The big thermoses in the basement?"

He pushed his face into a funny shape, like he had no idea what I was talking about. Then he reached into his thick jacket, fumbling around with all the grace of a walrus doing a tango.

Finally, he produced a wimpy little handgun. It was one of those numbers with an ivory handle, like painted ladies or Yankee-Doodle dandies always carried in old westerns. A derringer. It made me want to laugh, but it would put a hole in me just the same.

"Gunplay," I said. "You trying to make me homesick?"

"I must ask you to step outside, Mr. Chaka."

"I don't think so," I said. "It's cold outside. Almost as cold as those tanks down there."

"Please turn around."

I'd studied pretty much every style of martial arts at one time or another. Shaolin Kung Fu, Tai-chi, Kenpo Karate, Tae Kwon Do, Muay Thai Kickboxing. Judo, Jeet Koon Do, American Freestyle, Capoeira and many of the esoteric brands between. Each had procedures to counter being in a headlock, being grabbed from behind or pinned to the ground. They teach you all kinds of things to do when someone attacks with a knife, a baseball bat, a tire iron, a long sword, or a rolled-up annual report.

But so far, there was only one surefire method to deal with someone pulling a gun. And that was to do whatever they said.

I turned around.

"Walk."

I did, carefully avoiding the kittens. I listened for the sound of a shot, wondering if I'd even hear it before it hit me. I recalled seeing an S.A.T. question years ago about whether someone would hear a shot fired at X miles an hour from Y feet away before the person felt it. I couldn't remember the answer. Like most kids, I never believed those stupid tests would ever affect my future.

I was just about at the front door when one particularly tenacious kitten managed to get its claw stuck in my shoelace. It gave me an idea.

I flipped him into the air like a hacky sack. As he arched overhead, I spun around to face the Day Manager. He watched the cat sailing above, his face going slack as he unconsciously lowered the gun.

I snatched the kitten out of the air and pulled it to my chest. I grabbed its little head with my other hand like it was a sticky lid on a jar of pickles. The Day Manager's face was a rictal mask of ghastly disapproval.

"You ever heard the koan Nanzen kills a cat?"

The Day Manager's face quivered. I took it as a "no."

"It goes like this. Two monks were arguing over a cat when Nanzen came along. If one of you can say a good word, Nanzen said, you will save this animal. They couldn't. He cut the cat in half."

The Day Manager blanched. His hand fell to his side as his body went cataplexic.

"Say a good word, Mr. Day Manager."

"What . . . what do you mean?"

"Drop the gun."

He knelt and placed it carefully on the floor at his feet. A curious kitten darted over and sniffed the barrel.

"Kick it over here," I said.

"Please," he said. "Don't harm the poor thing. He's done nothing to you." He carefully nudged the kitten away from the gun with his foot, then sent the gun my way. I kneeled over, picked up the silly antique and let the kitten go. He scampered away, shaking out his matted fur.

A voice called out from the fog of airborn cat hair.

"You're wasting your time with him."

A figure in a white lab coat stepped out of the elevator. The figure was carrying a black medical bag. The Day Manager smiled. He didn't mean to, he just had no idea what to do in a situation like this. The figure moved from the elevator, walking into the shadows.

"He's just our landlord," the voice said. "He provides the Phoenix Society a little basement space. We give him enough money to keep the hotel running. But our mutually beneficial relationship has been forced to come to a premature end."

"Tell Takeshi Ishikawa about premature endings."

"Suspending Ishikawa was a very difficult decision," the voice said. "One of many we've had to make recently. It's been a very hectic time for the Phoenix Society, but we've learned a great deal. Complications are bound to arise, but I think from this day forward the Phoenix Society will be better prepared. This episode has been a setback, certainly, but no one said immortality would be a walk in the park."

The figure moved into the light. It was Setsuko Nishimura.

She was not at all the Setsuko I knew. Her voice was colder, distant. Even her face seemed hardened and drawn inward. My surprise must have registered, for Nishimura let out a light chuckle. "I guess I've played a little trick on you. But if it makes you feel any better, the Night Porter really was my grandfather."

"And let me guess," I said. "You're part of the emergency cryo team that bungled the Yoshi suspension."

"I wouldn't use the word 'bungled,'" she said. "The situation was out of control before we even arrived. But in the end, I think we acted ethically. I suppose after everything you've been through, you deserve to know what happened. And I *was* planning on telling you. Though not for one hundred years or so."

I kept the gun trained on her as she moved toward the center of the lobby. Even her stride was different. More purposeful, not so loose-limbed. I didn't know what kind of scientist Setsuko made, but she really should've been an actress. Or a screenwriter. The long speech that followed was right out of one of those bad movies where the master criminal gloats needlessly about his crime, allowing the hero one final chance to escape. The only difference was, the hero had the gun this time. And I wasn't gonna allow Setsuko to go anywhere.

"At approximately ten-thirty we received a call from Yoshi's emergency hot-button pager," she began. "Our four-person cryosuspension response team arrived at the Hotel L'Charm in Shibuya nearly half an hour later to find Yoshi unconscious from a heroin overdose, but still breathing. We loaded him into our van, and started toward our facility. As Yoshi lay in our transport vehicle somewhere between death and life, quite a debate raged among our team. Should we go ahead and begin cryonic suspension procedures before he dies? No, because this is illegal and unethical. Do we wait for him to die? No, because then we are complicit in his death, no better than murderers. Do we take him to the hospital? No, because if they failed to save him, it would be next to impossible to reclaim his body. The hospital would stall, allowing decomposition and massive tissue damage to occur in the meantime. The medical community and the authorities afford organizations like the Phoenix Society very little respect."

For once, the authorities may have been right.

"The situation was further complicated when we intercepted a police radio transmission dispatching an ambulance to the Hotel L'Charm. Someone had reported Yoshi's overdose. Now we had to worry about whether witnesses had seen our vehicle in Shibuya, and if police would be on the lookout for us. So we took a vote. Two voted to drop him off at the hospital. Two voted to let him die and begin suspension procedures."

"I guess four really is an unlucky number."

"One of the many lessons we learned. From now on, all cryo-emergency vehicles will be manned by five people, in case of ties."

"I think I can figure out the rest," I said. "You decided if you weren't going to take him to the hospital, and you weren't going to watch him die so you could freeze him, you'd leave him just like you found him. Only at the Love Hotel Chelsea, where no one would be likely to witness you checking him in. Then you made a second overdose call to the police. But they were slower this time, because of the false alarm at the Hotel L'Charm. By the time they got there, Yoshi was dead. You took a screwed-up situation and twisted it beyond repair. But why did you have to kill Takeshi?"

"Because of you," she said. "You set everything in motion by stealing my grandfather's identification card. When the local suspension team didn't find the card on his body, we got worried."

"What suspension team? No suspension team came."

"Didn't you wonder where the EMTs came from the night my grandfather died?" she asked. "There isn't a hospital around for miles. And you probably know that ambulances are forbidden to transport corpses in this country. Special vehicles are required. Then again, I doubt you saw an ambulance or any other emergency vehicle. Am I correct?"

I nodded. I hardly remembered anything about that night except the look on the Night Porter's face as he sat slumped against the wall.

"The missing ID by itself was a small risk. But when you made all those calls from Tokyo to our emergency number, we got worried. My grandfather was a little senile. He was capable of saying anything. That's why I invented the other Setsuko. To find out what you knew. Did you like her, by the way? I could never really tell."

"She was a little flaky," I said. "But I liked that Setsuko more than this one."

"I know your type," she said. "You like women in distress, demure little things in need of comfort. In need of saving. Such women reaffirm your basic prejudices."

"Sure," I said. The speech sounded like one Sarah might've made. I couldn't help but smile. I guess I missed her. "Next you're gonna say I have trouble showing my emotions and this gun I took from the Day Manager is really just an extension of my penis. Why don't we skip that and get back to Takeshi."

"Fine," she said, betraying no emotion whatsoever. "After you noticed Yoshi's tattoo on the magazine cover, the Phoenix Society decided you were getting too close. And we knew you were sharing information with Takeshi. We had him tailed when he went poking his nose around the Hotel L'Charm. We didn't need the publicity in light of the complications with Yoshi's suspension."

"So you killed Takeshi. And you tried to kill me."

"We *suspended* him," she said. "And yes, we planned to do the same to you. You were jeopardizing our operation, and we believe that scientific progress and the lives of our patients are more important than some story for kiddies. Unfortunately, those two hulking twins were able to beat our cryo-transport vehicle to the scene. You're very lucky not to be resting in our Cryotorium right this moment. Or unlucky. Just think—you could've been reborn, seen the future."

"I don't think I'd like the future," I said. "All my jokes would be a hundred years old."

The Day Manager suddenly interrupted.

"Please understand," he said haltingly. "I wanted no part in this. I only did it for the good of the cats."

"It was a gamble taking Yoshi on," Setsuko sighed. "In retrospect, we shouldn't have done it. He could have generated a lot of positive awareness for the Phoenix Society, but he was too unpredictable."

"Don't worry about the missed publicity. I'll make sure you still get plenty of ink."

"I don't think so," Setsuko said. "We'd come out looking like bumbling fools. Which we are not, regardless of what you may think. Our methodology is scientifically solid. Our facilities are top-rate. Cryosuspension is an idea whose time has come, and—"

"I've studied the literature," I cut her off. "Call me ignorant, but the whole idea makes about as much sense as putting a steak in the fridge and expecting it to come back a cow."

"You're right," Setsuko conceded. "You are ignorant. Yours is not even a good metaphor for a process as complex as cryosuspension. And if anything, the Yoshi crisis proves how skilled we really are. We overcame a lot of obstacles to keep Yoshi's secret. And I suppose you overcame a few to uncover it. But what good have you done?"

"I found out the truth."

"Maybe," she said. "But you lost your friend Takeshi.

And what will you do with this truth you hold in such high regard? The Phoenix Society will never be brought to trial. We've gone underground. After all these years of work, in only a few short days there will be no evidence we ever existed. All so you could give a bunch of pimply teenagers something to thumb through while they use the toilet. Kind of a waste, isn't it?"

"What about all those people in the cans downstairs?"

A troubled look came over Setsuko's face. She looked tired, defeated. For a moment she reminded me of the Setsuko Nishimura sitting at the sad little duck pond. "I figure you'll tell the police about our Cryotorium. The bodies will be exhumed and cremated. There won't be another life for them."

"I wasn't the one who promised them immortality."

"No one was promised anything," she said. "All of our patients knew the risks. Resurrection was never guaranteed. It's a young science, and we face an uphill battle. People have very stubborn attitudes toward death. I'm sure you'll probably notify the authorities. Even though it means your friend Takeshi Ishikawa will never live again."

I thought about the look on the Night Porter's face when he knew it was over. And I thought about Takeshi. Even if they were somehow able to bring him back to life in one hundred years, the interest on his loans by then would reach into the trillions.

Suddenly, I noticed several cats coming our direction. They were drawing in from all corners of the room, slinking toward us from the shadows, spotty pink noses turned up in the air, eyes blazing. My focus shifted to the Day Manager. He held a plastic bag filled with a greenish powder.

"I am sorry, Mr. Chaka," he said.

Before I could ask him what he meant, he whipped the bag at me. It exploded against my chest. I stumbled backward, holding fast to the gun. The powder coated my entire face, creeping into my mouth and my nose.

The smell was unmistakable. And from the thick odor, it wasn't just the regular old street stuff, but highly concentrated, refined catnip.

Kitty crack.

I was able to dodge the first two animals, but the third mutant cat stuck to my face, digging his claws in my swollen nose. I let loose a shriek and tore him off. His slower companions were upon me now, landing on my belly, thudding against my shoulders and chest. I convulsed and shook them off, their claws trailing down my body as they fell. But it was no use. There were too many of them.

I could have fired the gun. The Day Manager and Setsuko were still standing only a few feet away, and I might have been able to hit one of them. But I just didn't see the point.

Whirling teeth and claws, fur and blood, the thin ripping sound of my flesh. I went down and rolled onto my belly. More and more piled on, pinning me to the floor, burying me under a writhing mound of jonesing felines. I felt the cold wind blow in as the Day Manager and Setsuko Nishimura pushed through the front door. I heard the van doors open and close and heard the vehicle pull away. But mostly, I heard the screeches and warbles of the cats as they tore at my shoulders, at the back of my head, anywhere their claws could get to.

CHORUS

Interviewer: If Saint Arrow could be remembered for only one album, which would you choose?
Yoshi: The one I haven't made yet.

—(from *Power Chord Japan*'s
"The Last Interview")

26

Breathe on me."

Dr. Nick was in a creme-colored tuxedo jacket that looked made out of crepe paper. He was dressed down, either that or someone had stolen half his jewelry, but he still looked out of place in the locker room of the Yokohama Kickboxing Pavillion II.

For once, Suda didn't. His long blond-and-red locks were gone, a buzzcut in their place that made him look like an ostrich. Aki and Maki were giving Suda a rubdown and doing some strange good-cop bad-cop variation designed to get him ready for the fight tomorrow.

"You're the man. You are the fucking man!" Aki shouted.

"Picture the moon reflected in silent waters," said Maki.

"You're a killer, bro. A killer!"

"Become both the moon and its reflection."

"You're gonna rip this guy to fucking shreds!"

Suda just sat there listening to the twins, looking vaguely ill. It was twenty-four hours away from the opening bell of Suda's debut professional match, and the butterflies were already loose in his stomach.

"Breathe on me," Dr. Nick said again.

Even the doc couldn't help but wince at the sight of my face. Sarah liked to say eventually everyone gets the face they deserve and I didn't know if mine was the rule or the exception that proves it. I hadn't seen a mirror, but I could guess how my mug looked. *Like shit* were the words Inspector Arajiro had used that morning. My face was swollen, crisscrossed with cat-claw cuts and festering pustules, but *like shit* was the best Arajiro could do. And as much as Arajiro didn't like my looks, he'd never offered to get me a doctor. He was too interested in what I had to say.

I breathed on Dr. Nick. My chest felt constricted, my throat filled with glass. Dr. Nick's nose twitched around and he rocked back slightly on his heels.

"Benign lymphoreticulosis," he pronounced, rising and taking off a stethoscope he hadn't used. "Cat scratch fever."

Aki and Maki spun at the sound, each opening his mouth to beat the other to the reference. But neither was able to speak. For a moment they just stood there, eyes wide, mouths agape, twin images of confusion.

"Ted Nugent," I said. "The Motorcity Madman."

The comment cured their paralysis, but left them looking utterly dejected. I shrugged an apology and turned my attention to Dr. Nick. "How do you treat this?" I asked.

Dr. Nick arched an eyebrow and jangled some loose change in his pocket. Then he dug into his medical bag, the same antiquated black-leather number Setsuko Nishimura carried back at the Hotel Kitty, and produced the world's biggest wad of Ace bandages. He set it on the floor, took out a bottle of antiseptic, some gauze and a Q-tip and began swabbing my face. It stung like hell, but after the cat attack I didn't have any yelling left in me. Then he went to work with the gauze and the bandages. My face was completely mummified in a matter of seconds. I must've looked like Claude Rains in *The Invisible Man*. But at least I was back in some normal clothes. When Suda saw what the cats had done to Yoshi's Merzbow T-shirt and leather jacket, he'd dispatched the Fuzotao twins to bring me some respectable white button-downs and a new pair of pants.

Someone called from the doorway.

"Hey, Doc Nick?"

It was Sensei Fuzotao, Aki and Maki's old man. Dr. Nick turned to face him.

"You better check this out," Sensei Fuzotao hollered. "I think Ratanawong is gonna need a cut man any second." He looked back toward the gym and winced. "Yeah," he said. "He's gonna need a cut man."

Dr. Nick stood up and sighed. "Barbaric," he said, heading out into the gym. "Grown men beating each other senseless for sport."

"Agreed," I said. "We should all be beating cats."

After the doctor walked out the door, Suda suddenly broke his silence. With a look I couldn't quite decipher, he asked if I'd heard the new song. I shook my bandaged head and asked him what new song.

"The new Yoshi song," Suda said. "The new Saint Arrow song, that is. Seppuku are gonna release the single next Tuesday. The new album should come out about one month later."

"They found the demos?"

Suda answered by motioning to Aki. Aki strolled toward a boombox on the bench across from us and hit play. Suda watched me closely, awaiting my reaction, reminding me of a story I heard about Yoshi scrutinizing the record execs during prerelease listening parties. Supposedly, whichever two songs the suits liked best, he'd leave off the final release.

An empty hiss filled the room.

Then buzzed out guitars skittering over a throbbing bass line. Drums broke in, then more electronic percussion and some frantic scratching. It was a dark sound, minor key, but more overtly danceable than any Saint Arrow tune I could think of. Then the voice started.

> *She didn't leave me anything . . .*

The words were spoken rather than sung, and the voice didn't belong to Yoshi. I shot a look to Suda. He gave me a nervous grin and looked away. Disconnected bits of sampled dialogue drifted through the mix.

> *No key*
> *No kiss good-bye*
> *Nothing*

The tune dropped to a low rumble. Now Yoshi's voice came in, singing the words spoken beneath him.

> *No key, no kiss good-bye*
> *No key, no kiss good-bye*
> *Just up and broke*

All the instruments fell away except the drums. A distorted voice spoke with understated intensity.

> *This lonely heart of mine.*

A cannon shot ushered in a frenzied guitar assault and the instruments swelled in a whirling sonic blitzkrieg. The song would have given me a headache at any volume. Not because I didn't like it, but because just when I thought I had everything figured out, suddenly there's a dead man singing along to words I'd spoken only days ago. As I sat there listening to the rest of the song, I couldn't help but think Yoshi's death was becoming like one of those epic metal songs that goes on and on, one false ending after another.

The song came to a close. Aki turned off the CD player.

"What do you think?" Suda said.

"Funny, but I don't think Yoshi wrote that song. And unless he's found a way to come back from the grave, I don't think it's him singing, either."

Suda looked up at me, his hangdog grin back and bigger than ever. "I've got something even funnier," he said. "Remember Dark Essence, the Saint Arrow tribute band who played at the memorial gig? They just got signed to Seppuku."

I popped out of the Higashi-Ginza subway exit and hightailed it toward Ginza 13-chome. As I passed a bunch of people standing in line for the matinee at the Kabuki-za Theater, a little tyke in a green jacket with a picture of cartoon superboy Anpanman pointed up at me and started crying. His mom shushed him, smiling apologetically while taking in an eyeful herself. I was getting more funny looks than a black man in some Kyushu farm town, but I didn't take it personally. Hell, I'd stare, too. In all the bandages, I probably looked like Michael Jackson disguised for an afternoon jaunt to Toys "R" Us.

Seppuku already had a new video rolling on the screen above their building. It was a lightning-edited montage of Saint Arrow, mostly Yoshi. Grainy footage from inside Club Quattro during the early years. Yoshi posing with his guitar at the edge of the Nakadake peak in Mt. Aso. Yoshi in an S&M cowboy outfit, failing to seduce the camera. Then Yoshi climbing into a helicopter, waving good-bye. The final shot was an aerial view of the public memorial outside the Tsukiji Honganji Temple. I looked for myself in the crowd, but I wasn't there.

As the image faded out, the Saint Arrow logo came up. And then the words *Re/in/trospection coming soon from Seppuku Entertainment.*

I guess the period of mourning was over.

. . .

The security guard stood guarding the white Seppuku Entertainment sign with his usual dime-store Indian exuberance.
The mousy woman in the blue blouse had apparently uncovered her latent sexuality since my last visit. Today she sat
behind the desk, wearing a tight red sweater that told me the
room temperature and black skirt that told me she knew her
way around a StairMaster. The circle of her red lips told me
she was surprised to see me.

"May I help you?" The sound brought my neck hairs to a
stand. She had a voice made for busting glass.

"I'm here to see Mr. Sugawara."

"Who may I say is calling?"

"Michael Jackson," I said in a high voice.

She repeated the name in a voice even higher.

"That's right," I said. "Sugawara's tigers have been performing Beatles tunes without my permission. I'm here to
make them stop."

She stuck her lip out and cocked her head. She probably
thought I was making fun of her voice, but really I was just
doing the world's worst Michael Jackson impression. I've
always been horrible at impressions, but I can't resist doing
them. The way I see it, if Jon Bon Jovi gets to be in movies
and Keanu Reeves gets to play in a rock band, I get to do
impressions.

The secretary didn't see it my way. She picked up the
phone and dialed. Six feet to her left, the security guard's
beeper started beeping. As if someone had just dropped a
coin through a slot in his back, he suddenly came to life,
stepping forward and asking me:

"If you're Michael Jackson, where's your little monkey?"

"I'm looking at him."

The guard smirked. "Beat it," he said.

"Okay. But remember—it was your idea." Before he could figure it out, I slapped his face and yanked his magnetic key card from his breast pocket. I heard the receptionist gasp as I slapped him again and emitted a high-pitched yelp. The third time I started to slap him he grabbed my wrists, and I responded with the *tenchi-nage*, an akido throw that sent him halfway across the room. I could've followed up with any number of moves, but I was starting to feel guilty. Cops I'll throw around all day, but beating up security guards is like picking on stutterers.

I marched to the door and swiped the magnetic key through the slot, resisting the urge to dust off my moonwalk as I moved down the long and winding hallway. Seconds later, I was pushing open the door to Mr. Sugawara's office.

Sugawara was still wearing his yellow Mr. Rogers cardigan, standing at the far side of the room with his back to me. The fax machine was silent and the Navyblues were nowhere in sight. I shut the door quietly and locked it. No electronic devices, just an old-fashioned steel bolt. Sugawara remained still, looking out the window.

"I don't want to spoil the party," I said, starting toward him. "But for a guy with the hottest ear in showbiz you sure got hoodwinked by somebody."

Sugawara didn't move a muscle. I rounded the table.

"Next time you want to sample my voice," I growled, "you really oughta ask permission."

Still he stood there, gazing out onto the Ginza streets. I stomped toward him, but he didn't make a move. I clapped my hands together. Nothing.

I reached out and tapped his shoulder.

Sugawara spun around. His mouth hung open like an empty sock as his face erupted in a rubbery, terrified yawn. A billow of white facial powder obscured his features as he recoiled, moving like an octopus escaping in a cloud of ink. Even the moptop toupee seemed to shrink back in fear, shifting on his head as he stumbled backward. "Help!" he cried. "I need somebody!"

"Take it easy," I said, holding out my hands.

Once he saw I wasn't going to attack, he regained some measure of composure. His eyes focused through the haze of airborn cosmetics and he summoned a feeble smile. "Good morning, good morning!" he said nervously and far too loud.

I noticed how he reached out to the chair, like his balance was a little screwy. I noticed the way his funny bluish eyes focused on my mouth. Or where my mouth would be if it wasn't wrapped in bandages.

And suddenly, it all made sense.

"*I BURIED PAUL!*"

Sugawara just stood there as I shouted, curling his head forward, straining his eyes toward my mouth with that expectant half smile. He didn't get a word of it.

"Ob-La-Di Ob-La-Da," an amused voice behind me said. "Otosclerosis."

I turned to see Kizuguchi stroll in, replacing his keys in his pocket. He was wearing a stiff wasabi-colored suit to go with his freshly trimmed Caesar cut. I hardly even noticed those two scars on his forehead anymore. Maybe they lacked visceral impact compared to a severed tongue lying on the floor. But I was glad the scars were there, if only to remind me of the bite marks that covered Kizuguchi's body. It was important to remember what kind of sociopath I was dealing with.

The Navyblues followed right behind Kizuguchi. And last, but not least, there was everybody's favorite mute, the man who spins like a top and never lets a syllable drop, the one and only DJ Towa. Towa was still wearing his prison denims, but his huge reel-to-reel tape recorder was gone. He looked unsettled without it, his body vestigially stooped under the weight of something no longer there. His microphone was gone too, but he still wore his big-ass earphones. The wire dangled uselessly, plugged into nothing.

"Auto what?" I said.

"Otosclerosis," Kizuguchi repeated, wrapping his thick Osaka gangster accent around the word.

"That the clinical name for incurable Beatlemania?"

"Otosclerosis is a spongy, bonelike growth in the inner ear," Kizuguchi continued. "Affects only low-frequency sounds at first, but it makes a guy totally deaf in time. That's how Sugawara's ear specialist explained it to me, in exchange for making a certain malpractice suit disappear. Anyhow, Sugawara-san ain't been able to hear proper in years. The only human voice he can understand is his secretary's."

So that's how Kizuguchi had broken into the business. Did dirty deeds for a doctor in exchange for some good old-fashioned blackmail material. Sugawara's affliction explained some of the records Seppuku had released lately. It didn't explain why kids bought the stuff, but that was the kind of unanswerable question best left to Zen masters and endocrinologists.

Kizuguchi strode past me, walking up to Sugawara and his defective ears. Sugawara's head rolled from side to side as he tried to follow the conversation.

"Sugawara-sama will be stepping down with this record," Kizuguchi said, putting a hand on Sugawara's shoulder. "He's built an empire here. Now it's time to turn off his mind, relax and float downstream. Ain't that right?" Sugawara's smile looked anything but relaxed. He gazed at Kizuguchi as if searching for a meaning. "Mr. Sugawara,"

Kizuguchi said, mouthing it broadly. "The man in the bandages is Billy Chaka. You remember him?"

"Good morning! Good morning!" Sugawara shouted, brightening. "Nothing to say but what a day!"

"Sure is," Kizuguchi said. "Mr. Sugawara must excuse himself now. Time for his afternoon tea."

Tea time Sugawara understood at any pitch. He nodded happily as two Navyblues strolled across the floor to guide him out of the room. As he walked out the door, the illusion of agelessness fell away. It was impossible to think of Sugawara as anything but a tired old man. I wondered what would become of his tigers.

"And I suppose you're the new *oyabun*?" I said, turning my attention to Kizuguchi. I didn't much like the idea. Sugawara may have been deaf, but at least he was a music fan. And as far as I knew, he didn't kill anybody.

Kizuguchi grinned, pleased as hell with himself.

"Thanks in part to you, Mr. Chaka," said Kizuguchi. "And of course DJ Towa here. He's a bona fide magician. Turned those shitty demos into gold. If that's what drugs do to you, hell—I'm sending all Seppuku's producers to Amsterdam, to India, wherever the fuck. You heard the single yet?"

I cast a glance at DJ Towa. Towa's face twitched once and went back into zombie mode. I recalled how he'd pulled a hat rack in the corner of Launchpad Productions the first time I'd visited. Towa standing there, mic in hand, tape rolling, as Santa blabbed on and on and finally demanded the key. I guess that explained how my voice got onto the new single. Between this and Randy Chance, I was fast becoming an unauthorized multimedia superstar.

"I heard the song," I said. "Great beat and you can dance to it. But I thought DJ Towa was Hijime Sampo's right hand man. How'd you lure him away?"

"Didn't have to," Kizuguchi said. "Maybe you didn't hear, but Santa got attacked. He's dead. Murdered by one of his drug clients. Pretty brutal, what they did to him. Never seen anything like it. Not on the outside."

"So you saw it?"

"No," he said. "Read about it in the papers."

"But you said you've never *seen* any—"

"Don't tell me what I said and what I didn't say. 'Never seen anything like it' is an expression."

"A figure of speech," coughed a Navyblue.

"A figure of speech," Kizuguchi repeated. He let loose his dead blank prison stare again, and I thought about the little lecture he'd given inside the sauna. The one about the impermanent nature of secrets. I don't know why Kizuguchi didn't kill Santa right away if he really wanted to keep the plot to murder Yoshi under wraps. My theory was that Santa had kept himself alive by promising he could get the demos from Olga. When that didn't work out, Santa was nothing but a liability, especially as he wasn't the quietest guy around. I wasn't anxious for my tongue to get me in the same trouble, but I couldn't help pushing for just a little more.

"Word on the streets is that Seppuku signed Dark Essence."

"Who?" Kizuguchi asked.

"Actually," a Navyblue said, clearing his throat, "there is no Dark Essence anymore. They've changed their name to Phantom Limb. They're doing all originals, totally new material."

I realized then how the whole thing went down. The Seppuku gang had given up on finding the missing Yoshi demos. Instead, they convinced Dark Essence to make some quick and dirty recordings. What they didn't tell them was that this recording would be beefed up and sold as the new Saint

Arrow album. Seppuku had taken the sting out of it by awarding the band their own record contract, and I bet that somewhere in that contract was a clause to keep Dark Essence—er, Phantom Limb—muzzled about their "contributions" to the *Re/in/trospection* album. Or maybe Phantom Limb was in on the deception, and figured recording their hero's final album was the ultimate tribute. Maybe they figured the choice between playing covers all their lives and having a shot at the big time was no choice at all. Or maybe they were like most rock bands, and just never got around to reading the damn contract.

"Phantom Limb," Kizuguchi said emphatically. "We have high hopes for that band. We're positioning them to fill the void left by Saint Arrow."

"Interesting way to put it," I said.

Alarms started going off behind Kizuguchi's eyes. I just smiled at him. I smiled at each of them, one after another. Kizuguchi, DJ Towa, the three Navyblues. I smiled so long my face started hurting. But no one saw my smile. The bandages had me covered. Suddenly someone barked.

"Baby, you're a rich man!"

"Huh?" Kizuguchi said, turning around.

"Baby, you're a rich man!"

The voice was raspy, dust-choked, the words struggling out one painful syllable at a time. Even with all of us looking around, it took a while to find the source.

"Baby, you're a rich man, too!"

No one looked more surprised than DJ Towa himself. His limp body suddenly went stiff and angular and he cupped his hands over his headphones, a look of apoplectic terror on his face as his jaw vibrated with the words. He looked like a man possessed, a human antennae, receiving signals from a parallel astral plane.

"You keep all your money in a big brown bag inside a zoo!"

There was no mistaking who DJ Towa was talking to. His eyes were wide with amazement, jittering inside their sockets, but they were trained on me. My own eyes weren't as faithful. They wandered over the room, taking in all the reactions.

The twin scars on Kizuguchi's potato forehead wrinkled in dismay. "You said he couldn't talk," he mumbled.

"He can't," a Navyblue said.

"He hasn't spoken for years," added another.

"That's not exactly the same fuckin' thing," Kizuguchi hissed.

All eyes turned back to Towa, waiting for more. But nothing else came. Gradually, his eyes went back to normal as all the intensity drained from his body. His face twitched one more time then slackened. Slowly he bent until stooped again. It looked like someone doing *wilted flower* in a game of charades.

"The fuck was that all about?" Kizuguchi asked no one in particular. We all stood there looking at each other. Nobody had an answer.

27

I skipped down the stairwell. There was no music today. Maybe stairwell tunes were a Sugawara-era practice already being phased out. Much as I liked my wingtips, I didn't like the way they sounded echoing down the stairs. Before I knew it, I was whistling. Suddenly I realized it was the same song I'd been whistling back in that long empty corridor in the Hotel Kitty's basement. Then I thought about DJ Towa's outburst and realized exactly what song it was. The song that had been kicking around in my subconscious ever since Olga left Tokyo.

Star Festival Night. The Sunshine City Building. Two lonely foreigners and a whole lot of alcohol. Rain tapping on the glass of the Wild Strawberry, the Beatles playing over and over on the jukebox. Olga telling me about . . . what was she telling me about?

Baby, you're a rich man. Baby, you're a rich man, too. Star Festival Night, talking with a gorgeous Swedish woman. Glasses clinking, the sound of thunder. *You keep all your money in a big brown bag inside a zoo.* The zoo. She's telling me the song reminds her of her visit to the Ueno Zoo. Rain streaking against the windowpane. Zoos make her sad, she says. Zoo make her sad because the animals—the pandas, the tigers, the gorillas, the kangaroos, the flamingoes and all the beautiful creatures from every far-flung corner of the globe—the animals will never be able to go home again. They will eat in the zoo, they will sleep there, maybe even start families, but they will never belong there. And once they've been in the zoo for so long, they'll never really belong anywhere else. And so, she says, the animals will live out their lives dreaming of home. Sometimes, Olga tells me, Japan makes her feel the same way. Like a little animal in a giant zoo. I nod my head. I watch the ice melting in my glass. The Beatles keep playing, rain keeps tapping against the window. *You keep all your money in a big brown bag inside a zoo.* Star Festival Night on the fifty-eighth floor of the Sunshine City Building.

I reached into my pocket, felt the key, and figured out the quickest route to the Ueno Zoo.

The guidebooks won't tell you this, but when trying to hail a cab in Tokyo, it helps not to have your face completely wrapped in bandages. I tried for a while anyway, but no luck. If I was a cabbie forced to choose between svelte women with designer handbags and a guy with no face, I'd probably pass me by, too.

The Ueno Zoo closed in less than an hour. It was about three miles north, and I was in no mood to deal with the trains. I thought about stealing a car or a motorcycle, but I was trying to put those days behind me.

So I ran.

You wanna know what it was like running through downtown Tokyo, try it sometime. Only first, get your mug scratched up and develop benign lymphoreticulosis so your nodes swell and your chest constricts. Wrap up your face so you can hardly open your mouth to breathe and get your nose cracked so you can't breathe through that, either. Make sure you've only had about two hours of airplane sleep, then spend all night and most of the morning talking to a bunch of chain-smoking cops who think you're crazy and the afternoon with guys in the record biz who actually are. Just to disorient yourself a little, listen to a tape of someone pretending to be a dead guy singing along to a conversation you had last week. Then listen to a man who hasn't said a word in years quote the lyrics to a song that's been on the tip of your tongue for days because of a chance meeting you had on a rainy night a long, long time ago.

Do all this, and you won't even need to read this part. You'll know exactly what it was like.

I got to Ueno Park just as the sun was going down. Hundreds of leafless cherry trees etched a veiny pattern against the winter sky. Take all the skyscrapers out of the background and the throngs of people from the foreground and it was a view right out of a *suiboku* scroll painting. Unfortunately, I had no time to appreciate the scenery. I was concentrating on dodging and weaving through the pedestrians strolling through Tokyo's oldest park. Shinobazu Pond sprawled out on my left, looking like an ocean compared to the Night Porter's melancholy duck pond. Whatever else Setsuko said, I believed that part was true. Nostalgia for a place like that couldn't be faked. And I liked to believe she really missed her grandfather, too. Beyond that, well, it was safe to say that Setsuko Nishimura was even more mixed up than I gave her credit for. Murderously so.

Heads turned as I raced by. I ignored them, wondering to myself just what I would do if Olga's locker really did contain the Yoshi tapes. I don't know if Olga had lied to protect me or herself, but I felt certain the tapes were there. If they were, maybe I'd give them to Suda to hold on to in case the kickboxing thing didn't work out. Maybe I'd pass the demo on to Sarah, and let generasiax.com leak it all over the Internet. Maybe I'd release them myself, and send the proceeds to Takeshi's widow. Or the family of Rino Hana, the poor confused kid who'd hung herself over Yoshi.

When I finally reached the entrance to the zoo, my lungs were burning and my heart was ready to leap through my chest. I couldn't help but think how funny it would be if I were to just keel over and die on the spot, leaving Sarah to forever wonder why I'd been so desperate to see a bunch of caged animals. On second thought, maybe it wouldn't be so funny. Given the madness that had erupted after Yoshi's death, I figured it would be best to die in my apartment at a prearranged time, on worldwide television if possible, just so no one had any questions about what happened.

Two women in matching sailor suits and giant red hats gave me matching smiles as I approached the entrance. They kept smiling as they tried to dissuade me from entering, warning me the zoo would only be opened for another ten minutes. Gasping for breath, I told them I simply had to see Ling Ling and what's-his-name. That ended their arguments. The panda bears were two of the biggest celebrities in all of Japan—their procreative endeavors were followed as closely as those of the royal family—so the women could understand my plight. They ushered me right in, insisting on waiving the entrance fee. They probably also got on the phone to security as soon as I passed, but I didn't care. In minutes I'd have the final piece of the puzzle.

I found an information kiosk and looked on a map for all the various coin locker locations. They were color-coded. I could only hope the one I was looking for was on the west side of the park, because otherwise I'd have to take the mono-rail, and the last ride of the day had left five minutes ago. But I needn't have worried. The blue lockers, wouldn't you know, were only a few yards away. Right by the tiger enclosure.

An army of tiny schoolkids in matching yellow stocking caps paraded by, bundled in so much winter gear they looked like munchkins on an Antarctic expedition. As soon as they spotted me the pointing and giggling started. One lit-tle tyke started shouting *mīra mīra*, and I heard another one ask his teacher what mummies ate for dinner. I fought the impulse to turn around and growl "children."

I passed the tiger enclosure and gave it a quick glance. The placard out front said inside the dense faux jungle were four Bengal tigers, but they must've been in hiding. That was all right. Between Mr. Sugawara's animatrons and the Hand-some Tigers, I'd had quite enough of big cats on this trip, not to mention little ones. Moments later I found the blue locker bay. I found locker #910. I slid the key into the lock and turned. It didn't work. I turned the key the other way. It worked much better. The locker door swung open. Inside the locker was a slim white envelope.

> *Billy,*
>
> *When you are reading this, I am now gone.*
>
> *That you have come to the zoo means you must remember, too, all what begins at the Wild Straw-berry in the hiding from the rain. You remember too how I tell to you Tokyo is sometime make me feel like zoo animal. But I never know what is truly zoo animal feeling until I meet Yoshi.*
>
> *You must have many question about me and Yoshi, and I can only tell to you some answers.*

Yoshi was good person, but he is very sad, he is trapped. He is want to leave music business, he tell to me we run away together. Live in Gotenborg. He say this, but maybe in his heart he cannot think to be in Gotenborg. Maybe he is too long in the zoo, and now he can't leave. I think this is why he is take overdose. I believe he knew Santa wants to kill him, and he still take heroin. Maybe for him, is the only way out.

But Yoshi he plays a good trick before he died. Yoshi give to record company blank CD. True demos he is throw in the Sumida River. Like Rambo, he tell me, with his poetry. He want to be sure there is no turning back.

As for me, my life begins new. Yoshi and I have much money for plan to run away. Very, very much money. Not how I plan to be rich, but our lives and our plans seem to belong from different worlds, ne?

But Billy, one day you will know the world is not only Tokyo and the teenagers. You will know there is a life outside the zoo. When this day comes to you, come to me. Don't wait until it is too late, and you have nowhere to belong.

When you decide to come, look for the biggest house on Koningstrasse. Dewa mata, bastard.

   Olga S.

Along with the letter was one All Nippon Air nonstop to Stockholm, redeemable anytime. I read the note over and over, scrutinizing each and every word. Life had surprised me plenty the last few days, but apparently it wasn't through.

Olga had only cursed four times in the whole letter.

28

Later that night, I had Aki and Maki drive me to Yoshi's trash pad. I needed to hide out somewhere safe, somewhere no one could find me. Neither of the twins seemed to harbor any resentment about me attacking them with a guitar just days ago, though the ride was pretty quiet, and I noticed Aki walked with a limp when he led me up the stairs to Yoshi's detox hideout.

Once ensconced in the apartment, I cleared off the busted table, placed some stacks of LPs under it for makeshift legs and began to put my thoughts to paper. I wanted to get it all down while it was fresh in my mind, though the real writing wouldn't take place until I was back in Cleveland.

Sometime around 6:00 A.M., I decided to take a break. I found the remote control—which had been sitting on top of the TV the entire time—and flipped on the morning news. A female reporter bundled in a puffy blue coat and pink ear-muffs stood outside the Hotel Kitty, dazzling white flakes drifting in the air around her while the words "FROZEN CORPSES FOUND IN ABANDONED HOTEL" scrolled down the right side of the screen. Underneath was the subhead " 'Hokkaido Popsicles' Baffle Authorities."

The story was running on every channel. And why not? Thirteen frozen corpses found in a hotel overrun with bizarre cats, with no hint of how they got there and few clues as to who was behind it—it beat the hell out of hearing more depressing news from the Ministry of Trade.

I was in all the stories. Only they referred to me as an anonymous tip. As in, *an anonymous tip to a Tokyo detective led police in Hokkaido to a shocking discovery late yesterday evening.* I'd told Inspector Arajiro to credit Peoff the cartoon mouse as the tipster, but he just gave me that bureaucratic stare of his and proposed "anonymous" as a compromise.

The case was in the hands of the local authorities in Hokkaido now. They were teaming up with the Japanese National Police Agency for a massive nationwide manhunt for a woman named Setsuko Nishimura and a nameless chubby balding man with a pronounced fondness for cats.

I doubted they'd find either of them.

The stories never mentioned the Phoenix Society by name. I'd told the cops all about them, of course. I told him how they'd put Takeshi on ice, how they'd tried to do the same thing to me. All the while, Arajiro nodded along with that bored expression he'd perfected. When I finished, Arajiro asked what kind of proof I had such an organization even existed. So I started telling him about Yoshi's bird tattoo, about the Night Porter's ID card, about the brochure I'd seen but no longer had. Midway through my story Arajiro held up his hand and asked me the same question, putting lots of emphasis on the word *proof.*

Then I switched courses, and started telling him how the talent scout they'd found dead in a half-empty Shibuya office was murdered by a man named Yatsu Kizuguchi. I told them about how Hijime "Santa" Sampo and Kizuguchi had teamed up to kill Yoshi, how the plot had been called off too late, and how the Phoenix Society had interfered. That's when Arajiro started asking about proof again.

I told him finding proof was his job.

Thank you for your cooperation, he said. I couldn't tell for sure, but I think he might even have meant it.

As for the authenticity of the *Re/in/trospection* album, I thought of a famous samurai aphorism: *the most powerful weapon is the undrawn sword*. I decided to let the Yoshi fans hear the album and judge for themselves. I knew the kids weren't as stupid as Seppuku Records hoped. They'd notice something sounded fishy, and they'd wanna find out why. Once that happened, I could post a few hints in chatrooms, pointing them in the right direction. Hell, maybe the mystery would even get one or two kids interested in investigative journalism.

The reporter on TV said police would not be releasing the names of the frozen victims in Hokkaido until the immediate relatives were notified. There was also a hotline number set up for anyone who might have information on the crime or the whereabouts of the two fugitives.

Next up on the news, a friendly conversation with Ishao Tonda, acclaimed director of *Wildman for Geisha!*

I turned off the television.

The rest of the morning I spent wondering what Takeshi had done to deserve such a shitty fate. Of course, there's no answer to questions like that. But the fact remained that if he hadn't agreed to meet me—if he hadn't told me about the two separate emergency calls, if I hadn't told him about the picture in *Power Chord Japan*—he would still have been alive. He'd still be living in his cardboard box in the park, going to work at *Marquee*, downing Seven Happiness in the Golden Gai.

Of course, if the Phoenix Society would've had five people in their van, none of it would have happened. Or if the Night Porter hadn't died in my room. Or if I hadn't stumbled onto the guitar magazine. Or if Yoshi would've had the courage to leave it all behind and run away to Sweden, instead of becoming a suicide-slash-murder-victim-slash-casualty of indecision and disorganization, depending on how you looked at it.

There were all kinds of ways Takeshi could still be here, but he wasn't. And he wasn't coming back. No matter what the Day Manager believed about nine lives, no matter what kind of scientific immortality the Phoenix Society sold. The world is a chaotic place and all of us only get one ending. Takeshi deserved a better one.

And looking around at two splintered guitars, at the piles of CDs and LPs and cassettes and magazines and cigarette butts and beer cans and all the detritus Yoshi had left behind, I found myself wishing the Phoenix Society had been able to freeze the body of Yoshimura Fukuzatsu. I wished the cryonic suspension thing worked and they were able to bring him back in 2099, just like new. And I wished I would live well into my hundreds. Because I wanted to see Yoshi alive again, if only to give him a slap in the face for all the trouble he'd caused.

Then again, a slap in the face was what got me involved in this whole mess to begin with.

I arrived at the Yokohama Kickboxing Pavillion II about ten minutes before the opening bell. The barren gym had been transformed into a rowdy, smoke-filled arena and there was a pretty decent crowd for a fight with a bunch of nobodies and a former rock star on the card. While I waited at my ringside seat next to Sensei Fuzotao and his kids for the bout to begin, I overheard a rumor sweeping through the crowd. Seemed Yatsu Kizuguchi wouldn't be able to witness Suda's professional debut. The Tokyo Metropolitan Police Department decided they had a few things to discuss with him. I was still enjoying the good news when the bell rang to start the fight.

Suda shuffled towards the center of the ring, his hands up around his newly shorn head. In fight shorts his legs were as spindly as a newborn colt's and he looked lost in his own body. His opponent danced sideways, arms jangling around his hips, lazily skating the perimeter. Suddenly Suda lurched forward, sending a wobbly kick toward the other guy's midsection. His opponent coaxed it in before grabbing Suda's knobby leg and heaving it upwards.

The crowd gasped as Suda catapulted into the air, frozen for a moment before he came hurtling back to the mat. He hit hard, bouncing a good two inches off the canvas.

"C'mon, Isamu!" Sensei Fuzotao barked. "Don't get suckered!"

"Be a survivor!" Aki yelled.

"Eye of the tiger!" Maki followed.

Suda gave them a quick nod of recognition and hopped to his feet. Being sent onto his back so early opened the adrenaline floodgates and now he was skittering around the ring like a mouse dropped into a snake cage.

The other fighter casually moved to the center of the ring and dropped the anchor. As Suda came round the bend again, his opponent attacked.

The opening *roon hog klab* kick landed right above his knee. The *dap cha wa la* jab sailed over his head, but the *earawan soei nga* uppercut caught him in the soft spot just under his sternum.

His cheeks ballooned like Louis Armstrong's and his mouthpiece popped out. The little horseshoe of plastic boinked his opponent right between the eyes. It was Suda's best shot of the fight so far.

The bell rang. End of round one.

Suda picked himself off the canvas and shuffled to his corner. Aki and Maki jumped in to give him the rubdown while old man Fuzotao yelled instructions at him. "Don't be so direct in your attacks," he said. "Move like a butterfly, not a caterpillar."

A caterpillar this late in fall, still not a butterfly. Somehow, thinking of Sarah's poetic insult got me thinking of Olga. During the break between rounds, I tried to imagine life in Sweden. I didn't know anything about the place except what I'd seen in old Bergman films. Max Von Sydow and Bibi Andersson. I couldn't picture Yoshi hanging out in Gothenburg. I couldn't picture Olga hanging out in Gothenburg either, any more than she could probably imagine me in Cleveland. Whoever said the human imagination was unlimited had a pretty limited imagination. And what did people do in Sweden? Sit around in windswept seaside villages, look out dirty windows and flash back through all the bittersweet moments that defined their existence?

If there was one moment that defined mine, it was all those years ago when a nineteen-year-old Sarah walked into the *Youth in Asia* headquarters with a chip on her shoulder and a ring in her nose, demanding to see the hack who slagged off her favorite Hanoi riot-grrl band.

Sarah.

I thought about what Takeshi had said, about Sarah and I being meant for each other. About ending the game of cat and mouse. She was so much in my thoughts there must still have been something there. And maybe we could patch things up. Despite my Tokyo adventures, despite my belief that writing for teenagers was what I was meant to do. Despite, as Dr. Nick might say, my turgid personality. Deep down she had to know I'd probably never change. And deep down, I couldn't blame her for wanting me to.

And maybe, just maybe, this time I might. Who knew what might become of me when the cocoon of bandages came off? Caterpillars and butterflies. Cats and mice. Tigers and Beatles. Olga was right—but it wasn't just Tokyo—the whole goddamn world was a zoo.

But Tokyo, my beloved Tokyo. There was so much we still had to explore in each other, so many wounds left to inflict. Yet for now, I had to get back to Cleveland. Back in my cheap metal chair behind my nice wooden desk overlooking Lake Erie. Because I had one doozy of a story to write, one that teenagers—and maybe even a few older kids—wouldn't dare miss.

The second-round bell rang.

Suda practically sprinted to the center of the ring and managed to get knocked down in four seconds flat. Aki and Maki winced at the blow, but Suda quickly picked himself off the ground. He was smiling.

"Damn," Sensei Fuzotao said, shaking his head. "I knew he was one of them. I hoped he wasn't, but I *knew* he was."

I gave him a curious look, not that he could tell. Suda was staggering around the ring again, full of enthusiasm, a drunk dancing to his favorite song.

"You run across guys like this once in a while," Sensei Fuzotao sighed. "You can teach them the moves, get them into shape. They might even win a fight or two. But guys like that got one fatal habit you can't break."

I waited, watching the lights bounce off the silver bristles of his head.

"They want to get hit," he said. "They like it. Don't ask me why. It's a psychological tic. Like they're atoning for something. Like they got it coming. They think getting punched is some kind of reward."

Just then, Suda walked right into the *ten kwad larn*, a

sweeping low kick to the back of his legs. He went down again, rolling across the mat and managing to pop back up to his feet before his momentum stopped. His opponent sized up the situation for a moment then swaggered in for the knockout.

Suda's left eye was already starting to swell and blood trickled steadily from his mouth. But underneath all the wounds, he was smiling. Not his wry smirk or his hangdog grin, but a boundless smile of pure satisfaction.

He got one final reward, then it was all over.

Acknowledgments

Thanks to:

Dan Hooker for his knowledge, diligence, and good work at keeping my head screwed on straight.

Krista Stroever for her insight, expertise, and uncanny ability to ask all the right questions.

Jeff Diedrich for the Swedish swear words.

Alan Goldsher for sharing his music industry knowledge.

Chee-Soo Kim for putting up with me.

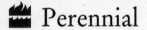 Perennial

Books by Isaac Adamson:

Tokyo Suckerpunch
ISBN 0-380-81291-6 (paperback)

Raymond Chandler meets John Woo when a ridiculously cool American reporter tries to track down the killer of Japan's worst movie director AND find the elusive geisha who has stolen his heart, all in the super-heated labyrinth of the Tokyo streets. No doubt about it: this is a pop culture potpourri of sub-epic proportions.

"This pop romp through the Tokyo of martial arts, yakuza and legendary geishas has more sly smarts than a Hong Kong gangster shoot-em-up. First-time novelist Adamson hooks the reader with fast action, clever dialogue and all-over atmosphere." —*Publishers Weekly*

Hokkaido Popsicle
ISBN 0-380-81292-4 (paperback)

An altercation between journalist Billy Chaka and the director of a movie loosely based on Billy's life places Chaka in Hokkaido on mandatory vacation. Here, at the Hotel Kitty, the elderly Night Manager stumbles into Billy's room one night and dies. Meanwhile, in Tokyo, the lead singer of Japan's most popular rock band was found dead in a sleazy love hotel. When Chaka goes to Tokyo to cover the story, he soon finds out there's more to the rocker's apparent drug overdose than meets the eye. Could it be that the rock star and the Night Manager share a very strange link?